PRAISE FOR JOSEPH

"Flynn is an excellent storyteller." — *Booklist*

"Flynn propels his plot with potent but flexible force."
— *Publishers Weekly*

Digger
"A mystery cloaked as cleverly as (and perhaps better than) any John Grisham work." — *Denver Post*

"Surefooted, suspenseful and in its breathless final moments unexpectedly heartbreaking." — *Booklist*

The Next President
"*The Next President* bears favorable comparison to such classics as *The Best Man, Advise and Consent* and *The Manchurian Candidate.*"
— *Booklist*

"A thriller fast enough to read in one sitting."
— *Rocky Mountain News*

The President's Henchman (A Jim McGill Novel)
"Marvelously entertaining." — *ForeWord Magazine*

The Devil on the Doorstep

A JIM McGILL NOVEL

Joseph Flynn

Stray Dog Press, Inc.
Springfield, IL
2013

ALSO BY JOSEPH FLYNN

The Concrete Inquisition
Digger
The Next President
Farewell Performance
Gasoline, Texas
Hot Type
Round Robin
The President's Henchman, A Jim McGill Novel
The Hangman's Companion, A Jim McGill Novel
Blood Street Punx
Nailed, A Ron Ketchum Mystery
One False Step
Still Coming
Still Coming Expanded Edition
The K Street Killer, A Jim McGill Novel
Tall Man in Ray-Bans, A John Tall Wolf Novel
Part 1: The Last Ballot Cast, A Jim McGill Novel
Part 2: The Last Ballot Cast, A Jim McGill Novel
Defiled, A Ron Ketchum Mystery
Short Cases 1-3, Three McGill Short Stories
Hangman, A Western Novella
War Party, A John Tall Wolf Novel

Pointy Teeth, 12 Short Stories
Insanity® Diary — A Sixty-Something Couple Takes Shaun T's Sixty-Day Challenge

Published by Stray Dog Press, Inc.
Springfield, IL 62704, U.S.A.

First Stray Dog Press, Inc. Printing, August, 2013

Visit the author's web site: *www.josephflynn.com*

Flynn, Joseph
The Devil on the Doorstep / Joseph Flynn
422 p.
ISBN 978-0-9887868-2-0
eBook ISBN 978-0-9887868-1-3

Printed in the United States of America

PUBLISHER'S NOTE
This is a work of fiction. Names, characters, places, and incidents are either the product of the author's imagination or are used fictitiously; any resemblance to actual persons, living or dead, events, or locales is entirely coincidental.

Book design by Aha! Designs

DEDICATION

For all the friends of Jim McGill and all his friends.

ACKNOWLEDGEMENTS

For Catherine, Susan, Anne, Caitie and everyone else who helps me keep my overhead low. Otherwise, I'd have to charge a whole lot more for these books. My thanks to Bernadette Cazobon-Wendricks for greatly improving my use of the French language. A special nod to Catherine, whose cover design for this book really knocks me out.

The Devil on the Doorstep

A JIM McGILL NOVEL

CHARACTER LIST

[In alphabetical order by last name]

Giles Benedict, artist, forger, fugitive conman
Richard Bergen, U.S. Senator [D, IL] Assistant majority leader
Gawayne Blessing, White House head butler
Philip Brock, Democratic Congressman from Pennsylvania
Tyler Busby, American billionaire and art collector
Edwina Byington, the president's personal secretary
Arlo Carsten, ex-NASA project manager
Gabriella "Gabbi" Casale, artist, security officer, U.S. Embassy
Celsus Crogher, retired Secret Service SAC
Byron DeWitt, Deputy Director of the FBI
Darren Drucker, American billionaire, art collector,
Carolyn [McGill] Enquist, first wife of Jim McGill
Lars Enquist, Carolyn's second husband
Elvie Fisk, daughter of militia leader Harlan Fisk
Harlan Fisk, commander of The First Michigan Militia
Laurent Fortier, French art thief
Cathryn Gorman, Chief of the Metropolitan Police Department
Patricia Darden Grant, President of the U.S., wife of Jim McGill
Andrew Hudson Grant (deceased), the president's first husband
Jeremiah Haskins, Director of the FBI
Sen. Howard Hurlbert, founder of True South Party
Bahir Ben Kalil, personal physician to the Jordanian ambassador
[SAC] Elspeth Kendry, head of the Presidential Protection Detail
Sheryl Kimbrough, Republican elector from Indiana
Duvessa Kinsale, New York art gallery owner
Donald "Deke" Ky, Jim McGill's personal bodyguard
Leo Levy, Jim McGill's personal driver
Charles Louvel, Pruet family employee
Père Louvel, French cleric, brother of Charles Louvel
Craig MacLaren, Chief Justice of the U.S. Supreme Court
Louis Marra, NYPD Detective

Jim McGill, president's husband, aka The President's Henchman
Abbie McGill, oldest child of Jim McGill and Carolyn Enquist
Caitie McGill, youngest child of Jim McGill and Carolyn Enquist
Kenny McGill, middle child of Jim McGill and Carolyn Enquist
Tommy Meeker, regional security officer U.S. Embassy, Paris
Bob Merriman, U.S. Senator [D, OR]
Roger Michaelson, former U.S Senator [D-OR]
Galia Mindel, White House chief of staff
Dikran "Dikki" Missirian, McGill's business landlord
Jean Morrissey, Vice President of the U.S.
George Mulchrone, retired Catholic priest
David Nathan, Director of the Secret Service
Artemus Nicolaides, White House physician
Stephen Norwood, White House deputy chief of staff
Merilee Parker, former press secretary for Senator Hurlbert
Peter Profitt, Speaker of the House
Augustin Pruet, Yves Pruet's father
Yves Pruet, French investigating magistrate
Joan Renshaw, director of The AHG Foundation
Osgood Riddick, FBI special agent on art crime team
Odo Sacripant, Yves Pruet's Corsican bodyguard
Putnam Shady, Sweetie's husband
Maxine Shady, Putnam's niece
Margaret "Sweetie" Sweeney, McGill's business partner
John Wexford, Senate majority leader
Ethan Winger, art forgery analyst
Mather Wyman, former VP of the U.S.
Kira Fahey Yates, Welborn Yates' wife
Captain Welborn Yates, the president's official investigator

CHAPTER 1

West Front of the United States Capitol

Patricia Darden Grant, President of the United States of America, placed her left hand on the Bible held by her husband, James J. McGill, and raised her right hand. Chief Justice Craig MacLaren also raised his right hand and intoned the first words of the presidential oath of office. The president began to repeat the oath as an estimated eight hundred thousand of her fellow Americans standing on the National Mall beyond the Reflecting Pool, looked on, many of them booing and jeering.

More than another hundred million Americans were watching on domestic television. That number was exceeded by those around the world viewing the event on international broadcasts and streaming Internet feeds. The president, sparing one glance at McGill, looked at no one except the chief justice.

She said, "I, Patricia Darden Grant, do solemnly swear ..."

Suburban Virginia

Minutes earlier, three miles south of the Capitol, two hands opened an upstairs window at the rear of an expensive but unremarkable tract house. A buzzing sound began and a UAV — unmanned aerial vehicle — flew out of the house and into the overcast sky. The device had the wingspan of a red-tailed hawk. The finish of the UAV was a mottled blue-gray. It all but disappeared against the backdrop of the sky. The soft buzz of its propeller was inaudible at a distance of a hundred feet.

The tiny aircraft banked to the north at near-rooftop level and set a course for the U.S. Capitol.

Suburban Maryland

The location of the Multi-Agency Communications Center was secret. The men and women who worked at MACC were responsible for the safety of everyone attending the presidential inauguration, first and foremost the president and her husband. The pecking order of the lives to be preserved, after those of the First Couple and the vice president, was also kept confidential.

The foursome in charge of coordinating the protective efforts consisted of: Major General Amos Stokes, Commander of the Military District of Washington; David Nathan, Director of the Secret Service; Byron DeWitt, Deputy Director of the FBI; Cathryn Gorman, Chief of the Metropolitan Police Department.

The three men at the top of the food chain fastened their eyes on the monitor showing the president taking her oath of office for the second time in two days. The official oath had been sworn yesterday in the White House on January 20th as prescribed by the Constitution. The public ceremony was just for show.

Chief Gorman was the one who noticed the skirmish start on the fringes of the huge crowd. Thousands of people who thought Patricia Darden Grant had stolen the election were no longer content to shout their objections. They pushed forward in the direction of the Capitol as if they hoped to prevent the public swearing in.

The police and the military had been warned of such a possibility. They stood at the ready to restrain such a charge. Only the protestors didn't reach the lines of uniformed resistance. Other members of the crowd, partisans of the president, pushed back against the protestors, keeping them on the far side of the Reflecting Pool. Within seconds, blood was being spilled as the largest brawl in the nation's history began.

Men, women and even adolescents threw punches, kicked one another and wrestled each other to the ground. In places where one combatant was clearly getting the better of another, he or she was quickly swarmed under by a group of the opposition. A terrible cacophony — shrieks of panic, curses and battle-cries — filled the air.

Chief Gorman yelled to her people on the scene, "Go, go, go!"

General Stokes ordered his soldiers, "Reinforce the police. Contain the situation."

Secret Service Director Nathan told SAC Elspeth Kendry, standing near the president, "Be ready. Get Holly G. and Holmes out of there on my word."

Only FBI Deputy Director Byron DeWitt refrained from issuing any directive.

He wondered if the melee might be a diversion.

He looked from one monitor to another to see what might be coming next.

Washington, DC

The UAV flew barely twenty feet above the roof where a Secret Service counter-sniper perched, trying not to be distracted by the riot taking place in the foreground of his vision. The cops and the soldiers were far from restoring order. If anything, the wave of violence rolled closer to the Capitol where the president and a large part of the federal government's elite remained in place.

The counter-sniper looked up when he heard the buzz of the UAV.

Nobody had said anything to him about the security forces using drones.

That left only one conclusion for him to draw: assassination attempt.

"Bogie, bogie, bogie!" he yelled into his microphone.

He gave the position, bearing and description of the small aircraft.

The UAV had moved hundreds of yards past his position by now, but he lined it up in his scope and took his shot, just as the damn thing began taking evasive maneuvers. The shot missed. He tried again, but the damn thing kept diving, climbing, juking one way and another.

All the while, though, it made forward progress.

The sniper kept repeating, "Bogie, bogie, bogie!"

He felt a chill go through him.

Holly G., Holmes and the chief justice were still standing in place.

Jesus Christ, he thought, they should be running for cover by now.

West Front United States Capitol

The president said, "… I will faithfully execute the Office of President of the United States and will to the best of my ability preserve, protect and defend the Constitution of the United States, so help me God."

The words were no sooner out of her mouth than a cluster of Secret Service agents grabbed her, Holmes and the chief justice and rushed them toward the nearby entrance to the Capitol. Forward progress came to an abrupt, stumbling halt when the chief justice tripped as he started up the stairway to the arched doorway. He took two agents down with him.

The crowd of dignitaries who had sat in the VIP section watching the inauguration tried to make their escape and slammed into the pile of bodies clogging the staircase. Secret Service agents shoved people aside as they tried to clear a path for the president.

SAC Elspeth Kendry pointed a finger at the sky and yelled, "There it is!"

No order to open fire was necessary.

Other agents also spotted the UAV and opened up with a ferocious barrage of automatic weapons fire. Their shots missed as the small aircraft was still executing evasive movements. Several of their rounds ended up killing spectators in the now hysterical crowd. The gunfire added to the panic on the West Front of the Capitol as Washington's governing class did their wailing best to escape the madness.

The sheer volume of the defensive fusillade finally hit the UAV, and it exploded with a bang hugely disproportionate to its size. The shock wave cut down those closest to the blast like a scythe. Still more were wounded by bits of shrapnel.

Holly G. and Holmes were unhurt and back on their feet. They were no more than ten meters from the entrance to the Capitol. The Secret Service had cleared a path for them.

They didn't make it.

A second mini-drone, launched from the north, found them in the open.

It had flown by propeller power up to that point.

Then a rocket motor ignited and the drone streaked toward its target.

Moving far too fast for the Secret Service to shoot it down.

The president and McGill barely had time to look up and see the end coming.

Everyone within a fifty-meter radius was killed.

CHAPTER 2

The White House — McGill's Hideaway
Monday, January 7, 2013

James J. McGill, husband of the president, father of three, former chief of police, current private investigator, friend to many and foe of others sat in his White House lair for his official portrait. The pose was a three-quarter turn to McGill's right, seen from mid-torso to the crown of his head. Working on McGill's likeness in oils on canvas was Gabriella "Gabbi" Casale.

By way of preparation, she had taken photographs, done sketches and executed an underpainting on the canvas.

The artist, an honors graduate of the School of the Art Institute of Chicago, a CIA dropout and a former regional security officer for the United States Department of State, had almost died under a bridge in Paris with McGill as they and three others had battled a gargantuan killer known as The Undertaker.

McGill had seen several of Gabbi's paintings and been impressed by them before that eventful night. Later, visiting Gabbi as she lay recovering in a Paris hospital, McGill had committed to having her do his official portrait. As the nation's first male presidential spouse, he thought he should set the bar high for those who might follow him.

Gabbi's first question, after arriving in Washington, was, "Which do you think is your better side?"

McGill shrugged. "Six of one, half-a-dozen of the other."

"Your face is fairly symmetrical," she agreed. "That's a common standard for good looks."

"Me and Rory Calhoun," McGill said.

The old-time movie star McGill thought he resembled. Gabbi had gone to the trouble of searching out pictures of the actor. There was some basis for comparison, but she thought McGill had more intelligence in his eyes, and just a touch of menace, too. She'd come to see that after he'd suggested they fight a giant armed with only sticks.

"But we don't want common, do we?" Gabbi asked.

"There might be a lot of people looking at this painting over the years," McGill said. "Better do something to hold the public interest."

They settled on the three-quarters pose.

"A majority of sunny Jim," Gabbi said, "with just a shadowed hint of trouble waiting around the corner for those who deserve it."

McGill laughed, but he liked the description.

He tried it out on Patti and Sweetie.

Got a kiss and a thumbs-up in response.

White House Library

The president's face was impassive as the lights came up in the White House library. She'd had the space converted into her private reading room, a retreat from the Oval Office. She did much of her obligatory study of threats to the nation and to her own life there. She also kept current about the possible plots against her husband and the McGill children in the room. Not that she mentioned that to Jim.

She looked at Secret Service Director David Nathan and SAC Elspeth Kendry.

"Computer generated imaging?" the president asked.

"Yes, ma'am," Nathan said.

Galia Mindel, the White House chief of staff and the only other person present, said, "It's amazing how realistic it looks.

That's what makes it all so frightening."

The president offered a thin smile. "This is the first movie I've been in where I die at the end. Can't say I care for the script at all, not with Jim and me ..."

She didn't finish the thought.

The president, Galia, Nathan and Elspeth had just finished watching the Secret Service's production of the threat it thought had the best chance of killing the president. The means would be an unmanned aerial vehicle, small but deadly. The place would be a public setting in which the president offered prolonged exposure, her inauguration.

The security array protecting her that day would be massive with the best people and technical resources doing their utmost to prevent a tragedy, but the challenge they faced would be equally great. Hundreds of thousands of people would be within a mile radius of the president. Many of those people would be openly hostile to her, thinking she'd either stolen the election or had been the beneficiary of an effort to steal it.

The leadership and partisans of the new True South party had been anything but conciliatory about the election's outcome. Despite their candidate, Senator Howard Hurlbert, having received fewer popular and electoral votes than the president, they claimed that if a "faithless" elector, Sheryl Kimbrough, hadn't switched her vote to the president, the election would have gone to the House of Representatives, and Hurlbert would have won.

They were probably right. But that wasn't what happened.

In earlier times, the political right had been fond of telling the left to get over tough losses. Now, True South was unwilling to follow its own advice. The new party was promising to battle the president every day of her coming administration. To make her life "a living hell," and assure history recorded her as a failed president.

The political dimension of the challenge lay outside the concern of the Secret Service.

The chance of another president being assassinated was what kept them up at night.

They had told the president the threat matrix was at an historical high.

To impress Holly G. with the seriousness of the threat, they'd produced their Inauguration Day assassination movie. Done a hell of a job with it, too, the president thought. She'd caught a glimpse of real fear on Galia's face as she watched the final scene.

Now the White House chief of staff asked Director Nathan, "Is drone technology so readily available that your scenario is plausible?"

Nathan said, "Our military and intelligence agencies have the best drone technology in the world, but the race to catch up has been underway for the past five years. As of now, China, Russia, India, France, Germany, the UK, Italy, Turkey, Israel and India all have drones. So does Iran, and their people have studied the drone we lost over their territory two years ago.

"Given the global dispersal of the technology and the fact that much of it is in the hands of people who are openly antagonistic to us or at least wouldn't mind seeing us suffer, we have to consider that a drone attack on the president is feasible."

Galia's face reddened. "But that would be an assassination, an act of war."

Nathan was about to respond when the president raised a hand.

"That might be just what an enemy or a provocateur intends, Galia. War might be a small price to pay, in some people's minds, for the bragging rights of saying they killed the president of the United States."

"Exactly, ma'am," Nathan said.

"But you're also considering the possibility that a domestic political enemy might have obtained a drone through some black market source, aren't you, David?" the president asked.

Nathan said, "Yes, ma'am."

"The melee your movie showed, that would have been a distraction to the security personnel. Have you considered that the violence in the crowd might be deliberately caused in concert with the drone attack?"

"We suspect that would be more likely than spontaneous mob action," Nathan said.

The president asked, "Are you recommending that I cancel my public inauguration?"

Everyone in the room knew that the official swearing in would happen on Sunday, January twentieth, inside the safety of the White House.

"We're asking that you weigh the risk, Madam President," Nathan told her.

"Thank you, all of you. I'll need some time to myself now."

Nathan, Elspeth and Galia all left. The chief of staff was the last to depart. She gave the president an inquiring look, as if to say, "Are you sure I can't be of help?" The president gently waved her out.

She was going to have to watch the damn movie again.

With Jim. So he could see it, too. Watch the two of them die together.

Get his opinion. Then make her decision.

Air France Flight 006 en route to New York

Investigating Magistrate Yves Pruet and his police bodyguard, Odo Sacripant, sat in the first row of *première classe* on the starboard side. Odo had informed the chic cabin attendant whose job it normally would have been to hover over them anticipating their every need that the two men required only their privacy. If they wanted anything else, he would press the call button.

Odo's voice was gentle as he delivered his message, but his hard Corsican face provided a clear subtext that his wish was to be respected. The seats behind the magistrate and his bodyguard were empty, as were those across the aisle. The closest company they had was an elderly couple on the other side of the plane, one row to the rear.

Both *monsieur et madame* had their seats reclined, wore sleep masks and buzzed quietly with the respiration of medicated slumber. The smooth flight did nothing to disturb them.

Even so, Odo kept his voice low.

"I would be happy to kill this man for you, Yves."

Revenge being a specialty of certain Corsicans.

Pruet gave his old friend a melancholy smile. "Of course, you would. Nonetheless, the task remains mine."

"Yes, but carrying it out will change you."

"Perhaps that would be for the best."

"You might not like who you become."

Pruet said, "I'm not so happy with who I am."

Odo sighed. He'd taken things as far as he could for the moment. If he pushed any harder, *Monsieur le Magistrat* might simply send him home. Not that he'd ever leave Yves alone. He would wait for another moment and try again to reason with his superior.

In the meantime, he pursued another angle.

"You are sure you don't wish to contact *Le Partisan de la Présidente?*"

The president's henchman, James J. McGill.

"I am certain of nothing," Pruet said, "other than the fact that neither of us has plied his trade in the United States before."

"Another hurdle," Odo agreed.

"We will do what we can," Pruet said. "Start our investigation in New York and see where it might lead us."

Odo nodded. "*Bon.* With any luck, we'll find the bastard, deal with him and be back in Paris almost as if we'd never left."

Pruet smiled again, more sadly than before.

He closed his eyes and said, "Of course, you and I, we are the luckiest of fellows."

Far from it, Odo knew.

He said, "If we have to engage the services of *Monsieur McGill,* he will not be so easy to deceive."

"We will tell him the truth. We are trying to recover an invaluable Renoir painting, stolen from my father's summer house," Pruet said.

Odo bided his silence.

Pruet opened one eye. Looked at his friend.

"You think that will not do?"

Now, Odo closed his eyes. "It is the truth, but it might not be enough."

"You are right. It wouldn't do to underestimate *Monsieur McGill.* We must *behave* as if all that concerns us is a painting."

Odo said, "Should we use *Monsieur McGill's* help to find our man, and he learns that you have killed the fellow, you will lose a friend."

"I know," Pruet said. "A terrible thing, but I have no choice."

The flight had left Paris early that afternoon. But both men had been hard at work for the past several days, and they slept fitfully for the rest of the flight.

The Chief of Staff's Office — The White House

Having been dismissed by the president, Galia Mindel invited Secret Service Director David Nathan and SAC Elspeth Kendry into her office. She didn't offer them anything to drink. It was within her purview to know of any existential threat to the president, but she knew how the guys and gals with the guns liked to keep their secrets.

Hell, secret was their first name.

So Galia looked each of them straight in the eye.

"I want to know what percentage of likelihood you ascribe to the assassination scenario you just presented to the president."

Not blinking, Nathan said, "Fifty percent."

"Even money?" Galia asked.

SAC Kendry nodded.

"Good God," Galia murmured. She pulled herself together and asked, "If there's no attempt at the inauguration, does the likelihood of some other attempt on the president's life decrease?"

Nathan said, "It does, but only slightly and it remains higher than normal threat levels for the foreseeable future."

"Break it down for me," the chief of staff said, "into foreign and domestic components."

The director looked at SAC Kendry. It was her turn in the batter's box.

She said, "Foreign threats are marginally higher, but that's to be expected for either a new president or a newly reelected president. Bad guys around the world see the first few months of a president's term of office as moments of maximum vulnerability. All the new people in the White House are getting their bearings and maybe things aren't working so smoothly yet."

"But you have things well in hand, don't you, SAC Kendry?" Galia asked.

"Yes, ma'am. Former SAC Crogher and I worked very hard to assure a seamless transition. I'm confident we're doing everything possible to keep the president safe."

"Mr. McGill, too?"

Elspeth bit her lip, then said, "I'm sure you know by now the unique problems that Holmes presents to us." Holmes being McGill's code name. "His exposure is greater because he insists on doing things his way. He doesn't answer to you or us or anyone I know of."

Galia had to agree with that assessment.

She knew from delicately worded discussions with the president that even the commander-in-chief couldn't rein Holmes in. That simply wasn't the way their marriage worked. Damnit.

She asked, "Does Mr. McGill share the president's elevated threat level?"

Nathan said, "Only insofar as the times he's at the president's side. On his own, his threat level has actually decreased. It's the inverse of his public approval ratings. Holmes has charmed a good portion of the country."

Elspeth said, "Saving your life on live TV gave him a big bump."

Galia nodded. She still had flashbacks to the moment she'd almost died.

"Mr. McGill now has former Special Agent Ky working for

him, as well as Leo Levy. So he's essentially as well protected as ever," Nathan said.

"You're okay with that?" Galia asked Elspeth.

"I accept it," Elspeth said. "I grew up in Beirut when people were dying in the streets by the dozens every day. You see that, you realize nobody can ever be fully protected, but some people walk away from situations you'd think would surely kill them."

Galia nodded. If James J. McGill had been a half-second slower in his reaction time, she wouldn't be alive today.

"You've said you think the main threat to the president is domestically based," Galia said. "Is there any evidence to tie it directly to supporters of Senator Hurlbert?"

Both Nathan and Kendry sat stone faced.

The director said, "We have no direct evidence implicating either the senator or senior members of True South."

Galia said, "That still leaves a lot of people who voted for Hurlbert and his new party."

The chief of staff held up a hand. She knew that she could poke her nose into the workings of a Secret Service investigation only so far. She didn't like it, but she had to live with it.

That was easier to do because she had her own network of spies.

She might pin down the threat to the president before anyone else did.

"Thank you for your time, David. You, too, SAC Kendry."

After they'd gone, she picked up her phone and made a call.

Captain Welborn Yates answered.

McGill's Hideaway — The White House

Gabbi Casale had tucked her easel into a corner, packed up her paints and took her brushes and the canvas with the portrait-in-progress of McGill with her when she left the room. McGill felt sure Gabbi was hiding the painting somewhere in the White House, but the building had one hundred and thirty-two rooms.

Even after four years of living in the place he hadn't seen all of them.

He felt sure the president's personal secretary, Edwina Byington, knew where the painting was kept, but that privileged knowledge was just the sort of nugget Edwina would withhold for her memoirs.

McGill was still working on solving the puzzle when Patti entered the room.

She had the Residence's head butler, Blessing, with her. Blessing had brought drinks, shots of Bushmills single malt, for the First Couple. The president told Blessing they were not to be disturbed for anything short of a family or national emergency.

McGill took all this in without a word.

Until he was alone with his wife. He raised his glass and said, "*Sláinte.*"

Irish for health. Appropriate to the whiskey and the mood McGill was sensing.

"God save the president," Patti replied. "Her henchman, too."

She clicked her glass against McGill's. They drank. McGill got an eighty proof presidential kiss and they sat close together on the room's huge leather sofa. The vibe was starting to make McGill feel uneasy. It wasn't that long ago that Patti had experienced a transient heart condition, one that might have killed her but hadn't.

"You're all right, aren't you?" he asked. "We don't need to call Nick?"

Artemus Nicolaides, the White House physician.

Patti put her glass and McGill's on an end table.

Not bothering about coasters. Worrying McGill all the more.

She took his hands in hers and he was somewhat reassured by their warmth.

"I'm in excellent health, as far as I know. I feel quite well. Physically."

"Then the problem is?" McGill asked.

"I've just sat through two screenings of a horror movie."

That one lost McGill for a moment, until he remembered the kinds of secrets to which a president was privy. It was a part of

Patti's job that had always left him feeling conflicted. He understood there were awful things his wife learned of almost daily. It wasn't his place to share in that knowledge. For the most part, he was glad to remain blissfully ignorant. But it was hard to comfort someone when you weren't allowed to know what was bothering her.

Simply trying to be a warm and fuzzy presence failed to satisfy either of them.

McGill always wanted to take steps to make things right. Rationally, he knew that the scope of the problems a president faced every day were beyond the ability of even the most motivated and able gumshoe to solve. Emotionally, that wouldn't have stopped him from giving it his best effort to meet the challenge.

If he brought Sweetie along, that just might be enough to overcome.

Assuming he was allowed to know what the problem was.

"How much can you tell me?" McGill asked.

"On this one? Pretty much the whole thing."

Patti looked around, even though she didn't need to do so. She knew Jim hadn't sneaked a TV into his hideaway. Doing so, even to watch a White Sox, Bears or Bulls game, would have allowed the world to intrude. He wouldn't have that.

There was, however, a television in their bedroom. Tucked away in a cherry-wood cabinet. But perfectly functional for viewing moments of tragedy or disaster before leaving bed to try to make the world all better. Might be just the place for the two of them to …

"Come on," the president said, getting to her feet, tugging McGill upright. "I need you to see the horror show, too. So you can give me your opinion."

McGill nodded. Put an arm around his wife's shoulders.

Old Ebbit Grill — Washington, DC

The restaurant was little more than a stone's throw from the White House, and it met Galia Mindel's requirement of the moment, anonymity. She'd never been there before. As far as she knew, no one working there knew her. Still, there was no telling if some politically astute diner might recognize her. This was Washington, after all.

To minimize the possibility of being spotted, she dressed down, far more casually than she did to stand at the president's side. The restaurant's dress code was informal. Blue jeans were acceptable. Galia had never owned a pair of jeans in her life, but that was what she'd asked Welborn Yates to wear. She definitely didn't want him to show up in uniform or even a suit.

Taking his cue from the suggestion of denim, Welborn had asked, "Sneakers or boots? Flannel shirt? Carhartt jacket?"

Galia had no idea of what a Carhartt jacket was, but if it went with a flannel shirt, that would be good. As to the shoes, Galia said, "Boots, unless they're the cowboy kind."

"Mine have more of a scuffed military look," Welborn said.

"Perfect," Galia said.

"Any other tips on wardrobe or grooming?" he asked.

The chief of staff knew she was being twitted, but as long as he'd asked, "Don't be disheveled, but don't have every hair in place either."

"Baseball cap?" Welborn asked.

Galia liked that idea. "As long as it's nothing too eye catching."

"Right. This is just between us, Ms. Mindel? No mention to Kira?"

"No mention to anyone, Captain Yates."

"Yes, ma'am."

Welborn showed up at the restaurant at two p.m. on the dot, as instructed. He asked the hostess for Ms. Bernstein's table, Galia having gone so far as to use an alias. He was shown to a booth with a fair amount of privacy. Good thing he had a sherpa. He wasn't sure he would have recognized Ms. Mindel. She had her hair pulled back in a bun, wore pointy plastic-framed glasses that looked like they came from a time-capsule sealed in 1959, and was dressed in a Rayon pantsuit the color of Kraft caramels.

Once the hostess had departed, Welborn asked, "Ms. Bernstein?"

Galia pointed to the seat opposite her. Welborn slid into the booth. She gave him a long once over.

"Too hayseed?" he asked "Or not hayseed enough?"

"A happy medium," Galia said. "Only I have to wonder, do you shave yet?"

"Yes, ma'am, quite closely, as both my upbringing and training require."

His wife required it, too, but he wasn't going to get into that. The whole hush-hush ambience of the meeting would have amused Welborn, if he wasn't getting a very uneasy feeling about all the costume drama.

Galia Mindel was the White House chief of staff, not some practical joker.

She had to have a *serious* reason to put on this show.

Galia asked, "So you could grow a … I guess a stubble would be what I'm looking for."

"Yes, ma'am, I could do that. I assume you'll tell me why."

Galia nodded, and told him to stop calling her ma'am.

Omni Berkshire Hotel — Midtown Manhattan

Yves Pruet and Odo Sacripant took a taxi from JFK to the Omni Berkshire Place on East 52nd Street. With the recent decline in the value of the euro, New York was not quite the bargain for Europeans that it once was. Money, however, was not a worry for the two visitors from France. Augustin Pruet, Yves' father and the head of the family business, was picking up the tab.

He had insisted that justice be done, no matter the expense.

Pruet was honored that his father had entrusted him with this duty.

Still, he suspected that Papa had made a side agreement with Odo. An additional reason why his friend repeatedly made it clear he was willing to dispose of the villain in question. Not that Odo needed more than one justification to protect a friend or strike down an enemy.

The two men had adjoining rooms on the third floor of the hotel.

Odo tapped on the connecting door and Pruet admitted him.

The bodyguard peeked into Pruet's closet and bathroom, looked beneath the bed, surveyed windows of the buildings across the street, all to make sure no evildoer was about to strike. Normally, the magistrate would have found such melodrama mildly amusing, worthy of a quip. Not now. Blood had already been spilled. A dear friend lay dead.

It would be foolish to think the malefactor would not expect a reprisal.

Satisfied all was well, Odo asked, "You will be comfortable here, Yves?"

"Oui."

The hotel was an elegant older building. It offered guest rooms not far above street level, Pruet's chief requirement when looking for accommodations. He said he found it impossible to sleep soundly if he knew there was a large number of people of dubious judgment lodging between him and the ground.

Smoking was forbidden in the hotel, but nicotine was an insistent demon. All it might take to cause a tragedy would be one fool flouting the rules and falling asleep in bed with a lit cigarette between his lips. Pruet knew this for a fact; he'd sent one such cretin to prison for the rest of his life.

Thinking of the matter of crime and punishment, the magistrate asked his bodyguard, "Have you considered the possibility one or both of us might end our days in an American prison?" A thought struck Pruet and he added, "Is this one of the American states that has the death penalty?"

Odo, always meticulous in his work, knew the answer.

"There is a law providing for executions, but a court has ruled it can't be used."

"Why not?" Pruet asked.

Odo shrugged. "Technical reasons that are beyond my understanding."

The magistrate frowned. "For us, they would likely make exceptions."

On that cheerful note, the two foreign visitors left the hotel for a late lunch, before they started their tour of the city's finest art galleries. They didn't expect to find the Renoir stolen from the Pruet family hanging on a gallery wall. They were looking for a broker.

Someone who sold stolen art to the unscrupulously wealthy.

There were many places around the world where such reprobates thrived.

For Pruet's money, though, New York City was the place to start looking.

Old Ebbet Grill — Washington, DC

Galia had forgotten one detail in implementing her plan and that annoyed her.

She didn't want to be called up before a Congressional committee someday and have to admit that she'd broken a national security law. That or commit perjury. She had legions of enemies in the capital who would like nothing better than to see her behind bars. Permanently.

So she asked Captain Welborn Yates, "Are you cleared to learn top secret information?"

Welborn was about to say, "Yes, ma'am," but he bit his tongue and merely nodded.

Adding in whisper, "Everything but the nuclear launch codes, per the president's order."

That sat Galia back in her seat for a moment, marveling at the degree of trust the president had placed in this young man. Without informing her. In a way, though, the strength of that bond would likely work in her favor. Captain Yates would want to repay the president's high regard for him. But Galia didn't get to that immediately.

Instead, she observed, "To my ear, you've lost a good deal of your Southern accent during your years in the White House."

Galia had lost none of her New York accent.

Unable to resist such an opening, Welborn said, "Overexposure to Yankees."

Galia parried without scolding. "Always a risky thing. What I'd like to know is, can you sound more down home, should you choose?"

Welborn assumed his best aw shucks smile. "'Course, I can. I jus' think of Mama makin' grits in the mornin'."

Galia smiled, liking the voice she heard.

"And how often did she do that?"

"Never," he said in his normal voice.

It had been a long time since anyone, other than James J. McGill, had cracked wise with her, Galia thought, but she liked Welborn's attitude. His acting ability, too. He likely would need both those qualities and several more to acquit himself successfully. The situation into which she wanted to send him could well involve mortal danger.

First, though, she had to get a better read on him. The worst thing would be to have him commit to what she wanted and not be able to follow through.

"Forgive me for asking," Galia said, "but how are things at home?"

Welborn's sense of unease soared. He had the notion to walk away there and then. Not worry if he might put the chief of staff's nose out of joint.

Before he could move, though, the waitress arrived to ask for their lunch orders.

That mundane inquiry made him feel his thoughts had veered into the melodramatic.

He was just having lunch, albeit an unusual one, with one of the most important people in the country. It was perfectly within the bounds of civil conversation to inquire about the well being of a junior colleague's family.

Only once they'd given their orders and the waitress had departed, the spirit of the rendezvous swung back to the ominous again.

That being the case, Welborn didn't think it out of place to respond, "Why do you ask?" He'd been about to say ma'am again, swallowed it and let the question hang.

Galia said, "You're still relatively newly married. You've recently become a father. I hope everything at home is going well, but I also understand domestic responsibilities can distract even the most dedicated professional from his responsibilities. The only losing political campaign I managed happened when my two sons were preschoolers and I was working from home. I overcommitted when I took that job. Never should have done it. I had to apologize profusely to the candidate. She should have won."

"I've been able to balance all my obligations," Welborn said in a quiet voice.

"Kira and your little girls are well?"

Welborn nodded.

Galia thought about that. Maybe what she had in mind was too much to ask of this young man, recently married and newly a father. Remembering her own youth, in the days of military conscription, she recalled that young fathers had been exempted from the draft. A rare example of social decency in those days.

Ironically, it was her reluctance to speak that piqued Welborn's interest, and prompted a bit of insight from him. In a whisper, he told her, "You want me to do something off the books. Something dangerous."

Galia nodded. "Exactly."

"What?"

Galia looked around. Seeing no one nearby she leaned over the table. Welborn responded in kind. If they'd been any closer, they would have been kissing.

"I want you to find out for me, personally, how real and how immediate the biggest threat to the president's life is."

Welborn Yates was a federal agent, a trained investigator. Beyond that, he'd become a protégé of James J. McGill and Margaret Sweeney, from whom he'd learned more than a few things. But he'd never worked undercover. He could only imagine the risks that might involve.

Losing his life, for one.

Leaving Kira a widow and Aria and Callista fatherless.

If he rejected Ms. Mindel's idea, though, and the president was assassinated, he'd never be able to live with himself. The president had plucked him from his desk at Andrews AFB and brought him to the White House. Without that, he'd never have met Kira, would never have had his twin girls melt his heart with their toothless smiles.

He told Galia, "I'll have to talk with Kira first."

Galia nodded.

"And we'll have to do this right," Welborn said.

"Meaning?"

"Meaning I'll need some backup, and Mr. McGill will have to know."

The President's Bedroom

McGill said, "I'm glad I didn't have to buy a ticket to that movie."

He and Patti reclined against their bed's headboard, a quartet of pillows cushioning them.

Patti looked at McGill and said, "That was the last time I'll watch that video. It's also the first time that I've thought to ask if the White House has a hypnotist on staff. I'm going to need some help to forget those images."

McGill picked up the remote control and clicked off the TV.

He put an arm around his wife's shoulders and drew her close.

"The best thing you can do," he told Patti, "is wake up the morning after the inauguration. Then you'll know that scenario was just somebody else's bad dream."

Patti nodded. "The way it was scripted, there was nothing you, I or anyone else could have done to prevent that awful ending."

"I think that was the point." McGill paused to consider whether he should say what he was thinking. Maybe not. But then he said it anyway. "Are you sure Celsus Crogher is out of the loop at the Secret Service? This is just the kind of thing he might concoct to scare both of us into falling in line."

"Jim, Celsus is officially retired. Off the payroll. Out of the building."

"He might have left a memo behind."

The president thought about that. "He might have."

McGill shook his head. "No, on second thought, I don't think he did."

"Why not?"

"He'd do it in a heartbeat if it was just to manipulate me, but he'd never do anything to scare you. A nervous president is not an effective president. Besides, in his own near-human way, Celsus is sweet on you. He's looking forward to that dance at the inaugural ball you owe him."

The president chided her husband. "Celsus is human, more than ever since he's learned to dance. Still more since he turned his worries over to SAC Kendry."

McGill feigned a shiver. "Poor Elspeth, to think she might turn out like Celsus."

"Careful," the president said, "or I might dance with her, too."

McGill looked at his wife and laughed.

"That might cause a bit of an uproar. Be fun to see who keeled over from outrage."

Patti smiled and then sighed. "We'd better save the fun and games for later. David Nathan asked me to weigh the situation. Decide whether to go ahead with the ceremonial outdoor inauguration."

"Or do a webcast of the real one on January twentieth from the safety of the White House?"

"Phone it in," Patti said.

"But you can't do that, can you?" McGill asked.

"No."

"Because if you do that you've surrendered. Might as well resign."

"Right," Patti said. "I have to be out there with my game-face on because, as someone just told me, a nervous president is an ineffective president."

McGill said, "Words of wisdom. I'll be right there beside you."

Patti bided a moment of silence and then she asked McGill, "Did you ever read any Greek and Roman mythology?"

"Yeah," he said, "we covered that at DePaul. Probably not in the same detail you did at Yale, but I know the broad strokes."

"That'll do. You remember the names Baucis and Philemon?"

McGill nodded. "Swell old couple, real nice people, had a long, happy marriage. Zeus and Hermes came to town in disguise one day and —"

Patti said, "Baucis and Philemon, poor though they were, were the only people in town to offer the gods shelter and hospitality for the night."

"And their reward was?" McGill asked.

"A warning. Get out of town because the gods were going to destroy everyone who had turned them away. Which they did with a flood."

McGill continued, "A flood that spared only the formerly humble home of Baucis and Philemon, which was transformed into a beautiful temple. Baucis and Philemon were granted the right to become the temple's guardians. Possibly the first jobs program in history."

Patti smiled. "What was the other favor the gods granted the sweet old couple?"

McGill said, "That when they died the same hour would take them both."

Patti kissed McGill's cheek. "Goes to show. You don't need the Ivy League to get a good education."

"Yeah, there's always Stanford," McGill said.

The two of them chuckled. Then McGill added, "For all the romance and comfort there is in the idea of two aged lovers departing at the same time, it's gotta be twice as hard on the people they leave behind. Assuming they survived the flood."

"No question," Patti said. "Let's send that myth out for a rewrite. Better yet, let's not die together or separately anytime soon."

"You know what my takeaway from that story is?" McGill asked. "A clean-living, hardworking couple like you and me, anything bad is about to happen, we'll get a warning from a higher power to beat feet or at least duck."

"You really think we're as virtuous as Baucis and Philemon?" Patti asked.

"Sure," McGill said, "if we work on our hospitality the next couple of weeks."

Lower Manhattan

After a meal at a Chinese restaurant on Mott Street — soup dumplings and fried fish for Pruet, pork in brown sauce for Odo — the two Frenchmen began their survey of Manhattan art galleries in the lower half of town. The prospect was daunting even for two keenly motivated investigators. There were four hundred art venues in the Chelsea neighborhood alone.

Galleries had sprouted in all manner of industrial spaces, in churches, in storefronts and in what had once been private residences. The possibilities would have narrowed dramatically if Pruet and Odo had limited themselves to showcases of museum quality masterpieces such as a missing Renoir, but they were looking for a shady middleman, a fence, and that sort of scoundrel might fetch up anywhere there was a profit to be made.

With the fickleness of the art market second only to that of fashion design, there might be huge sums paid for any artistic impulse imaginable: oils, pastels, watercolors, gouache, charcoals, abstracts, expressionism, representational art, street art.

The list was endless.

So was the extent of art theft and fencing.

Very little of what Pruet and Odo saw impressed them. That helped the two foreigners to play their parts, making their nationality and their sensibilities plain. They spoke exclusively in their native tongue, unless addressed in English. In that case, Pruet affected an accent thick enough to make the person addressing him strain to understand.

Giving Odo more than enough time to assess the other party's character.

They were approached by several gallery owners and other art hustlers. Pruet was polite to everyone, defying the stereotype that the French were haughty and rude. He was simply *moins qu'intéressé* — less than interested — in the art he saw and the sales pitches that came his way.

Papa might have disowned him had he brought home any of the paintings he was offered. And the schemers were far too small time in their propositions. They would have soiled themselves in their excitement had they come into possession of a Renoir, but they wouldn't know how to sell it to their advantage.

Fences were all about maintaining their advantage. They earned vastly more money than actual art thieves. In the area of antiquities, a looter might steal items of cultural significance, say, Mayan ceramics taken from a jungle site, and sell them for a few hundred dollars. The final buyer might pay six figures for the items. The fence and a willfully ignorant dealer would reap ninety-nine percent of the profit.

Neither Pruet nor Odo felt as if they'd been approached by anyone who played in the league that interested them. Most of the art they'd seen was dreadful, at least to their eyes. There was some, of course, that was both stunning and masterful. But even in those cases, the work was too new. Anyone buying it would be placing a bet rather than making an investment. Speculating that a painting's appeal would hold its allure indefinitely, with the artist's growing fame, the piece's lengthening history and inflation driving its price ever higher.

Pruet and Odo were looking for someone who traded in art that had already cleared that bar. As the evening wore on, they wore down. Even with the long naps they'd taken on the flight to the United States, jet lag was catching up with them. At what they thought would be their final stop for the night, a gallery owner with a mischievous sense of humor had filled trash cans with ice and bottles of Kronenbourg.

The idea of serving French beer rather than French wine amused both Pruet and Odo.

"Est-ce que cela vous dérangerait si j'avais une?" Odo asked. Would you mind if I have one?

Pruet said, *"J'en aurai une, aussi."* I'll have one, too.

Odo gave Pruet a look. *Monsieur le Magistrat* was not a noted beer drinker.

Still, Odo said, *"Bon, c'est bien."*

He brought two bottles and the gallery owner back with him.

She was young, no more than thirty, with ginger hair and a pert face. She addressed Pruet in French, spoken with a Belgian accent.

"Cosette Lenaerts. I hope you will forgive me for saying so, but you remind me of my papa."

Pruet offered a tired smile. "If you think well of your father, there's nothing to forgive."

"I love him dearly. You are comfortably situated in town?"

"Yes, thank you. We've found pleasant lodgings."

"You're recently arrived, right? You have that still tired from flying look."

Odo asked, "You are a detective in your spare time?"

"I notice things other people miss. That's how I succeed in business."

Pruet told her, "Your gallery is very lovely."

"But the art isn't quite what you're looking for."

Pruet shrugged, spread his hands. Saying no as politely as his fatigue allowed.

"Your tastes tend to the traditional?" Cosette asked.

"Do your father's?" the magistrate asked.

"Oui."

"So do mine, in the matter of paintings."

"I have just the place for you then." She took a business card from a pocket, gave it to Pruet. "This gallery is like a small annex of the Metropolitan Museum."

"Vraiment?" Pruet asked. Truly?

"Yes. Of course, the prices are set accordingly. If that's not a problem, I think you'd enjoy it. You'll have to be buzzed in. Please say I sent you."

She gave Pruet her business card.

"Will they still be open?" he asked.

"Of course, it's only eight p.m." Cosette smiled. "You're right off today's flight 006, aren't you? It's the wee hours for your bodies." Looking at Odo, she added, "Well, maybe not for you so much."

Pruet inclined his head to Cosette. "You are very kind."

She kissed Pruet on each cheek and told him, "I am just a good businesswoman."

She brought them two more bottles of beer.

Had her town car brought 'round to give them a ride.

East 78th Street — Manhattan

Duvessa Gallery was the name on the bronze plaque next to the front door of the townhouse.

"Odo," Pruet said as he pressed the doorbell.

"Oui." The bodyguard did a quick look around, saw no villains lurking nearby, took out his iPhone and concentrated on the task Pruet had set for him. Looking up the name on the plaque.

It was a trait Pruet had picked up from James J. McGill, a curiosity about the meaning of names. McGill felt, and Pruet had come to agree, the meaning of a name was a window onto a person's character. Even if the person in question was unaware of her name's meaning.

So Odo would look up the meaning of Duvessa, and see what else might be known about the gallery.

"Voilà," Odo said. "Duvessa. *Irlandais pour la beauté sombre."* Irish for dark beauty.

Pruet nodded and was about to ask if there was more when he saw a silhouette approaching from the other side of the frosted glass in the door. Odo put his phone away. A woman in early middle age opened the door and smiled at them. Duvessa? If so, she lived up to her name in every regard.

"Bienvenue, messieurs," she said. *"Je vous attendais."* I've been expecting you.

Pruet and Odo glanced at each other. Expecting them?

More of Cosette Lenaerts' business acumen? Calling ahead to alert her colleague to their imminent arrival? Or something else?

"Your French is lovely, madam," Pruet said in English, dropping the comic accent. "Especially the delicate Irish lilt you bring to it."

The woman introduced herself, Duvessa Kinsale, the mistress of the house.

She stepped aside to let them enter.

She explained her command of French. "A convent school in Normandy, refined by time at fourteen rue Bonaparte."

Pruet's eyebrows rose. He knew the Paris address of the Ecole Nationale Supérieure des Beaux-Arts. If there was anywhere in New York he might find what he wanted, the magistrate now felt, this would be the place.

Odo, as was his duty, had been the first to enter the townhouse.

Pruet had followed close behind.

Closing the door behind them, Duvessa said, "I'm sorry to say, I can offer you no beer."

McGill's Hideaway — The White House

The president frowned at her chief of staff.

McGill kept his face impassive.

Galia Mindel had called McGill, asked if she might have a moment of his time. The two of them had begun their relationship as the best of nemeses, at perpetual odds with each over who should have the final word in the president's ear. McGill readily conceded his place at the head of the line, if the matter at hand was purely political. He refused to budge, though, if he thought Galia was crossing the line into the Patti's personal life.

And God help the chief of staff if she tried to interfere with McGill's professional life, as she had a time or two.

With the intercession of the president and the passage of time, Galia and McGill had set down mutually understood boundaries and even come to regard each other with a wary trust. Then McGill had saved Galia's life, in front of television cameras that transmitted the heroic deed to the world. For her part, Galia had done favors for McGill, privately, that had aided more than one of his investigations.

With their relationship trending in a positive direction, Galia had some hope that McGill would help her out. He did, up to a point. He agreed to see her after business hours. He listened to her request. He even agreed to play along with her idea, conditionally.

"I think you're right, Galia," he told her as they sat in his hideaway. "This one should be done under the radar, but —"

Galia leaned forward on her chair. "We can't tell the president."

McGill shook his head. "I can't help but tell Patti. She's my wife."

Of course, back in his days as a Chicago copper, McGill had done plenty of job related things he hadn't told his first wife, Carolyn. If he had, she might have divorced him sooner than she had. Carolyn was a worrier. Patti had a far hardier composition.

The faint of heart didn't get elected president, twice.

"But the politics —" Galia started.

McGill put up a hand. "This isn't politics for me. It's being honest with my wife. That's why you won't be in the room when I talk with Patti. There will be no one who will ever be able to make either of us reveal what's said. That's the deal, Galia, take it or leave it."

Galia took it and left the room, before McGill asked the president to join him.

She envied McGill for the spousal privilege he enjoyed with the president. He was right. There wasn't a court or congressional committee in the land that could make him violate the confidence of a marital conversation.

There had been one time McGill had been called to testify before the House Committee on Oversight on a matter not directly involving the president, but that had worked out so badly for the chairman of the committee that McGill was unlikely ever to be summoned to appear before Congress again.

Galia would just have to —

Jump to her feet when the president opened the door to McGill's Hideaway and say, "Please join us, Galia."

Galia hurried into the room.

Saw the president frown at her.

Had the realization pop into her mind that very few chiefs of staff served two full terms of office under a president. But, damnit, after what she'd been through, almost dying on the job, making it through not just one but two elections of historical importance, she wanted to —"

Not let her knees buckle as the president took her shoulders and kissed her on the cheek.

Told her, "I love you, Galia. You're the sister I've always wanted."

The president being an only child.

The chief of staff felt tears well up in her eyes.

She was an only child, too.

Before she could start blubbering, the president told her, "Go home. Have a nice dinner. Call your sons. Tell them Jim and I say hello."

Clearing her throat, Galia said, "Yes, ma'am."

On the way out of the room, Galia saw McGill give her a wink.

That was all she needed to know. He'd smoothed the way for her.

Galia's plan would be set in motion.

Having the room to themselves again, Patti told McGill, "Galia thought I was displeased with her. I could see it when she first saw me."

McGill smiled and said, "Always good to keep the help on their toes."

The president gave her husband a gentle slap on the chest. Then she laughed and let him put his arms around her. She said, "I'm issuing a presidential order as of this moment."

"Should I snap to attention?" McGill asked.

Patti gave him a sly smile. "We'll get to that later. What I want to tell you now is that it will be your job for my second term of office to jolly me out of any funk I fall into. I'm going to need to have my spirits raised regularly, I fear."

McGill nodded. "I'll do everything I can. Except on truly solemn occasions."

"Of course."

McGill led Patti to his leather sofa and they sat hip to hip, holding hands.

"You're worried about Welborn," McGill said.

He'd explained Galia's idea to Patti, about having the young Air Force officer investigate the radical fringes of the new True South party to see if any conspiracy to assassinate the president amounted to more than just talk. In the normal scheme of things, that would be the job of the Secret Service, but after an election in which True South's presidential candidate had lost by one electoral vote, an official investigation would look like the president was trying to destroy her political opposition.

Something Nixonian like that, should it come to light, would only make the president's efforts to govern even harder. And the greater the number of people who knew about an investigation, the more likely it would be to leak to the press. A covert, unofficial operation — also Nixonian, come to think of it — would stand a better chance of going unnoticed.

Especially if the investigator had the regional background to blend in with the conspirators. That and expert guidance from a shrewd cop who'd been around the block more than once. McGill had seen the necessity of his playing the role of Welborn's mentor again.

He couldn't, however, get anywhere near the front lines.

His presence would look even more political than that of the Secret Service.

"Aren't you worried about Welborn?" Patti asked.

"I can't say he's like a son to me, but he'd qualify as a nephew."

"So you are concerned."

"Yeah, a guy with a new wife and two babies? I can identify."

"So what do we do?"

McGill gave his wife a look. She saw he had an idea.

"What are you thinking?"

"More often than not," he said, "undercover guys work alone. But it's not unheard of for two of them to pair up. Heckle and Jeckle. Or maybe in this case Homer and Gomer."

Patti thought she knew whom her husband had in mind. "Leo?"

McGill shook his head. "He'd do it and he has the right accent, but my money says there are lots of NASCAR fans in True South. They'd probably remember Leo from his racing days, and possibly know that he drives for me."

Patti had to agree. "But you can't mean Deke."

"No, former Special Agent Ky is too ethnically exotic to blend in."

"Then who?"

"A man of unquestioned courage. Someone off the payroll. Out of the building."

The president drew back, her eyes wide in surprise. "Celsus?"

"Bet he'd do it," McGill said.

East 78th Street — Manhattan

"Father was a bit of a scoundrel," Duvessa said.

She, Pruet and Odo sat in a private parlor on the first floor of the townhouse. The electric lighting was soft and a fireplace with dying embers added to the intimate atmosphere. As did the snifter of brandy each of them had in hand.

Pruet had refrained from sampling his. He did not wish to fall asleep before returning to his hotel bed. Odo and Duvessa had only sipped their drinks.

"What was the nature of his misdeeds?" Pruet asked.

"He rearranged numbers to add to his accounts while taking from others."

"A thief with an advanced education?"

"I'm afraid so."

Odo, always one to get to the point, asked, "He was caught?"

Duvessa said, "Not that I've heard, and I think his capture would make news."

Pruet, who knew about corruption on a grand scale, said, "He made an offering. Something to let the authorities save face. Gave them reason not to pursue him with full vigor."

Duvessa smiled. "Bravo, *monsieur.* Full marks. Eighty-five percent of what my father took was recovered. Fury was reduced to great relief and muted grumbling."

Odo shook his head. "There must have been no Corsicans harmed."

"That I can't say," Duvessa replied. "There might be one or two determined souls still looking for Father. In any event, Mother and I left England for France. I was quite young. Mother decided a convent school would be the safest place for me. When it came time for me to go to university, she married an American she had met and moved to California."

"And you went to art school and then to Beaux-Arts in Paris?" Pruet asked.

"No, I went back to the UK. The London School of Economics."

"Who paid for your education?" Odo asked.

"My stepfather."

Pruet and Odo shared a look. *Combien commode.* How

convenient.

"So you studied business, not art?" Pruet said.

"Exactly. But I've always loved art. When I was a little girl we had the most beautiful paintings at home. Before Father left, I spent hours every day looking at them."

"What happened to the paintings?" Odo wanted to know.

"I asked Mother. She told me not to think of the matter. I honestly don't know if my father still has them or they were seized as reparations. In any case, as I neared the completion of my studies, I saw an advert for a position with the business office at Beaux-Arts. It required someone who was fluent in French, possessed a broad knowledge of classical art and was well versed in modern business practices."

Pruet said, "The job might have been created with you in mind."

"I would have suggested a higher salary," Duvessa told him. "Paris is terribly expensive. I also would have made dealing with the bureaucrats less impossible, and asked the artists to keep at least one foot in the real world. I said *adieu* after two years."

"Surely, there must have been some benefits," Pruet said.

Duvessa nodded. "Seeing how a great art school should be run, learning how to deal with both budgets and artists, led me to think I could run a successful gallery. Feast on beautiful paintings and make a respectable living. I came here, worked for two other galleries for five years to make sure I wasn't deceiving myself and took the plunge on my own."

"Your stepfather helped with the financing?" Odo asked.

"He'd passed on by then. My mother is a partner in the gallery."

"A family business then," Pruet said.

"*Exactement.* Now that we've become acquainted, would you like to look at some pictures? We have a nice selection at the moment. I think you'll be pleased."

Duvessa led her prospective patrons up an ornately carved staircase to the third floor of the townhouse. She told them the work on the second floor was wonderful but of a more recent vintage. The third floor was reserved for her most discerning clientele.

She stopped on the stairs a moment to ask, "You do wish to see my best, don't you?"

Grateful for the momentary respite, a tired Pruet said, "Of course."

"Good. We've just had something extraordinary come in."

They renewed their climb. The third floor had been redone as one large open space.

The first painting Pruet and Odo saw, bathed in a spotlight, was a Renoir.

"Le Mariage d'Antoine et Jocelyne." Pruet's great-grandparents on their wedding day. A gift from the artist to Antoine Pruet in appreciation of his patronage. Until recently, it had never hung anywhere except his family's summer home in Avignon.

Pruet could sense Odo, behind him, start to become agitated.

The magistrate discreetly shook his head. Now was not the time.

Duvessa had her eyes on the painting. She turned to look at her guests.

"Magnifique, no?" she asked.

Pruet said, "Renoir has always been my favorite."

Omni Berkshire Plaza — Midtown Manhattan

Odo had wanted to walk back to their hotel through Central Park.

Hoping a villain would be foolhardy enough to attempt a mugging.

Giving him an excuse to thrash someone.

Pruet was too tired for a long walk and not in the mood for drama. They declined Duvessa's offer of a ride in her towncar and took a taxi. Odo sulked throughout the ride. He began his tirade only after they'd returned to Pruet's room at the Omni.

He'd wanted to rip the Renoir off the wall, Odo told Pruet.

After giving Duvessa's bottom a thorough paddling for toying with them as if they were children. Had she been a man, the punishment would have been far worse. Then they could have been off to the airport. Entrusted the painting to the cargo handlers of Air France, booked seats on the following evening's flight home and been done with the affair.

It was only after Odo had paused for breath that Pruet told his friend and protector, "The painting is a forgery."

Odo pulled his head back as if he'd been slapped.

"How do you know this?"

The magistrate sighed. "Duvessa Kinsale is not the only one who studied her family's paintings as a child. Of all my father's collection, the Renoir was indeed my favorite. It captured my heart from my youngest years. I imagined that someday I would have a bride as beautiful as Jocelyne and another great artist would paint my wedding day."

Odo's anger was displaced by sympathy for his friend.

Yves Pruet had grown up to marry a very beautiful woman, Nicolette Bisson. She had not only broken the magistrate's heart, she'd smashed his beloved guitar. There had been no more certain a way to show her contempt for the man she believed had failed her so badly.

Nicolette had expected social status and wealth from her marriage.

The love and music of a good man had been a poor substitute for her.

Odo shrugged and said, "Where would you have found another Renoir?"

"Nowhere, so far," Pruet answered, "and I've looked quite hard. Odo, old friend, I know every brushstroke of that painting. Over the years, I've memorized each of them. The painting we saw tonight was a respectable effort at reproduction. All the more so for being done in a short time. The forger has talent, but he does not have genius."

"Then why did you write a check for one thousand euros to Duvessa for the privilege of bidding on the painting when it is auctioned?" Odo asked.

"I wrote the check in the hope it would be deposited, creating a paper trail to follow."

Odo thought about that. "You think she would do such a thing?"

"Do you think Madam Kinsale is a thief or an honest saleswoman who has been duped?"

"A thief," Odo said with certainty. "Or an equally guilty accomplice."

Pruet said, "A cunning one. If we had accused her of dealing in stolen art, she would have asked what kind of a fool did we think she was, to lead us straight to a stolen painting. She would deny all knowledge of the theft and forgery. If we somehow managed to have her arrested, her lawyer would have demanded proof of guilt before she could be kept in custody. Lacking that, she would be released and disappear."

"Setting us back to the starting line," Odo said. "You were right, Yves. But if she's as clever as you say, why would she let us see the painting at all?"

"To taunt us, perhaps. Let us get ever so close to what we seek, then tug it out of reach. Of course, even if the police seized the painting, what would they have but a forgery?"

Odo's face clouded. Now he really wanted to make the woman pay.

"So she is cunning," Odo said. "Far too smart to cash the check, *n'est-ce pas?*"

Pruet said, "Thieves live to enjoy their spoils. Where is the pleasure in leaving an ill-gotten check uncashed? If she has unusual self-restraint, though, the check might make a pleasing keepsake. A reminder of how she outwitted us."

Odo's mood darkened further. "We might have just taken the woman to some out of the way place and *made* her tell us where the real painting might be found."

"And perhaps we might also have found the thief that way as well?" Pruet asked. "Is that what you are thinking?"

Odo frowned. Outwitting *Monsieur le Magistrat* was never easy.

"*I* will be the one to dispose of him," Pruet said.

"And I will be there with you, should you change your mind."

Pruet said, "*Mon ami,* these people who have wronged us are no fools. If we'd behaved rashly tonight, as you suggested, Duvessa would have had a countermove ready. Perhaps a small army of thugs, too many men for a lone Corsican to overcome. On the other hand, she might have needed no more than one corrupt policeman who would —"

A hard knock on Pruet's door cut the magistrate short.

He and Odo looked at each other.

They'd taken the taxi so Duvessa's driver wouldn't learn where they were staying.

Odo waved to Pruet to move out of line with the door.

With that done, Odo asked, "*Qui est là?*" Who's there?

A man's voice replied in French. "*Agent Spécial Riddick du FBI.*"

The Federal Bureau of Investigation?

Pruet and Odo looked at each other again and reached the same judgment.

It was time to call James J. McGill.

CHAPTER 3

Q Street — Washington, DC
Tuesday, January 8, 2013

Twenty-five years with the Secret Service hadn't so much as bloodied Celsus Crogher's nose, but one week after leaving the job, he started to think retirement might kill him. He found it impossible to sleep more than six hours a night, two more than he had for his time as head of the Presidential Protection Detail. That left three-quarters of a day to fill.

He worked out for two hours, running and lifting.

He devoted an hour to maintaining his townhouse.

He spent an hour at the firing range.

Invited to join his neighborhood watch, he reorganized its procedures and was quickly asked to assume its leadership. That took up another thirty minutes, including a daily call to the Metro cops to ask if there was any spike in criminal activity in the area of which he should be aware.

Given his former status, the cops told him things they didn't share with just anyone. He passed information on to his neighbors. Parceling it out on a need-to-know basis. Didn't want to scare them silly. Just keep them on their toes.

He spent ninety minutes a day working on his ballroom dancing. Alone.

There was no way he was going to embarrass either the president or himself when he danced with her at the inaugural ball. That was coming right up. Less than two weeks now.

The sum total of time required for all the activities he'd devised for himself occupied six hours. He had no clue as what to do with the remainder of his twelve hours of waking moments. He paced a lot, hoping his phone might ring. Praying it would be the White House with an offer of something for him to do. He'd have weeded the Rose Garden, had anyone asked him.

A package with no return address, but bearing a DC postmark, had arrived at his home a week after he'd left his job. Living dangerously, Crogher ripped it open, not caring if it was a mail bomb. Inside the box, he found two large needles, a skein of yarn and a copy of *Knitting for Dummies.* A former colleague's idea of a joke, though there was no note with the gift.

For a moment, Crogher wondered if Holmes — James J. McGill's code name — had sent the package to him. Decided he hadn't. For all their differences, Crogher had to admit to himself the president's husband had never tried to belittle him.

Other than to imply the former SAC wasn't totally human.

If only. He wouldn't be bored if he were a machine.

Crogher looked at the knitting needles on the side board where he'd left them. Some former law enforcement officers, when life after the job got to be too much or wasn't enough, did themselves in with their former duty weapons. Only Crogher's duty weapon had been an Uzi. He'd never want to leave that kind of mess for someone to clean up.

But those knitting needles. Somebody's idea of a joke. He wondered if he had the resolve and the strength to shove one of them in one ear and out the other. He didn't think that would leave too much blood. Cops who found him might even get a laugh, the way he'd look.

Only the prick who'd sent the package would feel sick about it.

Not quite ready to end it all in either a macabre way or a more mundane fashion that sunny, cold winter morning, Crogher decided to pass some time in a way said to lengthen the life of a useless old fart like him. He went out the front door for a walk.

Thinking he might not stop until it was time for the early bird dinner special at some chain restaurant.

He'd no sooner stepped outside and locked his front door than a classic old Chevy Malibu pulled up to the curb. A knockout blonde was behind the wheel. Now, there was a thought he'd never considered. Find himself a girlfriend.

Only not this particular woman.

Margaret "Sweetie" Sweeney was Holmes' partner in his private investigations agency. A government worker to his core, Crogher also had never considered a career in the private sector. Two new ideas in one morning. Maybe he ought to get out more often.

He descended his front stairs.

Intending to ask Sweeney if Holmes had sent her.

Before he could get a word out, she lowered the passenger side window and said, "Let's go for a ride."

Penn Station — Manhattan

"So your plan, Yves, is to motor up to the White House gates and ask if *Monsieur McGill* is receiving visitors this fine day?" Odo asked in French.

The Acela train bound for the nation's capital, with a stop in Baltimore, was just leaving the station. The car was all but full. A visual survey of their fellow travelers had shown row after row of what the two Frenchmen took to be domestic passengers, affluent business people moving from the country's hub of business to its political center. Neither of them had spotted the features, the manners or the wardrobe of any other foreign visitors.

No one had been speaking anything but English, Americans being the most determined of mono-linguists. That wasn't to say some well educated commuter might not have taken courses in French at his or her university. As a lark, if for no other reason. So, in the spirit of caution, Pruet and Odo kept their voices down.

"My thought," Pruet said, "is that it would be only polite to call in advance."

"Of course. You'll have to forgive my provincial manners. Do you have *Monsieur McGill's* phone number?"

"Several of them."

"I should have known."

"You might have guessed," Pruet said.

"D'accord."

The two men settled into a companionable silence. Odo turned his attention to the passing landscape. The normal position for him would have been the aisle seat, to fend off an attack on Pruet by another passenger. Pruet had accepted that logic until the morning he and Odo had boarded the Eurostar train at the Gare de Nord for a day-trip to London.

As they were making themselves comfortable for the journey, one of Pruet's political enemies happened to pass by outside the train and notice him. The man had stopped, given Pruet an evil grin and cocked his fingers at him as if he held a gun. The salaud — bastard — had gotten off his mimed shot and strolled down the platform before Odo had even turned his head in Pruet's direction.

After that, the magistrate and his bodyguard changed their seating arrangement.

On trains. Odo still took the aisle seat when they flew.

They had sat side by side last night at their hotel when Special Agent Osgood Riddick of the FBI had dropped by to speak with them. Pruet had taken the arm chair in his room, showing the nonchalance of an innocent man by putting his feet up on the accompanying hassock. Odo had pulled the desk chair over to sit next to the magistrate.

Riddick rested his backside on the edge of the desk.

With a smile, he'd asked, "Are you gentlemen visiting the United State to buy art, and before you answer, let me inform you it's a federal crime to lie to the FBI."

"All of you at the same time or individually?" Odo asked.

"Both," Riddick told him.

"We are here to *look* at art," Pruet said. "Perhaps we'll buy something, perhaps not."

Tired and coping with a portfolio of unresolved frustrations, Odo asked, "Is it the custom of the FBI to extend professional courtesy to colleagues from abroad?"

Before the fatigued Pruet could intercede, Odo displayed his *police judiciaire* — judicial police — identification. Riddick's eyesight was sufficient to read the credential from where he'd perched. A new smile creased his face.

"*Bienvenue,* gentlemen. Of course, we extend a warm welcome to our comrades in arms. Are you here in an official capacity? And you, sir," he addressed Pruet, "are you also with the police?"

Pruet said quietly but with authority, "The police are with me. I am an investigating magistrate." He produced his own identification.

"Okay. I'm not familiar with your country's justice system, but my guess is you're something like a prosecutor, on the state or federal level."

"The national level, yes," Pruet said.

"Got it," Riddick said. "Now, if you don't mind, can we get back to my other question? Are you and *Monsieur Sacripant* in the United States on official business?"

"No," Pruet said. "We are here on a matter of personal curiosity."

"You're not armed, are you?"

"No."

"That's good, but it also means you should be careful." Riddick paused to mull his thoughts for a moment. He decided to share, just a bit of information. "The bureau has Duvessa Kinsale under observation."

"It would be impertinent of us to ask why?" Pruet said.

"It would be more than I can tell you, except to say there would be an element of risk for you to return there."

Pruet and Odo shared a look.

Riddick wondered what that was all about. He asked, "Do you know any police officials in this country, someone who might advise you of the etiquette of dealing with the FBI."

"We are close acquaintances of a retired police captain," Pruet said.

"That's good," Riddick said. "He can give you the guidelines, if he was with a big enough police department."

"Chicago," Odo said.

"That'll do."

Pruet added, "And he was chief of police in a smaller town, I was told. Winnetka, Illinois."

That combination clicked into place for Riddick. For a moment, he regarded the two Frenchmen with a dubious look. Then he decided he'd better err on the side of caution.

"Do you mean —"

Pruet handed the business card McGill had given to him to the agent.

He inspected it closely.

The magistrate told him, "*Monsieur McGill's* private number at the White House is on the back of the card."

Riddick looked at the number and was suddenly glad he'd exercised good manners with the magistrate. He returned the card to Pruet. Got to his feet and nodded.

"Enjoy your visit to the United States, gentlemen, but it really wouldn't be a good idea for you to revisit Duvessa Kinsale."

Odo remained impassive.

Pruet asked, "If am not intruding too far, may I know your area of responsibility?"

Riddick told him, "I'm with the FBI art crime team."

McGill's Hideaway — The White House

McGill asked, "How's it coming?"

For the most part, he'd tried not to speak while Gabbi Casale was working on his portrait. When they'd started, it had been moderately burdensome for him to simply sit for an hour or two. Gabbi had taken some of the difficulty away by saying, "I've laid in the underpainting. So I'll work on your eyes now. I want to see the light in them, show what you're thinking, what you're feeling. So feel free to talk, softly. Just don't move your head, okay?"

That had worked for McGill. Helped the time to pass agreeably. He'd heard what Gabbi had to say about living in Paris. Was surprised when she told him she had given up the city for the first three months of each year, spending her time on the island of Saint Martin in the Caribbean.

"The light there is so much better than Paris in the winter," she said.

"Always a big consideration for a painter," McGill said. "Doesn't hurt that you can go outside in a T-shirt and shorts either."

"Doesn't hurt at all."

Then she confided she'd met someone who had led her to the island. They'd moved on, but she had grown fond of painting in a tropical setting and kept going back.

"A Gauguin thing?" McGill asked.

"A Gabbi Casale thing. I don't do bare-breasted island girls, but a young man at work or play without a shirt, that's another thing."

"Don't miss government work at all?"

"No."

"Ever give any thought to my idea of opening an office in Paris for me?"

"I've thought about it, but my paintings have started to sell at nice prices. After word gets out about my doing your portrait, the prices will go up. I'm happy holding a brush in my hand and having my bank account grow."

Then McGill's eyes were completed and he needed to be quiet.

Gabbi had suggested that a morning workout and a massage would help him meet her need for relaxed but not drowsy quietude from him. Patti had added the idea that he let go of his everyday concerns and let his mind wander to a future time when Abbie, Kenny and Caitie were all accomplished young adults, and the presidency was behind her, and all they had to do was relax in each other's company and perform the occasional good deed.

McGill had followed both suggestions and the time he'd spent posing for Gabbi had been moments of meditative bliss. The notion that his life could work out free from any major sorrow had left him feeling as tranquil as a child being tucked into bed. All of which had stopped upon viewing the Secret Service video showing Patti and him being obliterated by a missile strike.

Now, sitting immobile when he felt he should be *safeguarding* Patti's future left him antsy, unsure how much more time he'd be able to give Gabbi. His preoccupation left him looking stiff.

"I think I can finish without you," Gabbi told him, sensing her client's discomfort.

"The results won't suffer?" McGill asked, still holding his position.

"Might work out better."

"How's that?"

"You look … remote. Reminds me of that former boyfriend I told you about."

Before McGill could respond, there was a tentative knock at the door.

Gabbi said, "I'll get it. Feel free to move, if you want."

Blessing, the head butler at the White House, had come calling. Chagrin at the thought of disturbing a work of art in progress filled his eyes. Gabbi thought maybe she'd ask him if he'd like to sit for a portrait, after he retired. She was sure he'd have no time before then.

She told him, "No need to be concerned. We were just knocking off."

Blessing's eyes filled with relief.

He told Gabbi why he'd intruded. She said she'd give the message to McGill.

The president's husband was right where she left him, but clearly ready to hurry off if need be. "Everything okay?" he asked.

"*Monsieur le Magistrat* is in town," she told him.

"Yves Pruet?"

"*Lui-même*," she said, and then translated. "The man himself. Odo is with him."

"An official visit?"

"That part wasn't clear. Blessing did say they had talked to the FBI, and they'd like to inquire about retaining your services. They tried you at your office first."

The first thing that popped into McGill's head was Baucis and Philemon.

Whom the gods had favored for showing them hospitality.

McGill decided he'd better do no less with Pruet and Odo.

"I have to go," he said.

"Tell them I said hello."

As McGill was leaving the room, he tried to sneak a peek at his portrait.

But Gabbi had stepped between him and the canvas.

"Don't even think about it," she told him.

Wisconsin Avenue — Georgetown

Sweetie and Celsus Crogher walked along Georgetown's main shopping drag.

Sweetie offered to buy Celsus a cup of coffee and a pastry.

He said, "How about breakfast?"

"If you're hungry, sure."

They stepped into the Daily Grill and Celsus ordered bacon, eggs and a short stack of pancakes. Sweetie made do with a bowl of granola topped with berries. After Sweetie bowed her head and whispered a brief prayer of thanks for her food, they ate in silence. Then Celsus surprised her with his next request.

"You don't mind, before we get to whatever it is you have in mind, I'd like to look for some shoes." He said he wasn't satisfied with the pair he had for the inaugural ball.

Sweetie gave him a look, and saw he wasn't kidding.

The walked up the street to Soulier Shoes. Celsus saw a pair he liked in the window. He went inside and was pleased to find they had his size. He paid more for the shoes than any three pairs Sweetie had ever owned. Not counting the ones Putnam had bought for her.

They locked the pricy footwear in the trunk of her car and ambled along the street.

Celsus asked, "Holmes wants something, doesn't he? He sent you to talk to me."

Sweetie said, "He did, but the favor isn't for him."

Celsus stopped for a moment, looked at Sweetie and asked quietly, "Holly G.?"

The president's code name. Sweetie nodded. She resumed walking. Celsus kept pace.

He said, "If this is something serious, it should be handled the right way."

The official way, he meant. By *active* Secret Service personnel.

"If that's the way you feel, I'll tell Jim. He thought you might be interested."

Sonofabitch, Celsus thought. Holmes not only knew he'd be interested, he knew the former SAC would be unable to resist. He'd *still* give his life for Holly G. So the bastard was roping him into one of his off-the-books schemes.

Which, damn him, did have a way of working out.

Just about every stinking time he trampled on other people's turf.

Sweetie decided she'd given Celsus enough time to stew.

She said, "Let's turn around. I'll give you a ride home."

Celsus looked at her and asked, "How do you work with that man?"

"Jim? There's no one I'd rather work with."

"He calls the shots and you follow orders?"

Sweetie grinned. "It's not like that. Not even when we were cops and he outranked me. We talk things over, see who has a better understanding of a situation, a better fix for a problem. Go with the better idea."

"And if you can't agree?" Celsus asked.

"Then we disagree, and whoever has more invested in the situation gets to make the call. If we can't decide who has more skin in the game, each of us tries his or her own approach."

"And that works out?" His tone said he couldn't believe it would.

"So far," Sweetie said. "Maybe we're just lucky, but our luck's held out pretty well for over twenty-five years now."

The former SAC shook his head.

"I never count on luck."

"We don't *count* on it either. We do everything we can to *earn* it."

Sweetie thought steam might shoot out of Celsus' ears, with a whistling sound.

It was remarkable, she thought, that Jim and this man hadn't come to blows over the course of the president's first term. That or start shooting at each other. The absence of overt hostilities had to be attributed to God's grace and mercy.

Still, she thought maybe the Almighty could use a helping hand in this case.

"You wouldn't be working directly with Jim," Sweetie said.

The former SAC's eyes filled with suspicion. "No?"

"Unh-uh. For political reasons, he can't be seen getting involved. That's why he needs you."

"I'd be working alone?" Celsus asked.

He wasn't sure he'd be comfortable with that.

He'd always been part of a team.

The one with the most guns and money.

"No," Sweetie said. "You'd be working with Captain Welborn Yates."

Celsus knew Yates. Knew about him, too. He was the front man for Holmes' inside investigations. The ones, like this one, whatever it was, that wouldn't have looked good for the president's husband to do. But Yates was more than just a pretty face. He was smart. He'd tracked down the car thief who'd killed his three friends.

And he was always respectful when dealing with the Secret

Service.

That mattered to Celsus. As the president's pet, Yates could have lorded it over people.

"So he would be working for me?"

"*With* you. You'll work out your own professional courtesies. You can do that, can't you?"

Celsus paused to consider. Sweetie hoped he didn't need a manicure to reach a decision.

She played her last card. "You know from my visits to the White House that the president and I are friends, right?"

"Yeah?" Celsus said, feeling uneasy about what might be coming.

"So I know the woman. When we speak privately, I call her Patti. And I know Jim McGill as well as I know anyone. So when he asked me to talk with you, I knew both he and the president would like to have your help. Jim wouldn't ask without Patti's approval."

So there it was, Celsus thought. Out in the open.

Holly G. wanted him to go along with whatever McGill had planned.

"I'm in," he said.

Linnean Avenue, NW — Washington, DC

"You can't do this," Kira Fahey Yates told her husband, Welborn.

The two of them sat in Welborn's office in their new home. Welborn had had the privilege of visiting McGill's Hideaway in the White House and for the first time in his life had felt envious of someone else's circumstances. He wanted a space — a retreat — of his own, under his own roof, just like the hideaway. Somewhere he might go to think, plan or simply daydream.

So when Kira had come to him and said their townhouse, in which they'd lived for little more than a year, would soon be inadequate as their twin daughters came to need rooms of their own, and they should buy a house while the market was still relatively soft, he'd agreed without a quibble. Taking Kira by surprise.

Making her feel a little cheated. She'd written out a list of arguments to overcome his every objection.

She'd showed it to him. All five pages.

He'd kissed her and said, "Hang on to it. I'm sure you'll find new applications."

Kira was cheered by the thought, and the two of them went house hunting. They found just the place. A two-story white brick Colonial with a finished attic and a finished basement. Four bedrooms, five bathrooms, two detached garages, a sun room where Kira could hold court and an office for Welborn. He installed a huge leather sofa, as close as he could find to the one Mr. McGill had, opposite the room's fireplace.

The lot was a half-acre so the girls would have a big backyard to tear around in once they became self-ambulatory. It was everything Welborn and Kira could ask for in a new home. The price tag for domestic bliss was only one-point-five million dollars.

That sum was made doable by the fact that Kira had family money and Welborn had received a one-hundred-acre country estate in Virginia as a wedding present from the Queen of England, whom his father had served as personal secretary for twenty-two years. Welborn had used the property as collateral to secure a private loan from Mom and Dad.

What with Welborn's position at the White House secure for the next four years and Kira joining her uncle, Mather Wyman, the former vice-president, in his new political consulting business, working from home, Captain and Mrs. Yates felt sure there wasn't another young couple in the country luckier than they were.

Then Welborn came home to tell Kira he had to hit the road and hunt for assassins.

"You just can't do it," Kira repeated.

"It wouldn't be my first choice, either, but I think I have to."

"Why?"

"Practicality."

"What?" Kira asked.

"Well, if the president gets assassinated, I'm not sure Vice

President Morrissey would keep me on. If I lost my job, I couldn't repay the house loan. We'd all be thrown out into the snow."

Kira understood her husband was trying to humor her.

He reached a hand out to her. They were seated in the far corners of the sofa.

Kira didn't budge, leaving a one-cushion gap between them.

She said, "I have money. I'm working. I'll pay the bills."

Welborn dropped his hand. "Oh, sure. Then I'd feel inadequate. Turn to self-pity and bad habits. Be a poor father figure for our girls. They'd probably grow up and marry wastrels. Then you'd have to support those guys, too. A whole cycle of dependency could begin."

Tears appeared in Kira's eyes. Not from mirth.

She said, "I know what it's like to grow up without a father. I don't want that for Aria and Callista. I don't want to become a widow like my mother, either."

Welborn slid over to Kira, knocked off the kidding and took his wife's hand.

"I don't want any of those things either, but I honestly don't know how I'd live with myself if I didn't help out and some harm, or worse, came to the president."

"But that's what the Secret Service is for."

"True, but to be effective they need the best possible information."

Kira looked for another rebuttal, but she hadn't been given the time to work up a list of reasons. She thought she might not be able to dissuade Welborn in any case. Because if she succeeded in keeping him from doing what he proposed and the president was assassinated, the wound to their marriage might never heal.

Welborn had never seen Kira look so forlorn. It broke his heart.

He said, "I'm not going to try to be a hero. I'm not going to do anything more than see if I can find out if there's a real threat to the president. If there is, I'll beat a hasty retreat and tell the Secret Service. They'll do the heavy lifting."

Kira nodded, not that she really believed Welborn.

He wasn't the sort to bug out and let other people bear the burdens.

Kira took hold of Welborn's other hand.

"If you're going to do this, you've got to have help. Promise me that."

Welborn said, "I'll take whatever help I can get."

Never realizing he'd just agreed to work with Celsus Crogher.

McGill Investigations, Inc. — Georgetown

Investigating Magistrate Yves Pruet stepped through the front door of the building where James J. McGill had his professional offices and asked Dikki Missirian, who stood at his side, "This building has an elevator?"

"I am sorry, no," Dikki said.

"I am sorry also," Pruet told him.

He wondered if he'd picked up a virus on the flight to America. Airplanes were notorious for transmitting any number of maladies. It would be the height of irony if he were struck down by a virus while in pursuit of a killer.

Odo asked Pruet, "Would you like me to see if I can arrange for a sedan chair?"

Dikki gave Odo a look, wanting to help, but not understanding.

Odo tried to clarify. "A palanquin."

Understanding was reached and Dikki smiled, briefly.

"I don't think I've ever seen one in this country."

Pruet sighed. "Good litter bearers are so hard to find. Never mind, I'll walk."

He started up the stairs. To the *third* floor. *Sacre bleu.*

Odo trailed behind, serving as his rear guard. Ready to catch Pruet should he swoon.

Dikki called out, "I'll bring refreshments right up."

***

McGill greeted them with a smile at the door to his outer office.

"Yves, *mon ami.* Odo. It's great to see the two of you again."

He embraced the magistrate and shook the bodyguard's hand. He led the visitors into the reception area and introduced them to Deke Ky and Leo Levy. Handshakes were exchanged all around.

"Deke is a former special agent with the Secret Service. Leo was my White House driver, and is a former race car driver. Now, they both work here with me."

Dikki arrived with a tray of glasses and chilled bottles of sparkling water. Poland Spring. He set the tray on the reception desk. "Anything else you need, gentlemen, just call."

He bowed his way out.

Pruet asked McGill, "You own this building? That genial fellow is your employee?"

McGill said, "He owns the building. He's my landlord."

Pruet and Odo exchanged a look of surprise.

"You don't have landlords like Dikki in Paris?" McGill asked.

"Not that I have seen," Pruet said.

"I'll let him know. He has cousins looking to get into the business." McGill picked up three bottles off the tray. "Grab a glass and we'll go into my office and talk."

Pruet relieved McGill of a bottle and handed it and a glass to Odo.

The bodyguard recognized his cue.

"If you don't mind, Yves, I will stay here and talk with my new friends about the Secret Service and race cars. Tell them how we Corsicans do things."

"An excellent choice," the magistrate said.

He and McGill went into the inner sanctum.

Colonial Suites Hotel — Newport News, Virginia

The prayer breakfast in the hotel conference room became a prayer brunch due to the tardy arrival of both the pastor who would give the blessing and the member of Congress who would be the featured speaker. The two men had driven down Highway 64 from Richmond, keeping to the speed limit, looking at the countryside and wondering if the CIA was able to read their minds as they passed Camp Peary.

The camp was the Agency's training facility, also known as The Farm.

They joked about it, the idea of mind-reading, but neither of them put it beyond the realm of possibility. Spook shops and the mad scientists at DARPA consciously pushed themselves in the direction of science fiction, and then worked out ways to turn fantasy into fact. Not that they let the public in on what had been achieved with taxpayer dollars.

The pastor, George Mulchrone, sitting in the driver's seat, turned his thoughts to raising money for legal fees. Not for himself. For the abominable pederasts who not only trashed their vows of celibacy but also couldn't keep their filthy hands off young boys. The horrid creatures were bankrupting the church, and if he had his way —

"Pull off at the next exit, will you, George?" the politician, Philip Brock, said. "I'm going to be sick."

Mulchrone needed no more than a glance to confirm that Brock was going to lose the contents of his stomach, possibly from both directions, any moment now. They'd mutually agreed to decline the full coverage insurance at the car rental agency, both promising not to smoke in the vehicle as the cleaning fee was exorbitant.

God only knew what the charge would be to scour regurgitation and a flood tide of loose bowels. It might be cheaper just to purchase the car.

But Mulchrone made excellent time in reaching the filling station at a Walmart Supercenter. Brock bolted to the men's room and mercifully found it unlocked and unoccupied. He was in there long enough to make Mulchrone think he might have lost consciousness. Might be lying in his own foul mess.

The pastor had almost been forced to conclude it was his moral duty to see if his fellow traveler needed aid when the congressman emerged. He was pale but his face looked as if it had been splashed with water. His hair was freshly combed, and he'd popped a breath mint.

As far as Mulchrone could see, Brock hadn't stained any of his clothing. His suit was a bit rumpled but no more than could be explained by a highway drive. The pastor braced himself for an olfactory assault as Brock entered the car but he needn't have worried. All he smelled was the congressman's aftershave, which he had applied a bit thick.

"You'll be all right to continue, Philip?" Mulchrone asked.

"Yes, of course."

"And you'll be up to speaking?"

"Must have eaten something before I left home that disagreed with me. What's strange is, my digestive tract is normally tough enough to digest pig iron. Maybe somebody poisoned my groceries."

Mulchrone gave Brock a look.

With what they were up to, any number of people might want to stop them.

The priest drove on and the two of them arrived an hour late. Not a soul among the five hundred attendees in the conference room had left. Their breakfasts had been served on time and the pastries and coffee had kept coming. A spirited greeting welcomed the two visitors.

More than might be expected for two Yankees, one of them a Democrat, visiting Virginia, the cradle of the Confederacy.

But then George Mulchrone, retired Catholic priest, liked to emphasize that he'd been born in *South* Boston. He believed in the sanctity of life. Of the intrauterine sort. Leaving him free to preach that capital punishment was acceptable in the eyes of God who, after all, had set the example by flooding the world, drowning the wicked wholesale and sparing the lives of only Noah and his family. The pastor also condemned all sodomites and everyone who refused to see the evil of their vile ways.

His sermon and blessing were big hits with the crowd.

Congressman Brock, the first Democrat to represent Pennsylvania's ninth district in many years, began by asking the crowd, "You know what people say about Pennsylvania? It's Philadelphia and Pittsburgh with Alabama in between."

The audience laughed and slapped their knees.

"Now, I don't live in Philadelphia or Pittsburgh and my momma and daddy were *born* in Alabama."

Ma and Pa Brock were also graduates of Carnegie Mellon and Penn respectively, but their black sheep son didn't mention that. So he got another round of applause.

He went on to curry the audience's favor by castigating Patricia "Darn Her" Grant, the new leader of his party, for every sort of misdeed, maybe even stealing candy from babies. That got a laugh. But what she hadn't done, Brock said, was steal the last presidential election from True South and Senator Howard Hurlbert. The crowd wasn't expecting that and sat mute.

"It just looked like she did," he said with a wink.

Now, the audience rose to its feet and roared.

Among their number was Merilee Parker, one of Galia Mindel's spies.

But she wasn't included in the small group who met after the brunch.

To discuss regime change in Washington.

McGill Investigations, Inc. — Georgetown

McGill had a surprise for Pruet before they got down to cases. He gave the magistrate a Martin Golden Era 1937 Sunburst guitar. Pruet took the instrument gently into his hands, sat in the chair McGill offered him and looked as if he might cry.

"I can't let you keep that one," McGill said. He wrote off Pruet's obvious emotion as a French thing. "I borrowed it from a kid working at the White House. There's the case for it over in the corner. I thought you might enjoy playing in your spare time. While you're in Washington."

Pruet was a master classical guitarist. McGill had replaced the cherished instrument the magistrate had lost in Paris to his ex-wife's temper tantrum. The gesture had won him Pruet's heartfelt friendship.

"You are too kind," the magistrate said.

He couldn't resist plucking the strings and tuning the instrument. In a matter of moments, he began to play. McGill recognized the song immediately, "Puff the Magic Dragon."

McGill had suggested the Peter, Paul and Mary classic when Patti had asked for a duet, Pruet playing and McGill singing. The magistrate had rolled his eyes at the time, and they'd gone on to perform "Jail House Rock."

"You remember that, do you?" McGill asked with a smile.

"I learned it after you left Paris. I play it for my grandnieces and grandnephews. They are quite taken with it."

Pruet cleared his throat, got up and carefully placed the guitar in its case.

He returned to his seat opposite McGill and told him, "I need your help to find a painting that was stolen from my father's country house in Avignon."

McGill said, "Must be some painting, you and Odo coming all this way to get it back."

"It is a picture of my great-grandparents' wedding."

"Okay, I can see how you'd want that back," McGill said.

Pruet told him, "Its value is more than sentimental. The painting was done by Renoir."

"*The* Renoir?" McGill asked. "Pierre-Auguste?"

Pruet nodded. "My great grandfather, Antoine Pruet, was one of his patrons. The painting was a wedding gift, a token of appreciation. Renoir was still making his name at the time. In the years since, well, a conservative estimate of the painting's value today would be in the millions of euros. More likely, it would bring tens of millions."

That told McGill a thing or two.

The fact that the family hadn't sold the painting after its value had soared meant they didn't need the money. That it had been hanging in a country house, presumably a getaway from a main residence, likely meant that the painting hadn't been protected by museum-level security.

Then again, McGill remembered reading that some museums, especially those in Europe, had a quaint idea of security. They housed billions of dollars worth of art and trusted a sleepy guard or two to keep it all safe.

"You have a photo of the painting?" McGill asked.

The magistrate took one from a coat pocket and passed it to McGill.

Who looked at it and gave a low whistle.

"Gorgeous, both the painting and the young couple." McGill processed all the information he'd received thus far and said, "If this was my painting, I wouldn't have exhibited it in any public place."

Pruet bobbed his head. "From the day the artist presented it to my great-grandparents, it never left the family's summer home. It was not hidden from guests but neither was it publicized. Most scholars of Renoir's work have never heard of it."

"But the guests who visited the house would have seen of it," McGill said.

"Oui."

"Forgive me for asking, but are there any black sheep in your family? Someone in need of a large sum of money?"

The magistrate shook his head. "There is only my father, my brother, my sister, their spouses, children, grandchildren and me. I am the pauper of the family and I assure you none of us was involved."

"Is there any household help?" McGill asked.

He saw a flicker of pain, maybe even sorrow, in Pruet's eyes.

There was something important in that moment, but before McGill could pursue it, the magistrate answered his question.

"There is help, the Louvel family. They have been with us for over a century. They are well compensated and completely loyal."

If McGill had still been a cop, he would have pursued a line of questioning about the Louvel family. Under present circumstances, he simply flagged it in his memory, reserving the right to come back to it.

He said, "If it wasn't the family, it wasn't the help and the painting wasn't publicized, then somebody visiting the house had to talk about what he'd seen, and the word got back to the wrong person."

"Exactly the wrong person," Pruet said.

"You have an idea who the thief is?" McGill asked.

"An idea, yes. A certainty, no."

McGill said, "You'll have to clear that up for me."

"You remember when you visited Paris and you told me of an American myth? A man who wrestled bears."

"Grizzly Adams. He was a real person but the stories about him became legendary."

"Oui. I think what I am dealing with is a modern, French version of such a man. His name is Laurent Fortier. He is an art thief, but he doesn't steal from museums, auction houses or art galleries." Pruet paused to see if McGill could make the leap.

"He goes after easy pickings," McGill said.

It took the magistrate a moment to digest the American idiom. Then he said, *"Oui. Exactement."*

McGill followed up. "Your great-grandparents weren't the only patrons of the arts who supported unknown artists, people who later became famous, whose work is now worth millions. Some of those other patrons were given paintings as gifts or bought them cheap."

Pruet nodded.

"You didn't know about Fortier before your family's painting was stolen?" McGill asked.

The magistrate sighed.

He told McGill, "I heard his name but, as I said, I thought

he was a myth. He is a phantom; no knows what he looks like. I thought this was ridiculous, until it happened to my family."

"So how do you know his name?" McGill asked.

"In truth, I don't. No one does. A car with a flat tire was found abandoned near the scene of one theft. It was registered to a Laurent Fortier. It was a false identity that led nowhere. The police use that name because they have nothing else."

"What about the victims?" McGill asked. "Why haven't they spoken out?"

Pruet said, "What would we say? A thief has stolen valuable art from our homes? That might give other brigands the idea there could be more to take."

McGill had to concede that point. "So they asked the cops to keep things quiet."

"Demanded there be no public notice."

The next questions were hard, but McGill asked them anyway. "You didn't know how real Fortier is because you're still on the outs with your Interior Ministry? They don't share information with you?"

"I remain in disfavor," Pruet said. "Your dear wife won a second term in office. My good friend Jean-Louis Severin had to resign and flee the Élysée Palace one step ahead of a scandal placing him in the boudoir of the German chancellor, Erika Kirsch."

McGill hadn't heard that tidbit. Publicly, the former French president was said to have left office due to a serious, unspecified problem with his health. McGill wondered if Patti knew the real reason. Decided he'd need to find just the right moment to ask.

"So you lost your protector," McGill said.

Pruet nodded.

McGill got back to the missing painting.

"What makes you think Fortier brought the Renoir here?"

"Our police assume he either solicits customers among the unscrupulously wealthy or they commission him to look for work by preferred artists."

McGill said, "Okay, but wouldn't his customer base be global?"

"I'm certain it is, but two things lead me to think your country is where I will find the painting. The first is that my great-grandmother was American. Her name was Jocelyne Hobart. She was betrothed to a wealthy American from New York named Hiram Busby. The summer before she was to marry Busby she came to Paris on holiday and met my great-grandfather."

McGill grinned. "*Adieu,* Hiram?"

"*Oui.* But *Monsieur Busby* did not yield so easily. His marriage to Jocelyne was to be the cornerstone of a grand business alliance. Busby came to Paris thinking he would take his fiancée home by force if necessary. He was certain his wealth would allow him to have his way with any Frenchman who tried to thwart him."

"But it didn't work out that way," McGill said.

"No. He hadn't anticipated that he would confront a man of equal position and fortune, and one who was more than equal in his determination to have my great-grandmother. Theirs was a match of grand passion not business interests. Busby had also overlooked that my great-grandfather had all the political connections that wealth confers. When Busby tried to break into my family's country home, where Jocelyne had taken refuge, he was given a thorough beating by the Louvels and the police put him onto a vessel carrying German immigrants to Texas. He jumped ship in New Orleans and made his way back to New York from there."

"Carrying an animosity he bequeathed to generations of his family?" McGill asked.

"*Oui.*"

McGill could accept a multigenerational grudge, if not outright feud, as a reason to suspect the Renoir painting of the magistrate's forebears had been brought to America. That left one more point to examine.

"What's the other reason you think your family's painting is in the United States?" McGill asked. "You said there were two."

"Yesterday, Odo and I were in New York. We visited a number of art galleries there. In a handsome space called the Duvessa

Gallery, I saw a forgery of my family's Renoir."

That took McGill by surprise.

"You could tell it wasn't genuine?"

"Yes. I know it as intimately as the fretboard of my guitar."

A detailed understanding indeed, McGill thought.

"Was it a *good* forgery?" he asked.

Pruet said, "It was skilled, yes."

"When was the painting stolen from your father's summer house?"

"A week ago today."

"Is that enough time to do a skilled forgery?"

Another question to think about. Pruet said, *"Je ne sais pas."* I don't know.

McGill remembered enough French to understand. He said, "Neither do I. But I'd think a forger trying to copy Renoir's style would take more than a week to do a credible imitation."

"So do I," Pruet said, "now that you've enlightened me."

"I'm not personally involved," McGill said. He was tempted to ask about why Pruet had reacted emotionally to his question about the Louvels. Maybe the loyal family retainers had produced a prodigal son. Someone who had needed cash in a pinch. But McGill didn't get the feeling the time was right to ask that kind of question. Instead, he said, "Have you ever seen anyone, a guest I mean, use a mobile phone at your father's country house?"

"Yes, of course. France is a very modern —"

Pruet caught up with what McGill was suggesting.

"Someone could have photographed the Renoir without being obvious."

"Photographed it and emailed the picture to the forger."

The magistrate drew a deep breath and let it go slowly.

"I was foolish enough to think Odo and I might handle this matter ourselves. Our conversation has destroyed that illusion. Do you have the time to help me, *monsieur?"*

McGill thought about the need to find out how real the threat against Patti was.

That came first. If he took Pruet's case, he might have to table it at least momentarily.

But the fact that he'd be working for Pruet would give him cover, should anyone eventually ask if he'd been poking his nose into the affairs of the president's political opponents. And then there was the matter of hospitality paying dividends.

"I can give you at least some of my time. Enough, I think, to help you."

"*Bon.* Then there is one more thing I should tell you."

"Okay," McGill said, wondering what else was coming.

"Odo and I were visited by an agent of the FBI last night. His name, he said, is Osgood Riddick. He strongly advised Odo and me not to return to the Duvessa Gallery, even though I told him I'd put a deposit of one thousand euros down for the right to bid for the forgery."

"You did that because?" McGill asked.

"Owning the forgery might be the first step to finding the forger."

"Good idea," McGill said. He felt better about working with Pruet than he had a moment earlier. The man might be distracted by something he'd yet to share, but he still had his moments.

"The other thing you should know about this Riddick fellow," Pruet said, "he told Odo and me he is a member of the FBI's art crime team."

So, by coming to him, the magistrate was buying a little political insurance, too, McGill thought. Riddick, whoever he might be, could bully a foreigner, but he wasn't going to push McGill around. Another example of good thinking.

If Pruet got over his funk, he might be a real help with this case.

Pruet told McGill that he and Odo had booked rooms at the Four Seasons.

McGill said the magistrate and his bodyguard should get settled in at their hotel. He would confer with his partner, Margaret Sweeney, and they'd take things from there. McGill gave Pruet the Martin guitar to take with him.

Might be good for Pruet's mood, McGill thought.

But he didn't tell the magistrate that Gabbi sent her greetings.

McGill thought there might be a covert role for her in this one.

The Oval Office

"You can go right in, Senator," Edwina Byington, the president's personal secretary, said to Senator Richard Bergen, Democrat of Illinois.

"Thank you, Edwina."

"Please give my best wishes to Senator Wexford's family, if you get the chance."

"I will."

The assistant majority leader of the United States Senate stepped into the Oval Office, the door closing gently behind him. The president got to her feet upon seeing him. Her face reflected the weight of yet another burden being added to her endless list of concerns.

"How is John?" she asked.

"Still in surgery as of ten minutes ago, Madam President. I was told we won't know anything about an eventual outcome for some time."

"My thoughts and prayers are with him. He was at his desk when the stroke hit?"

She gestured to Bergen to sit and returned to her own seat.

"Yes, ma'am. He was alone in his office, but he was on the phone to his wife at home in Michigan. Word from Senator Wexford's staff is that Mrs. Wexford heard what she described as her husband gasping for breath while trying to speak to her. Then she heard the phone drop and immediately broke the connection and called his reception desk. Told the staffer to call the Senate medical office immediately and get help for her husband."

Patti Grant shook her head in sympathy. "The poor woman. She must have been terrified."

"She was, according to what I heard. She's on her way to Washington right now."

"Commercial flight?" the president asked.

Bergen shook his head. "A friend's plane. She'll make good time."

"Please let me know if there's any way I can speed her journey. I'll pull out all the stops."

The senator nodded. "That's very kind of you, ma'am." Bergen sighed. "I was told that Mrs. Wexford said John had called her just because he felt the need to hear her voice."

Neither of them could decide whether that was comforting or all the more heartbreaking. It would depend, they both supposed, on whether the majority leader survived long enough to see his wife again. Then, inevitably, given their professions and location, their thoughts turned to politics.

"You'll act in Senator Wexford's stead as majority leader, Dick?" the president asked.

"As long as that's appropriate."

Meaning as long as he still drew breath. If Wexford either died or survived but was unable to fulfill his duties for the remainder of his term, two years, that was when things could get interesting. As number two in the Senate hierarchy, Dick Bergen might simply be the choice of his caucus to take over as majority leader.

Democrats, however, rarely did anything the easy way.

Senators in the numbers three, four and five spots in the caucus pecking order might want to play leapfrog. Go for the top spot. A fight would be divisive.

The president told Bergen, "I'm new to the party, and it really isn't my place to say whom I might prefer to replace Senator Wexford, if that should become necessary. But if you want the job and ask for my endorsement, I'll give it to you."

Without ever having said so, she preferred Bergen to Wexford.

And to the other alternatives as well.

"Thank you, Madam President. I really don't know how I feel at the moment. If I didn't feel I owe it my supporters at home and in the party to stay on the job, I might retire before my term expires. I'm no kid, myself. The idea of spending time with my family holds a great deal more attraction at the moment than personal ambition does."

"That's only natural," the president said. "I'll understand whatever your choice may be."

"Thank you. As long as I'm here, I should pass along the news that bills will be introduced in both the Senate and the House to amend the Constitution."

Before the president could respond, Edwina buzzed her.

"Madam President, I'm sorry to intrude but Chief of Staff Mindel is here with me. I told her you're speaking with Senator Bergen. She asked if the two of you might spare her a moment."

The president looked at the senator. He nodded.

"Send Galia in, Edwina."

The chief of staff entered the Oval Office. She told the president, "I'm sorry to intrude, ma'am."

The president nodded in understanding.

Galia turned to Bergen. "I'm so sorry about Majority Leader Wexford."

"Thank you."

The president said, "Have a seat, Galia. Senator Bergen was just about to tell me that bills to amend the Constitution will be taken up soon in the Senate and the House."

"To abolish the Electoral College," Galia said.

"That's right," Bergen said.

The president asked, "Was that legislation to be introduced today?"

"Yes, ma'am," Bergen said, "until the news about Majority Leader Wexford became known. The Senate, at my direction, will defer all business through the end of this week. The House, as my colleagues in that body tell me, will put the matter off for twenty-four hours as a sign of respect."

"True South went along with that?" Galia asked.

"They didn't want to at first, I was told, but cooler heads

prevailed."

The president said, "The White House will have no comment on the proceedings of the House in this matter, but I'll tell you right now, Dick, as long as both bills support a direct popular election of future presidents, *and* language is included in the amendment to provide for orderly and reasonable voter registration and uniform early voting dates across the nation to make the greatest voter turnout likely, I'll support the amendment wholeheartedly."

Bergen nodded. "That's pretty much what our party in both chambers has in mind."

Galia exchanged a silent message with the president and received permission to speak.

She said, "May I offer a suggestion for Congress to consider, Senator?"

"Of course," Bergen said, if only to be polite.

"As long as an historical change will be considered here, why not either change Election Day to Saturday or if it remains on Tuesday declare the day to be a national holiday. Also, give everyone who votes a fifty-dollar credit to apply to their federal tax liability."

The president liked both of Galia's ideas but she said, "Make it a hundred-dollar credit. Come down to fifty only if the other side balks."

The assistant majority leader, long one of the best vote counters in Congress, was running the numbers in his head. "I think we can get all of that, if we all play our cards right."

Telling the president she'd have to get out front and lead the way.

Mobilize the state legislatures to ratify the amendment after it was passed by Congress.

"Do you have something else for the assistant majority leader, Galia?" the president asked.

"I do." The chief of staff turned to the senator. "If you are able, sir, will you please give me your candid reading on Representative Philip Brock of Pennsylvania?"

Dick Bergen had begun his career in national politics as a

member of the House. It was widely known he kept up his contacts with colleagues who remained there. That was both a measure of true friendship and smart politics.

It took a moment, though, for the senator to respond.

He asked, "What I have to say will stay strictly between us?"

"It will," the president said, speaking also for her chief of staff.

"I don't like the man. He often plays the rabble-rousing buffoon, but he's quite smart. He knew enough to distance himself from the GOP at a time when —" Bergen realized he'd just put himself in an awkward spot.

"When even the president thought it was time to change parties?" the president asked. "That's all right, Dick. I'm fairly smart, too."

"Yes, ma'am. Give me just a second and I'll try to get my foot out of my mouth."

Both the president and Galia laughed.

"Anyway," Bergen continued, "he still managed to get himself elected in a district that's been voting Republican for decades. Most of us, of course, tell the voters what we hope they want to hear. But with Brock … it's like he knows people's worst impulses and can cozy up to them without quite crossing the line. If you look at the polls for his two runs for the House, he was way behind both times, but he won by double digits."

"And how do you explain that?" Galia asked.

She had her own idea, but she wanted to hear what the senator had to say.

"What I think is," Bergen said, "a lot of people are ashamed to admit they like his ideas, but when they go to vote, are alone in the booth, they cast their ballots for him and his ideas with a sense of glee. Like they just put one over on everybody else."

Bergen sighed, as if he'd just articulated another reason why he might retire early.

He shook hands with the president and Galia on his way out.

When they were alone, the president told her chief of staff, "Good ideas on the amendment, Galia. So, tell me, why do we need to worry about Philip Brock?"

Galia told the president that she'd heard from Merilee Parker.

The chief of staff's spy was formerly the press secretary for Senator Howard Hurlbert, founder of the True South party and the man who came within one electoral vote of winning the election. Galia told the president of Reverend Mulchrone's benediction and Representative Brock's speech in Virginia and the private meeting afterward.

Then she added, "Merilee knows all the important players in Southern far right politics. She recognized two men who are active in militia movements. She also saw a former NASA project manager. These men met briefly with Representative Brock and for a longer time with Reverend Mulchrone after their public appearance."

The president's face tightened. "These militias, do they advocate violence against the federal government?"

"They're a bit more sophisticated than most. But they are very unhappy Howard Hurlbert won't be sitting in this office as of January twentieth, and say so at every opportunity."

"Which falls under their First Amendment rights," the president said.

"Exactly. They say they're arming themselves to the teeth only in preparation for the day *we* come after *them*."

"Meanwhile," the president said, "they interpret the law to suit themselves, and if one of them clearly violates a law, as Burke Godfrey did when he conspired to kill Andy, they retreat behind lines of armed followers and blame us when they come to grief."

Galia could hear the pain and anger in the president's voice.

The loss of her first husband remained an unhealed wound.

The chief of staff said, "It's bad enough when bands of yahoos go out into the woods to play Rambo, but when they have a rocket scientist giving them who knows what kind of help, it's time to worry."

"Let's not forget True South," the president said. "A new political party is trying to shape political opinion in their favor."

Well, Patricia Darden Grant thought, I'm not without resources or the will to use them, either. She told Galia, "I want to see the Director of National Intelligence and the Chairman of the Joint Chiefs of Staff this afternoon. Four o'clock."

Galia got to her feet and said, "Yes, ma'am."

"But first, Galia?"

"Yes, ma'am?"

"Put all your spies on full alert," the president said.

"Already done, Madam President."

SE Washington, DC

Sweetie met her husband, Putnam Shady, outside a construction barrier surrounding a gleaming new four-story building of rose tinted marble and gleaming glass. Only glimpses of the structure could be seen from street level, just enough to pique everyone's curiosity. Even Google Earth and media snoops in helicopters were prevented from getting overhead looks by a black tarp stretched taut over the roof of the structure.

A robust private security force kept busybodies, vandals and publicity seekers from either defacing or climbing the barricade. On the few occasions the private cops had to intercede they were quickly supported by Metro police. The speedy response time got reporters to ask the mayor if he knew what the building was.

His honor would only smile and tell everyone, "You're going to like it."

Trying to guess what the building was became first a local and than a national guessing game. It was rumored that everyone who worked on the building would be given a substantial bonus, but only if the news of what they'd labored on didn't leak.

With construction all but complete, it hadn't.

Margaret "Sweetie" Sweeney had been as curious as anyone else.

Having the firmest sense of boundaries, though, she contented herself to wait to find out.

But then Putnam had called and said, "That new mystery

building in Southeast? How'd you like a sneak preview?"

Also having an abiding sense of priorities, Sweetie put an obligation to duty ahead of self-gratification. So she'd told Putnam, "I'd love to, but let me see if I can clear something up first."

She called the office, McGill Investigations, Inc.

Leo Levy answered. Sweetie said hello and asked if Jim was available.

"He's in with *Monsieur le Magistrat,* Yves Pruet." Sweetie heard Leo ask someone how his pronunciation was. "That's close enough for rock 'n' roll, I'm told, Margaret. You want to leave a message?"

Some secrets Sweetie couldn't share even with Leo or Deke.

Welborn and Celsus were about to put their butts on the line.

The fewer people who knew about that the better.

She wondered what the guy from Paris was doing in town.

Jim had told her all about what had happened over in France.

"Tell him I'll get back to him, Leo."

"Will do."

There, Sweetie thought. Now she could meet Putnam with a clear conscience. She drove over to Southeast, parked and saw him standing, mid-block, outside the construction barrier. She walked over and gave him a kiss. He knocked softly on the barrier and a door Sweetie hadn't even noticed opened. An armed guard nodded to Putnam and said, "Please step inside quickly, Mr. Shady. You, too, ma'am."

They complied and the guard closed the door behind them. Sweetie felt as if she'd crossed the threshold to a dazzling new world. The lines and proportions of the building she beheld all but took her breath away. What really captured Sweetie's attention, though, was when they went inside and she saw a row of paintings on an interior wall.

Sweetie glanced at Putnam and turned back to the paintings.

"Monet," she said. "Manet, too. Is that a Modigliani?"

Putnam walked up to his wife's side. "It is."

Sweetie put a hand on Putnam's shoulder.

"What is this place?" she asked.

"The world's next great art museum."

"And how did you get us in here?"

Putnam said, "It was my idea, sort of."

"What?" Sweetie asked, suspecting a joke was at hand.

"Really. Well, sort of. I wrote a guest column for the *Post* maybe eight years ago, suggesting how the overprivileged might do a bit of good for the American public. Never thought it would amount to anything. But …" Putnam gestured at the building.

"Don't tell me it's going to be named after you," Sweetie said.

Putnam laughed. "The Putnam Shady Museum? No."

"Well, what's it going to be called?"

With a broad smile, Putnam said, "Inspiration Hall."

Grand Street — Manhattan

The man known to the French police as Laurent Fortier sat on a stool in a SoHo loft and watched an artist, currently calling himself Giles Benedict, complete a painting. It was hard to say which of them had the better critical eye when it came to evaluating a forgery's proximity to an original work. Fortier got to his feet and stood shoulder to shoulder with Benedict.

"What do you think?" the forger asked, wiping off his brush.

Resting on an easel, the canvas Benedict had just completed glowed gold and green, a field of ripe wheat, under an intense blue sky filled with crows. Next to it stood the Van Gogh masterwork from which it was taken. Not the double-square painting that hung securely in the Amsterdam museum named after the artist, but a smaller preliminary study, one the artist sold for the price of some paints, the material for the larger canvas and perhaps a meal.

The study for "Wheatfield with Crows" was officially listed as missing. Not stolen. That classification got things exactly backward. Until the early 1990s, the painting had been the property of a family of diamond dealers in Antwerp. They'd taken great pleasure in owning the painting and keeping knowledge of their possession a closely, but imperfectly, held secret.

It was the first painting Laurent Fortier ever stole.

Being new to his craft at the time of the theft, Fortier had been forced to kill the diamond dealer's groundskeeper who had foolishly stationed himself in the driveway, hands on hips, between Fortier's automobile and the road on which the thief intended to flee. There were still times when Fortier would awaken from a sound sleep with the image of the man's shocked face in his mind, that awful moment when the groundskeeper realized the car speeding toward him was not going to stop and his life was at an end.

In Fortier's career of more than twenty-five years, that was one of only two times he'd had to take such a drastic measure to make his escape. The second life he'd taken to remain at liberty had been on his most recent theft.

He saw the two killings as bookends. The mistake of a beginner. The clumsiness of a professional in decline. He hadn't told anyone, because there was no one to tell, but he was all but finished with his work. There was little else to accomplish.

He would live out his days in comfort and self-satisfaction, knowing there had never been an art thief to match him. Likely never would be anyone to compare. Only Benedict could come close. But even he was an implementer not a creator.

"It's marvelous," Fortier said of Benedict's effort. "Except you left out one crow."

Depending on interpretations of Van Gogh's suggestions of birds in flight, the accepted number of crows in the painting was thirty-seven.

Benedict grinned and said, "Really? Which one?"

Fortier said, "A very obvious one. Just to the right of the path through the field. At the bottom of the diagonal column of birds."

"Oh, that one. Well, if it's as obvious as all that, I'd better put it in."

He did so with a brief, precise turn of his wrist. "Better?"

"Perfect."

Rays of sunshine from a skylight fell equally on both paintings.

Now, the only difference to be seen was the sheen of fresh paint on the forgery. That would be overcome by time sitting in a kiln turned to low heat. A more sophisticated analysis of paints and canvas would quickly unmask the forgery but that was never going to happen because Benedict's creation would have a lifespan measured in days.

A door to the loft opened and woman's voice asked, "Is it done? May I see, Father?"

The two men looked behind them. Both smiled.

"Of course, my dear. Your opinion is always invaluable."

"Bonjour, madame," Fortier added with a nod.

"Bonjour, monsieur. C'est toujours un plaisir de vous revoir." A pleasure as always.

Benedict and Fortier made room and Duvessa stepped forward.

She studied both paintings in detail. A smiled formed on her face. She kissed her father's cheek and said, *"Bravo, Papa."*

Benedict grinned. "I'm only as good as the geniuses I copy. But not bad, all in all, for an old businessman."

"Gauguin was a stockbroker," Duvessa reminded him.

"Among other things," Fortier added.

Benedict concluded the capsule bio. "Yeah, he had a thing for little girls, booze and drugs, contracted syphilis and died at fifty-four."

"No one's perfect, Papa," Duvessa told him. "You stole billions of dollars in your hedge fund days. Managed to hang on to a hundred million."

Benedict shook his head and laughed. "Less than I could have made honestly, if I hadn't gotten so bored. My blessing and my curse was the day I thought I needed a hobby and first picked up a paint brush. Found out I was a great copycat but wasn't creative at anything but juggling numbers on a balance sheet."

"You've managed to lead an interesting life nonetheless," Duvessa said.

"There is that."

Fortier thought it was time to get back to business. "Has

Monsieur Pruet found you yet?"

"Oui, hier soir." Yes, last night. She told Fortier and her father of the meeting with Pruet and Odo and how the magistrate had put a deposit of one thousand euros down on the Renoir. "I explained that this would merely allow him to enter the bidding on the painting should I decide to auction it."

"He didn't make any claim to the canvas?" Fortier asked. "Didn't threaten to call the police?"

Duvessa shook her head.

"Maybe he has a better eye than either of us," Benedict said. "Spotted it for a fake."

Fortier wasn't happy with that idea. "Why would he offer *any* money to bid on a forgery?"

"Maybe he doesn't want us to know he's not a rube." Benedict said.

Both men turned to Duvessa for her evaluation of Pruet.

"It was hard to get a good reading other than to say he's careful. He was tired from the flight to New York. He didn't take even a sip of his drink. He had trouble climbing the stairs. He didn't show any sign of outrage when he saw the painting." She thought for a moment and added, "He could be biding his time. Setting up a play of his own."

Fortier said, "I'm halfway tempted to ship the painting, the real one, back to France. Have his family call him home. Tell him all's well."

Benedict said, "He still might want revenge."

Fortier nodded glumly. He asked Duvessa, "What is your opinion of the Corsican who travels with the magistrate?"

"Dangerous."

Merde, Fortier thought.

Duvessa turned to her father. "You're playing one of your little jokes."

"What?" Benedict asked, playing the innocent.

"You left out a crow," she said.

The forger gave her a wink. Didn't bother to ask her which

one. In the upper right hand corner of the knockoff, where the blue sky shaded darker, nearly black, he added the last crow. The tonal difference was so slight the bird was all but invisible.

That didn't comfort Fortier at all.

He never should have missed the omission.

Wasn't happy at all that Benedict had pranked him.

Had left *two* crows out of the painting.

FBI Headquarters — Washington, DC

Deputy Director Byron DeWitt welcomed McGill into his office.

The first thing McGill noticed was DeWitt's new haircut. Shorter and tapered. Less free-flowing SoCal surfer dude. The next thing he saw was a photo of Patti on the wall. It had replaced the Warhol serigraph of Chairman Mao. DeWitt, it looked like, had even gotten himself a manicure.

Two explanations came to McGill's mind. The powers that be had cracked down on the free spirit that had infiltrated their ranks. Or the deputy director had fallen under the influence of an ambitious woman who was grooming him for greater things. Neither possibility pleased McGill.

He'd always gotten along well with DeWitt.

Hoped that wouldn't change.

"Care for coffee, tea or a soft drink?" the deputy director asked.

"Black coffee, one sugar, thanks."

DeWitt passed along the request through his intercom.

"Ms. Sweeney won't be joining us?" the deputy director asked.

McGill said, "We keep missing each other today. I'll bring her up to speed later."

DeWitt nodded. McGill's coffee was delivered by a serious looking young woman whose college coursework probably hadn't included waiting on tables for private eyes. She didn't even seem impressed that he was married to the president. Oh, well. The newly buttoned-down DeWitt understood the pecking order.

"Is there something I might do for you?" he asked McGill.

"It's more a matter of us not stepping on each other's toes," McGill said. "I've been hired by a friend to look for a painting that was stolen from his family." He gave DeWitt a summary of his relationship with Yves Pruet and the particulars of the case that had brought the investigating magistrate to the United States. "*Monsieur Pruet* also informed me that one of your people, Special Agent Osgood Riddick of the art crime team, visited his hotel room in Manhattan for a chat."

DeWitt made a note of that.

McGill continued, "Riddick strongly suggested that my client not return to a gallery in New York where he saw a forgery of the stolen painting and gave the gallery owner a check for one thousand euros for the right to bid on the forgery."

The deputy director took a beat to think about that.

"*Monsieur Pruet's* job title suggests that he's used to conducting his own investigations."

McGill nodded.

"But when the FBI came calling he decided to call you."

"Wisely, I'd say."

DeWitt asked, "Can you tell me whether your client might have any interests beyond recovering a painting?"

Now, McGill needed a moment to consider the question. As a cop, he'd been protective of his snitches. When he'd started working in the private sector, though, his attitude about confidentiality had become more flexible. He wouldn't reveal anything that might harm a client, but he wouldn't let a rigid adherence to principle screw up a case either.

"I think there is," McGill said. "I don't know what it is, but I have a feeling there's more at stake than just a painting."

"Your client is an honest man, as far as you know?"

McGill smiled. "His reputation is that he's too honest, and I've seen nothing to contradict that."

"How can someone be too honest?"

"When it costs you your marriage. Puts a brick on your career, too."

Chicago jargon for putting an end to professional advancement. Used mainly by cops. McGill saw that DeWitt understood.

He said, "Okay. Point taken. So what is it you'd like from me?"

McGill said, "Guidelines, I guess. So I can do my job without messing up anything your people are working on."

DeWitt said, "Would it be too much to ask you to put your case on hold?"

"What, indefinitely?" McGill asked. He got the uneasy feeling DeWitt was trying to get him to fall into line instead of working with him, as if the deputy director really had been co-opted by the bureaucracy. He repressed a sigh. "I could do that, but then *Monsieur Pruet* would likely proceed without me. I think it would be better for everyone if I were involved."

McGill couldn't put it more politely.

He wasn't going to be muscled off the case.

"I suppose you're right," DeWitt said. Then he thought to ask, "Has *Monsieur Pruet* met the president?"

"He has. They became fast friends in Paris."

McGill saw DeWitt relax.

He knew why. If DeWitt caught any grief from the director of the FBI for not trying harder to shove McGill aside, all he had to do was invoke the president's name. Nobody pushed her.

"Will you give me just a moment, Mr. McGill?" DeWitt asked.

McGill took his coffee into DeWitt's outer office.

He finished his java, set the cup and saucer down and was about to ask the serious young assistant if the Bureau had the current issue of *Sports Illustrated* for visitors to read when the intercom buzzed and he was sent back into DeWitt's office. The deputy director's peace of mind had vanished. He looked like a man in a corner awaiting bad news.

To his credit, DeWitt spoke bluntly. "Mr. McGill, if you were anyone else, the FBI would tell you at this point to advise your client to return home immediately and for you to steer well clear of this case."

McGill nodded and gave it a beat. Then he said, "Okay, but I'm not anyone else. So what can the FBI tell me?"

"Nothing at all. Except my generic advice is well worth considering."

The White House Putting Green

Neither Patti nor McGill played golf. That put them outside the mainstream of First Couples. Most presidents from Woodrow Wilson onward played the game. Ike had a green built outside the Oval Office. That was scrapped by Kennedy, even though he played, bad back and all. Patti's predecessor, a fifteen handicap, had a new green installed among the trees just north of the tennis court. Word was he put it there so his favorite foursome wouldn't know how hard he was working on his game and would give him extra strokes on their wagers. Sometimes even the world's most powerful man wasn't above hustling his friends.

Many a First Lady played golf, too.

But neither McGill nor Patti found it in the least interesting.

Hadn't set foot on the putting green in their four years at the White House.

They'd kept it in deference to their successors.

But that late afternoon in January with darkness closing in and the air taking on a cold edge, McGill was out there putting, trying to remember the form he'd used the few times he'd played miniature golf as a kid. He'd left a message with Edwina Byington asking to have the president join him there at her earliest convenience.

"Just her with a putter, Edwina," McGill said. "Tell Elspeth and the uniformed people we don't want anyone too close to disturb our concentration."

Total pro that she was, the president's secretary said, "Of course, sir. The gallery will be most respectful."

McGill tried to figure out the way the green broke as he tapped the ball toward the hole. Seemed right to left no matter where he started. He sank more than a few putts. Wondered if the guy who sat in the Oval Office right before Patti might have grooved the damn thing. Be just like him. For McGill, it only made the exercise even less interesting.

His cell phone chirped and he hoped it wasn't Edwina saying Patti couldn't make it.

It wasn't the White House at all. His daughter Caitie was calling.

"Everything all right, honey?" he asked.

"Everything's great, Dad. I just called to say goodbye."

"Why? Where are you going?"

"Los Angeles, to make a movie, remember?"

Now, he did. The film in which his daughter had been cast originally had been scheduled to begin shooting in late May, but the director had a conflict come up. If the producers wanted to keep him on the project, they'd have to start —

"Next week, Dad. That's when principal photography begins. Everyone has to be in L.A. tomorrow to get ready. Did you forget?"

"Guess I did. We have this little inauguration thing coming up. Tends to crowd out other thoughts. But I should have remembered your movie, too."

"It's not *my* movie, but I do have a good part."

McGill saw Patti approaching. He laughed. She'd found a pair of knickerbockers and tam o'shanter to wear. Carried a putter under her right arm. Gave him a wink as she drew near.

"What's so funny?" Caitie asked.

"Patti's coming. She's kidding around with me."

"Can I talk to her?"

"Sure, but remind me, you're not going to fall behind on your schoolwork, right?"

"No way, Dad. I'll have tutors."

Just what his youngest needed, McGill thought, an *enhanced* sense of entitlement.

What he said was, "You'll send me an autographed glossy?"

Caitie laughed and promised she would.

McGill told his daughter he loved her and handed the phone to Patti, saying, "Caitie. She's about to leave for L.A."

Patti said hello and embarked on a spirited conversation of best wishes and step-maternal advice. It warmed McGill's heart just to watch Patti's face. Every president needed a ray of sunshine on a daily basis, and nothing beat seeing your child do well.

McGill had told Patti from the start to consider his children hers.

Just as Lars Enquist, the second husband of McGill's ex, considered them his.

Patti had been hesitant to accept that role at first. She didn't want to step on any of Carolyn's prerogatives. McGill's ex had been leery, too. It would be tough, if not impossible, for her to compete with the president of the United States, and Carolyn knew kids, like anyone else, could be overwhelmed by glamour and power.

After Patti's bone marrow donation had saved Kenny McGill's life, though, Carolyn's misgivings about her perceived rival evaporated. Her gratitude to the president was too profound to allow for petty jealousies. She could acknowledge that her children had a stepmother, too.

She even found comfort that their futures were more secure because of that.

Patti wrapped up her conversation with Caitie, expressing herself in classic show biz form. "Break a leg, kiddo."

She handed the phone back to McGill.

He told her, "I've always wondered if that expression didn't originate with loan sharks talking to their pet thugs."

"Funny, but not very," Patti said.

"I might be a bit off form," McGill admitted.

"I know. I heard from the director of the FBI. That's why I dressed up. Thought it might amuse you."

"It did, until just now. I suppose the director didn't hold out on you the way the deputy director did with me."

"Do you really want to putt golf balls?" Patti asked.

McGill shook his head. "Just wanted a little privacy."

"I have my moving bubble with me. Let's go for a stroll."

She gave McGill her putter. He tucked it and his club under his left arm. The White House grounds covered eighteen acres. Trees provided a privacy barrier for most of the South Lawn. McGill and Patti stuck close to the woodland on the western side of the lawn. Ready to duck into the trees should a drone appear overhead.

The darkening sky remained peaceful. The moving security cordon kept even the squirrels at bay. For a moment, McGill wondered if Galia Mindel would have been allowed to barge through. He scanned the nearby surroundings looking for a more immediate concern.

People with pointy ears. Eavesdroppers.

He didn't see any uniformed Secret Service officers close enough to overhear anything he and Patti might say, if they kept their voices down.

As if she knew just what he'd been thinking, Patti said quietly, "The FBI couldn't talk to you because national security is involved."

"So you shouldn't say anything either?"

Dropping her voice further, Patti said, "I shouldn't, but I'm going to. If I can't trust you, I'm really sunk."

McGill linked his free arm to Patti's near arm and drew her close.

"What do you know about the connection between stolen art and terrorism?" she asked.

McGill had never given the question a moment's thought, but he saw the connection easily. "Terrorists need money. Stealing art and selling it seems like a way to make a bundle."

"Not as much as you might think," Patti told McGill. "But stealing art, cranking out forgeries and selling them in bulk is the real profit multiplier."

He informed her about Pruet spotting a forgery of the painting his family had lost.

Patti sighed. "That's another thing. Residential thefts make up more than half the losses to art thieves. Usually, the thieves net only a small fraction of the value of what they've taken. But they can get better deals from terrorists than private collectors."

"Why's that?" McGill asked.

"The terrorists have better access to the knockoff artists and to the people who fund their atrocities. Delivering stolen art as a token of appreciation to their bankrollers can bump their so-called charitable donations."

That puzzled McGill. "Guys who fund jihad like infidel art?"

"Irony knows no borders. Of course, sometimes the recipient of the stolen art makes a gleeful show of destroying it."

McGill shook his head, remembering how the Taliban dynamited the two giant Buddhas in Afghanistan. "What a world," he said, "and this is what Pruet's family is caught up in."

"So it would appear."

"How should I handle this?" McGill asked.

Patti stopped and looked her husband in the eye. "Knowing you, you're not going to extend your regrets to Yves and beg off."

"No, I'm not."

"Would you mind giving me a daily update? I can let you know if you're about to put a foot in something stinky. But I'd rather not lay things out in detail, if that's not necessary."

McGill agreed. "That works. Too much information might make me feel hemmed in. Stifle my creative impulses."

Resuming their walk, Patti said, "Can't have that."

"Shall I give *Monsieur le Magistrat* your regards?"

"Better than that, invite him to dinner."

"Let the word spread through town the two of you are buds."

Patti smiled. "Couldn't hurt."

Linnean Avenue, NW — Washington, DC

Welborn Yates was in his daughters' bedroom doing dirty-diaper duty, while Kira was in the kitchen uncapping jars of organic goo for the twins' dinners, when the doorbell rang. Welborn called out, "I've got it," and tapped the control that brought up the view from the front door videocam. He saw a face he'd come to know from his years at the White House, former SAC Celsus Crogher.

Prior to becoming a father, he'd thought Crogher would make

an excellent bogeyman, so deathly pale and filled with barely restrained menace, with which to frighten children into proper behavior. Having held his infant daughters in his arms, cooed to them and watch them fall into blissful sleep as Kira nursed them, he discarded the idea of using anything but sweet reason and maybe a firm tone of voice to guide them through life.

He keyed the intercom and said, "Good evening, SAC Crogher. What brings you out this way?"

"I'm here to pick you up. Galia Mindel says we should head out tonight."

Whip smart, Welborn understood the implication, but it still registered in his mind as a question. SAC Crogher was going to be his partner? He was certainly white enough, but hardly came across as a Southerner. Giving it just a moment's thought, Welborn couldn't really place what part of the country Crogher and his forebears might call home.

"You still there, Yates?" Crogher asked.

"Yes. Just changing diapers."

Welborn saw a look of incomprehension appear on Crogher's face.

"My daughters," he elaborated.

That made only marginally more sense to the SAC, the idea of having children and tending to their needs.

"I'll be right down," Welborn said.

"Who're you talking to?" Kira called up to him. "The goo is just about room temperature."

Welborn decided it wouldn't be comforting to his better half to have her open the door to the pallid figure who used to protect the president. She knew him by sight, of course, having spent almost four years working in the White House, but Welborn doubted they'd exchanged ten words. What she knew of SAC Crogher was that he'd worked in a dangerous world she didn't like to think about.

Welborn opened his front door and was pleased that his baby girls didn't recoil at the sight of Crogher. He was the one who took a step back when both infants reached a hand out to him.

"What do they want?" Crogher asked.

Welborn said, "I'm not sure, but my guess is a boyfriend the other one won't steal and bragging rights the other can't match."

Crogher looked as if Welborn were speaking Swahili.

"I mean now," he said.

"That I can't tell you. They're pre-verbal and I'm post-gurgle."

Crogher started to have a bad feeling about what he'd let himself in for.

Things didn't get any better when the front door was opened wide and Kira saw who had come calling. She immediately jumped to the wrong conclusion, which only agitated Crogher.

"Something happened to the president?" Kira asked.

Missing her inflection, Crogher replied, "What happened to the president?"

Welborn stepped between them before things got out of control. He handed Aria to her mother and looked at Crogher. "Nothing has happened to the president," he told Crogher. Turning to Kira, he said, "SAC Crogher has come for me. I have to go."

"Now?" Kira asked. "Before we've fed the girls, bathed them, put them to bed?"

Welborn asked Crogher, "Can you spare one more hour?"

The request seemed reasonable to Welborn.

The man had showed up at his house unannounced.

"It's not me you'll keep waiting," Crogher said.

Welborn understood. Crogher had said Galia Mindel had sent him.

"She'll understand," Welborn said.

Or she could find herself another boy, he thought.

Then he asked Crogher, "Have you heard from Holmes about this?"

The former Secret Service agent stiffened.

"What's *he* got to do with it?"

"We should probably talk later," Welborn said. "Where will we meet?"

Crogher scribbled an address on the back of one of his old business cards, gave it to Welborn. He read it and gave it back, avoiding an attempt by Callista to grab it. Told Crogher, "You probably ought to get rid of those cards before we head out."

Crogher wasn't used to having people tell him what to do, but he understood the logic and nodded. He walked back to his vehicle, a late model stripped down sedan that screamed government vehicle or maybe rental car. No way was it a good ol' boy's ride. For that matter, neither was Welborn's Porsche Cayman.

Closing the door, he and Kira took care of their girls' evening routine.

Even managed to sneak in a quickie, Welborn kissing Kira's tears away.

He promised he'd be careful.

He almost added that she shouldn't be surprised if the purchase of a used pickup truck appeared on their next credit card statement. Then he changed his mind. Too much information would only worry Kira more.

Besides, he should pay cash for the truck.

The Constellation Club — Washington, DC

The club's dining room was uninspired. The bar was nothing short of magnificent. Both were reserved for members and their guests. The club had been part of the Washington establishment scene long enough to have counted Teddy Roosevelt and Mark Twain as members.

A wag, not Twain, had once said the Constellation Club hearkened back to a time when people expected politicians to be modestly intelligent and judges to be relatively honest, but to operate in the black membership requirements had to be relaxed.

As if to validate the quip, Senator Howard Hurlbert, True South, Mississippi and Representative Philip Brock, Democrat, Pennsylvania had cleared the membership bar and sat with their drinks at a quiet, remote, softly lit corner table. Many a sly legislative deal and an illicit romance had been hatched at that very spot, but Hurlbert and Brock conspired on a far more serious matter.

Assassination.

Each waited for the other to speak first.

Having a lesser character and what he felt to be the greater grievance, Hurlbert gave in first. "They killed Bobby Beckley, you know, the Grant Administration did. I wouldn't be surprised if that bastard McGill did the job himself. Probably screwed that Indiana elector senseless, too, before she cast the vote that put his damn wife back in the Oval Office."

Brock sipped his drink and grinned. "Must be quite a man to accomplish all that. He doesn't change into blue tights and a red cape before he goes to work, does he?"

Hurlbert glowered. He had come within *one* vote of becoming president. He shouldn't be mocked by anyone, much less a second-term member of the House. Millions of people still held the opinion he should be the one taking the oath of office less than two weeks from now. A new activist group called American Right 2013, aka AR-13, had sought him out to lead a Million-Man Shout Down at the inauguration.

Their idea was to occupy the half-mile of the National Mall closest to the Capitol. When it came time for Patti Grant to take the oath they would drown her out with shouts of thief, fraud, cheat and several other choice words. No one would ever hear her pledge to preserve, protect and defend the Constitution.

Having failed to meet that requirement, they thought, she couldn't be a real president.

It pained Hurlbert greatly, but he had to tell the oath deniers that the public swearing in would be only a ceremonial event. The actual oath of office would take place on Sunday, January twentieth as specified by the Constitution. That event would occur inside the White House and there would be no chance to shout it down.

Even the damn calendar was working against him, Hurlbert thought.

He did, however, urge the oathers to shout their protests at

Patti Grant when she did make her public appearance. There was no law against raising your voice outdoors. They should give it their all. Hurlbert saw that his followers regarded his advice as weak tea.

They wanted him to lead the charge. To storm the ramparts.

Frontline confrontation, though, was never his style. That was where people got clubbed, tased and gassed. In the event of a stampede, they even got trampled to death. Hurlbert said that he had to preserve his dignity for a possible future run for the White House.

Nobody had laughed aloud. Not yet. But he felt it wouldn't be long before his name became a joke of historical proportions. "You remember ol' Hurlbert? Poor bastard came within a whisker of the White House. After that, though, his new party collapsed, his wife left him and took all his money and he went to work as a greeter at a Biloxi casino. Shaking strangers' hands was all he had left of his old life."

A paranoid fantasy, maybe, but with each passing day, Hurlbert was ever more sure his worst fears would be realized, if he was even lucky enough to find a casino that would have him. They might figure he was bad luck and turn him away.

Far better to go out in a blaze of … probably not glory.

Notoriety would do.

He would have his defenders. Wouldn't he? Surely, he wouldn't be completely abandoned.

With a start, Hurlbert became aware Brock had just said something similar to what he been thinking. He asked, "What did you say?"

Brock told him, "I said you could probably peddle that horseshit if you don't leave your fingerprints all over it."

Straining to maintain some stateliness, Hurlbert asked, "What exactly do you mean?"

"Your fairy tale about McGill killing Beckley and banging Sheryl Kimbrough. Half the people who voted for you are —" Brock was going to say ignorant assholes, but he didn't want Hurlbert to get his back up. "Highly suggestible."

Just hearing the name of the faithless elector, Kimbrough, set Hurlbert's teeth on edge.

The idea of using her to ruin McGill's name, though, held great appeal.

If he and Brock couldn't manage the real thing, for some reason, character assassination would be the next best option. Taint Patti Grant's legacy by making her husband a toxic figure. Yes, that idea was fascinating. Hurlbert felt a smile form on his face.

His moment of uplift lasted only until he saw Brock smirking at him.

Who *was* this bastard sitting so close to him, Hurlbert wondered.

How had they become partners in treachery? That question, he could answer. Brock had approached him. Offering his sympathies. Commiserating with him on being the victim of the greatest political theft since Lenin stole Russia from Czar Nicholas.

It wasn't long before Brock turned the conversation to encouraging him to find ways to seek retribution. Hurlbert couldn't honestly remember, though, who first brought up the idea of killing the president. He *might* have been the one.

The two of them had been drinking, more than a polite glass or two.

One thing Hurlbert was sure of, he hadn't asked Brock the most basic of questions.

So he brought it up now. "Why did you get into politics?"

The congressman told the senator, "I'm not musical, but I love having groupies."

Despite his sour mood, Hurlbert had to laugh.

Brock's answer rang true to him. So many people in Washington longed for the perks of being a rock star: celebrity, power, money and sex. So few had put in the time to take music lessons.

Reassured that Brock was a kindred spirit, the two men got back to discussing the possibility of making an attempt on the life of Patricia Darden Grant.

***

The National Mall — Washington, DC

The Mall stayed open to the public twenty-four hours a day. Park rangers, however, knocked off at 11:30 p.m. It wasn't always the wisest of ideas for either tourists or District residents to pay casual visits well after dark. The Metro cops worked around the clock, but the police department was not exactly overstaffed with patrol officers, and muggers tended to be opportunists, robbing when the robbing was good.

Galia Mindel, in the company of Welborn Yates and Celsus Crogher, was not concerned about random thuggery. Looking at the construction work for the upcoming inauguration that had already begun outside the West Front of the illuminated U.S. Capitol, she worried on a far grander scale. Welborn and Celsus, having seen the video showing the drone killing of the president and McGill on a tablet computer Galia had brought with her, now shared that trepidation.

After having summoned both men earlier in the evening, the White House chief of staff had to keep them waiting after being detained by other duties. Galia said it would be better that they meet after the park rangers went off duty anyway.

She apologized for the delay.

Celsus thought the apology was unnecessary.

Welborn appreciated it.

Galia turned away from the Capitol and looked at her two companions.

"We can't let anyone even come close to killing the president, gentlemen."

"No, ma'am," Welborn said.

"Coming close would encourage others," Crogher said.

"My thought exactly," Galia replied.

"Where are SAC Crogher and I headed, ma'am?" Welborn asked.

Galia told them, "A meeting was held this morning at a hotel in Newport News, Virginia. Its public purpose was to insult the president and raise funds for her political opponents. Both of those goals are standard practices in party politics and Constitutionally protected activities. But after the public meeting there was a small private gathering. Among its participants were a member of Congress from Pennsylvania, a retired cleric from Boston, a banker from Dallas, a former NASA project director from Florida, and the so-called commanding officers of two militias, one from Louisiana and the other from Michigan."

Both Welborn and Crogher understood the implications.

A cabal had been formed, one that implied violence.

"The Secret Service knows all this?" Celsus asked.

"I just briefed SAC Kendry," Galia said, "that's why I was late for our meeting."

"Then she should be handling this," the former SAC said.

"Handling what?" Galia asked. "Investigating a perfectly legal gathering of the president's political opponents? That might be just what the other side wants. A chance to claim the president is a tyrant who's trying to establish a police state."

Welborn said, "There'd be a much better chance of a leak if we did this by the book."

Galia nodded.

For a long moment, Celsus Crogher closed his eyes. He stood so still Galia and Welborn thought he might have fallen asleep on his feet. The onset of narcolepsy perhaps. Just before either of them could call his name, he raised his right hand as if to ask a moment's indulgence.

As he lowered his hand, he sighed and opened his eyes.

"You're right, Ms. Mindel," he said. "A situation like this requires subtlety. A regimented approach would not only be seen coming, it likely would make things worse."

Galia leaned forward to see if Celsus was playing some sort of trick on her.

"Are you all right, SAC Crogher?" she asked.

He said, "That's just the thing. I'm not a special agent anymore, and I'm not in charge of anything. Near the end of my time at the

White House, I was starting to change the way I saw things. Once I retired, though, my sense of organization was all I had to hold things together."

Galia had sometimes wondered what she'd do with her life after the president left office. She could empathize with Celsus. Still, she had to know if he'd be up to the task at hand.

"You think you'll be able to do this job safely and effectively?" she asked.

"I do. Certainly better than if I tried to be the man I used to be. No question I'll be less of a pain in the ass to Captain Yates."

That led Welborn to ask, "What caused these changes at the end of your career with the Secret Service?"

Crogher hesitated to say, but then he realized he had no reason to be embarrassed.

"I started taking dance lessons."

"Because?" Galia asked.

"The president said she'd like to dance with me at the inaugural ball. Right after she dances with Hol — with Mr. McGill. After the first dozen or so lessons, my instructor managed to get it through my thick skull I was going to have to loosen up or I'd embarrass both myself and the president. As I got into the flow of the dance, it took some of the starch out of my thinking."

Galia and Welborn looked at each other. Both smiled.

"You're still tough as nails, right?" Welborn asked.

"Ten-penny nails," Crogher said.

"You don't mind my asking," Welborn continued, "what part of the country do you come from?"

"Casper, Wyoming."

Welborn did his best to keep a straight face.

The whitest man he'd ever seen came from *Casper?*

He covered up by asking another question.

"Don't people out that way have a little different tone to their voices?"

"I kin talk cowboy," Crogher said in a drawl he'd never used in the White House.

This time Galia and Welborn made a point of *not* looking at each other.

"Anything else we should know about you?" Galia asked.

"I'm fluent in Latin."

The chief of staff shook her head in wonder.

"Not a problem for me," Welborn said.

"Good, so the two of you will be able to work together. We'll need some sort of cover story for you," Galia said. "I was thinking —"

"I have a summer home down that way," Welborn said. "A house on a hundred acres of land. We could pose as hired hands."

Now, the looks of surprise were directed at Welborn.

Somewhat abashed, he said, "The queen — the one in London — gave it to Kira and me as a wedding present."

"Okay," Galia said, feeling a bit like Alice in Wonderland, "that should do. Now, as to what you should look to do —"

"Infiltrate the bad guys and learn everything we can as fast as we can," Celsus said.

"With emphasis on the guy from NASA," Welborn added. "He's most likely the one to head up any drone assault, if that's their game. But is he still around?"

Galia said, "His name is Arlo Carsten, and as of late this afternoon, yes, he's still in Newport News. Staying at the Colonial Suites where the meeting with the others was held." She gave them a phone number for Merilee Parker. "Ms. Parker works for me, covertly. She'll provide you with the latest information she has once you arrive. Please don't do anything to call undue attention to her."

Both men nodded.

"Now, all we need is a pickup truck," Welborn said. "Something that looks like it belongs to a couple of working stiffs but runs like a hot rod."

Showing why she was chief of staff, Galia said, "I'd think Leo Levy would know where you could get something like that."

CHAPTER 4

McGill's Hideaway — The White House
Wednesday, January 9, 2013

Doing his best not to be bothered by the presence of Patti and Sweetie, McGill held his pose as Gabbi Casale put the finishing touches on his official portrait. The way his head was turned, his focal point was looking out a window. Aside from bare branches and a gray sky, there wasn't a lot to see … except in his peripheral vision.

Patti and Sweetie were both smiling. Each of their faces expressed the particular affection she held for McGill. He should have been pleased. Warmed that he was held in such esteem. Not today, though. He was miffed that he wasn't the first to see what Gabbi had wrought.

Childish, he knew, but he didn't see ever sitting for a painted portrait again.

Seemed like he should have gotten the first look.

Then the better part of his nature came to the fore.

Told him to get over himself. He relaxed. Without slouching.

"Much better," Gabbi said, noticing the change immediately.

McGill refrained from laughing at himself.

"Better yet," Gabbi said. "The light in your eyes is perfect. Hold that thought."

Ms. Casale was yet another amazing woman he was privileged to know. McGill thought he had to be doing something right. He must have drifted off into reverie because some time later he heard Gabbi say, "*Voila.*"

"Done?" McGill asked.

"Except for the signature," Gabbi said.

A few turns of her wrist added that.

"Does it look like Rory Calhoun?" McGill asked Patti and Sweetie.

They both shook their heads.

"May I?" he asked the artist.

Gabbi bobbed her head and stepped back.

McGill walked over to look at the painting. Patti and Sweetie stood at one shoulder; Gabbi stood next to the other. McGill couldn't find the words to express his feelings. It was him, all right. The level of detail was astounding. Each line, curve and plane of his face was immediately familiar. Exactly right. The palette was perfect, too. The texture of his skin, hair, even eyelashes, and the light in his eyes, were all made real by the most subtle shadings of color. His colors.

All in all, the portrait made him feel he'd have to become a better man just to be worthy of it. Have the people who knew him say, "That was Jim McGill, all right. On his better days."

Now, he knew how Yves Pruet could feel so invested in the Renoir he'd lost. It wasn't just the monetary value of the work or the prestige of the artist. A good painting could capture a moment dear to those most involved. A great painting could share the feeling of that moment with the world.

"So I've left you at a loss for words," Gabbi told him. "Try to let me down gently."

An unexpected wellspring of sentiment took hold of McGill.

He kissed Gabbi on each cheek and embraced her.

The artist turned red, what with the president standing three feet away.

Patti understood and took pity on Gabbi. "He does that with me all the time."

Sweetie added, "Yeah, me, too."

McGill stepped back from Gabbi and said, "I try not to get mushy with Deke and Leo. It's a wonderful painting, Gabbi. I didn't know you could make so much of so little."

"Faux modesty is part of his act, too," Patti said.

"But you captured that beautifully," Sweetie said.

McGill laughed and told Gabbi, "Those two had a lot of time to work up their routine."

"You forget," Gabbi told McGill, "I've seen you when things got rough and tumble. I think I've got a good fix on who you are. That's why I'm pretty sure the check for my fee won't be late."

Patti said, "Another kidder."

Gabbi extended her hand to Patti, "Madam President, it's been so good to see you again." Shaking Sweetie's hand, she said, "A real pleasure to meet you, Margaret. Please let me know if you and your husband ever come to Paris."

McGill said, "But you're heading to Saint Bart's, right?"

"After a few days in Chicago to see my family," Gabbi said.

"Of course. After that, though," McGill asked, "do you think you might lend me a hand for a few days?"

Having just completed McGill's portrait, Gabbi drew the only available conclusion.

"You want me to help you with an investigation?"

Patti and Sweetie decided to say their goodbyes, leaving McGill and Gabbi alone.

"It involves Yves Pruet," McGill explained. He told her about the missing Renoir and how he felt the magistrate was holding something back on him. "I could ask him what it is, but I'd hate to have a lie come between us. Worse than that, I don't want something to go badly wrong for him while he's visiting our country."

Gabbi didn't want that either.

"I'll delay my trips to Chicago and Saint Bart," she said. "What do you want me to do, remembering that I'm just a civilian these days."

"But you still have friends in the State Department, right?"

Gabbi had been a regional security officer for the State Department the last time she'd worked with McGill.

"Yes," she said.

"And maybe you still have a friend or two among the French police?"

"I do. This is starting to sound like more than an art theft."

"That's what I want to find out. The Pruet family's summer home is in Avignon. That was where the Renoir was stolen. The man suspected of taking it, I was told, is known as —"

"Laurent Fortier. Is that a good guess?"

"You've heard of him?" McGill asked.

"The joke among the lower ranks of artists in France is that one day you'll be good enough to have Fortier steal your work."

McGill grinned. He thought he had Gabbi hooked now.

"You're more than good enough," he said.

"But there are still days I wake up sore from that beating I took under the *Pont d'Iéna*."

"Me, too. If you're not up to it, I'll understand."

"Yeah, right." Gabbi shook her head. "You're lucky I've got soft spots for both you and *Monsieur le Magistrat*. Okay, I'll go to Avignon. But I'm not going to get into any fights."

"Please don't. Stealth is what I want."

Gabbi was happy to hear that.

Bonifant Cafe — Silver Spring, Maryland

Representative Philip Brock sipped his espresso. He was saving his pain au chocolat for the moment. A copy of the *Washington Post,* minus the sports section, occupied the opposite half of the small corner table. The two women running the shop, sisters Brock thought, would give him a look every few minutes. They were keeping track of his needs, more coffee, another pastry, but they were also trying to place him. He seemed familiar but they weren't sure why.

Brock looked like he was born to be on television: full, neatly trimmed dark hair topped an oblong face with a strong jaw. Features of average size were symmetrically placed. A bright, broad smile courtesy of Dr. Kepperman's orthodontic labors was easily displayed. Most business days he was dressed by Brooks Brothers. Today, Ralph Lauren did the honors.

The default choices for guessing his occupation, that close to Washington, were politician, lobbyist or the new TV anchorman in town. It was only when someone got a good look at Phil Brock's eyes that the range of possibilities broadened to include the intelligence community or possibly a military contractor.

Once, a particularly forward woman to whom he was introduced at a fundraiser for a colleague had whispered into his ear, "Do you kill people?"

"Not yet," he replied.

Seemingly disappointed, she went away.

He wondered if his lack of homicidal experience was limiting his dating opportunities. He didn't have any particular objection to the idea of taking a life. But he'd never felt a personal grievance against anyone so great as to move him to murder.

He hadn't suffered any childhood scarring at the hands of either his mother or father. They were good people, smart, too. All of them had gotten along well enough when he was young and dependent. As soon as he reached the point where he could earn his own way in the world, though, it became clear he didn't really love the people who'd raised him. Couldn't really think of *anyone* he loved.

He *appreciated* his parents' efforts. He returned their investment in him as if he were a blue-chip stock that paid quarterly dividends. The first check he sent home was for twenty-five hundred dollars, and none of the ones that followed was ever for less. While the money he sent home arrived like clockwork, birthdays, anniversaries and professional honors were never acknowledged.

For their part, Mom and Dad eventually stopped trying to interest him in their lives. They signed his checks over to their preferred charities, a development Brock found amusing. He started sending the checks directly to the charities, in honor of his parents, he wrote, to make sure they knew what he was doing.

By the time he left banking and went into politics, as a *conservative* Democrat, he was sure Mom and Dad felt a great relief that he didn't try to involve them in his campaign. Or even ask them to wear campaign buttons. Their politics were decidedly to the left of the positions he espoused. They considered themselves refugees from Dixie, fortunate to have gotten out early.

He didn't favor right-wing positions just to twit his parents. The way he saw things, the Republicans, especially the True South variety, were going off the deep end. The Democrats were taking their turn being the grown-ups. But, at heart, he thought, people wanted things to change slowly if at all. The middle class had hit an iceberg but the band was still playing and no one wanted to admit it was time to run for the lifeboats.

What a lot of people did want was to cling to the remnants of the lives that remained to them: their jobs if not the salaries they used to make; their devalued health insurance plans which they still preferred to uncertain government alternatives; their social standing which allowed them to think they were keeping their heads a bit higher above water than people they didn't like anyway.

Brock stepped into that social context of gnawing insecurity not with the promise that he would make things better — even the gullible would have trouble swallowing that one — but that he would manage the decay so that things would get worse a little less quickly. The path to oblivion would be a slow slide rather than a horrifying plunge.

Small comfort, he felt, was better than none at all.

Thing was, he was able to sell his message, and win votes, because he really believed his take on the world and the U.S. in particular was right on the money. He might have scrambled along with so many other politicians to latch onto the hind teat of the great cash cow that was the ever diminishing number of ever richer plutocrats.

The problem with that, it was a short-term game. The fat cats would become bigger targets in the end, that was all. They and their toadies would all come to grief. Once a critical mass of people woke up on a given day and realized that all their futures held was more misery, they would look to make someone pay for letting things getting to that point.

The guy living on the top of the hill in his palace — mansion, if you preferred — was the obvious target. But the people who lived on the slopes of the hill who fetched and carried for the wealthy, they'd get it in the head, too.

Brock had jokingly compared that fool Howard Hurlbert to Czar Nicholas, but that was an apt example of how bad things could get. When the Bolsheviks decided that the old order had to go, they not only executed the royal family, they killed all the Romanovs' servants, too.

Right down to the royal family's cook.

What had that poor sonofabitch done?

Cooked for the wrong people was what.

There were lots of cooks in Washington these days. They might call themselves lobbyists, lawyers or fair and balanced journalists. But when push came to shove, they were all cooks. They fed the machinery of a corrupt system. The only way out that Brock could see was to amass some money, spread it around in some small, warm country, endear yourself to both the government and the locals. Then as the end approached at home make your getaway with enough cash, though gold would really be better, to live comfortably if not lavishly in your chosen retreat.

Brock found Costa Rica agreeable.

He wasn't waiting for the end to come to the U.S. either. He was doing what he could to hasten the day. That and build up his traveling money.

A man stepped into the café. He had a perma-tan complexion, an aquiline nose and had gone Brock's Ralph Lauren one better by wearing Pierre Cardin. In his hand, he carried the sports section of the *Post.* He spotted the congressman, smiled and stepped over to his table.

He tucked the sports section into the middle of Brock's newspaper.

Letting the congressman know his money had been deposited. Brock got to his feet and moved the paper aside to clear table space for his guest. The two men shook hands.

Doctor Bahir Ben Kalil was the personal physician to the Jordanian ambassador to the United States. Jordan, of course, was America's most trustworthy Arab ally. The two men had met at a State Department function the ambassador, a frail fellow, and his doctor had attended. One handshake and a look in the other man's eyes was all it took for Brock and Ben Kalil to recognize a kindred spirit.

Brock felt sure that while the good doctor was on his government's payroll, his loyalties lay elsewhere. It was a short jump to guess where. Brock might have picked up a phone and suggested to the FBI that Ben Kalil deserved to be watched for terrorist connections either at home or abroad. But he didn't.

The doctor knew Brock saw him for what he was, but the opposite was also true. He recognized the congressman not as a patriot but as a wrecker. Ben Kalil thought it might be useful to cultivate such a man. He was the one who had reached out to Brock.

His intuition was rewarded.

Brock came up with a truly stunning idea.

The outsourcing of acts of foreign terror to American dupes.

The Oval Office

Vice President Jean Morrissey entered the room looking as grim as either the president or Galia Mindel could ever recall seeing her. She'd just come from her office. The Secret Service, at the president's direction, had given her a private screening of the drone assassination video.

That wasn't strictly necessary.

A good vice president did what she was told without needing

to know the reason why. But that wasn't the way Patricia Darden Grant did things. She wanted her number two to know she was a full partner, not an afterthought.

In response to that consideration, and what she'd just seen, the vice president stepped up to the president and gave her a hug. She said, "Madam President, that had to be a horrible video for you to watch."

"It was. Please have a seat, Jean."

The president took her place behind her desk, smiled and shook her head.

"Look at us," she said. "Three women running the government."

"Long overdue," Galia replied.

"No," the president said, "we had to wait for the country to tell us it was time. That and maybe wait for women to become a majority of voters."

"That and have women make up their own minds, not just echo their husbands' votes," the vice president said.

"In any case," the president said, "hooray for us. Here we are. Unfortunately, as you've just seen, Jean, there are bastards who can't stand the idea of us, well mostly me, being here. Would like to blow us to bits. That being the case, Galia will spend the day with you bringing you up to speed on everything you'll need to know if they should get their way."

Jean Morrissey nodded. Didn't protest that such a thing would never happen.

The president appreciated that. Planning for the worst case was imperative.

"The Secret Service would be greatly relieved," the president continued, "if I canceled the ceremonial inauguration on January twenty-first. I'm not going to do that. Allowing myself to be seen as intimidated would be bad for the country, bad for me, bad for you and bad for the chance of another woman being elected president in the next hundred years."

Jean Morrissey said, "I agree, Madam President. Every tinpot tyrant and dung-beetle terrorist would think he'd just been given the green light. Maybe, ahead of the inauguration, you should think of some overseas jerk whose attitude would be improved by a cruise missile or a naval shelling. A preemptive slap across the face might make a would-be terrorist or his sponsor think twice."

The president and Galia looked at each other.

Neither of them had thought of that idea.

Then, again, neither of them had played collegiate ice hockey as Jean had. The vice president had been both the high scorer on her team and its chief enforcer. You messed with one of Jean Morrissey's teammates, she'd mess you up.

The actual breaking of a nose, and suffering the same, might be useful experience for someone who wanted to sit in the Oval Office, the president thought. She felt a new level of comfort with her vice president. If she should perish — perish the thought — the country wouldn't lack for a strong leader.

In fact, the vice president's suggestion about attitude adjustment implied there would be hell to pay for anyone behind an assassination. That also pleased the president.

"That's certainly something to think about, Jean. But here's what I have in mind in the meanwhile. While we will have the ceremonial inauguration as planned, you and I won't be in plain sight at the same time. You'll be sworn in while I'm still inside the Capitol. Then you'll step inside and a few minutes later I'll make my appearance."

"Sort of like the State of the Union strategy," the vice president said.

At the president's annual speech to Congress, assessing the well-being of the country and offering plans for its future, the president, vice president, speaker of the House and just about everyone else in the line of presidential succession was in one place, the chamber of the House of Representatives. A catastrophic attack might take all of them out. So one member of the president's cabinet watched the speech from an undisclosed location. That person, in the worst case, would become president.

"Yeah, it's sort of like that," Galia said, "only we'll insist Speaker

Profitt remain at ground zero the whole time."

Peter Profitt was second in the line of presidential succession And the leading member of the opposition party.

Vice President Morrissey laughed.

The president limited herself to a smile.

Four Seasons Hotel — Washington, DC

Their body-clocks still not fully adjusted to the time zone in which they found themselves, Pruet and Odo rose early. The magistrate called Paris and spoke with his father.

"Papa, do you recall ever seeing anyone use a mobile phone in our Avignon library?"

"Why would anyone do that?" Augustin Pruet asked. "It is a place to read, to think or —"

To look at Renoir's painting of Antoine and Jocelyne.

Augustin's voice caught in his throat.

The wound he had suffered was not just fresh it was still bleeding.

"Papa, I have found a forgery of the Renoir in New York."

The elder Pruet's voice returned, filled with excitement. "A forgery? You've called the police?"

"Not yet, but Odo and I were visited by an agent of the FBI's art crime team. He urged us to stay away from the gallery where we saw the forgery, even though I told him I had put a deposit down on the painting for the right to bid on it."

"Why would you —" his father began. Then he understood, "You think the forgery is the initial step in your pursuit of the thief."

"Yes, but not in the same fashion as I first thought."

He explained McGill's thought that a respectable forgery could not be painted, shipped to the United States and hung in a New York gallery in less than a week.

The magistrate said, "If someone visiting our house used his phone and sent the photos of the painting to the United States, the forgery could have been done here, perhaps over a period of months, and hung in the art gallery with much more subtlety."

There was a long moment of silence. Pruet understood it. His father was mourning the idea that one of his guests must have betrayed his hospitality.

"I will ask Emmeline," Augustin said. "She knows everyone who has visited us."

Emmeline Louvel was the wife of the the *maître d'hôtel.* The head butler.

"I can call her, if you prefer, Papa."

"That is very kind of you, Yves, but it is my responsibility."

"As you wish. Please let me know what you learn."

Pruet didn't presume to tell his father how to speak with Emmeline.

He had learned his manners from his father, not the other way around.

The senior Pruet said he would be in touch. Even with an ocean between them, Pruet thought he could hear his father's heart breaking. As he ended the call, the magistrate saw Odo looking at him.

"I know," Pruet said, "you would still be happy to provide vengeance."

"Oui."

"Be careful of what you wish for," Pruet told him.

The two of them went down to an early breakfast in the hotel's Seasons dining room. A Belgian waffle with berries for Pruet; corn beef hash and poached eggs for Odo. The bodyguard said with a slight taunt that one of them had to keep up his strength.

Rising to the bait, Pruet suggested they get some exercise.

He proposed they go for a walk and see the American capital.

Williamsburg, Virginia

Welborn Yates and Celsus Crogher pulled onto the driveway of what Kira called the Yates' country manor in the early hours of the morning. Working on short notice, Leo Levy had needed a few hours to find the pickup truck they wanted, a faded blue Ford F150 SuperCab Short Bed. The odometer showed 136,859 miles on the pickup.

Leo said, "Pay no mind to that." He lifted the hood, showed them the gleaming monster that lurked within and told Welborn, "This engine will make you think you're back in one of your jet planes."

He also showed them a concealed storage compartment beneath the rear seats.

In it, held in place by tension clips, were two Beretta 92s and a Remington Compact Camo shotgun. Leo said, "I guarantee you nobody who doesn't take this truck apart bolt by bolt is ever going to find these weapons. But if you want to head out unarmed, I'll take them off your hands."

Welborn and Celsus chose not to go gentle into that good night.

Celsus was only sorry Leo hadn't brought him an Uzi.

They didn't ask where Leo got the truck or the guns. Welborn told Leo he'd receive cash for whatever the rental fee was. Leo just shook his head.

"This one's from a good ol' boy who owes me more than one favor. Just try to bring the truck back if you can. And be sure to use only high-test gas. You're going to need a *lot* of it."

Arriving in Virginia, Celsus was amazed that anyone he knew owned such a large piece of land. Not that he could see the dimensions in the dark. The countryside outside the limits of the former colonial town of Williamsburg was illuminated only by their headlights. Beyond the beams the night was as dark as the devil's sense of humor. Celsus judged the size of the property by the distance they traveled after turning off the small country road.

"It's not a really big property," Welborn said. "A little less than six times the size of the White House grounds."

"Is that all?" Celsus asked and snorted.

Coming from Wyoming, he knew all about vast ranches and farms, but those were working properties. Businesses. People raised livestock or crops. He knew they did that in Virginia, too. Some well-to-do types also raised horses, and that'd take some room. But Welborn had told him that since the early days of the nation his property had been used as a "getaway."

Self-indulgence on any scale made Celsus' upper lip curl.

Having a hundred acres just to stretch your legs was beyond him.

"Give it a try," Welborn teased, "maybe you'll like it."

Celsus found the very idea threatening.

Some values were beyond even the power of dance to change.

It came as a comfort to him that in keeping with their cover identities Welborn said they should stay in the blacksmith's cottage. The former SAC could relate to someone banging heated steel into horseshoes. It was the privileged gentry thing that set his teeth on edge.

Which led him to think of Kira Yates

He told Welborn, "Sorry if I upset your wife back in DC."

"She's tougher than she likes to let on," Welborn said, "but thank you."

The two men pulled up in front of a humble structure behind the main house. They got out carrying the duffel bags holding their changes of clothing. They also brought their firearms. Wouldn't do to be caught unaware and unarmed. On that, they were in complete agreement.

Welborn, being a federal agent, wouldn't have had to sweat a weapons' charge.

Celsus, being a *former* federal agent would have to rely on a presidential pardon.

As they approached the front door, Celsus asked, "What's that little lean-to section over there?"

"That's the smithy," Welborn said.

The former SAC's face brightened. "You weren't kidding? This place had a real blacksmith?"

"Hammer, tongs, anvil, bellows: the works. You can give it a try after the sun's up. Right now, though, I need some sleep."

Accommodating Celsus' Spartan sensibilities, Welborn gave him the smaller bedroom, a space with a narrow cot, a small window and a chamber pot. He took the moderately larger, more comfortable room with access to the water closet.

Both of them fell asleep in minutes.

Being accustomed to functioning on fewer hours of sleep than Welborn, Celsus rose first. The chamber pot did not pass muster for his needs. He used the water closet, but the toilet refused to flush. While far from genteel, Celsus was devoted to hygiene.

With the sun just over the horizon, he headed out to the smithy to look for tools that might be applied to plumbing problems. He didn't get that far. Parked next to the pickup was a black BMW 320i. The woman behind the wheel was filing her fingernails and looked like she was whistling along to a song.

Celsus couldn't hear the music and the woman didn't hear him approach.

Not until he rapped on her window and she levitated a good three inches.

After settling back on her leather seat, she looked at him, smiled and lowered her window.

"You must be SAC Crogher," she said.

She extended her right hand and he shook it.

"And who are you?" he asked.

"I'm your new girlfriend."

Celsus nodded and said, "Can't blame Santa for not bringing you on time."

Where the hell had *that* come from, he asked himself.

Then he knew. It came from four years of listening to Holmes talk. Still, the woman didn't take it wrong. She got out of the car beaming.

"Well, aren't you the sweetest thing?" She kissed his cheek and told him, "I'm Merilee Parker, and tonight you're going to beat up the man who's been pestering me."

Celsus said, "Sure, I can do that."

***

Washington, DC, Southeast

Odo interspersed his usual surveillance of his surroundings with glances at the brochure he'd picked up from the concierge at the Four Seasons. He asked Pruet, "Did you know that the original plans for this city were drawn up by a Frenchman?"

"Pierre Charles L'Enfant," Pruet said. "He served in the Continental — that is Revolutionary — Army under Major General Lafayette. He also served under General Washington as a Captain of Engineers."

Odo was impressed. "I bow to your superior knowledge. My pamphlet does not go into such detail."

Pruet said, "My father has always had a fondness for Americans and a disdain for the leftists who filled Paris' streets in the 1960s. I was educated accordingly."

"So your share his views?"

"When I was young? Of course not. I was never a communist and only mildly a socialist. Having the luck to be born into privilege, I wanted to secure my position in life. But I never flaunted my good fortune. I dressed, talked and acted like most university students. The Americans had been foolish enough to follow us into Vietnam. I could not believe how blind they had been not to learn from our mistake."

Odo said, "Obviously, they thought they could do better."

"And they paid a terrible price for such pride. No, in my early days I did not think much of this country."

At that point, the magistrate saw a building under construction. Rather, he saw a construction barricade around a building. From what little he could discern of the structure itself, it seemed to be near completion. He also took notice that he and Odo had exited from what he knew was termed *official* Washington, the area containing the White House, the Capitol, the plethora of government offices and national museums.

"Where are we?" Pruet asked Odo.

He knew there were parts of this city where visitors were advised not to tread.

Odo found a map in his brochure, pointed and said, *"Ici."* Here.

They had not wandered too far off the path regarded as safe.

Pruet nodded. "What do you think that building up there will be?"

"The one with the barricade? If construction does not rise higher, it's not likely to be a hotel or an office structure. Perhaps some sort of cultural site. That would be about the right scale."

Pruet nodded, agreeing with the assessment.

They continued to walk toward the building.

Pruet said, "It was American culture, music, films and, television, that forced me not to underestimate these people. That and their technology. It seemed for several years, decades really, that every new thought in the world came from here."

Odo said, "They do seem energetic."

"In recent years, our country has lost several of our best academics to America. That made me both sad and envious, but I couldn't blame this country for making itself so appealing."

"Others have," Odo replied.

"True, but I have enough burdens to carry without piling bitterness on my shoulders."

"And then you met *Monsieur McGill.*"

"Oui. He was a revelation, and *Madame la Présidente* is a delight."

Odo smiled. "After she paid for the holiday Marie and I took in Hawaii, my dear wife told me that never being able to vote for Patricia Grant will be one of her rare regrets."

"Her regrets are rare only because she married such a stalwart fellow."

Odo laughed. "It's not too late for you to find someone new, Yves."

"She will have to find me. My energy is not what it once was. Let's find a taxi to take us back to the hotel."

"If you don't mind, I'd like to take a closer look at that building up ahead."

It was less than a block distant now.

"Very well," Pruet said.

"Have you given any thought about telling *Monsieur McGill* the other reason we are here?" Odo asked.

Pruet sighed. "The question torments me endlessly."

"You could put it to rest."

"I could, but I am still too foolish to do so. Yet another of my failings."

Odo refused to contribute to his friend's self-pity. As they waited for a green light at the corner across the street from the new building, a large truck passed in front of them. On the door of the cab was a small crest bearing the word FAT in Gothic script. Otherwise the vehicle was an anonymous white, as uninformative as a blank sheet of paper.

Pruet and Odo watched as a section of the barricade around the building swung open and the truck drove into the enclosed space. The barrier swung back into place, restoring a sense of secrecy to the site.

The traffic light turned green and the two Frenchmen crossed the street. A security guard stood watch in front of them. Pruet stopped a polite distance away and asked, "May I inquire what purpose this building will serve?"

The man smiled and said, "I get that question a hundred times a day. I tell everybody that's the sixty-four thousand dollar question."

Neither Pruet or Odo knew the idiom. Incomprehension showed on their faces.

The guard read their looks easily. "Just means I don't know. Whoever is putting this place up wants it to be a big surprise. I can say, I think it's going to open pretty soon."

"Merci," Pruet said.

The guard understood he'd been thanked. He'd visited Montreal.

"Yeah, welcome to the United States. You fellas have a nice time now."

Pruet and Odo hailed a cab, asked to be taken to the Four

Seasons.

They continued their conversation in French.

"Now, I think the building is a mall, a collection of small but prestigious shops," Odo said.

Pruet shook his head.

"No?" Odo asked.

"The truck that entered the construction site? Did you notice the initials on the cab?"

Odo missed very little. He said, "F-A-T."

"Have you ever noticed such a truck in Paris? The initials there would be T-B-A."

Odo wrinkled his brow. "I think I have, but I don't recall ever giving it any thought."

"No reason you should."

"But you'll enlighten me now, Yves?"

"Yes, the letters stand for *Transport de beaux-arts*."

In English: Fine Art Transport. FAT.

Something to think about for two fellows looking for a Renoir.

Dupont Circle — Washington, DC

Laurent Fortier gave the paintings hanging in Gallery Trois far more attention than he felt they deserved. He was waiting for a client who was late. He couldn't imagine why the man had asked to meet him in the gallery above the two-story bookstore. Every painting he looked at only depressed him more.

The problem was not a lack of technical skill. For the most part, the craft of applying paint to canvas was adequate. Composition was proficient. Color balance was clearly understood. An eye for anatomical detail and proportion was demonstrated. Yet when all the elements were put together the sum of their parts was barely worthy of a shrug.

Where was the vision? An understanding of real people and the ways they truly lived. Where was the passion, the toil, the frivolity, the competition, the kindness and even the cruelty? In short, where was the *life* in any of the figures and settings he saw?

Fortier wondered if the fault lay with the shallow daubers whose efforts hung on the walls or in a world grown so horrible that superficial reflections were the most anyone could bear to make of it. In both France and the United States, soulless lunatics had recently chosen small school children as the victims of their murderous madness. Would it have been possible for even the greatest artists of the past to attempt a painting that would capture such profound heartbreak?

His well-educated mind quickly produced an answer.

Picasso could have done it.

In another vile time filled with a wholesale contempt for life, he'd created "Guernica."

Thinking of that masterpiece raised another question in Fortier's mind.

Was there a painting anywhere in the world of such significance that he would not steal it? Would not deprive either the public or its private owner of the right to have access to it? The way he'd always rationalized the thefts he'd committed, he told himself the former owners should have donated the paintings to museums, preferably ones that had sufficient security to retain possession of them.

By continuing to keep great paintings to themselves, private owners were saying two things. I was lucky enough to make this mine. I will continue to be lucky enough to keep it. Fortier saw it as his task to prove those smug bastards wrong.

Someday, his true name would be revealed.

Perhaps, he would be thought of not as a thief but a hero.

"See anything you like?" a man asked him.

Fortier turned and saw Tyler Busby. The client for whom he'd waited.

"No, nothing. Why did you bring me here?"

"I own the place," Busby said, grinning.

Fortier's English was perfect, but he still failed to understand.

"What?" he asked.

"I come here at least once a week. Then I go home and appreciate my collection so much more," Busby said. "I also turn a tidy profit here. It's amazing, the stuff people will buy."

Fortier shook his head.

Busby laughed. "It's good to see you again, Laurent." Switching to French and dropping his voice, he continued, "Benedict's work has been masterful, and his output prodigious."

Fortier was still disgruntled that Benedict had twitted him, leaving out two crows in the Van Gogh. He said, "The man is a *technician,* adequate to his task and nothing more."

"Having troubles, are you? I hope not. Your partnership with Benedict is too valuable to discard casually."

The thief was not of a mind to tell Busby of his plans to retire.

He was sorry he'd uttered the thought to Benedict.

On the other hand, Duvessa might try to persuade him to keep going, once she learned what he'd said to her father. Her means of getting him to reconsider were predictable. Welcome, too.

Busby interrupted the moment of reverie.

"I understand a Magistrate Yves Pruet is visiting Washington at the moment."

Fortier looked at the wealthy American. It was only natural that such a man would do his best to stay informed of anything that might inconvenience him. That being the extent to which people of his class were ever bothered by anything.

"You heard that from Benedict?" the thief asked.

"From Duvessa."

For a moment, Fortier felt a pang of jealousy, thinking Busby must be bedding her, too. Then he dismissed his emotions as misplaced, bourgeois. Duvessa was a businesswoman in every aspect of her life, including her sexual affairs. She always made him feel like a Spartan, if not a god, and she had never passed so much as a sniffle along to him.

Why should he care if she'd slept with Busby?

Having a mistress in common with a billionaire only made him more colorful.

Busby continued, "It occurred to me that having a Pruet nearby at this particular moment has to be more than just coincidence."

"So you bought the answer from Duvessa."

"No, from Benedict. You stole a Renoir from the Pruets. I didn't know they even had one."

"Would you like to buy it?"

"No, thank you," Busby said. "As delightful as his work is, I have my fill of the man."

Fortier grew tired of playing Busby's games. The only thing the man liked more than money and art was scheming. Having others play the fool to his Machiavelli. With the number of forgeries he'd had Benedict do for him, he had to be about to perpetrate his greatest swindle yet.

Honoré de Balzac had said, "Behind every great fortune is a great crime."

As vast as Busby's fortune was, there had to be a *history* of great crime.

Fortier was sure that there were many other villains involved in Busby's machinations and … looking at the man in that moment, he thought Busby meant to kill him.

The billionaire deepened the thief's chill with a knowing laugh.

"Benedict tells me you're thinking of retiring."

"That is a possibility, not a firm decision."

"Laurent, you will soon understand what I'm working on these days. It will make news around the world. I have to rely on your discretion not to, as we Americans say, rat me out."

The idea had never occurred to Fortier, though maybe it should have.

"I would never do such a thing," he said, using his initial impulse to convey sincerity.

"Good, but just to be sure I've wired a little money to your Swiss account. Ten million euros. Think of it as a retirement gift, should that be your choice."

A fine gift indeed. "*Merci, monsieur.* That was not necessary, but is deeply appreciated."

"The money will also tie you to me and what I'm about to do. If I go to trial, so will you. If I'm found guilty, so will you. If I get the death penalty, so will you."

That last caveat made Fortier's eyes grow wide. Not just the thought of his own death. The idea that a multibillionaire could be executed anywhere in the civilized world.

Busby could see what he was thinking and said, "It's going to happen to one of the super rich before long. If things keep going the way they have. The mob will demand it. After all, the king got the chop in your country."

Louis the Sixteenth had indeed lost his head.

After supporting the American revolution and reform in his own country.

"But there's one thing I want you to keep in mind above all else, Laurent."

"What?"

"If you betray me, if you take my little parting gift and don't keep silent about our dealings, you won't have to worry about the government doing you in. My people will take care of that, and they specialize in cruel and unusual punishment."

The White House Mess

McGill bought lunch for Gabbi Casale before she left for France. She ordered the Harvest Fresh Vegetable Platter and a glass of sauvignon blanc. McGill went with the West Wing Burger and a White House Honey Ale.

He would sign for the tab.

The Navy culinary specialist who would serve them didn't expect a tip.

McGill had made it a point to remember the entire Mess staff every Christmas.

After clearing the gesture with the Chief of Naval Operations.

Gabbi asked, "Are you writing this lunch off as a business expense?"

"No. For me, this would fall into a gray area. I mean, we will discuss some business, and if we were dining in a commercial location, I would. But as contentious as the politics in this town are these days, I'll pick it up on my own dime."

"We didn't get around to the question of paying for my time and expenses."

"You're right. You can't be expected to go without compensation."

"I might do a freebie. You just gave me the biggest art commission I've ever had. Once the public gets to see the painting, I expect I'll have more offers to do portraits than I'll really want to accept."

"You didn't have fun?" McGill asked.

"Oh, I did. Painting your likeness, I feel I've gotten to know you better."

"More than when we were whacking Etienne Burel with sticks?"

"This was a different side of you. I enjoyed seeing that. It added to a more complete understanding of the man in my painting. But I don't know if I'd find portraiture nearly as engaging if I were painting someone I didn't know or who didn't interest me."

McGill could understand that.

"So what else do you want to paint? Landscapes, still lifes, city scenes?"

"All of that."

"And you've said you're starting to make it pay?"

"In a modest way, but things are looking up."

"So do a portrait every now and then. Cover your overhead. Pay for winters in the Caribbean. Do your other stuff to please your soul."

"That's pretty much my plan," Gabbi said.

"You could throw a little investigative work into your schedule every now and then."

"So you are going to pay me?"

"Of course. Money's not the first thing I think of. Sweetie keeps our books. But we'll pay you fairly."

"Good, because I've been doing a little thinking."

"And you've come up with an idea you like," McGill said.

Their meals came and they paused while they were being served.

Gabbi sampled her veggies and sipped her wine. "Very nice."

McGill took an enthusiastic bite of his burger. "Mmm."

Gabbi told McGill, "Besides looking for the particulars of the Pruet theft, I thought it might be interesting to do some parallel research. See if I can find out who some of the more generous patrons of the French arts were at the time Antoine and Jocelyne Pruet were married."

McGill informed her that he'd also thought other families or individuals must have unpublicized paintings by famous names in the arts.

"That's one path," Gabbi said. "See who else might have been robbed and look for any connections."

"What's the other path?" McGill asked.

"Look for the person who's already done what I'll be doing, the historical research."

McGill smiled. "That's a great idea. If there is someone who's been down the same path, and he didn't write a book on the subject—"

"Then he was casing potential victims," Gabbi said. "What I'm thinking, 'Laurent Fortier' could be more than one person, one of them an academic and the other an actual thief."

McGill thought about that. He liked the possibility. He also appreciated the fact that Gabbi had come up with such a good idea so quickly. Painting wasn't her only gift. She had a good investigative mind. But McGill did have one caveat.

"Might be two people," he said, "but I don't think we'll find more than that. You have three people, the ability to keep a secret falls off a cliff."

"And the potential for treachery goes up, two people pairing off against the third."

McGill and Gabbi looked at each other and smiled.

Pleased that they were on the same wavelength.

They clinked their glasses together in a silent here's-to-us toast.

That was when Pruet was shown to their table. Surprise filled his eyes. He'd yet to be told Gabbi was in town. Being a man of sophistication, he underplayed McGill's ruse. "Am I late?"

McGill and Gabbi stood. He said, "Not at all. We were just hungry. I hope you don't mind."

Before the magistrate could answer, Gabbi hugged him and said, *"Bonjour, monsieur. C'est bien agréable de vous revoir.* It's so good to see you again.

Pruet cheeks turned a bright pink but he responded in kind.

Then he told McGill. "I'm quite hungry myself. Is the kitchen still open?"

"It's always open for certain people," McGill said.

For a moment, Pruet thought McGill was stepping out of character and boasting until he saw who else had joined them at the table.

With a bow, he said, *"Madame la Présidente, je suis honoré."*

I am honored.

"She gets that a lot," McGill said.

"But it never gets old," Patti replied.

McGill Investigations, Inc. — Georgetown

McGill got SAC Elspeth Kendry to give Pruet and him a lift to his office. Leo Levy and Deke Ky had taken Odo Sacripant to the Secret Service's shooting range while their boss was lunching at the White House. Pruet was delighted to speak French with Elspeth, who spoke that language along with English, Arabic and Farsi.

Not wanting to interrupt the flow of the conversation, McGill contented himself to sit back and listen, see how many words he could recognize as cognates or vocabulary he'd learned on his visit to Paris. Wasn't a lot but more than he had suspected. He was beginning to think he should take a Rosetta Stone course. Keep his mind sharp.

As engaged as she was in the conversation, McGill saw that

Elspeth hadn't lost professional focus. He'd have bet she could have executed an evasive driving maneuver and fired a controlled burst from her Uzi without dropping the thread of the conversation. Having people that able look after your safety was comforting.

They arrived at McGill's P Street address without any dramatics.

Standing in the doorway to the building were Dikki Missirian and a man in a black trench coat who looked like he'd stepped out of GQ fashion shoot: three-day beard, matte pomade to keep his hair spiky and a custom-made suit and shoes. Both he and Dikki were smoking and smiling.

"Who's the guy with Dikki?" Elspeth asked.

McGill said, "A cop."

"That guy's a cop?" Elspeth found McGill's assessment dubious.

"From the NYPD."

"Oh."

"Major Case Squad."

"Okay."

"Works on art thefts."

"That explains everything."

Or the guy could be Dikki's cousin, McGill thought, just in from the old country.

But he didn't think so. Once McGill had learned the FBI would be of no help, he had called his old friend Clare Tracy, one of the most prodigious political fundraisers in New York and asked if she had any friends on the NYPD who knew something about stolen art. She'd told McGill of course she did.

She gave him a name, Louis Marra. Promised she would have the copper call.

The call hadn't come but now this guy showed up at his office. What else was a private eye to think?

"I didn't know Dikki smoked," Elspeth said.

"Neither did I," McGill said. He turned to Pruet, who'd been observing everything with care. "Let's see if we can find your painting."

McGill got out of the car and called out, "Louis Marra?"

"People call me Lou," he said.

Ever the cordial host, Dikki provided freshly made coffee to Pruet and Marra and a bottle of Poland Spring sparkling water to McGill. Then the landlord left the others to their business.

Neither Pruet nor Marra was disappointed by his coffee.

"That guy's a prince," the New York detective said.

"More impressive with each meeting," Pruet agreed.

McGill thought about that. Decided he'd come to take Dikki too much for granted.

He'd have to mend his ways. Maybe invite Dikki to the White House for dinner.

He told Marra. "It was very good of you to come to Washington, Detective. You had some time you could spare?"

Marra smiled, and McGill thought the guy could have been a model.

Maybe even did some in his off hours.

"Are you kidding, Mr. McGill? Every cop in this country knows about you. Catching Erna Godfrey for Andrew Grant's murder, overnight. Taking down Speaker Geiger. Bagging Damon Todd and those other two loons after they escaped from the CIA. You do damn well for a retired copper. Couldn't pass up a chance to meet you."

"I have a lot of help," McGill said. "Don't mind reaching out to people."

"That's smart, and I'll be happy to help if I can."

McGill said, "My friend here, Magistrate Pruet, had a Renoir stolen from his family's summer home in France. It was a gift from the artist. *Monsieur Pruet* had reason to think it might have been taken to the United States. While visiting New York two days ago, he saw a forgery of the painting hanging in the Duvessa Gallery in Manhattan."

Marra's eyes narrowed. He put down his coffee cup and turned to Pruet.

"Bet you got a visit from the FBI," the detective said.

Pruet nodded. "Special Agent Osgood Riddick."

Marra said, "Ozzie can be a pain in the ass, but he's good. Recovers a lot of stolen art. Wouldn't be surprised if he turned up your Renoir."

Pruet looked less than sure of that.

McGill told Marra, "I usually have a fairly good working relationship with the Bureau."

The New York detective smiled. "They know they can't muscle you."

"True," McGill said, "but they can try to shut me out."

Marra asked, "You can't make them talk?"

"Wouldn't be smart to try. All sorts of people are waiting to pounce on the president for the least little political mistake."

Every big city cop knew about politics. They dealt with it on a departmental level every day. Marra said, "So what is it you'd like from me? A little insight into what's going on with the FBI?"

McGill said, "Yes, if it won't put you in a bad spot."

Marra picked up his cup, drained the last sip of coffee.

"Well, truth is, the NYPD and the FBI work with each other because we have to; it's not a cordial relationship."

"I had the same experience in Chicago," McGill said.

Marra returned his cup to its saucer.

"Okay, a little primer here, first. Art theft is exploding. The annual loss approaches six billion dollars per year. Only drugs and guns pull in a bigger haul. The proceeds from art theft used to go almost entirely to traditional organized crime, guys who are in the rackets for money. Then along come the terrorists, who think, 'Hey, this could work for us, too.' Especially with governments around the world cracking down on their traditional sources of funding."

"Are you saying there's a terrorist angle at work with my friend's stolen painting?" McGill asked. He wanted to see if the New York cop backed up what Patti had told him.

"You know," Marra replied, "if I get too specific, I *might* be in a world of hurt, but if you think about what I just said, and why the FBI gave you the cold shoulder, you should have a pretty good idea why Ozzie Riddick warned *Monsieur Pruet* to steer clear."

Pruet asked Marra, "How do you explain the forgery? What purpose does that serve?"

"That's easy," Marra said. "Why sell a painting once when you can sell it twice?"

"But I recognized it as a fraud immediately," Pruet said.

"How many times have you seen that painting?"

"Ever since I was a child, more times than I can remember."

"Can you do the same with paintings you've seen once or twice?" Marra asked.

Pruet sat back in his chair. "No."

Marra took matters a step farther. "Would you say the forgery you saw was good enough to fool a private collector, if not a museum expert?"

The magistrate gave the question a moment's consideration.

"Yes," he said. "I think it would."

"There you go. The thieves could sell the knockoff to some rich creep with the morals of a weasel and sell the real thing to a museum."

"Wait a minute," McGill said. Patti hadn't covered that point. "Wouldn't a museum want to know where a previously unknown Renoir came from?"

"Sure. One of the big, established museums in, say, New York, Chicago or L.A. would operate that way. Thing is, museums pop up like dandelions in the spring these days. Any place you find new wealth, somebody will be opening or planning a new museum. That's both here and abroad. Might surprise the average Joe, but people like high culture. A new museum that's just assembling its collection likely would jump at the chance to get a Renoir, and not look too closely at its provenance."

Pruet shook his head, his expression grim.

"I know," Marra said, "and maybe it's worse than that. Your Renoir was a gift from the artist? I'd guess that would mean there was no bill of sale. Who's to say *you're* the legitimate owner?"

Both Pruet and McGill were stuck for an answer.

Marra took pity on them. "There is this," he said. "If you can produce witnesses who say that the painting has been hanging on a wall in your family's home for umpteen years, and no one else can show that he or she held it early on, your claim probably would prevail in court."

"But only if we can recover the painting," Pruet said.

"Yeah, that's the first step. Your best chance is the feds. The FBI, tightlipped bastards though they may be, do a pretty good job at getting things back."

The New York cop chuckled.

"What's funny?" McGill asked.

"*Monsieur Pruet,* you should definitely report the theft of your painting to the FBI. You have a photo or two of it?"

"Yes."

"Make some copies. Attach them to your report. That will give the feds more to work with than just a description."

"Still don't see the humor," McGill said.

Marra replied, "If the FBI is officially put on the case, and they don't produce results *toute de suite,* they can't complain if you keep looking, too. And if they keep coming up short but they get cranky about your efforts, who could legitimately lean on them?"

Now, McGill grinned. "The president. That's very good, Detective."

Marra got up and gave business cards to McGill and Pruet.

"Things lead back to New York, give me a call. I'll see what I can do."

He shook hands goodbye, then told McGill, "Clare asked me to tell you she says hello."

"My best wishes to her, too," McGill replied.

Colonial Suites Hotel Bar — Newport News, Virginia

Arlo Carsten thought rocket science was easy compared to figuring out women. For one thing, rocket science had textbooks. They were based on proven principles of physics. They listed data out the wazoo, and numbers didn't lie. Women, on the other hand …

Well, there were books on how to understand them, too.

Of course, those things were all guesswork. Nothing you could prove in a lab or on a launch pad. A woman writing a book on what women liked was really telling you what she liked. But if you tried to apply one woman's advice across the board, brother, you were asking for trouble.

The advice books *men* wrote about women? They were more likely to land you in jail than in bed. You put just one hand, lightly, in the wrong place, you were looking at an assault charge or worse. Christ, one time, he'd just brushed the back of a woman's bare upper arm — a long neglected erogenous zone, according to the book he'd been reading — with a few fingers, accidental like, and she planted her elbow smack on his nose.

Left him sitting on the floor of a flashy nightclub, blood running down his face.

The bouncers threw *him* out of the place. Said they'd call the cops if he came back.

Of course, he'd been a lot younger then. In the intervening years, he'd overcome his disdain for *soft* sciences like anthropology and sociology and did all sorts of field work on the subject of adult male-female relationships in the United States, Canada and Western Europe.

Without being obvious about it, he observed couples in public places, the women being the type he'd love to have for his own, the guys being, maybe, something he could aspire to. He watched their body language, where and how often they touched each other. He listened in to conversations while looking the other way. He made notes on cocktail napkins.

Hell, half the world's technological advances and big marketing ideas had started with scribbles on napkins. Nobody ever thought he was doing anything wrong.

If somebody asked what he was writing, he said he was making notes on a new rocketry ideas. Sometimes that was even the truth. Guys thought it was cool when he told them he was a NASA project manager, had his PhD from Georgia Tech.

Women rolled their eyes if he started talking math and science.

At the end of a good night, he'd have two or three pockets stuffed with notes on napkins. After twenty years of work, though, he'd distilled everything he'd learned into two conclusions he might have guessed in ten seconds. Women were interested in a guy with looks and money.

They were also crazy about a man with rhythm.

A guy who not only could dance, but was lighter, quicker and more sure on his feet than anyone else in the room, and could make a woman look like a good dancer, was halfway home.

To have the kind of women for whom he lusted, Arlo understood he'd have to offer them at least two of the three qualities they prized most in a man. He wasn't a bad looking guy, and hair grafts, dental bonding, Lasik and facials made the most of what he had.

That was part of his trouble, though. He looked like he was trying too hard. Like, at any moment, a spell might be broken and he'd be revealed for the toad he was. Worse still, he didn't look comfortable in his carefully managed skin.

At his peak NASA salary, he'd made good money, just under two hundred thousand dollars a year. He'd owned two homes, bought a new car every other year. Then came the federal pay freezes. That was bad. He had to sell one of his houses to fatten his nest egg.

Bad went to worse when that goddamn woman in the White House all but put NASA in mothballs. Ended the whole manned space program. The only way for Americans to get into space these days was to hitch rides with the goddamn Russians. That galled him no end.

Not as much, though, as when he was laid off after nineteen years on the job.

One year short of what it took to guarantee a full pension. So his take was reduced by five percent for each year between his age at termination and sixty-two. He got the axe when he had just turned fifty-two. That meant his pension got chopped in half because the cost-cutting bastards wouldn't let him stay one goddamn more year.

By then, the bottom had dropped out of the housing market and there was no way he could sell his remaining house for more than pennies on the dollar. So he sold his Lexus and bought a used Prius. Now, there was a ride to make a woman weak in the knees.

Still, he had a roof over his head, enough to eat and formerly stylish clothes to wear.

Put him three notches up on a lot of guys in Florida.

Didn't make him a bit less bitter. He was well educated, ambitious and had nowhere to go. There was talk about private companies getting into things like space tourism. The goddamn Russians — them again — were taking millionaires up for joyrides. But no one in the U.S. was anywhere close to doing that.

He might well starve to death before another job opened up for him.

Not that he'd ever find another job. He read like crazy to keep his skill set from becoming obsolete, but reading wasn't close to doing. He was losing his professional edge. He might as well stop showering and getting his hair cut for all the chances he had of getting even an interview. Only a dogged nature kept him going.

He happened to be at the public library, his main job-hunting resource, when he came across a magazine article that expressed the government's concern about all the nuclear physicists in Russia — there was no getting away from the bastards — who were unemployed and might be lured into working for rogue states and terrorists.

Arlo laughed at the idea that there were skilled and possibly dangerous professionals more desperate than he was. He thought maybe he should start a placement service. Put Russian bomb-makers together with American rocket scientists. Call the company Super Power in a Box.

He could offer their services to whomever could pay.

Top dollar required. Health and dental benefits, too. Six weeks paid vacation.

He was giggling to himself about the idea, trying not to be

obvious and look too crazy, when he thought, why the hell not see what his skills could fetch on the black market? He opened a Gmail account in the username BRogers2419. He used that to write a position wanted post and put it up on craigslist. *Rocket scientist. PhD. Big government, big rocket experience. No job too small.*

He copied the message to every location the site had around the world.

That was on a Saturday. The library was closed on Sunday due to budget cuts.

He showed up at the library first thing Monday morning, along with homeless people who needed the chance to use a bathroom and relax in a cushioned chair for an hour or two. Arlo shook his head, thinking the country never should have come to this point. People using libraries for basic needs because they didn't have homes.

There had to be somebody who could run a government that would take care of its own.

The current damn bunch sure weren't getting the job done.

He tried not to think that he might soon be among those looking for a place to pee.

He beat out a bag lady to a computer station and pulled up his Gmail account.

Five hundred and seventy-two responses awaited his attention.

One of them asked, "What do you know about unmanned aerial vehicles and the missiles they fire?" For just a second, Arlo thought the email might be a sting, the kind of thing the feds used to trick dumbass wannabe jihadis.

He decided he didn't care if it was. If the feds locked him up, it would cost them, what, fifty-to-a hundred K a year. He'd get free health and dental, too.

That'd make up, at least in terms of money, for the pension they'd taken away from him.

Turned out not to be a sting, though. It was a real, if criminal, job. Paid great and the politics of the situation were pleasing, too. He knew more than enough of what the job required to justify his new salary. His first mission was getting ready to launch, and there was the promise of more.

So there he was sitting in a nice hotel bar, drink in front of him, money in both his pocket and the bank, and …

Here she came now. The sweet-talking Southern belle he'd met the day before in this very same drinking establishment. She'd been happy to engage in conversation, but wouldn't go any farther, not on a first meeting. Her resistance only made him want her more.

That was probably her game.

His was not to waste a minute.

He knew he was playing with fire these days. Might very well be locked up for the rest of his life. Killed even. His days of note-taking were o-ver.

So as soon as she —

Sonofabitch. She had some guy with her. Looked like a shit-kicker.

No way was he dressed nice enough for the bar. But just as the trio that provided live music started their set, the shitkicker led the belle onto the dance floor, and had every damn pair of eyes in the place on them. Arlo's most of all.

He'd never wanted even a fantasy woman as badly as he wanted the belle now.

He was going to have to do something about that shitkicker, no question.

Capital Hilton — Washington, DC

Laurent Fortier returned to his room at the Hilton after an agreeable meal at a French restaurant in DuPont Circle. He judged the restaurant would be given one star by the Michelin Guide. To the uninformed, that might sound damning. In fact, it meant a very good restaurant in its category.

The French loved understatement and could be a bit stingy with their praise.

Two stars from the MG, which still might seem underwhelming

to American sensibilities, meant excellent cooking, worth making a detour to have. Three stars meant exceptional cuisine, surroundings and service, worth seeking out as its own destination.

Fortier never ate at three-star restaurants. The patrons there tended to attract the attention of the media, and he never wanted any public notice. His privacy was far more important to him than his taste buds.

The same thinking guided him to the Hilton, a perfectly pleasing hotel.

One almost certain, however, never to have paparazzi lurking in its vicinity.

The Hilton, among its other virtues, was close to the cluster of first-class museums that filled central Washington. Visiting the National Portrait Gallery had been the highlight of the thief's day. Unlike those in Paris, admission to the museums in Washington was free to the public. So curious, these Americans. Providing such a wealth of culture without a fee while charging a veritable fortune for basic medical services and health insurance.

Ah, well. *Chacun à son goût.* To each his own.

The National Portrait Gallery, Fortier thought, revealed the face of America to any who cared to see it. See them, more accurately. The faces were famous and anonymous, rich and poor, historical and contemporary. The diversity was staggering. Some of the images were dignified or even reverent. Others were caricatures that made one laugh aloud.

That was also a distinct aspect of the American character. Making fun of the high and mighty and using public funds to do it. The French also loved to satirize the upper classes of government and society, but they left it to the private sector. At least when it came to museums.

Fortier saw several pieces in the National Portrait Gallery he would love to have as his own. But stealing from museums, in his opinion, was an exercise best left to cinema or madmen whose daring far exceeded their intelligence. Not that some of them didn't get lucky. But even those who did had policemen around the world looking for them.

The game he played was far more subtle, far less risky, but still rewarding.

Fortier had pursued an academic career in art history, winning admission to *L'École du Louvre.* He'd studied art from its origins in prehistoric times to works with paint that had yet to dry on their canvases. The scope of the curriculum was global not merely Western. After eight years of study, he'd received his *diplôme de recherche approfondie.*

Diploma of thorough research, The School of the Louvre's equivalent of a Ph.D.

For all the breadth and depth of his studies, it was the paintings of the Impressionist Period that claimed his heart above all others. He was a longtime fixture at the Musée Marmottan Monet in the sixteenth arrondissement of Paris. He haunted the Musée d'Orsay like an inconsolable ghost who refused to be put to rest. His despair had to do with money.

More specifically, the lack of it in sufficient quantity.

The paintings he loved most were forever beyond his reach financially.

Then again, such works were unavailable to anyone who wasn't hugely wealthy.

That couldn't have been the intention of the artists who created them, he was sure.

Whenever he studied his favorite pieces, he wondered what it must have been like to be a young man in the late nineteenth century when such masterpieces were available for a song. From the start, though, some people — all too often foreigners — saw the beauty in the paintings that the leading arbiters of French culture openly scorned.

As a result of foreign interest and local disdain, boatloads of France's cultural heritage were shipped off to Chicago, Baltimore, Philadelphia and New York, bought more often than not by the wives of rich merchants. These women consumed the works of Manet, Monet, Degas and Toulouse-Lautrec as if they were the latest styles of hats and dresses, meant to be shown off to friends and rivals who couldn't be bothered with traveling to Europe.

These grand dames were bourgeois plunderers, Fortier thought.

In a just world, the paintings would have been returned to the city where they were created. But such thinking was folly. With the exchange of francs for canvas and oil paint, great art had become mere merchandise, legally bought and sold and for the most part now bequeathed to American museums. In his youth, Fortier did entertain fantasies of slipping into the world's great museums and making off with the iconic works of France's master artists.

Even then, the practical side of his nature indulged these delusions at bedtime, but forbade them during daylight hours — until the Isabella Stewart Gardner Museum in Boston was robbed in 1990. The thieves made off with a Manet, a Vermeer and four pieces by Rembrandt, among others. Their success electrified Fortier. Gave him reason to think that he could do the same.

Then his spoilsport sensible side reminded him that he was no longer young; his youth had been spent in scholarly not gymnastic exercise. Even as an art historian, though, he had yet to make a name for himself. What chance would he have to enter a museum after hours undetected, rip paintings from the walls and elude both the museum guards and the police?

The answer was none at all. He was unable to deceive himself about that. His despair returned and grew to the point that one night he couldn't even be bothered with drinking himself to sleep. He lay abed and decided that at some point exhaustion would claim his consciousness and with any luck he would never wake up. Suicide by refusal to open one's eyes.

The first half of his plan worked. He crashed into the depths of a sleep so dense he felt as if he were suspended in a sea of thick black ink. He didn't know where the surface lay or if there even was one. Finally, he saw a light. He did not swim to it; he pulled himself toward it, unsure why he was motivated to move at all. He reached out to grasp the light, and the moment he had it in his hand he woke up.

With the most brilliant idea of his life.

Certainly, not all the great works of Impressionism had been bought by the doyennes of American society. His two favorite Paris museums were stuffed with them and — here was the good part — other masterpieces had to hang in the homes of the patrons of the Impressionism, the canny *native* bourgeoisie whose commercial instincts had told them that here was the chance to get in on the ground floor of something that would become fabulously valuable.

In a way, those patrons had been the venture capitalists of their day.

Monet had been their Apple Computers; Manet had been their Google.

Surely, some of those investors must have held onto their shares of stock.

With his background in scholarly investigation, Fortier didn't have any difficulty searching out the men and women in France who had supported the great artists of their times. The ones who foresaw the merit of the Impressionists in the times of the artists' poverty, the days when they didn't have a *sou* to call their own.

Once he had compiled a long list of names, Fortier did what any smart burglar would do: He cased the houses he intended to rob. He looked for a happy medium, a property that indicated relative prosperity but was not surrounded by high walls or festooned with signage indicating the services of a private security company.

Fortier was always scared when he broke into a home, but he was pleased, too, that his body while no longer youthful was still relatively supple and strong. The remnants of the athleticism of his boyhood was still adequate to break into an unguarded home — and he felt positively Herculean whenever he got away with a painting.

He suffered no remorse for the pain he inflicted on a painting's former owner. That selfish bastard and his family had hoarded it for more than a century. Generations of greedy swine had kept to themselves art that, rightfully, the French public should have been able to see on any day they chose. Before putting his plan into effect, Fortier decided that shortly prior to his death, he would send every painting he'd stolen to the Musée d'Orsay.

He had no doubt the so-called *rightful* owners would charge forward to claim them. Perhaps they would even retrieve them. But before that happened there would be a loud national debate whether great art should ever belong to anyone but society as a whole. There would undoubtedly be those who would criticize him not only for his thefts but also for his holding the paintings for his personal enjoyment.

Fortier did not care. He would be dead by then.

His posthumous reputation would take a far greater blow should his other secret be discovered. For every painting he stole, he commissioned a brilliant forgery that he sold to the gullible, greedy, amoral rich. Thus he struck twofold at the bourgeoisie. He stole great art from them and sold knockoffs to them.

In more than a few cases, he sold a forgery of, say, a Gauguin to the same fellow from whom he'd taken, say, a Cézanne. The stupid bastard consoled himself over the loss of one treasure by buying what he thought was another — that he surely had to assume was stolen from someone else.

The idea was brilliant, but it was not his own.

He was standing in the Musée d'Orsay one day, as he so often did, and was studying Caillebotte's *"Les Raboteurs,"* The Floor Scrapers, when a beautiful, dark-haired young woman walked over to his side and whispered, "You're up to something."

A chill ran through Fortier, but he did his best not to let it show.

The woman continued, ever so quietly, "It's almost certainly illegal."

Fortier's head started to swim, but he kept his balance.

He'd just been thinking he needed someplace better than his small Left Bank apartment to hide his growing collection of fine art. Only the night before, he'd made off with a Degas. He would have loved to hang it, and the other two masterpieces he'd taken, on his wall, but he knew if he did that his next living quarters would be a prison cell. He needed the money to buy a home of his own, a place with high walls around it and guard dogs to patrol the grounds.

He was considering selling one of the paintings he'd stolen to buy such a place.

Then the woman said, almost directly into his ear, "If you tell me what you're doing, I'll not only sleep with you, I'll probably know a way to increase your profits."

Fortier finally turned to look directly at her. She was stunning, someone who never would have given him a second glance if all she'd been seeking was a handsome face. But she wanted something more and recognized that she could find it in Fortier. He'd never felt so flattered by a woman before.

Feeling unusually sure of himself, he replied, "Sleep with me first and I might tell you."

That was how he'd met Duvessa Kinsale and, later, her father, the former Wall Street swindler who now called himself Giles Benedict. Before his scheme of massive fraud had been discovered, Benedict had learned he was a painter of great technical skill, but he had no sense of creative inspiration at all.

His gift was for duplicity. Once he learned that his daughter, Duvessa, had found a chap in France who'd come up with the idea of seeking out and making off with the unknown works of some of the most famous names in art, it was only natural that he suggest a scheme to benefit both of them while bilking rich suckers. It had all the appeal of selling worthless securities to pension funds, while letting him wield his paint brush, too.

The plan was: Fortier stole a painting, Benedict knocked off a near perfect forgery and Duvessa sold it out the back door of her gallery. After a short time, Benedict foresaw the need for both protection and an inside source of law enforcement information, just in case any customers or coppers caught on to their game. Duvessa roped in a special agent working for the FBI's art crime team. Brought him over to the dark side.

Benedict had never been more proud of his little girl.

While reminiscing in the National Portrait Gallery, Fortier saw the man who'd told him about the Renoir hanging in the home of Augustin Pruet. The two men never acknowledged each other. When no one else was nearby, Fortier placed a paperback book he'd bought in the museum gift shop down on a bench. The receipt for his purchase acted as a bookmark. He walked away. The other fellow strolled over and picked up the book, opened it to the indicated page.

There, he found a key. An address was written on the back of the receipt.

In a storage locker in Alexandria, Virginia, the fellow would find his Renoir.

Well, a very good facsimile thereof.

McGill Investigations, Inc. — Georgetown

Leo took Pruet and Odo back to their hotel. McGill sat behind his desk with Sweetie and Deke for company. He shared his concern about the magistrate with them.

"I hate to dredge up a private eye cliché, but I'm pretty sure my client is holding something back on me."

"Like what?" Deke asked. He was peeking out the window behind McGill's chair.

You could take the boy out of the Secret Service, but you couldn't take the Secret Service out of the boy. Circumstances did, however, take Deke's Uzi away from him. Left him with a Beretta semi-auto, a situation he admitted often left him feeling undergunned.

McGill, hearing that, had been tempted to tell Deke maybe he ought to do an ad for the NRA. Except he'd never want to see that happen. Most cops around the country hated the fact that they too often found themselves outgunned.

Wouldn't do to have an ex-fed make things worse.

At first, McGill had thought, it might seem reasonable that the bodyguard of a high profile character like him might ask for an exception to the no-fully-automatic-weapons law. But if that was granted, the people guarding other pols — outside of those who rated Secret Service protection — would want their Uzis, too. No governor or big city mayor would fail to have a security detail armed for war.

From there it would be only a short jump for titans of industry, superstar athletes and marquee entertainers to demand their own mini-militias.

McGill told Deke to tough it out.

Remembering that he, Sweetie and Leo were also armed.

Deke grudgingly had agreed, but he didn't like it.

McGill answered Deke's question, "It's more like … Yves Pruet has lost *someone* rather than something."

"Do we know he didn't?" Sweetie asked.

McGill said, "I have —"

"Someone coming," Deke said from his vantage point.

McGill turned his chair around and got up for a look.

"Where?" he asked.

"Just entered the building," Deke said.

Sweetie got to her feet, too.

McGill felt the sudden tension in the room. His first impulse was to dispel it with a wisecrack, except he had a sense of foreboding, too. Without any obvious reason why.

Except for the fact he received death threats the way most people got junk mail.

Even so, he was about to suggest that maybe the person who'd entered the building was going to stop in at Wentworth & Willoughby, the accounting firm on the second floor, to get an early start on doing his tax return.

But then everyone in McGill's office heard Dikki's voice yell, "No, no you may not … No, please, don't! Do not shoot me!"

Hearing those words, McGill led the charge out of his office.

He, Sweetie and Deke all had their guns in hand.

Colonial Suites Hotel Bar — Newport News, Virginia

Celsus Crogher and Merilee Parker stepped onto the dance floor while everyone else was still in their seats. The trio on the bandstand started their set with Kenny Chesney's "No Shoes, No Shirt, No Problems." The Caribbean-influenced country tune had just the hip-swaying, easy-listening lilt to get the crowd in a dancing mood.

The unlikely first couple on the dance floor only added to the spirit of the moment. She was tall, slim and graceful. A cascade of chestnut hair with streaks of gold framed an oval face alight with joy, and maybe something a bit more lustful. The tight little black dress she wore would have been daring in New York City let alone Tidewater Virginia.

He was dressed like a cowboy, the working kind. Wore a Stetson, a Western cut shirt, low-riding jeans and scuffed Durango boots. But the way he led that lady around the floor they might have been ice skating. Smooth, brother. You could tell he was looking forward to later that night, too. The crowd saw the magic, whistled and cheered.

All except for Arlo Carsten.

And Welborn Yates.

Welborn divided his attention between his compatriots and their target. Thought things were working out just fine. Arlo didn't appear to be the type to start a bar fight, but he did have a glass in front of him. Looked like a whiskey and soda.

Alcohol, Welborn's mother had instructed him, was a depressant.

Trampled nothing faster than common sense.

Welborn had no doubt that Celsus could handle Arlo easily in any kind of fair contest, but that didn't mean the little creep might not hurl his rock glass at the back of the former SAC's head. He might even miss Celsus and hit Merilee.

To forestall any sneak attack, Welborn moved closer, leaving only two empty barstools between Arlo and himself. The former NASA project manager never noticed. He was too busy staring at the dancers and clenching his fists. The fellow clearly felt a rising sense of anger.

Hated to lose the woman he regarded as his, even if that was an ill-conceived notion.

It had been Celsus' idea to get Arlo to come after him.

They'd talked things over with Merilee at the blacksmith's cottage.

"You led the guy on, right?" Celsus asked after Merilee explained how she'd talked with Arlo the night before, following Galia Mindel's directions.

"I flirted with him," she said. "Just a *little.* Anything less would practically have been impolite. I did leave an open seat between us."

Welborn asked, "Did you lean his way? Put your hand on the stool between you?"

"You sound like you know the game," Merilee said to him with a smile.

"I've played it a time or two."

Celsus hadn't. He asked, "What comes next?"

Merilee deferred to Welborn.

He said, "If a lady leans your way, the only polite thing to do is lean her way. The better to look into her eyes. Or down her blouse if she's the type to forget a button or two. While your attention is elsewhere, one of you might just happen to put a hand on top of a hand."

Celsus was following the scenario intently.

"Yeah," he said, "then what?"

Merilee took it from there. "Well, that first point of contact might sometimes be thought of as the beginning of a greater physical intimacy."

Before the idea might be misconstrued, Welborn added, "The next step is generally thought to be a kiss."

"Oh," Celsus said. He nodded. The progression making sense to him. The kiss first and then … He asked Merilee, "Did you kiss the guy?"

She shook her head. "Not *this* guy. I knew just when he'd make his move. So I sat back and took my hand with me. The moment had passed. But I allowed as to how I might be back tonight."

"Wow," Celsus said. "You played him just right."

"So when he goes a little too far this time you can break it up?" Merilee asked.

"No, no," Celsus said. "We don't want to go to him. We want him to come to us."

"Us?" Merilee asked.

"You and me," Celsus said.

"How are you go to manage that?" Welborn asked.

"Well … do you dance, Merilee?"

Her eyes sparkled. "I certainly do."

"And *you* dance, too?" Welborn asked Celsus, his voice filled with disbelief.

"I do." Celsus paused to consider his next words. Then he spilled his secret. "The inaugural ball that's coming up? Where the president dances the first dance with Holmes?"

"Who's Holmes?" Merilee asked.

"James J. McGill," Welborn said.

He wondered where this was leading.

"I've got the second dance," Celsus said.

Merilee and Welborn looked at each other.

They said in unison, "With the president?"

Celsus nodded, looking more than a little smug.

"That's amazing," Merilee said.

That's bullshit, Welborn thought.

But he said, "Maybe you can show Merilee and me a step or two."

"What'll we do for music?" Celsus asked.

They went out to Merilee's BMW, opened the door and brought up The Righteous Brothers doing "You're My Soul and Inspiration" on her iPod. And they danced on cold Virginia earth for three minutes and four seconds like they were teenagers in love.

Without missing a beat, Celsus turned to Welborn and said, "When we're done dancing, we'll leave like we've got better things to do, and you don't let the creep jump us from behind."

After the trio finished its Kenny Chesney number, a stunning young African-American woman stepped out onto the dance floor. She put a hand on Merilee and on Celsus. She had some words and a couple of laughs with them. As a few other couples approached the floor, she waved them away.

"This next one's just for this lovely couple. Y'all can join in after that."

Welborn didn't know if what happened next was serendipity or Galia Mindel had somehow managed to put in the fix. But the other people stayed on the sideline, a tightly focused spotlight hit Merilee and Celsus and the young woman fronted the trio and began to sing "I Will Always Love You."

The Whitney Houston cover.

To Welborn, it seemed liked Celsus Crogher had become a wholly new man, a cowboy with soul. He danced with Merilee as if they were celebrating their twentieth wedding anniversary. They certainly had to be falling in love, if only for the night. Welborn had a sudden intense longing to hold Kira in his arms, to sway in time to the music with her.

Then, with a start, he remembered he was the guy who was supposed to be watching Celsus' back. One look at Arlo Carsten's grim expression told him that was going to be a necessity. The man looked ready to kill. Didn't matter if he'd spent only a few minutes talking to Merilee the night before. No way was he going to graciously step aside.

Welborn caught up to him just as Celsus helped Merilee into the cab of the pickup.

He put his gun to the back of Arlo's head and told him, "I think my friend and the lady are old enough not to need a chaperone."

Then he took the steak knife out of Arlo's hand.

McGill Investigations, Inc. — Georgetown

"I wasn't going to shoot him," the man holding the gun said, speaking of Dikki. "I wasn't going to let him stop me, either."

Five steps up the staircase, McGill, also with his gun in hand, said, "Holster your weapon."

"You first," the man said. "You and your friends."

The guy still had his gun pointed at Dikki.

Wisely, Dikki didn't precipitate any gunfire by attempting to flee.

For the moment, McGill thought keeping the conversation going was the best course.

"Who are you?" he asked.

"FBI," the man said.

"Osgood Riddick?" McGill asked.

Surprise registered in the man's eyes, but he nodded.

McGill put his gun away. Sweetie and Deke didn't.

"You can go now, Dikki," McGill said.

"I meant no trouble," the landlord said.

"It wasn't your fault," McGill said. "You weren't the one who overreacted."

Dikki nodded and disappeared into his little office under the staircase.

McGill told Riddick, "Put your gun away, if you want to come upstairs. If you don't, get the hell out. If you ever come here again waving a gun around, you and I will get together on your next day off and have a little talk."

McGill turned his back on Riddick and climbed the stairs.

McGill sat behind his desk and watched Riddick enter his office, preceded by Sweetie, followed by Deke. Going by the scowl on his face, he failed to appreciate all the personal attention he was getting. Made him feel less than the reigning power in the room.

Something the special agent wasn't used to when dealing with civilians.

As he stood in front of McGill, Sweetie and Deke moved to flank him.

"You going to ask me to sit down?" Riddick asked.

"No. You must have something to say or you wouldn't be here.

Be concise, then go."

Riddick nodded. "You're working a case for a client looking for a painting. Stop."

McGill grinned. "Well, you know how to follow directions."

"Yeah. Otherwise, I'd have said, 'Stop or I'll arrest your ass.'"

"Has the Bureau recovered Magistrate Pruet's painting, the original not the forgery? If you have, and return it to the magistrate by, say, nine a.m. tomorrow morning, my work is done."

Riddick barely moved his lips when he said, "We don't have it."

"That's a shame," McGill said. "I'd have liked to help, but now I can't. I have an obligation to my client, and so far I've heard no legitimate reason to desist."

Riddick glared at McGill, taking a moment to share his expression of unhappiness with Sweetie and Deke, and said. "You're all civilians here."

Deke understood what was coming next and said, "Are you really that stupid?"

Sweetie said, "Worse than that, he's a zealot."

McGill knew Sweetie was attuned to extremism, religious or otherwise.

He said, "Let me guess, Riddick. Not only do you not want me anywhere near your investigation, you were none too pleased with the candidate who won the last two elections for president. Especially the last one."

Riddick's face grew red, persuading Deke and Sweetie that McGill was right.

But he wasn't finished.

McGill said, "You backed off after Magistrate Pruet told you he was a friend of mine and of the president, and that's been eating you ever since, hasn't it? Damn woman *stole* the presidency. You shouldn't have to worry about what she might think. So you decided you wouldn't, and you came here to … do what? Try to intimidate me?"

"Get on your feet," Riddick told McGill, "you're under arrest."

The special agent looked at Sweetie and Deke and said, "You

try to interfere, I'll arrest both of you, too. And don't tell me you were Secret Service, pal," he said to Deke, "because that doesn't matter. You aren't shit now."

Deke started to move, but McGill held up a hand, forestalling him.

He looked at Riddick. The man did have the power of arrest. Even if he hadn't offered a reason for doing so, he might have some sort of justification in his back pocket that would let a judge side with him. Resisting arrest would make things a bigger mess for Patti. It would be a bad enough if the story that he'd been taken in hit the media at all.

Only McGill didn't judge the special agent to be in a rational state of mind.

If he submitted to —

"I said get up, goddamnit!" Riddick shouted.

He started to reach for his weapon when Elspeth Kendry appeared in the doorway behind him, gun in hand, and said, "Secret Service. Show me your hands right now or I will blow your fucking head off."

McGill rolled his chair to the right to give Elspeth a clean line of fire.

Riddick had no way of knowing who was behind him.

The woman might be just who she claimed or a secretary with balls.

Riddick went for his weapon, and collapsed in a heap when Elspeth slammed the butt of her Glock into the back of his head. She kicked Riddick's weapon away from him. He twitched and she dropped a knee on the small of his back.

Everybody in the room heard the sound of a bone breaking.

Unfazed, Elspeth cuffed him and turned to make sure Holmes was unhurt.

"Dikki called me," she said.

***

McGill's Hideaway — The White House

"I honestly didn't have a good answer," McGill told Patti.

He was standing at a window, looking out at the grounds and the city beyond the fence.

"If the guy had seemed halfway rational, I'd have let him put handcuffs on me and take me in, count on you and the other powers that be to straighten things out. But the bastard had pulled his weapon on Dikki Missirian, for Christ's sake. Might not make him textbook crazy, but it comes pretty damn close."

Sitting on the room's leather sofa, the president looked at her husband. Saw his shoulders were still hunched with tension. His mind was still running the horror show of all the things that might have gone wrong that evening.

"From what you told me," Patti said, "you also promised to fight the man if he ever came back to your office."

McGill turned from the window and walked over to the sofa, sat next to Patti.

"Came back and waved his gun around," he said.

"Even so, you implicitly challenged his authority in front of witnesses. Having done that, allowing yourself to be bound, placed in his custody and taken from public view would not have been a smart thing to do."

"I didn't know he was going to concoct a false arrest because I wouldn't knuckle under."

Patti nodded. "But you've at least heard stories of other federal or local officers doing similar things."

McGill took a beat and admitted he had.

"Maybe my experience is what led me astray. Coming from Chicago, cops know better than to arrest the wrong people. Meaning people with the clout to take their jobs from them."

"Someone like the president's husband?" Patti asked.

"Yeah, exactly. Especially when he was sitting peacefully in his place of business. Not having broken so much as a littering ordinance. As for challenging his authority, I'd have busted the

SOB's head if he'd actually hurt Dikki."

"Which, of course, you know how to do. That might not have looked so good for either of us."

"I know. I keep thinking of all the things that might have gone wrong." A new thought occurred to McGill. "There's no chance Elspeth will be in trouble for what she did, is there?"

A chill smile appeared on Patti's face.

"She might have been permanently in my dog house, if you'd gotten hurt because she didn't shoot the bastard. As things stand, with the only three witnesses to the incident supporting her action, and the fact that Dikki placed his call to Elspeth because he was concerned for your safety, I think she'll be fine."

A knock sounded at the door to the room.

Presidential instructions had been given for no interruptions. Patti said, "I'll get this."

McGill stood and went back to his spot at the window. He could hear Patti speaking with Galia. Had to be either her or Jean Morrissey. No one else would intrude. He heard the conversation end and the door close. A moment later Patti stood beside him.

"Tidings of comfort and joy?" McGill asked.

"Riddick was not acting on anyone's orders. His superiors didn't even know he was in Washington. The director is trying to decide what to do with him. Unless I seriously disagree with his conclusion, I'm going to leave the matter to him."

McGill asked, "What he did isn't grounds for dismissal?"

"Of course, it is. It's the terms of separation that need to be clarified. Medical expenses and the like. Elspeth fractured the man's lumbar spine. It looks like he'll be paraplegic."

"Ah, hell."

"She was justified in landing on his back?" Patti asked.

"He jerked or twitched or something. He was moving. In the moment, I don't know if anyone could tell if the movement was voluntary. I'd say she was fully justified."

"Then she'll be all right," Patti said.

All McGill could do was shake his head, and stop the motion

abruptly.

Patti noticed and said, "What is it?"

"That damn Inauguration Day assassination video just popped into my head. I just realized what's wrong with it?"

"What?"

"Well … the reason I didn't know what to do about Riddick was because the very idea was so unexpected, a federal agent staging a phony bust on the president's husband."

Patti said, "Okay, and that leads to?"

"You always have incredible protection because you need it. But on Inauguration Day it gets ratcheted up over the moon, everybody from cops to feds to the military is on alert. The Secret Service showed us that drone attack getting through, but you can bet they'll be as ready for that as anything else."

"You really think so?" Patti asked.

"I do. But before Inauguration Day your protection might be a little off its form because everybody's looking ahead."

"And afterward there's bound to be an inevitable letdown," Patti said.

"Right," McGill said. "So if there is going to be an assassination attempt, it's going to happen before or after January twenty-first."

"Before," Patti said, grasping the situation clearly now. "So I won't even get to take the official oath of office at the White House on January twentieth. If I die before then, they'll have made me a one-term president, nullified my reelection."

McGill's thoughts didn't concern political consequences.

He thought if anyone killed Patti, they'd better get him, too.

Or his vengeance would be both certain and monstrous.

CHAPTER 5

Number One Observatory Circle
Washington, DC — Thursday, January 10, 2013

The presence of James J. McGill in the White House should have been a lesson to the Secret Service. Namely that the world was changing and they would have to adapt. As with most institutions, however, the status quo was always to be preferred. Without expressing any partisan leanings, the men and women who protected the life of the president hoped that the administration of Patricia Darden Grant would be a singular exception, at least long enough for everyone currently on the job to retire with a full pension.

Most, if not all, of their number longed for a return to traditional norms: a male president who understood the need to put security concerns before personal whims; a dutiful first lady, not employed outside the home and certain to respect the limits on her freedom of movement; children, ideally none. Failing that a small number of young ones still under the influence of their parents so special agents need not become either the good or bad nannies.

An identical wish list applied to the vice president.

Former VP Mather Wyman had been the ideal package, a mature responsible man with a deceased wife and no children. Couldn't ask for better. That he turned out to be gay mattered not at all as his behavior had been impeccable and his secret came out only after he'd resigned.

Vice President Jean Morrissey, the current office holder?

She was the next step in evolutionary change. Another *woman.* A *single* woman. One whose oath of office didn't include a vow of chastity. Good God Almighty. The Secret Service realized it would have to check out her every boyfriend. Right back to the day they were christened, assuming that was their faith tradition.

If the Secret Service found out something they didn't like about a guy, what were they supposed to do? Tell the VP, "Sorry, Ma'am, your boyfriend doesn't make the grade?" Why? Well, he has a record of: illegal drug use, nonpayment of child support, improper use of an expense account. And those were just the kinds of things that had tripped up members of Congress.

What if Madam VP fell for a seriously bad guy?

Like a visiting academic who was really a computer hacker for the Chinese army. A Wall Street banker who was a Bernie Madoff disciple. An Arizona rancher who'd married six times without ever getting a divorce.

Imagining awful pairings for Jean Morrissey briefly became a popular exercise in black humor at the Secret Service. Suggestions came in from offices around the country. Other federal agencies got wind of the game and asked if they could play, too.

Just before one foolhardy agent could take "Who's Kissing the Veep Now?" global on social media, the vice president called the director of the Secret Service into her office and had a little talk with him.

"I know the problems my social life might cause for your people," she told David Nathan. "So here's what I propose to do. I'll keep things polite with any man I might meet. If I think there's a chance I might like to know someone better, I'll talk with the special agent in charge of my security detail. Ask to have the man vetted, confidentially. If there's a reason why I shouldn't take the relationship to a personal level, all you have to do is put up the stop sign.

"I won't ask you the reason why I shouldn't go forward. Likewise, if the gentleman in question is cleared, I won't ask you about his particulars either."

Nathan said, "Madam Vice President, don't you think any perceptive man would realize he'll be checked out before he's allowed to get close to you?"

"I do. If he's somebody with something to hide, he'll back off fast, and so much the better. If he's a good guy, a standup guy, he'll shrug it off, and he'll go up in my estimation."

The director understood, without saying so, that a venerable agency of the federal government had just morphed into a dating service.

"Yes, ma'am."

"I'll also try to make things easier for you by never dating a politician, a lobbyist or a member of the military. That should eliminate a lot of possible conflicts of interest."

"Very wise," Nathan said.

"Any suggestions as to other limitations I might consider?"

The director took a breath, thinking, "As long as you've asked."

He said, "It might be a good idea to avoid temperamental types."

Jean Morrissey smiled. "Wouldn't be smart to get into shouting matches and force your people to decide when it was time to step in."

"Exactly."

"That's reasonable. I'll also impose a curfew, say one a.m. to eight a.m. No overnight male visitors. Let your people dial it back just a little during the wee hours."

"That's very kind of you, Madam Vice President. Will that be all?"

"I think we've got it covered. Thank you, David."

The director got to his feet and offered one last thought, "I hope you'll find someone who makes you very happy."

"Me, too," Jean Morrissey said.

She knew the director's sentiment wasn't entirely selfless.

Fourteen vice presidents had gone on to sit in the Oval Office.

Protecting a president who was still dating would be a much stickier problem.

***

True to her word, no man got to spend the night at the vice president's official residence, but so far two lucky gents got to stay until closing time and one of them, Mark Naughton got invited back for breakfast twice. Including that morning. He brought his Volvo S60R to a gentle stop at the gate to the grounds of the United States Naval Observatory.

Naughton had indeed been christened, but Director Nathan had decided that wasn't good enough. The Secret Service had checked out his parents as well to assure they were loyal Americans without the taint of either mental instability or criminal activity. The worst that could be said of any of the Naughtons was they all seemed to have the gifts of effortless brilliance, cinematic good looks and self-deprecating humor.

Mark Naughton was the youngest headmaster of DC's elite Cameron School in its one hundred and forty-eight-year history. He'd charmed the vice president by telling her that he always behaved in a way that would make his student body proud.

She'd responded, "Good thing your school doesn't have a girls' ice hockey team."

They'd hit it off so well that the new Secret Service betting pool was when the date of the couple's wedding engagement would be officially announced.

Even the prospect of marriage, though, didn't mean Mark Naughton could skip a security check. He might be Jack Armstrong 2.0, but that didn't mean some bad actor might not try to use him to further an evil design. Say by attaching a remotely triggered explosive device to his car.

The agents on the gate rolled mirrors under his car to check for that possibility.

Cleared of that concern, Mark popped the lid of his trunk so the Secret Service could make sure that —

He heard an agent exclaim, "Jesus Christ!"

Right through the raised window with Eva Cassidy singing on eight speakers.

The next thing Mark knew, his car was surrounded by half-a-dozen agents, two of whom had their Uzis pointed his way. He'd never done an illegal drug in his life, but he felt certain he must be undergoing a hallucinatory episode. He thought it must be the consequence of a stroke or some other catastrophic brain dysfunction.

Then the driver's door was pulled open and he was yanked out of the car.

The sensation of his body in flight also had a dreamlike feeling.

When his feet hit the ground hard enough to make his teeth click, though, he knew he was experiencing a horrible reality. He was frog-marched to the rear of his car and forced to take a good look at what was in his trunk. At first, he wasn't sure of what he was seeing.

Then his mind began to interpret the visual input.

It was a body … in a bag. Transparent but fogged plastic. A woman, he realized. He couldn't see her face because something obscured it. A baseball cap. With the cursive C of the Cameron School above the bill.

He'd given one just like it to —

Mark Naughton's legs suddenly refused to carry his weight.

Two agents had to catch him.

He'd given that cap to his sister, Meghan.

He screamed in anguish, "Meg! No!"

Jean Morrissey had just come downstairs for her breakfast date when she heard a piercing cry of heartbreak. The nearest Secret Service agent had to sprint to catch up with her as she ran out the front door of her official residence.

Making herself a perfect target.

Williamsburg, Virginia

Arlo Carsten awoke with a terrible crick in his neck from being chained like a dog to an anvil. His hands were bound behind his back and, Jesus, his shoulders hurt almost as bad as his neck. A rope fastened his ankles together, but he felt nothing from the waist down. Sweet Mother of God. Was he going to lose his legs?

Put a bullet in my brain right now, he thought.

He retracted that idea the moment he felt a twinge in his right hip.

He revised his silent plea to a more common entreaty.

Get me out of here.

Deliverance failed to arrive on demand. Arlo used the early morning light to assess his plight. He'd been able to see very little last night, after they'd taken his blindfold off. He had the feeling he was in some decrepit enclosure built in days long past, little better than a lean-to. He felt drafts of cold air. The temperature and his predicament made him shiver.

One of the two men who had kidnapped him, the one with the cowboy twang, said, "Don't get to shakin' too hard. You'll pull the anvil right down on your melon, and wouldn't that make a fine mess?"

Just the thought made Arlo's gorge rise. He repressed the urge his dinner had to flee his stomach. Abdominals spasms were certain to bring the great weight down on him.

"You have a pleasant night now," his other captor told him.

The one who'd put the gun to his head. Bastard.

Arlo did the best he could to relax. He'd never done yoga, meditation or any of that other hippie horseshit. He was a man of science. He needed a rational point of focus to calm his mind and still his body. Took him only a minute to find what he needed: money.

He would *buy* his way out of this fix.

He had a quarter-million in a Bahamian account these days.

If that wasn't enough, he'd sign over his house. Damn real estate market was finally on the upswing again. The house would bring in another two-fifty K. Lump it with his bank money, that'd be more than two shitkickers could ever imagine stuffing into their flea-ridden mattresses.

They'd go for the deal.

Hell, they'd accept … He fell asleep trying to decide how hard a bargain he might drive.

Fully awake now with sunlight coming through a dirty window, he got his first good look at the anvil. Damn thing looked like a relic from the O.K. Corral. Pitted steel. Had to weigh hundreds of pounds. Some crusty sonofabitch with a bald head and a handlebar mustache ought to be banging out horseshoes on the thing.

Be cheaper to pay just one asshole to let him go, Arlo thought.

He saw that the anvil sat on a roughly hewn cube of oak maybe three feet high. Closer inspection showed him the dense chunk of steel overhung the oak by half-an-inch or so. He didn't know if he'd tugged it out of place as he slept, but he sure as hell didn't want the damn thing to reach its tipping point.

Fucking anvil even had a pointed end. Pointed his way. It came down on him, it'd crack his skull like an eggshell. His stomach started to roll again. In a fevered whisper, he began to chant, "Money, money, mo —"

The door to the enclosure opened and the guy with the cowboy hat, Mr. Smooth Dancer, and his friend with the gun stood there.

The friend asked, "I hear you say something about money?"

Four Seasons Hotel — Washington, DC

Magistrate Yves Pruet and his bodyguard, Odo Sacripant, had their breakfasts served in Pruet's room that morning. The magistrate had two griddle cakes; Odo ordered more eggs, this time with honey-cured ham. Each drank freshly squeezed orange juice and Kona coffee.

They finished eating at eight a.m. With the six-hour time difference between Washington and Paris, the moment was just right for Pruet to call his father after the elder Pruet had finished his lunch and before he began his afternoon nap. Madam Billaud, his father's secretary, told the magistrate that his father was hoping he'd call and put him right through.

"You have news, Yves?" Augustin Pruet asked his son.

"I have spoken with a detective from New York City."

"You have returned to New York?"

"No, Papa. He came to Washington to meet *Monsieur McGill.*"

"The president's husband is helping you?"

"Oui."

"Have you met with Madame la Présidente?"

"Yes, we had lunch at the White House. She is as charming as ever."

"That fool Jean-Louis should have had his affair with her not the German."

Pruet's father still had not forgiven Germany for World War Two.

"Papa, Patricia Grant loves her husband, and I think *Monsieur McGill* might have dispatched the former President of France had he intruded in his marriage. Where would that have left all of us?"

"With an immortal love story," Augustin said. "Romance, revenge and unimagined consequences."

That sounded familiar, Pruet thought. The names Antoine and Jocelyne leaped to mind … and something else nibbled at the edge of the magistrate's reasoning process. The notion of unimagined consequences.

But of what sort? And for which couple?

The president and McGill or his great-grandparents.

He shelved those questions for the moment to pursue another.

"Papa, the detective from New York raised a potentially important question. Did great-grandfather receive a bill of sale from Renoir?"

Antoine Pruet chuckled. "Of course, he did. I meant to show it to you when you entered the family business. Then you chose a different path and I … well, by the time I got over my pique with you, I forgot to tell you about it."

Pruet shook his head. He supposed parents and children never stopped learning about one another. He asked, "But how could there be a bill of sale if the painting was a gift?"

"The receipt, written in Renoir's own hand, was part of his

gift," his father explained. "It say's, 'One painting, in token repayment for the immeasurable kindness and generosity of *Monsieur Antoine Pruet.* Pierre Auguste Renoir.' He also describes the painting."

The magistrate swelled with pride.

He said, "The document itself is a treasure."

"*Exactement.* Which is why it resides in my safe."

The news of the bill of sale led directly to the magistrate's next question.

"Papa, I have never inquired into your business affairs, but does the Pruet family still support the arts?"

"Yes, of course. The shame of it is, there are no Renoirs painting these days."

"Still, you must have earned some good will in the arts community. Do you know anyone connected with the fine arts transportation company, TBA, or its American operation, FAT?"

"*Oui.* Jules Favre, the chairman, and I dine quarterly. Why do you ask?"

"Odo and I saw a FAT truck arriving at a new museum in Washington." Pruet gave his father the street address. "I would like to know everything I can about this museum."

"Your interest is more than cultural?" Augustin asked.

"The detective from New York told me new museums are not so particular how they acquire their art. They might easily pay a high price for an authentic, newly discovered Renoir and ask no questions about its origins."

A moment of silence ensued, followed by, "Bravo, Yves! That is brilliant. I shall call Favre immediately. You will have all the information you need. I have never been more proud of you, *mon fil.*" My son.

"Thank you, Papa. Please keep the bill of sale safe. With luck, we may soon need it."

The two Pruets said their goodbyes. Odo looked up from his copy of Le Monde, having lingered over a cup of coffee.

"All went well?" he asked.

"Oui. Nothing to bring a family together like facing a common enemy."

Odo nodded. "We are all Corsicans at heart."

"Possibly," Pruet said.

"I have a thought for you, Yves."

"Yes?"

"I don't want to see you with blood on your hands. You don't want me to do what you feel is your duty. There is one solution we have both intentionally overlooked."

"I know," Pruet said.

"The Louvel family is the truly injured party here. Perhaps the answer is to find our villain and let them determine his fate."

After a moment's silence, Pruet said, "I will consider the possibility."

Then he called his father back and asked him to find out everything he could about a woman named Duvessa Kinsale who claimed to have worked at *L'Ecole Nationale Supérieure des Beaux-Arts* and now owned a gallery in Manhattan.

"Tout de suite," Augustin said. Immediately.

Pruet heard a note of glee in his father's voice.

He devoutly hoped Papa's interest in detection wasn't growing too keen.

Inspiration Hall — Washington, DC

Representative Philip Brock and billionaire Tyler Busby stood before a painting of a vase filled with wildflowers hanging in the Busby Gallery of Washington's new mystery museum. The painting was signed Van Gogh. Brock leaned forward, careful not to break the plane of the security sensors.

Might be interesting, though, he thought, to see how quickly the museum locked itself down. How fast the guards came running. Whether the whole antitheft system was up and running.

Not that he could afford to indulge himself. As things stood, he was now on a very short list of people who had gained admission to the museum before its official opening. His presence would be judged as Busby currying the favor of an up-and-coming member of the House of Representatives. The similarity of their political views made the idea plausible.

It was publicly known the two had met two years ago at a PAVES, Preserve American Values, conference in Charleston, South Carolina.

Busby had been one of the many mega-rich present; Brock had been the lone Democrat elected to federal office. They agreed on many points of policy, but what had made them fast friends was each recognized in the other a buccaneer's sense of entitlement to anything he wanted. Plunder was to be taken by any means available.

Influence buying and peddling were the tools they held common.

Shedding blood, in a pinch, was another shared trait.

Brock leaned back and told Busby, "I can't tell the difference. Is the painting butter or margarine?"

Busby smiled, liking the metaphor. "It's real. I bought it early on, as an investment. Never really cared for the work."

"You like any of Van Gogh's stuff?"

"Mostly his self-portraits. He really captured the feel of the world closing in on him. Poor bastard was lucky to last as long as he did. Made the most of his time, though. Did a hellacious amount of work."

"And sold what, one or two paintings to his brother?"

"One painting out of nine hundred, 'Red Vineyard at Arles.' It's now in the Pushkin Museum."

"Poor sap," Brock said, "but imagine all that potential wealth he left behind, just sitting around waiting to be discovered. It's mind boggling."

"That's the real reason I run my little gallery. My idea of a lotto ticket. Some clueless genius waltzes in with a warehouse full of treasure. But no jackpot so far."

Brock laughed.

The two men moved on to the other major galleries in the museum.

Busby whispered which paintings were real, which were superb forgeries.

Brock asked him, “What matters more to you, the taking or the having?”

“Each reinforces the other. You can’t have what you don’t take. So taking is grand. But having is both its own pleasure *and* it reminds you what you’re capable of taking.”

“So, in common parlance, it’s all good.”

“It’s all wonderful. And how’s your *rancho* down in Costa Rica coming along?”

“I’ve taken title to the land, begun construction and started looking for people to work the fields and guys to man the battlements.”

Busby chuckled. He didn’t share Brock’s view of a coming apocalypse, but you never knew. With what they had planned, things would be shaken up big time. Might be a good idea to have a fortified foreign hideaway. Maybe even stash some of the art he’d acquired offshore.

The original masterpieces.

Not the forgeries hanging in the new museum.

The Oval Office

Galia Mindel’s face was chalk white when she handed the photograph to the president. The picture had been sent to the Secret Service. Also present were James J. McGill, Vice President Jean Morrissey and SAC Elspeth Kendry. The photo had been attached to an email sent to the White House. McGill had seen the image when he’d stepped into Elspeth’s office on another matter.

Though McGill had no official position in anyone’s chain of command, and rarely threw his weight around, he suggested that Elspeth bring the photo first to Galia rather than take it directly to the president. Regarding his suggestion as reasonable, the SAC complied. At first sight, the photo made Galia's eyelids flutter, as if she might faint. McGill steadied her. The feel of his hands on her helped Galia to right herself.

She called the vice president, who was en route to the White House, and asked her to meet them at the Oval Office. McGill informed the three women that he'd be sitting in on this meeting, if that was all right with the president.

Without a word passing between them, Patricia Darden Grant decided that if McGill wanted to be present he must have a compelling reason. It never crossed her mind to ask him to leave. She took the photograph Galia offered her.

It was a sharply focused, tightly cropped head-to-toe shot of Jean Morrissey running out the front door of her official residence. The angle made it clear the picture had been taken from above, from an aircraft. Superimposed crosshairs left no doubt a fatal shot might have been taken as easily as a photograph. A message superimposed across the bottom of the image emphasized that point: *We haven't forgotten about you. Leave while you can.*

"May I?" the vice president asked the president.

She had yet to see the photo.

The president handed it to her and stepped out from behind her desk. Patricia Grant took the middle seat on one of the room's sofa. McGill sat to her right. Galia was gestured to sit to the president's left. Jean Morrissey and SAC Kendry remained standing. In contrast to Galia's pallor, the vice president's face turned crimson.

She looked at the president and said, "Fuck them. The only way I'm leaving office is at the end of my term or in a box."

McGill kept his seat, but he wanted to give Jean a high five.

The president said, "Please give the picture to SAC Kendry and have a seat, Jean."

Taking and releasing a deep breath first, the vice president did as she was told.

"What can you tell us about what happened this morning?" the president asked.

Before the vice president could respond, Elspeth asked the president, "Would you mind if I record this, ma'am."

"Only the vice president's recollection of this morning's events. The rest of our discussion will remain confidential."

"Yes, ma'am." SAC Kendry took her smart phone out and began recording.

Jean Morrissey gave her account of what she'd done prior to running out of her house. Then she said, "I'd never heard a man scream in such pain before. I thought someone was killing Mark. I didn't think, I just reacted."

Everyone in the room, including the vice president, knew that her response, while perfectly natural, was foolhardy. No one criticized her for it, though. They'd all have done the same. That was the scary thing. The people behind the threat had had the cunning and the means to kill one of the best protected people in the world. They'd simply chosen not to do so.

While still rattling everyone's nerves but good.

The vice president continued, "The body in the car was not Mark Naughton's sister, Meghan. From her appearance, she was a longtime street person approximately the same size as Meghan. The baseball cap that had covered the poor woman's face *was* the one Mark had given to his sister."

"Where are the Naughtons now?" the president asked.

The vice president said, "Mark said they'd be going to the family's summer home in upstate New York, but he said they're both too busy to stay away from their jobs for long, no more than a week."

"Do you think they'd accept Secret Service protection for the time being?" the president asked.

"I think that would be a comfort … until they get angry," Jean said.

"We'll try to resolve the matter before that happens," the president said. Turning to SAC Kendry, she added, "Please get contact information for the Naughtons from the vice president when we're done here, Elspeth, and now is the time to turn off your recorder."

Turning to McGill, she asked, "What do you think, Jim?"

"There's a no-fly zone around the Naval Observatory just like the White House, right?"

The president nodded.

"So, I have to think," McGill said, "the picture wasn't taken from any obvious aircraft like a helicopter. That suggests the creeps used a small UAV. If that's the case, and they'd intended to kill Jean instead of photograph her, they'd have fired a missile rather than a gunshot."

Elspeth Kendry nodded; Galia grew pale again.

Jean Morrissey got mad once more.

McGill continued, looking at his wife, "So what they had in mind could be twofold. Make a misplaced attempt to get the vice president to resign and show us they have the ability to carry off an assassination on Inauguration Day. Scare you into staying indoors. Especially if Jean wasn't as tough as she is and did resign."

The vice president snorted at the idea.

Everyone laughed and for a moment the tension was broken.

The mood quickly turned serious again when the president said, "Maybe the thing to do then would be for Jean and me to make an unscheduled public appearance, a show of solidarity, maybe make a policy point or two along the way."

A grim smile appeared on Jean Morrissey's face.

"Damn right, Madam President," she said. "That's just the thing to do."

McGill said, "I'm all for shaking up the schedule, except for Inauguration Day, but let's review the rest of the activities planned for you and Jean over the next eleven days. See if we can figure out the times when we could throw the bad guys a curve or two."

This time it was Elspeth Kendry who agreed emphatically.

After asking for and receiving a moment alone with the president, McGill told her, "I need a favor."

The two of them were still sitting next to each other. Patti squeezed McGill's hand, "You deserve one. Bringing Galia into this situation in advance was the right thing to do. She'll likely have an idea or two that wouldn't have occurred to you or me."

McGill said, "I just wanted to make her faint so I could catch her."

Patti grinned. "She didn't and neither did you."

"She almost did and I did. You can ask Elspeth. Mostly, though, I wanted to get everybody together to show Jean we're all behind her, and we need her."

"In case anything should happen to me?" Patti asked.

"You *and* me," McGill said. "I think you had a good idea, the two of you making a surprise appearance somewhere, but you have to know I'm going to be on hand, too."

Patti said, "I'd have mixed feelings about that. I'm not the only one who needs you."

McGill sighed. He knew Patti was thinking of the kids: Abbie, Kenny and Caitie.

"We've got to have faith things will be okay for all of us. But right now being close to you, in case help is needed, is what I have to do."

Patti said, "All right. But let's increase the security on the children for the time being."

"Absolutely," McGill said.

"So what's the favor you want?"

"I'm going to ask Deke if he can stand going back to the Secret Service."

"While continuing to be your personal bodyguard."

"Yes," McGill said. "That was why I went to see Elspeth, to smooth things over with her about the idea of Deke coming back. I'm still uneasy that Special Agent Riddick came along and tried to arrest me. I need someone with official standing to tell anyone trying to do the same sort of thing again to buzz off."

Patti nodded. "Politics in this town have gone beyond being nasty. Threats to assassinate both Jean and me. An attempt to arrest you. It makes me wonder if —"

McGill shook his head. "No, it doesn't. You know the country would be worse off by far if the House had elected Howard Hurlbert president. Sheryl Kimbrough did the right thing."

Patti kissed McGill. "You are so good for me."

"All part of my master plan."

"Your objective being?"

"More kisses, other shows of affection and a long, happy retirement, both of us knowing we did our best whenever called upon."

Patti smiled. "Would you like to be my speechwriter?"

"Only if you'll use the cuss words I write for you."

"Maybe we'll hold off on that. Do you think we should increase Sheryl Kimbrough's security?"

"I do, and her daughter's, maybe even her ex's, too."

"I'll see to it, and if you can persuade Deke to take his old job back, I'll fix that, too. Is there anything else?"

McGill nodded. "Welborn called me this morning. He and Celsus had an interesting time last night."

"Tell me all about it," the president said.

Williamsburg, Virginia

Welborn fetched two left over milking stools from the estate's garage, formerly a barn for dairy cows. The new lord of the manor had asked Kira whether they should buy a cow and be independent of the nearby chain stores for milk, butter and ice cream. His dear wife had told him, "Sure, if you want to get up in the dark to milk Elsie, churn the butter and … do whatever the heck you do to make ice cream, be my guest."

The Yates family continued to shop at the Williamsburg Fresh Market.

Despite bowing to modern convenience, Welborn had kept the milking stools he found in his garage. He intended to get around to refinishing them, but had yet to do so. Neglect paid in this case. The weathered look was right in keeping with the personas he and Celsus had adopted.

They sat in the smithy five feet away from Arlo Carsten's head.

A sufficient distance that any unfortunate tremor on their captive's part wouldn't bring the anvil down on one of their feet.

"C'mon, guys," Arlo whined, "I'm really hurting here, and now that I think about it my bladder's stretched pretty good."

"Shoulda thought of that before you tried to put a knife into my friend's back," Welborn told him.

Celsus had yet to speak to Carsten.

But his gaze under the Stetson's brim was pitiless.

"I wasn't gonna stab him. I … I just wanted to scare him."

"He look to you like the type that scares?" Welborn asked.

"Well, no, not now that I get a good look at him." Adding quickly to Celsus, "Not that there's anything *wrong* with the way you look. You're a fine looking man."

Arlo paused to consider his last comment.

"Look, I didn't mean that the wrong way either. Aw, shit, I'm just making things worse."

Welborn told Arlo, "A man in your position doesn't have a whole lot of room for things to get worse, does he? Messin' with a man's fiancée, then trying to stick him."

Arlo winced at the news. Looking at Celsus, he said, "Oh, hell. I didn't know she … Hey, you know, you're a lucky guy, mister. Gonna marry a woman like that. First time I saw her, I thought —"

Celsus leaned forward. The better to hear Arlo or maybe to slit his throat.

Looked like it could go either way.

Arlo decided to take the conversation in a new direction.

Turning to Welborn, he said, "You were right. I do have some money, and I'd be happy to give it to you if you let me go."

"How much money?" Welborn asked.

Before Arlo could answer, Celsus said in his cowboy voice, "Don't matter."

"Why not?" Arlo asked, the fear plain in his eyes.

Celsus told him. "This is a smithy right? All we got to do is heat up a few coals, get 'em glowing red and yellow."

"White's good, too," Welborn said. "Can't get hotter'n white."

"That's right. Maybe we'll start at red, go to white. Pick up a coal with the tongs. Drop it right on you."

Arlo started to shudder. He stopped when he realized he was tugging on the anvil.

"Shouldn't take more'n two or three, he tells us how to get his money." Welborn said.

"Never has," Celsus agreed.

A shiver ran through Arlo. The moment passed and took the bound man's fear with it. He looked both Welborn and Celsus in the eye and didn't blink.

"You know what? Fuck you both. You kill me, just see what happens to you. The people I work for, they'll roast both your asses. Feed you to their damn dogs."

The two captors sat back and looked at each other.

"Kinda funny he should just now think of something like that," Welborn said.

"Well, he has to pee," Celsus reminded Welborn. "That mighta distracted him."

Both of them laughed, something Welborn had not suspected the former SAC was capable of doing. But they sounded good. Like two homicidal cretins just about to have some fun.

Arlo's fear came back, but he was still in there pitching, "You shitkickers wouldn't laugh if I told you what I'm a part of, a big part."

Welborn and Celsus fell silent.

Gave Arlo looks so cruel they scared him worse than ever.

Welborn said in a menacing whisper, "Oh, yeah? What's that?"

Celsus leaned in close again like he didn't want to miss a word.

Arlo knew he'd better come up with something good now.

So he went with the only thing he had that qualified.

The truth.

Aboard Air France

Gabbi Casale's flight from New York to Paris got off to a

bumpy start. The pilot asked everyone to remain seated for "just a moment or two," promising he would find some smooth air before too long, which turned out to be an hour and a half later. Gabbi would bet that every passenger aboard experienced the same rise in blood pressure she did, but the adults on the plane did their best to remain stoic.

From the rear of the cabin, though, came the cries of an infant. The dips and shudders of the aircraft upset the child as much as anyone else. The baby's distress added to the general sense of unease. A senior flight attendant took a blue blanket back into economy class and a moment later the little one stopped bawling.

Gabbi drew the logical conclusion. Mom was nursing her child, discreetly, under the cover of the blanket. The comfort of a warm, nourishing breast and the shelter of the soft blanket had trumped the erratic progress of the plane.

The kiddo seated next to Gabbi in business class looked like she could use some reassurance and distraction, too. Eight years old or so with shining dark hair and heart shaped face, she was doing her best to keep her fear in check, but tears had formed at the corners of her brown eyes. Mom and Dad occupied the seats directly across the aisle. Their daughter had wanted to join them, but she was too big to sit on either of their laps.

They all had to keep their seatbelts buckled to be safe.

The parents looked almost as scared as their daughter.

Gabbi was on edge herself. There were moments when it almost seemed as if the plane was flying backward. As long as she didn't see a flight attendant openly weeping, though, she was determined to maintain her composure.

She asked the flight attendant who'd brought the blanket to the nursing mother, *"Auriez-vous une autre couverture pour ma jeune amie?"* Would you have another blanket for my young friend?

"Oui, Madame."

The girl, who hadn't done more than glance at Gabbi, turned to her now.

"Parlez-vous français?"

"Oui."

"Je m'appelle Madeleine."

Gabbi extended her hand. *"Je m'appelle Gabriella. Mes amis m'appellent Gabbi."*

Madeleine shook hands but frowned.

"That last part," she said in English. "Your friends call you Gabbi?"

"Très bien." The compliment came from the flight attendant.

She wrapped the blanket around the girl.

Then the pilot asked all the flight attendants to please be seated.

Madeleine looked at her parents. They smiled as bravely as they could.

Gabbi said, "You're American, right?"

Madeleine looked at her and nodded.

"You want to do something fun?"

"What?"

"I'm a pretty good artist, but when a plane is bumping around like this, I find it's the best time to do really funny drawings."

"What do you mean?" Madeleine asked.

Gabbi took two sketch pads and pens out of her carryon bag, handed one of each to her young friend. She flipped Madeleine's pad open to a blank page. Put the bag back under the seat in front of her.

"Now, hold tight to your pad and pen," she told Madeleine. "What you want to do is draw the face of a friend or maybe a boy you know and when the plane bounces around you'll get all sorts of funny lines. Let's see who can do the funnier drawings before the pilot finds that smooth air he was talking about."

Gabbi started. Madeleine watched with fascination, the way people do when they see an accomplished artist at work, and laughed when a bump in the air made the line she was drawing take a crazy detour.

"That made your drawing's nose real big," the girl said.

"Well, let's see what I can do with it," Gabbi told her, working the unplanned line into her sketch.

Madeleine watched and followed Gabbi's lead, choosing, no surprise, to make a hilarious drawing of a boy. His eyes, mouth, ears and hair style all took unplanned directions, provoking much laughter. There were still scary moments, but Madeleine focused on completing her drawing, returning to it after each jolt.

By the time they'd each completed three comic portraits, the pilot made good on his promise and found calm air. The plane's movement went from a thrill ride to a lily pad floating on a pond. There were a few audible sighs of relief and smiles throughout the aircraft.

Madeleine grinned at Gabbi and asked, "Do you have some of your drawings in here?"

In the sketch pad, she meant. Gabbi nodded.

"May I look at them?"

"Sure," she said.

Mom and Dad smiled at her from across the aisle. Mom mimed a "Thank you."

"These are great," Madeleine said, leafing through Gabbi's sketches. One pencil portrait stopped her cold. "I know him."

"You do?"

"He's the president's husband, Mr. McGill."

"That's right."

"Do you know him?"

"He's my friend."

"Really?"

"Really." Gabbi saw Mom and Dad were listening now. She didn't want to get into a political discussion, pro or con, with them. She wanted to keep things light. So she told Madeleine. "He and I fought a giant under a bridge in Paris."

Madeleine's eyes grew big. Mom and Dad repressed laughter.

Minutes later, the little girl fell asleep with her head resting against Gabbi's arm.

When the plane taxied to its gate, Dad leaned in and gave his business card to Gabbi.

He said, "Thank you. You were great. We're starting a year's stay in Paris. If there's ever anything we can do for you, please give me a call."

Edward Baxter was a senior VP in a commercial realty firm.

He'd handwritten a personal phone number on the back of the card.

Gabbi said thank you and tucked his card in a pocket.

Charles de Gaulle Airport — Paris

Tommy Meeker, an old pal from the U.S. embassy who had succeeded Gabbi as regional security officer, met her as she deplaned.

He held a card inscribed *Belle Madame d'Artiste.* Beautiful Artist Lady.

Gabbi laughed and gave Tommy a hug. He whisked her through customs and drove like a cabbie to the Gare de Lyon. Perks of diplomatic status.

En route, he told her, "You said Yves Pruet's family has a villa just outside Avignon, right? You've got a first-class ticket on the TGV and a room at Hôtel Cloitre Saint Louis. I booked two nights for you but there should be no problem adding nights or cutting back to one. It's off-season. But all this is on my AmEx, so you'll be able to reimburse me before the end of the month?"

"Right away, Tommy. I'm doing a favor for James J. McGill."

"Ooh-la-la," Tommy said.

"Yeah. I intend to be on my best behavior, but if I need a little weight behind me ..."

Tommy gave her his card, saying, "My new mobile number and the consul general's personal number in Marseilles."

"You're the best," Gabbi said.

"Only when you're back in the States."

Gabbi smiled, kissed his cheek when they stopped for a red light.

"Any headlines on Pruet or his family?" she asked.

"Not that the national French media or *Herald Tribune* have to report. Maybe a local journal down in Provence has some news. So how'd Mr. McGill's portrait turn out?"

"He likes it and I like it. We'll have to see about the critics and history."

Tommy pulled up in front of the train station, handed Gabbi her tickets and hotel reservation.

"So you're what now," he asked, "a painter and a private eye?"

Gabbi laughed. "Yeah, just like Mom and Dad always wanted."

The National Mall — Washington, DC

"It turns out my family does have a bill of sale for our painting," Pruet said.

McGill directed an inquiring look at the magistrate.

Pruet explained the situation as the two men walked west on the Mall.

"That is too cool," McGill said with a smile. "A thank you note from Renoir. I think my parents have some gold-star Crayola drawings I did in kindergarten."

"Each one a masterpiece, I'm sure," Pruet said with a straight face.

"Not bad. It was my early Jackson Pollock period."

Pruet grinned.

"Abstract expressionism being just the thing for five-year-olds," McGill said.

"You are a never-ending surprise, *monsieur.*"

"I like to keep people on their toes."

Knowing that other people, some with hostile intent, felt the same way, McGill kept a watchful eye on his surroundings. The sky overhead, too. He thought of the old George Carlin bit about radar picking up thunderstorms and Russian ICBMs. Punchline: Don't sweat the thunderstorms. These days, mass destruction had yielded to personalized obliteration and a Hellfire missile's flight time didn't allow anyone the chance to duck into a bomb shelter.

Made it damn hard to fight back.

To help cope with more manageable threats, Sweetie and

Elspeth walked ten paces ahead of McGill and Pruet; Deke and Odo followed by ten paces. Leo was at the wheel of an eight-passenger black Chevy SUV on Constitution Avenue, pacing Pruet and McGill.

The vigilance stayed intact but the spacing changed as the group of six came to a halt in front of the Lincoln Memorial. McGill and Pruet climbed the steps and looked intently at the enormous seated statue of the sixteenth president of the United States.

"Magnificent," Pruet said, "both the man and his likeness."

McGill told his friend, "The sculptor's name is Daniel Chester French."

"*Vraiment?*" Truly?

"*Oui.*"

Turning to McGill, Pruet said, "Odo and I made a discovery the other day, a moment of serendipity perhaps in light of what Detective Marra from New York told us."

"He said a few things, as I recall," McGill replied.

"I refer to the willingness of new museums to be less than circumspect in their purchasing decisions."

"You found a new museum here in Washington?"

The magistrate nodded.

"I thought Marra was talking about places — museums — that opened in the Middle East or Asia. Countries with relatively new money."

Amusement brightened Pruet's blue eyes. "*Mon ami,* you must not forget that to those of us in Europe, there's no greater repository of new money than America. China is having its moment, and is certainly not to be underestimated, but before long the government in Beijing will either have to crack down on growing middle class demands for freedom or give way. In either case, there will be a period of upheaval. The world's capital will rush to your country as never before. Rivers of new money will flow your way."

McGill wished he felt that optimistic about the future.

"I haven't read about any new museum opening here. What's its name?"

"I don't know," Pruet admitted, "but I have made inquiries."

He told McGill about the fine art delivery trucks pulling onto the building site and quickly being shielded from view.

"That place?" McGill said. "Everybody in town has been wondering what it is."

"All the better to make a first impression," Pruet said.

"A real splash," McGill agreed. "And you think your Renoir will be part of the new museum's collection?"

The magistrate shook his head.

"No?" McGill said. "Then what —" That was when he got his friend's idea. "You think the forgery of your Renoir will hang there."

"Oui."

McGill rolled that idea around in his head, and took matters a step farther.

"Why stop at one forgery?" he said. "The more knockoffs you can use to fool the public, the more real masterpieces you can sell to private buyers."

Pruet suggested they step outside as a large group of tourists entered the memorial.

Finding a spot with some privacy, the magistrate continued, "I do not think money is the object here."

"Why not?"

"Because the man behind this whole affair has more money than he will ever need."

"You still think it's one of the Busbys, because of what happened a long time ago."

"Tyler Busby and, yes, that is what I think."

McGill still thought Pruet was holding back something, but he respected both the magistrate's intelligence and his instincts.

"What about this delivery company?" McGill asked. "Would they get involved in criminal activities?"

"From all I know, they would not. They are entirely reputable."

"Okay, so what's going on then?"

Pruet said, "I had to give the matter some thought. Then I decided if a Renoir can be forged, so can a truck."

McGill bobbed his head. He liked the idea.

Pruet asked, "If we can find a connection between Busby and the new museum, you will have more confidence in my theory?"

"I will," McGill said.

"Will you devote some of your energy to me on spec? Do I have that figure of speech right? Spec means speculation? Not that I am asking you to work without pay, of course."

McGill grinned and said, "I've already signed on. Just tell me how may I be of help, *Monsieur le Magistrat*."

"If Tyler Busby is using the new museum to display forgeries, he will need —"

"A place to hang all the originals," McGill said, "assuming Fortier stole them for him."

"*Exactement*. A private viewing space. Perhaps with only a polarizing skylight to illuminate his treasures. Certainly, in a discreet location. Possibly on a large estate with high walls and its own security personnel."

"Or a moat, portcullis and a dragon," McGill said.

Pruet played along. "Of course. America is famous for its many castles."

"Snooping on a billionaire would be a tough job for most private eyes, you know."

"I can well imagine, but then you are *le partisan de la présidente*."

The president's henchman.

McGill said, "*Oui, je suis*." Yes, I am.

Pruet said, "I've yet to really play the lovely guitar you've lent me. Perhaps spending an afternoon with it might inspire another idea or two."

Leo dropped Pruet and Odo at the Four Seasons.

McGill and his friends returned to his office.

Nobody fired a missile at any of them.

***

The Oval Office

"How is Special Agent Riddick doing?" the president asked.

Sitting opposite her, on the other side of the president's desk, FBI Director Jeremiah Haskins said, "It looks pretty certain that he's lost the use of his legs, but advances in medical technology leave some room for hope."

Haskins' voice was a smooth baritone. He could discuss the onset of Armageddon in even tones. Suggest it might be time to purchase some life insurance. His eyes, if you could meet them, revealed his emotions plainly. The president had years of practice, looking strong men in the eye, and saw that Haskins was angry.

The question was, angry with whom?

"Has Special Agent Riddick tried to justify his actions?" the president asked.

"He said he was trying to protect the integrity of the investigation he was working."

"Did he tell his supervisor on the art crime team he'd be coming to Washington to speak with Mr. McGill?"

"No, he did not."

"Did Special Agent Riddick seek or get permission from any other superior to come to Washington?"

"No."

"As far as you know, Director Haskins, does Special Agent Riddick have a record of making unilateral decisions when working cases?"

In other words, was he a loose cannon?

Jeremiah Haskins certainly would have looked into Riddick's record before coming to the Oval Office. He would know that pleading ignorance would not be acceptable. Nor would it be in character for the director.

"He's been reprimanded twice for exceeding his authority," Haskins said.

Patricia Grant didn't show it but she felt a sense of relief.

"Does his record include any criticism for excessive use of

force?"

"There's one such instance, yes."

Now, a spark of anger flared in the president's eyes. Anyone wearing or carrying a badge was vested with the power to change peoples lives forever. That power had to be exercised with great care and judgment. It was never intended to be a bludgeon used to coerce and intimidate.

The president knew that was an idealistic view of police work. Jim would probably be the first to tell her so.

That didn't matter right now. She wouldn't knowingly have any bullies, especially ones who pulled their guns on people without a damn good reason, working for her.

She said, "I can only imagine that Special Agent Riddick's career has been allowed to continue because he's been productive in some regard."

"Yes, ma'am. He's recovered a lot of stolen art, arrested some dangerous people whose criminal activities were funded by selling that art."

The president nodded but said, "That's no longer good enough. The special agent had no cause to arrest Mr. McGill except to intimidate him, to get him to stop doing a job he was legally entitled to do. Had there been a compelling need to ask Mr. McGill to desist or at least delay his own investigation, Special Agent Riddick should have appealed to his superiors and they, or even you, should have appealed to me. I find Mr. McGill to be quite amenable when presented with a reasoned approach."

"Yes, ma'am. That's exactly what —"

"Instead, Special Agent Riddick pulled his gun on my husband, Jeremiah." Any good president knew there were times when it paid to let her senior people see her get mad. Remind them with perfect clarity just who the boss was. "Goddamnit, you point a gun at someone, you're all but begging for a tragic outcome.

"I've spoken with SAC Kendry. She was a heartbeat away from killing Riddick, and who knows if her gunshots might have hit more than one man. I don't know if Riddick bears me or my administration any personal enmity. I won't ask, but I would hardly be surprised.

"What I can and will do, though, is insist that you have your people look long and hard at any special agents whose records indicate that they regard themselves as cowboy sheriffs out to clean up Dodge. Anyone who thinks they don't have to follow the law to enforce the law can damn well find another line of work. Am I clear?"

"Yes, ma'am, entirely. Will that be all?"

"No, we're not done. You will follow disciplinary proceedings as to Special Agent Riddick's future with the Bureau exactly as they are written. You will not take into account that Mr. McGill is my husband. Nor will Riddick's record of achievement in any way mitigate the outcome. Give him exactly what he's got coming, neither more nor less."

The director gave a brief nod, his face now tight.

The president continued, "You're probably angry with me by now, Mr. Director, and you ought to be angry with Riddick, but your displeasure should not extend to SAC Kendry. From everything I've learned, she acted with restraint. She'd have been the one looking at a bleak future if she'd allowed my husband to be shot. She protected the man I love more than life. Special Agent Riddick brought the outcome on himself, including his paralysis, if it comes to that.

"There will be no hostility between the FBI and the Secret Service. You will make it your job to see that interagency cooperation is better than ever. If that's a problem for you, let me know right now and I'll accept your resignation."

Jeremiah Haskins got to his feet.

"I serve at your pleasure, Madam President. I hope it will please you to allow me to clean up the mess I permitted to happen."

Dialing her ire back a notch, the president said, "It would please me greatly."

"Will that be all, Madam President?"

The director clearly hoped it would.

He was disappointed.

The president said, "Please sit down, Jeremiah. I want to hear the details of the investigation that precipitated this sad state of affairs."

Portland, Oregon

Retirement from elected office greeted Roger Michaelson, former U.S. Senator, with offers of employment from a second-tier think tank in Washington, a *local* TV station and the head basketball coach position at a suburban high school that, athletically, had been down on its luck for the past ten years.

A former All Big Ten basketball player during his collegiate days at Northwestern, Michaelson was leaning toward the coaching job. Not for the money, certainly, but for the opportunity to get back on the court. He'd told his wife what he was thinking, hoping to get a laugh from her. Maybe even a riposte.

Like he should hold out for a junior college team.

Instead, she'd said, "Whatever makes you happy, I'm all for it. You're my guy and you always will be."

Michaelson kissed her, but when she went out to shop for groceries, he retreated to his bedroom, drew the curtains and wept. Even his wife, whom he still loved, found him to be a figure of pity. It was almost too much to bear.

If he didn't think suicide was such a chickenshit move, he might have been tempted to end it all. So with nothing better to do, he lay in his darkened bedroom and tried to summon the energy to be good and pissed off. At Patricia Fucking Grant. She was responsible for his plunge from power and position.

She'd been kicking his ass politically since he first ran for the House back in Illinois.

Her and that hag, Galia Mindel. The two of them had worked him over left and right.

Even so, those defeats had been more or less fair fights. Brass knuckle matches but with the understanding that they were opponents from the opening bell. What happened this last time was nothing less than *betrayal.* He had been led to believe that he would be the president's pick to become vice president after Mather Wyman resigned. Then the two of them would run together on the same ticket for her second term.

After she served out her second term, he would be the leading candidate for the Democratic nomination for president.

That was the plan, until Patti Fucking Grant dumped his ass, picked Jean Morrissey to replace Wyman and to run with her in 2012. Roger Michaelson was left standing on the side of the road with his wienie in his hand. He didn't like it? That made it all the funnier.

After all, what the hell could he do about it?

What Michaelson longed for was a *national* platform he could use to blast every move the president made. Problem with that was, everybody who mattered in major media knew he couldn't even *pretend* to be objective in what he would say. Anything he had to say would come across as sour grapes.

Big goddamn deal, Michaelson thought. The desire for vengeance had never stopped people from getting big TV gigs before. Everyone had to get religion right when it was his turn to cash in on dishing bile? Shit.

Somewhere in his self-commiseration, Michaelson must have fallen asleep, in the middle of the damn day, because his phone rang and woke him up. The ID screen read: Sen. Merriman. Another damn traitor.

Bob Merriman, his former chief of staff.

The guy who took his old Senate seat. After assuring him that the fix was in with Patti Grant for him to become vice president.

"You've got a lot of fucking nerve," Michaelson said by way of answering his phone.

"I'm sorry, sir," a young female voice replied.

For a moment, Michaelson was at a loss.

Then the truth slapped his face with a wet dishrag.

Bob Merriman had been too smart to place the call himself.

Or he'd decided that Michaelson didn't rate such courtesy any longer.

Somehow he found the presence of mind to say, "I'm the one who's sorry, young lady. I thought you were that turd who used to work for me."

Apparently, that line hadn't gone over too well either. The silence that followed was long enough for Michaelson to think the connection had been broken. Just as he was about to hang up the phone an older, tougher female voice spoke to him. "Senator, this is Toni Ciszewski, Senator Merriman's chief of staff. Senator Merriman thought you might like to know that Representative Philip Brock will be on MSNBC tonight at 9:00 p.m. eastern time. Word is, he's going to mention your name. In what context, we don't know. Senator Merriman thought you might like a heads-up. You've got all that? Good. Goodbye."

The chief of staff hung up on him with a bang.

Teach him to mind his phone manners.

Roger Michaelson didn't care.

Phil Brock was going to raise his name on MSNBC.

Who knew? Maybe they'd call and ask him to say something on national TV, too.

Florida Avenue — Washington, DC

Deke listened to McGill's pitch about rejoining the Secret Service in the kitchen of Sweetie and Putnam Shady's townhouse. McGill assured him that if he chose not to go back into government work he'd still have his job as a private investigator. Only problem would be, McGill would have to find a new special agent and break him in. Just in case there were any other misguided feds out there looking to arrest him.

As Deke thought about that, Sweetie added, "Could be a conspiracy for all we know. People in government who don't like the president and will try to get at her through Jim."

"Something I never had to worry about before," McGill added.

Deke told him, "If SAC Kendry hadn't come in when she did, I was going to put Riddick down. Not just smack him on the head. Shoot him. Dead."

McGill gave him a look.

"Someone presents a deadly threat to a package," Deke said, meaning a protected person, "that's what we're trained to do. You've been my package for quite a while now."

McGill asked, "You think Elspeth should have shot Riddick?"

Deke said, "I won't second-guess her. Things probably worked out better her way."

Sweetie wanted to know, "You think she did the right thing dropping her knee on the guy?"

"Yes. I saw him move, too. Maybe it was just a twitch, but at that point he'd brought whatever happened on himself."

McGill said, "If you want, take a while to think about it. The president said she'd fix it if you want to go back. We can probably work something out where you'd have some extra freedom of movement."

"No," Deke said, "if I go back I'll play by the rules. I will think about it for a while. I'll go sit with Leo out front."

McGill nodded.

Sweetie waited until Deke was out the door before saying, "He's right. If he goes back, he has to be subject to all the usual regulations. That'd be best for him as well as you."

Sweetie's instincts were on the mark as usual, McGill thought.

"You're right. I just hated to ask him. It seemed like he's enjoyed being a member of our team."

"Might be an alternative," Sweetie said.

"Yeah? Like what?"

"Well, talking with former SAC Crogher, I got the feeling he might be having second thoughts about retirement. If it turns out he doesn't enjoy his private sector work with Welborn, he might agree to rejoin the ranks."

McGill looked at his old, dear friend as if she'd started speaking in tongues.

"Are you saying, Margaret, that Celsus should displace Elspeth and she should become my personal Secret Service bodyguard?"

Sweetie shook her head. "It would be unfair to Elspeth to demote her. I was thinking you and Crogher might be able to work out your differences if *he* worked more closely with you."

"Yeah, that might happen or, far more likely, we'd kill each other."

"Just an idea," Sweetie said. "No need to get dramatic. Deke will probably bail you out."

McGill almost felt like sulking. Time was, he hadn't needed *anybody* to help him take care of himself. He was more than self-sufficient. If something really big came up, he could always count on Sweetie to help out. Only now that she was married, most of her protective energies were directed toward Putnam. That was natural enough. He didn't resent it.

He did, however, feel a sense of loss.

And maybe a touch of concern that his backside might be exposed.

To anyone who might care to come by and kick it.

But, good God, rely on Celsus Crogher?

McGill interrupted his reverie when he saw Sweetie looking at him. She knew just what he was thinking. That he was considering her suggestion. It was time to change the subject.

He asked Sweetie, "Have you heard anything about that new mystery building going up in Southeast?"

"I have," Sweetie said. "It was all Putnam's idea."

"What is it?" McGill asked.

"It's a new art museum, but I'm not supposed to tell anyone."

Even so, Sweetie was telling him, McGill thought. Their bonds might not be quite as tight as they once were, but they were still close. Quick as a finger snap, he felt a lot better.

"Is there anything else you can share?" he asked. "Without going too far?"

"Let me see," Sweetie said. She picked up an old-fashioned phone that was hard-wired into a wall. "Putnam's in Omaha right now visiting Darren Drucker. I'll see if he'll forgive me for what I already let slip, and we'll take it from there."

Let slip, my Aunt Fannie, McGill thought. He now realized Sweetie had an ulterior motive for sharing that tidbit. Maybe Putnam had been having a hard time measuring up against Sweetie's nearly continuous state of grace. So she'd created a flaw for herself that would benefit both McGill and Putnam.

Margaret Mary Sweeney's cunning was never to be underestimated.

She said hello to her husband and McGill saw a joyful softness round the planes of her face. Before she'd gotten married, he'd seen that expression from Sweetie only when she talked with children, his or other people's. That Putnam could bring out the same feeling in her was worth a prayer that the two of them would have a long and happy marriage.

After a moment of conversation, Sweetie confessed to letting a bit of their secret slip to McGill. She asked if having transgressed already she might tell McGill a little more. Sweetie listened to Putnam's reply, said okay, told Putnam she couldn't wait until he got home.

Sweetie hung up the phone and looked at McGill.

"Putnam says hello and he's sorry but I can't blab anymore than I already have."

"Okay," McGill said, respecting spousal privilege, "I'll just have to do some detecting."

"I can give you a clue," Sweetie said.

"Clues are always good."

"Putnam said to ask Patti."

"Patti knows?" That surprised McGill.

"Maybe not," Sweetie said. "But she should be able to find out."

"Because she's the president," McGill said.

"Because The Andrew Hudson Grant Foundation is one of the new museum's major benefactors," Sweetie replied.

***

Williamsburg, Virginia

Arlo Carsten's conditions of bondage had improved to the extent that his ankle was now bound to a U-bolt screwed into the wooden floor of the blacksmith's cottage. The heft of the chain that had been draped around his neck still weighed on his memory. He also looked up frequently to see if some crushing weight might descend upon him.

Shitkicker bastards had inflicted psychological damage on him.

Had learned his big secret, too.

But who the hell was he going to complain to?

If he told anybody connected with law enforcement what was going on, they'd set him up in the Timothy McVeigh suite at that Indiana prison where the federal government executed people. Thinking in terms of McVeigh, Arlo realized he'd sold himself cheaply. He didn't want to end up being responsible for killing a bunch of innocent people just doing their nine-to-fives.

He sure as hell didn't want any little kids in a day-care center to get killed.

The president and the other budget-slashing politicians who didn't believe in manned space flight and cost him the only job he'd ever dreamed of, them he'd kill in a heartbeat. But as precise as drone-fired missiles were, they weren't *that* accurate.

You could nail an SUV going down a dirt road in some third-world garbage dump of a country, sure. But you couldn't program your weapon to kill the guy in the rear seat on the passenger side and leave everyone else in the vehicle alive. Maybe it'd come to that someday. Be kind of an interesting problem to solve, really. But that wasn't the state of the art today.

So, yeah, it was a pretty good bet he was about to become a mass murderer.

Shit. His mama hadn't raised him to be like that. Good thing she and daddy were already gone. They'd be horrified that things had already gotten as bad as they had. Him staked out like a judas-goat in some old tumble down shack.

He hadn't eaten in long enough he felt like something was chewing on *him* from the inside.

All because he'd lost his fool head to —

The woman who walked through the door that very moment. His breath caught in his throat, seeing her again. She wasn't all dolled up liked the two times he'd seen her at the hotel bar. She was wearing sneakers, blue jeans, a UVA sweatshirt and a pink leather jacket.

Appropriate clothing to a chilly night that promised to get colder.

And she still looked mighty fine.

Arlo expected one or both of the shitkickers would be with her, but she left the door ajar and came in alone. He didn't see anyone outside. He was tempted to … shit, that didn't matter. What his temptations were.

He was chained to the goddamn floor, had enough slack to lie on the narrow bed the two assholes had dragged in for him. Of course, if he criticized his accommodations, the shitkickers might hook him back up to the anvil.

"I brought you some food," the woman said.

She dug into her jacket pockets and pulled out a granola log, a jumbo size Snickers bar and a cardboard container of Juicy Juice Punch Splash. She tossed the items to him while standing out of reach. It surprised Arlo anyone could think he was dangerous at that point.

Made him feel a little bit good the woman did.

Think he was a threat.

That made him wonder. Maybe he could trick her into coming closer. See what happened then. Not that he could see how taking her as a hostage could work out to his advantage. He didn't have it in him to kill a woman. Except for the president, and her only from a distance.

"You're all confused, aren't you sugar?" she said. "I can see it on your face. You only sorta know how you got here and you don't have a clue how you can get out."

In a damn nutshell, yeah, Arlo thought.

All he said was, "You mind closing the door? It's cold enough in here."

She smiled at him and went to the door, stepped outside. He thought she was about to leave, and forget to close the stinking door. But she didn't go. She only looked around. Like she wanted to make sure the shitkickers weren't nearby.

Then she came back inside and closed the door.

Why would she do that?

What the hell was going on?

Arlo had the feeling he was being set up. Something bad was about to happen. He was *not* going to like the way things turned out.

"I just want to tell you how sorry I am, sugar," the woman said. "This is all my fault. I'm such a terrible tease. I know I shouldn't do it, but I can't help myself. I must be insecure or something." She paused before adding, "You'll never guess what I have in mind now."

"You're going to stand me up for a date?"

The snappy comeback cheered Arlo. If one of the shitkickers burst in and killed him right now, at least he'd die knowing he got one good lick in.

"No, silly." The woman was smiling. Took no offense. "I was going to show you what you'll be missing. Undress for you. Down to my lingerie, anyway. Might've been more than that if it was warmer."

Arlo looked at her with suspicion, and a flicker of hope.

"You're engaged to that cowboy?" he asked.

"At the moment," she said. "Things can change, you know."

He shook his head, "I'm afraid I don't."

With a bit of a pout, she said, "Well, you should. That's the way all you guys are. Reaching out to grab any girl that gets close enough. You want your way with all of us. Well, that's what I'm like, too."

Arlo gave the idea fair consideration. There was some truth to what she said.

"So would you like to get a peek at me or not?" she asked.

He decided it was time to keep quiet again.

Didn't look away, though.

As if reading his mind, the woman said, "Okay, here's how we'll do it. I'll start stripping and maybe I will go all the way. Or you can make me stop any time you want. You just say so, I'll get dressed and be on my way."

Arlo couldn't stop himself from asking, "You get a thrill from me being all chained up?"

She gave him a big smile and nodded, like she was getting the chance to act out a favorite fantasy. A sudden thought chilled him. Maybe this crazy woman and the shitkickers had done all this before. Lured some sad sack into a trap, brought him out into the boonies and …

Well, shit, if they were going to kill him, he might as well enjoy the show first.

He unwrapped the Snickers bar and took a bite.

While chewing, he said, "You know, I forgot your name from the other night. You care to tell me what it is?"

"What's your favorite lady's name? The name of the girl you always hoped you'd end up with?"

Arlo knew that right off. He said, "Dolly."

She smiled. "You like those real big boobies, huh? Well, I'm not in that league, but I do okay. You can call me Dolly, if you want."

He didn't call her anything. He just lay back with his hands under his head and watched. She took her jacket off first, shimmying as she worked her arms out of the sleeves. It didn't have the polish of a real stripper doing a number, but Arlo didn't complain.

She put the jacket down on a rickety old table.

Arlo heard a jingling sound and a thunk.

Like some keys, coins and a heavier object had fallen out of a pocket.

Dolly didn't pay any attention to that. She was too busy trying to get him worked up. She did a little hip-swaying number in front of him, like she was dancing with that cowboy again. She moved a whole lot better when she didn't pretend to be something she wasn't.

Then she started to pull her sweatshirt up, an inch or so at a time. Wasn't long before he could see her nice flat tum-tum. All speckled with goose bumps from the cold, too. Damn, he was getting excited. Wouldn't be long before she got her shirt lifted high enough for —

Her to turn her back and look at him over a shoulder.

Grinning to show she sure as hell knew how to tease.

But she kept going with her back to him. Got the sweatshirt up all the way to her shoulders. Her damn back, with a million more goosebumps and no bra straps in the way, was enough to get him breathing fast. He hoped she'd turn around and give him a real show. Take everything off, like she'd said. Then the high beams of a car or a truck swept through the dirty window.

In a high-pitched squeal, the woman said, "Oh, shit!"

She pulled her shirt down, grabbed her jacket and was out the door in a heartbeat. Christ, Arlo thought, he'd been cheated out of having fun with the damn woman again. His shoulders sagged and he was tempted to beat his head against the wall. Save the shitkickers the trouble of doing him in.

Only he didn't have the energy to kill himself just then.

Maybe he could find the grit to do it later.

At least the goddamn woman had closed the door on her way out.

Then he noticed something else. The stuff that had fallen out of Dolly's jacket pocket onto the table. She'd been too scared, in too much of a hurry, to notice it when she'd run from the shack. He'd been right about the keys and the coins.

And the thing that had gone thunk?

Well, it turned out that was a cell phone.

***

Four Seasons Hotel — Washington, DC

Pruet's typical guitar repertoire ranged from classical pieces, Chopin's Prelude in D, to French folk ballads, *"J'ai vu le loup."* I saw the wolf. The folk music was usually reserved for festive family occasions when the wine flowed freely and the magistrate chose not to object to Odo's off-key singing. The classical pieces were played when serious analysis or introspection was required.

Odo had never heard Pruet play blues numbers, especially not following along with someone else playing on the radio. Or in this case a laptop computer. The magistrate's room came with wireless connectivity. Electronic communications and Internet research comprised the normal uses for Pruet's computer.

With Jean-Louis Severin no longer the president of France, and Pruet's political cover gone with him, *Monsieur le Magistrat* also had to stay abreast of any political intrigue that found its way into the electronic pages of *Le Monde* and other online journals.

When the machine was not otherwise occupied, Odo used it to Skype with his wife, Marie, and their children. It invariably astonished Pruet to see Odo's hard Corsican face transform itself into the visage of a warm, wise papa whenever he spoke with his children. Not that any of them would ever think of disobeying him.

Odo had explained to each child that he didn't need a computer to see them and know if they were obeying their mother. *Père Noël* had nothing on him. Wasn't the only one who kept a list. Checked it twice.

And that was the extent to which the laptop was used, until Pruet took the borrowed Martin guitar out of its case, intending to work through his usual playlist. Then a brochure fluttered out of the case along with the guitar. Pruet picked it up and took a look.

Spotify. *"Qu'est-ce que c'est?"* he asked Odo. What's this?

The bodyguard could only shrug.

Opening the brochure, Pruet saw a headline: The Soundtrack of Your Life.

With a rueful smile, the magistrate thought that would be a

somber medley indeed. He was about to put the brochure back in the case when he saw a code that offered a free forty-eight hour trial to Spotify's premium service. Music for every mood and moment, it said.

Who could resist such an offer?

He signed up. Browsed an astounding variety of musical offerings and decided to go with American blues. Thus did the music of Stevie Ray Vaughn, Joe Bonamassa and Kenny Wayne Shepherd make his acquaintance. At first, Pruet was content to listen as he cradled the Martin on his lap. Then his toes started to tap. His fingers kept time gently on the body of the guitar.

When he thought he understood a melody, had a feel for where it might go, he started to play along. He took many a wrong turn, but after an hour he stopped thinking about what to do and just played from his heart. More often than not, he got things right, note for note.

Even when he didn't, he felt he'd achieved an improvisation that worked well with the original composition. He couldn't remember the last time he felt so alive. So vibrant.

Watching from the equivalent of a front row seat, Odo didn't know whether his old friend, smiling ear to ear, bobbing his head, sweat forming on his brow, was being reborn or losing his mind. Then the spell broke. Pruet stopped playing. Turned off the computer.

Still holding the guitar, he looked at Odo and asked, "What do you think will become of us when we are forced to leave our current employment?"

"Nothing too difficult," Odo said. "I will have my pension and your family is quite rich."

"My family but not me. Even if money is not a concern, what will we do? Meet at a café each morning? While away endless hours until we forget we once had a purpose in life?"

"I can think of worse things. You forget, of course, I have children to look after."

"Yes, you do," Pruet said. "I should have acquired one or two for myself by now. May I buy one of yours?"

Odo said, "For the right price, you can take them all."

The two of them laughed.

"I suspect we will find ways to fill our time," Odo said.

"I hope you're right. While I was trying to play along with all this new music, it came to me. *Monsieur McGill* knows we have more on our plates than just recovering a Renoir."

"As I told you from the start," Odo said.

"He will do what any good policeman would do. Look for the truth."

"D'accord."

"I saw the painting Gabriella Casale did of *Monsieur McGill.* It is masterful."

Odo said, "I am not surprised."

"She would also be most helpful to him in pursuing an investigation in France."

"I would *not* be surprised if she were in Avignon at this moment," Odo said.

"So the question is, what should we do about that?"

"Call the Louvels."

"And?"

"Tell them to extend every courtesy to her," Odo said.

He'd fought the giant under the bridge along with Gabbi, McGill and Denys Harbin. Any of those four would always watch the others' backs. Pruet had also been there, but he'd been on the bridge not beneath it.

"You're right, of course," the magistrate said. "No point delaying the inevitable."

Dumbarton Oaks — Washington, DC

Galia Mindel didn't need a heads-up phone call to know that Representative Philip Brock would be on MSNBC that night and mention the name Roger Michaelson. Galia's spy network had penetrated mass media decades ago and was more efficient than

Google Alerts at calling programmed topics of interest to her attention. The must-see TV notation was on her desktop computer, tablet and smart phone that morning when she woke up.

She'd spoken with her sons, Aaron and Josh, earlier that evening. They and their families were all well, thank God. It reassured the White House chief of staff that her own little corner of the world was snug and secure even if it looked like the rest of the planet was swiftly going to hell. She'd let both her offspring know that she had work to do that night. So they wouldn't interrupt her for anything short of a life-or-death crisis.

She'd also texted her deputy chief of staff, Stephen Norwood, and told him he'd need to handle all calls from anyone short of the president. If he caught a call that needed her personal attention, it would have to wait until after ten p.m.

With all that settled, Galia had her notepad and pen on her lap as she used the remote control to turn on the TV from her bed. She tuned in five minutes early in case there was any cross chat about Brock or Michaelson between Gar Moses, the host of the preceding show and Deirdre "Didi" DiMarco, who would interview Phil Brock. Galia had also set the DiMarco show to record in case she wanted to review any bit of dialogue.

Two minutes before the Moses show ended, Galia's phone rang.

When it didn't explode from the look she directed at it, she answered the call.

"Madam president?" she asked.

"Next best thing," came the reply.

"Mr. McGill. I am really quite busy right now."

"I'll be brief then. I need to see the president's schedule, the real one, starting from tomorrow morning and running through January twenty-first. I'll be up at seven a.m. I'd like to have it by then. Okay?"

Gar Moses was talking to Deirdre DiMarco, as the baton was passed from one show to the next. Galia thought she heard Roger Michaelson's name mentioned, but she wasn't sure. Damnit, she hadn't wanted to miss a thing.

She also wanted to keep the president's hard and firm schedule to herself.

McGill would know better than to be satisfied if she told him to get the schedule kept by Edwina Byington, the president's secretary. That was a tentative outline of the president's day. Subject to change by whim or necessity. Galia was the keeper of appointments that only catastrophic events would change.

"Galia?" McGill said. "I thought you were in a hurry."

"Can you tell me why you need that information?"

"Sure, I could, but I'm not going to right now. I could also ask Patti directly and get what I want, but I thought I'd be mindful of your position and ask you."

Damnit, the chief of staff thought, the man had done the right thing.

"Will you tell me if I need to know?" Galia asked.

"Of course. I had Elspeth bring the photos of Jean Morrissey being targeted to you first, didn't I?"

"You did," Galia admitted.

"I'm trying to play nice, Galia, but you know what? I'd like to watch the Didi DiMarco show in a minute or two. So give me an answer or I'll do things my way."

He wanted to watch DiMarco? Galia was tempted to hang up on the man.

And she did.

After she said, "Okay, you'll get it."

McGill's Hideaway — The White House

Determined not to lift the ban on having a television in his lair, McGill watched the Didi DiMarco show streaming live on his laptop. Patti entered the room, sat next to her husband and handed him a glass of pinot grigio. He'd have preferred a Goose Island 312, but sometimes, he knew, you drank what your wife was drinking to show spousal solidarity.

Looking at the computer screen, the president said, "Brock hasn't come on yet."

"No. Didi's still doing her buildup."

Deirdre DiMarco, in her mid-thirties, had already left behind a position lecturing the rising elite at Harvard to bring political enlightenment to the masses via cable television. That and make more money than anyone in academia, while still affecting the blazer and blue jeans look of a grad student ten years her junior and getting away with it beautifully.

"She's a bit effusive for me," McGill said.

The president replied, "Overcompensation. She's sharp as a scalpel. If she skipped the stage dressing, she'd scare off most of her audience."

McGill looked at his wife.

"What?" she asked.

"How much of that do you do?"

"We've been married almost five years. You tell me."

Before McGill could respond, Didi DiMarco introduced Representative Philip Brock. McGill had his own source of information about Brock's appearance. Ellie Booker, former producer with WorldWide News, had informed McGill, hoping he'd have a comment for her after watching the program. He'd said thanks but made no promises.

Patti had heard of the interview from Galia.

Only after she'd heard of it from McGill, though.

Her husband having scooped Galia was a thought to conjure with.

Didi DiMarco stood to welcome her guest and greeted him with a handshake firm enough to impress the commandant of the Marine Corps. Brock managed not to wince. He smiled and took his seat. There was no Lucite desk between them, only a reasonable amount of legroom. Didi had explained in many media interviews that furniture shouldn't be allowed to intrude on a good conversation.

"Welcome to the show, Representative Brock. I'm so glad you decided to accept my invitation."

Brock said, "Not a problem. Happy to be here."

The star of the show gave him a wide smile.

One a former guest had characterized as Didi's "Big Bad Wolf" look.

The better to eat you with.

"Let's start with the most important question," Didi said. "Do you regard President Patricia Darden Grant to be legitimately reelected as president of the United States?"

Brock said, "I do. She won the electoral vote; she won the popular vote; the process was found to be without any Constitutional defect by the Supreme Court. She's our president now and for the next four years."

Brock sipped from a glass of water that had been placed next to his chair.

"Well, that wasn't so bad," he said, "if that was your most important question."

He refrained from smirking, but every viewer with a background in either politics or the media knew the guest had just twitted his interrogator. For her part, Didi chuckled. As if to say, you poor, sad, foolish man.

"It was far from my only question, Congressman. Would you say your Democratic caucus stands solidly behind the president? Do they share the validity of the presidential election to the same extent you say you do?"

"Well, I'm neither the minority leader nor the minority whip in the House. So it's not my job to either count or line up party members when a vote comes before us. But I still have to think that every Democrat in both the House and the Senate has to stand behind the president because without her we'd all be in trouble. And when I say 'all' I mean everyone in the country not just those of us who work on Capitol Hill."

McGill turned to Patti and said, "I didn't know he was such a big fan."

"He's not. Just keep watching."

Didi DiMarco said, "You sound like a good political soldier, Congressman, but you've voted out of step with your party on any number of issues from birth control to gun control. Many of your critics call you a DINO, a Democrat in name only. You said only two days ago in Virginia that the president didn't steal the election, it only looked like she did."

Brock didn't cross his arms or his legs. Made no attempt to equivocate.

He leaned forward and told Didi, "I also winked when I said that."

The congressman demonstrated for the camera.

"I was having a little fun."

"So who were you trying to fool, Congressman? Your audience in Virginia, my audience here tonight or the president?"

"If you've met the president, you know there's no fooling her. I doubt I could put one past you or your audience either. So I hope you'll allow for the possibility that the people I spoke to the other day also are smart enough to recognize a joke when they hear one."

Brock's calm demeanor began to annoy Didi.

She decided to try another tack.

"Let's assume the Democrats are united behind the president. Your party controls the senate, but you're the minority in the House and —"

"For the moment," Brock said.

"What's that supposed to mean?" McGill asked.

Patti shushed him, wanting to hear what came next.

"What's that supposed to mean?" Didi DiMarco asked.

"Well, it's true," Brock said, "that the GOP and True South have decided to caucus together at the start of the new Congress, and for the moment that puts us Democrats in the minority. Now, True

South will never make common cause with us Democrats, but if our party could moderate its position on some of the more important issues to the country, why, you never know what might happen. Some GOP House members might want to get things done and caucus with us."

Didi laughed. "You're serious?"

"I am."

"What you're suggesting would turn Congress into Parliament."

"I know," Brock said. "The Founders probably wouldn't like it, but it beats the alternative."

"And what would that be, Congressman?"

"Gridlock, dysfunction, the world passing us by, laughing as it leaves us behind."

"Quite the grim picture. Would it be just a happy coincidence that you're essentially advocating that the country adapt your political point of view to avoid catastrophe?"

"What I'm saying, Didi, is if there's to be any way forward for our country, it will be found in the center of the political spectrum not at either end."

Brock took another sip of water.

"This guy's trying to box you in," McGill said.

"Not just me," Patti replied.

Didi asked, "Would it be reasonable to assume you'd like to move up in the world, Congressman? Maybe become the speaker of the House in a new coalition majority there?"

"No, that would not be reasonable," Brock said. "I'm not looking for personal advantage."

Didi paused to regroup. No pol advanced the kind of ideas Brock had done without seeking some sort of opportunity. If not directly, then what he had in mind was …

"Congressman, do you have someone else in mind who might help bring about the kind of bipartisan middle ground you're advocating?"

Brock said with a straight face, "I'm sure there's any number of people who might be helpful. The one name I'll put forward, since you've asked …" Like he was doing Didi a big favor. "That name is Roger Michaelson."

"Sonofabitch," the president said.

"What I've heard," Brock continued, "Senator Michaelson was seriously considered as a candidate to replace Mather Wyman as vice president. We all know that Jean Morrissey got that call, but the fact that Senator Michaelson was even considered shows that the president must value his abilities, and the fact that he's a good deal more conservative than the president should make him relatively appealing to the GOP."

"But Senator Michaelson is out of office, out of politics," Didi said.

"All the more reason he would be seen as an honest broker."

Didi thanked her guest and that segment of her show was over.

"That Brock guy is dangerous," McGill said, closing his laptop.

Portland, Oregon

For the first time in his life, Roger Michaelson wanted to kiss another man on the lips. He'd have done it right there on camera, if he'd been there with Brock and Didi DiMarco in New York. Of course, maybe that was why Brock hadn't had any direct contact with him. He didn't want to be embarrassed by a foolish, emotional overreaction on Michaelson's part.

Didn't want to give anyone the impression they were in cahoots.

The former senator would have to modulate his elation.

Present a sober, serious face to the nation. He had no doubt television cameras would arrive at his house … he was going to say in the morning. But it was only seven p.m. now on the West Coast. He might hear from the local network affiliates tonight.

Michaelson thought he'd better get a coat and tie on.

No, no. That would look like he knew what Brock was going to say. It would be better if the TV people found him looking just the way he was. Wearing a Northwestern sweatshirt, jeans and tennis shoes. Maybe just ask his wife to spiff up a little. She'd appreciate the chance to look her best on camera. Yeah, she should be the one to open the door.

Christ, he thought, I've never been given a gift like this one.

He wouldn't be able to take any money for brokering a peace treaty between the left and the right in Congress. Not right away. But the exposure he'd get should be worth a fortune, especially if he could pull off a power shift in the House. Lobbying firms would be brawling with one another to sign him up.

Michaelson was nearly giddy at the idea of all the good fortune his future might hold when he forced himself to hit the brakes. Just because one junior congressman from Pennsylvania had pitched his name for consideration, that didn't mean he would get the job. Hell, it would be a long shot that either the Democrats or the Republicans would ever go for the idea of joining forces.

Unless, of course, the TV people did come to solicit his opinion and he made a persuasive argument why the two major parties should work together in a centrist fashion. He thought he could spitball that one. He could also, he was pretty sure, make himself look like the only man for the job.

In a totally self-effacing way.

Modest saviors always went over the best.

Just then Michaelson's phone rang. He looked at the caller ID. KGW-TV, the NBC station in town. Things were happening already.

His wife called out, "I'll get it, dear. Are you taking any calls?"

Michaelson replied, "Sure. Why not?"

He never thought to ask why Philip Brock, a near stranger, had singled him out. Not just then. As a former jock and politician, given the least motivation, he tended to think well of himself.

Williamsburg, Virginia

Welborn and Celsus watched the blacksmith's cottage through night-vision goggles. Their bluetooth headsets allowed them to communicate with each other and with Merilee, who was watching the cottage from the main house. An hour had passed since Merilee had fled the cottage and left her cell phone.

That hadn't been a mistake made in a moment of panic.

The phone had been rigged to allow the eavesdropping and recording of any call made from it. Their hope was Arlo Carsten would use the phone to call for help. Welborn and Celsus were confident that call would not be made to the police. Arlo had already told them he was part of a group that planned to attack Washington with a "squadron" of drones.

The size of the attacking force had yet to be determined because Arlo had been told six drones had been ordered, but so far only three had been delivered. Each of the aircraft was capable of firing two missiles. The missiles weren't much to look at but the amount of damage they could do was mind bending. Death was a given to anyone within the primary blast radius.

The six missiles that were good to go, and the twelve they were aiming for, fired in concert at a single edifice built to normal civilian specifications would penetrate a roof, collapse walls, penetrate floors and ignite a conflagration. Anyone close to the point of impact would be blown to bits, crushed by falling building materials or consumed by the ensuing fire.

Even those who didn't perish immediately might succumb to what the medical people called overpressure injuries. Ears, lungs, intestines and blood vessels were highly vulnerable to shock waves. A person who exhibited no external wounds could easily be dying inside. Pulmonary contusion was the most common cause of death among people who initially survived an explosion.

Besides having received only half the promised drones, the forces planning the attack on Washington now faced another setback with Arlo's capture. He hadn't completed training the other two would-be drone pilots. They could fly the birds all right, but it wasn't a sure bet their missile launches would be dead-center perfect. Arlo was just getting good on the simulator himself.

Welborn and Celsus had been happy to hear that. The big problem from their point of view was that Arlo said he hadn't been given either the targets in Washington or the date and time of the attack. Pushing too hard for that information would have blown their cover as rustic thugs. So deception had to be their plan.

They thought they had everything covered.

Right down to measuring the chain that tethered Arlo so he could reach the table where Merilee's cell phone lay. It'd be a helluva mistake if they'd gotten their arithmetic wrong. Or if Arlo turned out to have street smarts that approached his book learning.

Whatever the reason, more than an hour had now gone by and the renegade NASA scientist had yet to attempt a phone call.

Celsus grew impatient before the others, breaking radio silence.

"Maybe he's afraid to call," the former SAC said.

"Afraid of what?" Merilee asked.

Welborn wanted to tell the two of them to be quiet.

Problem was, he didn't know how to demand that without raising his own voice.

Celsus elaborated. "Afraid to let his friends know he screwed up. Got himself in trouble. Maybe they're supposed to do themselves in if that happens. I didn't check the dipstick for any cyanide capsule."

Welborn hadn't either. Now, that would be a really sick joke. The three of them playing their slick little game and Arlo lying in the cottage dead, a swollen purple tongue sticking out of his mouth.

The thought must have bothered Celsus, too, and led him to a further worry.

"You still with us, Dubya?"

Double-you. Not a bad spur of the moment cover name for Welborn, Welborn thought.

He had just barely whispered, "Yeah," when a piercing high-pitched squeal followed by two more high register notes sounded in the bluetooth earpieces Welborn, Celsus and Merilee all wore.

Merilee shrieked, adding to the din.

"What the hell was that?" Celsus asked, pain clear in his voice.

Welborn shook his head and winced. "My guess is Arlo figured out a way to send out his own special 911 call."

Or he's just trying to mess with us, Welborn thought.

"Let's make sure he doesn't try to run for it while our ears are ringing," he said.

"Watch for more bad guys to show up, too," Celsus added.

That had been part of the original plan, after all.

The flaw in that part of the plan was a lack of triangulation technology on the part of Arlo's fellow conspirators. They weren't able to pinpoint his location, and having arrived at his present location only after being blindfolded, Arlo didn't know where he was either. So they called back, not suspecting the call was being monitored, and one fellow with a deep voice did the talking.

"You still there, Arlo?"

"Where the fuck else would I be? I'm shackled to the goddamn floor in some old tumbledown shack."

There was a pause as several voices quietly conferred in the background.

"The place is as run down as you make out, try yankin' the board you're pegged to outta the floor."

"Sonofabitch," Arlo muttered. "Hold on."

The phone went down onto the table in the cottage with a clunk. A series of grunts, curses and pleas to the Almighty followed. A prolonged creak, a sharp snap and a dull thump concluded the sound effects.

Arlo, breathing heavily, came back to the phone.

"You still there?" he asked.

"Yeah. What the hell happened?"

"I knocked myself on my ass, but I did it. Pulled the board out of the floor, split it right where my chain was bolted to the floor."

"So you're free?"

"The chain is still fastened to my ankle, but I can move."

"Then you better run, boy."

"Yeah, but where to?"

"Any-goddamn-where you can."

"Yeah, yeah." Arlo was thinking as fast as he could. "Listen, I think the shitkickers who grabbed me took me west. I'll work my way east and —"

"How you gonna know which way's east?"

Arlo took a quick peek out the window. Didn't see the assholes who'd kidnapped him or the woman who'd caused him all his trouble. But the sky was clear and he could see the stars.

"Celestial navigation," Arlo said.

"What?"

"The goddamn stars, I'll use them to guide me. I can't be more than a few miles from Highway 64. I'll hide out by the side of the road, jump up when I see you coming."

"Yeah, okay. Hey, they done anything to you that'd make you hard to recognize?"

Arlo laughed bitterly. "Just the fucking opposite. I'll be the only hitchhiker wearing chains."

The other man laughed. "Yeah, that oughta be a tipoff. You better scoot right now."

Arlo did, making the mistake of taking Merilee's phone with him, thinking the shitkickers would never have the triangulation technology to find him.

He was wrong.

Though Welborn and Celsus were delayed momentarily.

McGill called them to say, "It's time to bring in the FBI."

Neither Welborn nor Celsus was inclined to argue.

But as long as McGill was available, Celsus had a request for him.

"Ask Holly G. if I can bring a date to the inaugural ball."

***

McGill's Hideaway — The White House

McGill and Patti had moved to opposite ends of his large leather sofa. Not as a result of an argument or hard feelings. There were times when they, like any married couple, had their disagreements, but they respected the right to dissent, even from each other. They could do that comfortably, knowing that far more bound them together than divided them.

Sometimes, though, the topic of discussion and the need for objectivity precluded whispering into each other's ears. Such was the case at the moment.

"It was Byron DeWitt's idea originally," Patti said.

"What was?" McGill asked.

"That the sneakiest thing the jihadis could do would be to use our most trusted friend in the Arab world for cover. That would be Jordan, in case your subscription to the *New York Times* has lapsed."

"Never had one," McGill said. "Snubbing New York is an article of faith for all true Chicagoans."

Patti smiled. "Anyway, there's been a long history of cooperation between our government and Jordan's royal family."

"That's not risky, backing a monarch? Didn't we get our start rebelling against one?"

"We did, but you work with the best partners available, and that's what we've done."

"Okay. Seems I don't remember hearing the Arab Spring hitting Jordan too hard."

Patti said, "Relative to other countries in the Middle East, it hasn't. There is an Islamist movement in the country, but given all the bloodshed and destruction next door in Syria, they're showing self-restraint. Nobody in Jordan wants civil war in their country."

McGill offered a surmise. "But maybe, as Deputy Director DeWitt thinks, some of the people who might otherwise be leading mass demonstrations in the streets have infiltrated royal headquarters. Posing as defenders of the status quo."

"Our intelligence people think so. Deputy Director DeWitt had a good idea, it turns out, and it dovetails with another point he raised: Militant Islam and the militant right in this country want the same thing."

McGill knew that one. "The destruction of the federal government."

"Exactly. After 9/11, it became impossible for jihadists to enter our country in large numbers, cohere as military units and mount an attack on an even bigger scale than those that took place against New York and Washington."

McGill could see that and he knew what was coming next.

"On the other hand," he said, "there are so-called militias of Americans armed with assault weapons, fifty-caliber machine guns, shoulder-launched missiles and who knows what else already in the country and well represented by the gun lobby on Capitol Hill. Am I sensing that an unholy, interfaith alliance has taken place between people who'd otherwise shoot each other on sight?"

Patti said, "You never heard it from me, but yes. The FBI got their first lead by discovering that some domestic hate groups have started receiving funds that originated in Jordan. The Bureau also learned that a portion of those funds came from the proceeds of selling stolen art."

"Well, hell," McGill said. "No wonder DeWitt couldn't talk to me."

"He would have been in serious trouble if he had. Attempting to discourage you was the only right thing for him to do."

"You didn't know about this conspiracy of dirtbags?" McGill asked.

"No." Patti sighed. "Jim, if I told you how many threats I have to keep my eye on it would give you gray hair. The way my priorities get set, the worst come first."

McGill hadn't noticed any gray in Patti's coif.

Then again he wasn't sure she didn't color her hair.

Wouldn't begrudge her the artifice if she did.

"You're sure you want to do this second term thing?" he asked.

"You could leave this whole mess to Jean."

"Okay, and you'll leave Yves Pruet to work out his own problems?"

"So we're stuck," McGill said.

"Only four more years," Patti reassured him.

McGill sighed.

"You do see the problem the government faces here, don't you?" Patti asked.

McGill said he did. "The domestic dipshits get the deep personal pleasure of attacking the government they revile. Maybe killing you and me in the bargain. The foreign dirtbags claim responsibility, diverting the investigation and gaining glory from other foreign dirtbags. Then they see how many more times they can pull off the same trick."

"That's the way our people see things now," Patti said. "The end game goes like this. Each side turns on the other. Once the local zealots get their hands on the really big weaponry, they think they'll wipe out the jihadis. The jihadis figure the militias need help tying their shoelaces, won't be able to run a competent military and will be easy pickings."

McGill shook his head. "You know, I believe in evolution, but it seems to leave an awful lot of people behind."

"I think that's the point," Patti said. "Natural selection and all."

"Damn tough on the rest of us."

"Only the strong survive. Meanwhile, I think it's time we call Captain Yates and former SAC Crogher, have them return home."

"Make use of any information they've gathered?"

"Of course."

"And what should I do?" McGill asked.

"See if you can wrap things up as quickly as possible."

McGill said he would, and made his call to Welborn.

CHAPTER 6

Williamsburg, Virginia— Friday, January 11, 2013

Having received new orders from James J. McGill, Captain Welborn Yates did the sensible thing. He followed them, and went them one better. First, he called the FBI office in Richmond, fifty-three miles away, and gave his and Celsus' current location, their description, the make and model of the truck they were driving and the description of the suspect they were pursuing.

The special agent taking the call at that wee hour of the night, Brenna Ahern, listened to and recorded every Welborn's word. Then she responded, "You know it's a federal offense to prank the FBI, don't you, mister?"

Welborn said as a federal officer himself, he knew that quite well.

He added, "Call Deputy Director Byron DeWitt if you want to check my bona fides. But don't take a coffee break first." He gave Special Agent Ahern the number where DeWitt could be reached. That got her attention.

"I'll leave my cell phone on so you can track us," Welborn said, and ended the call.

Celsus was driving and tracking Arlo's movements on a computer app not available to the public. He pointed to a map on their iPad. "The dope is smart enough to run cross country. Let's just hope he doesn't fall into a ditch in the dark and break his neck."

"Let's hope he leaves Merilee's phone on, too."

"Right. Looks like he's heading for Highway 64. We should be able to get there first, but then what? Just grab Arlo again and wait for the FBI?"

Celsus was already doing twenty miles per hour above the speed limit.

That was when Welborn decided to take the additional step.

"Let's call the local cops, too. Wouldn't do to get stopped for speeding and let the bad guy get away while our story's being checked out."

Celsus laughed. "Never entered my mind *anybody* would try to stop me. Guess I'll need to make a few adjustments."

"Uh-huh," Welborn agreed.

He called the cops in both James City County and York County. Gave them his spiel. Undercover federal officers pursuing a terrorist suspect. FBI was en route. Local help was requested to capture and hold suspect until the FBI could arrive.

The county police didn't think he was pranking them. They responded with professional courtesy and promises of immediate action. What slowed Welborn and Celsus was the entrance to the highway they had planned to use was closed for construction. That fact had not been updated on the app they were using.

Celsus cursed, then said, "Next entrance is only a mile away."

Welborn saw Arlo was just about at the highway.

"Let's hope our boy's ride is late, if he has one coming."

Celsus pushed the Ford F150 and the acceleration made Welborn think the damn thing, souped up the way it was, just might outrun his Porsche Cayman. Celsus looked like he was handling the high speed comfortably. No doubt, he'd taken the Protective Services Driver's Training Course at Fort Leonard Wood, Missouri. Students not only learned how to drive at redline speeds, they also were taught how to turn their cars at high speeds, ram another vehicle without causing injuries and drive in reverse at up to fifty miles per hour.

Welborn knew all that but, as they entered the highway, he still wished he was the one behind the wheel.

Cresting a rise in the road, Welborn saw, ahead in the distance, a small car pull to the side of the road. A man standing there hurried into the vehicle, the driver taking off before the door was shut. The passenger had to try twice to close it before he succeeded.

"That's Arlo," Welborn said.

"You sure?" Celsus asked. "You recognized him from this far off?"

"Saw the chain on his leg. He had to pull it inside before he could shut the door."

"Right," Celsus said. He'd seen the problem with the door, too. "Hold on, we'll see what this thing can really do."

The F150 could do a lot more than the little car. The gap between the vehicles closed quickly. Flicking a glance at his rear view mirror, Celsus said, "Got cops running hot behind us." With a smile, he added, "But they aren't gaining on us."

Welborn said, "That little bug up there is a Mini Cooper. It'll never —"

Get away, Welborn had intended to say.

But as Celsus moved left to pass the little car it swerved in front of him, making Celsus ease back on the gas pedal. The police cruiser behind the pickup made up ground.

So did Celsus. He caught up to the Mini and rode its rear bumper hard.

He said, "I learned how to nudge another vehicle into a spin, but not when the difference in size was this big. One mistake, I might just run that flyspeck clean over."

"We don't want that," Welborn said.

"Right, so we'll try this other idea I just thought of."

"There's a bridge just ahead," Welborn said, wanting to be helpful.

That was, not wanting anyone to die.

"I see it," Celsus said. "Hold on tight."

He dropped back maybe ten feet, just enough to sell what he was going to do next. He turned the steering wheel left, just a bit and only for a split second. That was all he needed. The driver of the Mini, quick as a cat, cut him off. But while the Mini was doing that, Celsus moved right and slammed the gas pedal to the floor.

The F150 shot past the Mini. The driver of the tiny car would have been risking suicide to attempt another blocking maneuver. Both vehicles were on the bridge now. The police cruiser was coming up hard behind the Mini.

Celsus said, "Here we go. Hope this thing has monster shocks."

He slowed just a bit and put the pickup into a sideways skid, blocking the Mini from dodging around them on the narrow bridge surface. Welborn saw the Mini coming straight at him now. The little car looked too small to smack directly into the truck's passenger door, but it was far too big to slide under the truck and emerge unscathed.

Welborn feared any collision between the two vehicles would end in a gruesome tragedy.

The F150 was not meant to skid sideways at high speeds for an indefinite distance. If it tore free of the road surface and started tumbling, that would likely leave him and Celsus dead and dismembered. Welborn didn't see his life flash before his eyes, but his mind conjured images of Kira, Aria and Callista. They all looked at him mournfully.

Then the idiot driving the Mini brought him back to reality by honking the tiny car's horn. Really? Like that would clear things right up. At least, the damn little pest was braking, leaving tracks of burning rubber behind it.

That was when Welborn realized he had his Beretta out and pointing at the Mini. If it had been a living creature, he would have shot it. But he didn't think he could kill the car's engine, didn't even know if the damn thing was in front or back. That left him nothing to do but wave his gun at the car and its occupants.

Which, seemingly, by the grace of God, appeared to work.

The nose of the Mini dipped toward the road surface, and it slowed so drastically the police cruiser almost ran it over from behind. In the end, all three vehicles stayed upright and almost, but not quite, made themselves into a Mini Cooper sandwich.

"We good?" Celsus asked, not sounding particularly anxious.

Welborn only nodded. His legs were wobbly, but he managed to get out of the truck, stay upright and yell to the cops, "Federal officer."

The cops kept their guns pointed at him.

"Y'all can put your weapon down anyway," one cop said.

Welborn did, and that was when the driver of the Mini emerged, hands up.

A girl, not quite as young as a pre-schooler, but about the size of a Keebler elf.

She yelled, "Don't nobody shoot me, I'm a minor."

Arlo Carsten didn't try to get out of the Mini.

Not until he threw up all over himself.

Avignon, France

When Gabbi Casale entered the lobby of the Hôtel Cloitre Saint Louis that morning, intending to ask if the desk clerk might recommend a place to eat breakfast outside the hotel, the clerk had a question for her.

"Are you a cyclist, madam?"

"You're asking about bicycles?"

"Oui."

"Yes, I know how to ride."

"There is a gentleman, a priest, waiting for you. His name is Père Georges Louvel. He would like for you to accompany him on a bicycle tour of Avignon."

Gabbi ran that idea through her mind. She was acceptably dressed for a ride and in decent shape, but not nearly as fit as when she worked for the State Department as a regional security officer. Avignon was hilly. In January, there were also other concerns for cyclists in Provence. Cold rain and a colder wind known as the Mistral.

A look out a window showed the soft glow of winter sunlight.

"Is there wind this morning?" Gabbi asked the clerk.

"Very little, madam. Becoming quite strong this afternoon."

"Bringing rain with it?"

"*Oui.* Will you be our guest another night?"

"Check-out is midday. I'll let you know before then."

The clerk told her where she could find Père Louvel. He would have a bicycle and a helmet for her. She stepped out of the hotel expecting to see a wizened little fellow in clerical garb, perhaps a Gallic knockoff of Barry Fitzgerald. What she found was a fellow who more closely resembled Bob Hoskins, a short thickly muscled man with a dusting of steel gray hair on a great dome of a head. His eyes were a soft blue but his shoulders, arms and knuckles suggested he'd been his seminary's middleweight boxing champion.

Gabbi extended her hand to him. "Père Louvel? I'm Gabriella Casale."

He smiled, clasped her hand and asked, "Your people are from the Italian Piedmont?"

"Not for a hundred years, Father. But originally, yes."

"You are American, then."

Gabbi nodded.

"Will the hills be too much for you on the bicycle? We can always walk."

"I'll try to keep up, but I am hungry. I could use some breakfast."

"I know just the place."

Gabbi wasn't the least bit surprised. She donned the helmet dangling from the handle bars of the bicycle Father Louvel held for her. She swung onto the seat and they were off. The priest set the pace and Gabbi followed behind, thinking she needed to hit the gym more often.

Châteauneuf-du-Pape — France

The ride to the village of Châteauneuf-du-Pape — the Pope's new palace — was a little more than ten miles. More uphill than down. To Gabbi, it felt like a hundred-mile stage of the Tour de

France through the Maritime Alps, without the benefit of performance enhancing drugs. The effort was grueling despite Father Louvel's far from scorching pace.

He just kept going and going.

Not herky-jerky like an Energizer bunny.

Implacably, like a man — a priest — on a mission.

The saving grace for Gabbi was the weather. The sun, rising in the sky, did a fair imitation of summertime radiance, but the temperature was just fifty degrees. Good for sustained aerobic effort. The breeze came from the Northwest, holding just a hint of greater coolness and the promised change in the weather scheduled to arrive that afternoon.

Narrating the ride over his shoulder, Father Louvel, told Gabbi that Châteauneuf-du-Pape's *raison d'etre* was to sell its famous wine and every second shop in the village did just that. Still, the priest managed to find a storefront in the lower reaches of the village that not only wasn't a wine shop, it didn't have any signage at all to announce its purpose.

When the proprietor and his wife noticed Père Louvel's arrival, however, they brought a table out to the sidewalk, along with two chairs and menus. They took the bikes inside so they would not clutter the narrow lane, and brought two huge cups of coffee.

Black. No cream or sugar.

Gabbi would have preferred a gallon of lemonade but the promise of a caffeine rush was not to be overlooked. She and Father Louvel dined on sweet crepes, fresh strawberries and more coffee, this time *avec crème et sucre.*

Apparently, the good father had given his silent consent to such indulgences.

At the end of the block, the road curved, offering a view of the resting vineyards below.

Not a soul, either on foot or in mechanized transport, passed them as they ate.

Between bites, Gabbi said, "You've heard from *Monsieur le Magistrat.*"

"Oui."

"The content of his message being?"

"That you are a woman of true courage and integrity. You should be treated with the greatest of respect. Nothing should be withheld from you, at least regarding the reason for Yves' visit to America."

"Very flattering, but how do you feel about that?" Gabbi asked.

Père Louvel wrinkled his brow and thought a moment.

He said, "I take it your family thinks of itself as American, after such a long time away from the Old World."

"We do, but I've lived and worked in France for years."

"Bon, then you might know how our country folk are."

"Country folk are pretty much the same the world over, Father. No one has any secrets, from each other. Where outsiders are concerned, very little is shared, and then grudgingly."

"Exactement."

"So how would Magistrate Pruet persuade you to do otherwise?"

"You know of our revolution, of course, occurring as it did so soon after America's own. We disposed, to put it mildly, of our monarchy. For all our *liberté, égalité et fraternité,* though, we are still a hierarchical society. Position matters to us. Some people are simply situated to do certain things better than others."

Gabbi asked, "Are you saying the magistrate has taken on an obligation that in other circumstances would be yours?"

The priest's face clouded. In that moment, he looked ten years older.

"The Pruet and Louvel families have lived and worked together for a very long time. We don't share bloodlines, but in all other ways we are one family. Many years ago, one of us, no one quite remembers who, came up with an expression: the devil on the doorstep."

Gabbi thought she could guess the meaning, but she wanted to hear the explanation from the priest in his own words.

"By this, we are saying that one of us is facing an irresistible temptation to commit an irredeemable act."

"What's the solution to such a problem, Father?"

"It is quite simple. You don't open the door to the devil."

"And if restraint isn't possible?"

"Then you kick …" The priest paused to search for the right words.

Kick his ass, Gabbi wondered. But that wouldn't be hard to remember.

"This is an American expression, I believe," Father Louvel said, "the one I seek."

Now, Gabbi knew what he wanted. "You kick him to the curb."

The priest smiled and made the gesture of blessing her.

"Just so. You give the devil a good, hard kick to the curb."

In the conviviality of the moment, Gabbi asked, "Father, will you tell me, please, what the nature of the irresistible temptation facing Magistrate Pruet is?"

Somber again, he said, "When Laurent Fortier stole the painting by Renoir from the Pruets, he killed the *maître d'hôtel* of their villa. He was my elder brother, Charles. Whenever Yves had one of his many differences with his own father, Augustin, he turned to Charles, a second father, if you will, for comfort and guidance."

Gabbi said, *"Je suis si désolée, Père Louvel."* I'm so sorry.

"As are we all. The only reasons we did not insist a Louvel be the one to find Fortier is because Yves and Charles were so close, and Yves would be far more likely to succeed."

With the definition of success being … arrest or vengeance?

Only one of those choices seemed irredeemable to Gabbi.

Père Louvel's silence on the matter was all the answer she needed.

Solving the problem Magistrate Pruet had taken on would require …

"Madam," the priest said, "are you all right?"

Require beating the devil at his own game, Gabbi thought.

Tempt him into making a fatal mistake. She thought she knew just how to do it.

"Father, do the Louvels know other families in Provence, in Paris and around the country, for that matter, who have the same relationship to the bourgeoisie that you have with the Pruets?"

The priest was reluctant to answer, but he finally nodded.

Gabbi said, "Good. I have an idea that might save everyone from damnation. Except Laurent Fortier."

They discussed it on the ride back to the hotel.

Père Louvel grew quite excited by the notion.

He promised Gabbi all the help he could muster.

He gave her another blessing and kissed her on both cheeks.

She was on the TGV to Paris by the time the Mistral blew into Avignon.

FBI Offices — Richmond, Virginia

The pint-sized hellraiser who tried to drive Arlo Carsten to freedom refused to give her name to any of the feds. Took pride in her defiance. As if she'd laughed off a month of sleep deprivation and listening to nothing but "Dancing Queen" and other ABBA hits. Welborn and Celsus stood in the far corners of the interrogation room while the FBI had at her.

Washington, DC was only a hundred and seven miles away, but Richmond hosted a much smaller media contingent, and the higher ups decided there would be a lesser chance of a news leak of the arrests of Ms. Don't Nobody Shoot Me and Arlo Carsten if they were confined in central Virginia.

After five hours of attempting to get the imp to open up about anything, Welborn stepped forward and said, "You know what I think? We could all use a milk shake. How about it? Can we send someone out for shakes?"

The FBI agents in the room looked him blankly.

So did the prisoner.

The others feds played along when they saw Celsus give a small nod. Welborn was an unknown quantity to most of his federal brothers and sisters in arms, but just about everyone knew that

Celsus Crogher had been the SAC of the Presidential Protection Detail for four years. He had obvious connections; his opinion mattered.

The FBI followed Welborn's lead. He took the orders of everybody who wasn't incarcerated and then said, "You want one, kid?"

"Screw you."

"Yeah, sure." Welborn shook his head. "Like you'd know anything about that."

The little punk turned bright red, but she claimed, "I know, all right."

"Maybe so. The kind of pinheads you hang with do like their jailbait."

"Fuck you."

"We're getting into a loop here. You want a shake or not?"

"Strawberry," she said.

Welborn led the other feds out of the room, leaving the kid to stew on her own for fifteen minutes. When they returned each of them held a large cup with a Dairy Queen milkshake in it, including whipped cream, a maraschino cherry and a straw. Welborn plunked the strawberry shake down in front of the kid and took a step back.

She looked at the cup and asked, "How do I know you didn't put something in it?"

"You don't, but no one's forcing you to drink."

While the prisoner pondered, the captors drank. Loudly. One finishing his shake and slurping the bottom of the cup. Welborn consumed his more slowly. When he got to the halfway point, he told the punk, "You don't want yours, I'm going to take it. I'm hungry."

She grabbed her cup in both hands, chomped the cherry off the top.

Got whipped cream on her nose and chin.

Welborn leaned in and laughed at her.

She looked at him, her temper rising as she sucked up some of the shake.

The others joined in with Welborn, laughing at the kid. Wasn't long at all before she'd had enough of their crap. Her muscles tensed and Welborn started to retreat, but not so fast that she didn't splatter the front of his shirt with the milkshake she threw at him.

He did get his left hand up in time to catch the gobbet of saliva and DQ's finest she spat at his face, caught it neatly like an infielder snagging a line drive. One of the FBI guys stepped up and scraped the globule into a clear plastic bag.

"That enough?" Welborn asked him.

"Plenty." He left the room with the bag.

Welborn drew close to the kid again.

"Thank you for the DNA sample," he said. "Even if you've never been arrested before, my guess is someone in your family has. Your daddy maybe. We'll find the connection, learn who you are and go looking for your kin."

"You asshole! You cock—"

Welborn held up a finger and shook his head.

The kid was smart enough to know she'd better hear him out and bit her tongue.

"We could have gotten a court order to force you to provide a DNA sample, taken a swab from inside your cheek. But what you did, throwing your cup at me, spitting at me, that was an assault on a federal law enforcement officer. The straw in your milkshake might've put my eye out. You know how much prison time you can get for that?"

The kid had no idea, but she knew she was in more trouble than ever.

"Truth is," Welborn told her, "I don't really know myself. It might be as little as three months or as much as sixty years."

"Sixty years?" The fight went out of Elvie. She slumped in her chair.

"The judge has a lot of leeway," Welborn said. "Depends on the kind of crime the people you're running with have planned. The worse it is, the longer your time. It'll also depend on how much you piss off the judge, and pissing people off seems to be your specialty."

The kid started to cry.

Small as she was, it looked like they were keeping her from her nap.

Nobody said, "There, there, it'll be all right."

What Welborn said was, "On the other hand, you work with us, your future will look a lot brighter. Judges like people who help us out."

A gleam of hope entered the kid's eyes.

Welborn told her, "Let's start with Arlo."

FBI Headquarters — Washington, DC

After FBI Director Jeremiah Haskins promised the president he would clean up the mess he allowed to happen, he did what any good top executive would do. He delegated the task to his most able assistant. That person was Deputy Director Byron DeWitt.

DeWitt took on the task of poring over the life of Special Agent Osgood Riddick.

The matter of weeding out any "cowboy sheriffs looking to clean up Dodge" who might be employed at the FBI, DeWitt passed along to his most trusted assistant, Special Agent Abra Benjamin.

DeWitt closely read Riddick's file from the time he applied for his position at the FBI to the day he pulled his duty weapon on the president's husband. What the hell could he have been thinking, DeWitt wondered. That he'd lock up James J. McGill for interfering with an official investigation? That he'd get McGill alone for a moment and rough him up? *Intimidate* the president's henchman? Jesus. The guy had to be nuts.

Or suffering from an overabundance of testosterone.

As a matter of policy, special agents of the FBI had to submit to random drug tests throughout their careers. Riddick had always tested clean for recreational hallucinogens, narcotics, cannabis, steroids and human growth hormones, but his testosterone numbers always bumped up against the high end of normal, sometimes nudged over the high end.

Of course, there were several legal testosterone supplements on the market. But they were generally intended for guys approaching grandpaternity. Sometimes, though, if a younger man suffered from an abnormally low production of the hormone, a supplement might be a legitimate medical prescription. The bureau wouldn't have had a problem accepting that.

But Riddick said, no, he didn't take any testosterone supplements.

He claimed he made enough of his own and his readings were consistent from the time he came on the job. Thing was, those numbers remained high into his forties, when they should have started to decline. But the polygraph said he was telling the truth.

Government regulations, especially those of the FBI, tried to take everything under the sun into account, but it had never occurred to anyone to require that certain male employees take prescription drugs to *reduce* the amount of testosterone in their bloodstream. Had they tried, people might have laughed. On the other hand, the correlation between raised testosterone levels and competitive behavior, including aggression, was widely recognized.

So maybe a testosterone-lowering drug wouldn't have been such a bad idea.

The excessive force complaint against Riddick was filed by an NYPD patrol officer. Both men were off duty, having drinks in a bar. The cop went off on his girlfriend when she criticized him for not leaving his wife, as he'd promised. Riddick was the only person who saw fit to intervene. The cop tried to scare Riddick off by flashing his badge.

Riddick then showed his ID and told the cop he was under arrest for abuse of authority.

The cop resisted and got the worse of it, by far. Witnesses said Riddick might have been overly enthusiastic in subduing the cop, but the jerk had earned it. The NYPD made no fuss. Word was quietly passed they were glad the guy, also a wife beater, was no longer their problem. The New York County D.A.'s office didn't pursue any charges against Riddick.

The only one who complained was the guy who took his lumps.

He shut up, too, when his attorney said his sentences for assaulting his girlfriend and a fed would be a lot longer if he kept yapping.

So that was Riddick's official episode of competitive-aggressive behavior.

Until he walked into McGill's office.

Thinking Riddick might try to use his abnormally high testosterone levels as an argument to defend his actions against McGill, DeWitt delved further into his research. He found that testosterone levels rose naturally when a male found himself in mating situations, and declined in child rearing situations.

Riddick was single and had no children. That left mating behavior.

The guy had gotten into a serious bar fight over a woman's well being.

Maybe he liked to look for companionship in night spots. DeWitt looked to see where that might lead. He didn't limit himself to searching police blotters or criminal justice journals. Riddick was an FBI agent who worked on art thefts and had made some big recoveries. Maybe he considered himself a dashing character. Someone who could date above his pay grade.

DeWitt scanned TMZ, Celebrity Gossip, Hollywood Gossip and half-a-dozen more websites. Didn't find any shots of Riddick with actresses or supermodels. But, yessir, there he was with a real looker at a benefit for a children's orchestra.

The woman with him was named Duvessa Kinsale.

The accompanying story said she owned a Manhattan art gallery. That was a natural fit, Riddick being with the art crime team. But McGill had told him Riddick had come to warn his client, the French magistrate … what was his name? DeWitt couldn't think of it, not after working all night. What he did remember was the Frenchman had said he was looking for a stolen Renoir and found a forgery of it in a gallery run by a woman named Duvessa Kinsale.

No problem remembering that name.

So now DeWitt had an art dealer with a forgery on her wall.

A hotheaded agent who was photographed with his arm around that art dealer.

A visiting official of the French government who got a warning from that agent.

And James J. McGill who got threatened with arrest at gunpoint by that agent.

Gee, maybe there was a connection. DeWitt would have liked to call McGill and talk about things, but he played it safe. Did the bureaucratically correct thing. Picked up the phone and called Director Haskins' office.

As he waited for Haskins, DeWitt looked up at the portrait of the president on the wall. It was a terrific likeness. He doubted Patricia Darden Grant had ever been the subject of an unflattering picture. Still, he felt disgusted with himself. What a chickenshit he'd become.

He decided it was time to put his Warhol serigraph of Chairman Mao back on the wall.

Opposite the photo of the president. Anybody gave him any grief about it, he'd quit. Go back to California and teach. Get some serious surfing time in again, too.

The director came on the line.

DeWitt said, "I think I've come up with something, sir."

The President's Private Dining Room — The White House

Chief of Staff Galia Mindel sat at the dining room table in the Residence. She had a cup of coffee, a glass of orange juice and a bran muffin in front of her. James J. McGill, phone in hand, stood across the room speaking quietly to someone. He'd apologized for interrupting their breakfast meeting.

Galia had appeared in the Residence that morning at seven a.m. with the president's official schedule in hand for McGill. She'd intended to drop off the document and warn McGill not to let it fall into the wrong hands. She was certain he wouldn't; he'd never be so careless. Still, she felt compelled to give voice to the caution.

McGill had accepted her admonition with good grace and then had surprised her by saying, "Let me buy you breakfast, Galia."

For a moment, she thought he meant taking her outside the building to eat and intended to beg off. She wanted to get to work. The president was already in the Oval Office. But McGill said he had the private dining room in mind. That was different.

The implication was the chief of staff was considered family.

Even by McGill. A far cry from their early days.

She agreed but said she couldn't spare too much time. McGill kept a straight face and said not to worry. He got great service because he tipped well. The food came promptly and with a smile. Galia had even let McGill talk her into getting two bran muffins. The second one for lunch or to take home with her for a late snack, he'd said.

She'd already eaten the first one and now was eyeing the second.

Galia, formerly a well-cushioned figure, had lost weight and inches due to the relentless stress and the sleepless nights of the president's reelection campaign. She'd liked the way she looked when she hit the svelte stage of her weight loss. Zipping past that to being gaunt hadn't pleased her. Now, she faced the greatest eating challenge of her life. How to add just the right number of calories to her diet without getting carried away.

She'd been considering eating a fraction of the second muffin when McGill had to leave the table to take the first of *two* phone calls.

She was trying to arrive at the denominator of the fraction she wanted, when McGill said, "I think a half should do it, Galia. You're looking terrific these days, by the way."

The chief of staff looked at McGill as he rejoined her at the table.

"I never thought I'd say this," Galia told him, "but I'm too thin."

She'd *never* been underweight before, not even as a little girl.

"Oh," McGill said, "I thought maybe you were going for the fashion model look."

The very idea made Galia grin. McGill liked that.

"No?" he said. "Well, maybe a body double for the president then."

McGill thought Patti had lost too much weight during the campaign.

That idea made the chief of staff laugh out loud.

Then she thought she'd better watch out. She'd been immune to McGill's charm up until now. She didn't want to let that armor fall away. She needed any edge she could get on the man to maintain a rough parity with him when it came to influencing the president.

Composing herself, she asked, "What can I do for you, Mr. McGill?"

McGill stirred a spoonful of sugar into his cold coffee and said, "I was told that The Andrew Hudson Grant Foundation made a substantial contribution to a new art museum here in Washington."

That tidbit caught the chief of staff by surprise, but she processed the information quickly.

"That new mystery building in Southeast?" she asked.

McGill nodded as he leafed through the events on the president' schedule.

Galia said. "I hadn't heard about that."

McGill looked up. "Don't you generally keep an eye on anything that might affect public opinion of the president?"

"Of course, but the reputation of the Grant Foundation is immaculate. There's never been a hint of wrongdoing in its administration. Haven't you ever talked with the president about this?"

McGill shook his head. "It might come as a surprise to some people, but I didn't marry Patti Grant for her money."

"Of course not," Galia said, repressing another smile, "but it doesn't hurt that she's, shall we say, quite well off."

McGill said, "We keep our financial affairs separate, not that it's anybody's business. I'm lucky enough to have two pensions and my business income."

Galia had never pried into that area of the First Couple's life. Doing so and getting caught would have cost her her job. But it was good to know McGill was financially independent. He'd shown from the start he couldn't be bought as a means to influence the president. The fact that he had his own cash flow meant he couldn't be portrayed as a predatory husband either.

"Do you know how the Grant Foundation works?" McGill asked

Galia said, "It's a family foundation with an IRS 501(c)(3) tax exemption. The president is the chairwoman of the board of directors. She's paid one dollar per year for her services. During her presidency, she's turned her duties over to an acting chairwoman, Alison Monahan."

McGill didn't know the name. He said, "Not someone from her Hollywood days?"

Galia shook her head. "The president's first roommate at Yale."

"Good. What else can you tell me?"

"Only general information. Private foundations generally make grants to recognized charities such as religious organizations committed to public service. Other beneficiaries might be educational, scientific or cultural institutions. Disaster and poverty relief efforts might also be recipients. On an individual basis, scholarships may be provided to deserving people. Overall, the IRS requires that the foundation pay out at least five percent annually of the previous year's net assets for charitable purposes."

McGill summed up, "So the sole purpose of a legitimate foundation is to help others."

Galia hesitated.

"What?" McGill asked.

"In most cases, I'd say yes," Galia said.

"But in some cases?"

"Well, there's always the matter of legacy. A foundation that carries a family name is a way for people to be *seen* doing good works. There can be public relations benefits that carry over to other activities, for-profit enterprises. Also, the gloss of a foundation's name might mitigate the misdeeds of the founder's descendants."

"Huh," McGill said. He'd never thought of that. Spoiled rich kids catching a break because of Mom and Dad's charity. He decided that didn't apply in this case. "I didn't know Andy Grant very long, but I got the impression he genuinely wanted to make other people's lives better … and he and the president had no children to consider."

Galia said, "I agree. I knew Mr. Grant for ten years. His philanthropy was heartfelt."

"So any contribution the foundation made to the new museum would be strictly on its merits?"

"I would say so," Galia told him. "You know, I'd like to get a sneak peek at that place."

"So would I," McGill said.

Pennsylvania Avenue — Washington, DC

McGill and Leo Levy made the drive to his office unaccompanied by an armed guard, either privately or federally employed. Of course, both of them were carrying.

"Where's Deke?" McGill asked.

"Said he had a chore to finish up. Asked me if I was good giving you a ride my ownself."

"You said, 'Of course.'"

"I said. 'Damn straight.'"

The Chevy sedan Leo drove was armored and had bullet-resistant windows and tires. Despite the added weight, it traveled faster than bad news. Its top end speed was a secret Leo had refused to share with McGill, telling him, "That number might scare you."

"Yeah?" McGill had asked. "Is it measured in warp drive, like Star Trek?"

Leo laughed and said, "Just about."

Even so, the vehicle did have its vulnerabilities.

A fifty caliber round from a sniper rifle could pierce its protective layers.

McGill had raised that possibility with Leo. Hadn't ruffled him one bit.

Leo had told him, "You know what snipers shoot? People. Usually standing still, walking or moving at a light trot in a straight line. You put one of them boys a thousand yards off, he'd have a hard time hitting a man who was sprinting in an evasive fashion. As fast as this car can go, the way I can make it stand up and pirouette, good luck."

McGill had thought to ask what if they were stuck in traffic. Before he did, he remembered they'd never been stuck in traffic. The car had continuous online traffic reporting. Backups and bottlenecks were foreseen and avoided. As far as simple inconveniences like red lights went, they got zapped by a control on Leo's steering wheel. Green was the only color they ever saw.

Stop signs were an analog technology not subject to digital override, but Leo had a presidential get-out-of-jail-free pass anytime he felt it best to run one.

All that left for McGill to worry about was the subject he brought up.

"What would you do if a drone attacked us?" he asked Leo.

"Cry for mama?"

"How about something a little more likely to get us through the day?"

Leo went uncharacteristically silent. McGill made the logical inference.

"What? That's like the top speed question?" he asked.

Leo answered with his own query. "You do know this is a new car, right? Took delivery just a couple weeks ago."

McGill had noticed a new car smell but hadn't commented on it.

"Yeah, okay, it's new. So?"

"You know who talks with General Motors about the specs for your cars? I'll give you three guesses."

McGill didn't have to think about it. "You, the Secret Service and the president."

"Uh-huh. So think about that for a while."

McGill did. Patti would call upon every resource at her command to protect him. She'd told him plainly she didn't want to become a widow again. She'd involve the military, the spy agencies and … well, anybody else who might know about drones and how to evade them."

Still, McGill had another question. "I know the missiles a drone fires are fast as hell, but the aircraft themselves, especially the little ones, aren't too speedy, are they?"

"Unh-uh," Leo said.

"You think if you had the right long gun you might shoot one down? Like skeet."

McGill saw Leo's smile in the rear view mirror.

"Now, that's a right interesting question," Leo said.

They way Leo said that, McGill wouldn't be surprised if his car sported a rifle rack before long.

FBI Offices — Richmond, Virginia

Arlo Carsten, former project manager at NASA, didn't like his career prospects as he sat alone handcuffed to a table in the interview room. He thought he'd been so damn clever with his craigslist job wanted ad. Shit, he'd been lucky he hadn't gotten caught within ten minutes of posting the damn thing. The government's spook shops had to be reading that website around the clock. If they weren't, they damn well ought to be.

He couldn't be the only jackass to use it the way he had.

If he was, maybe he could trade that morsel of information for some kind of consideration. Like they'd shoot him up with some real good dope before they gave him his lethal injection. He'd float along on a cloud before he wasn't ever doing anything again.

Christ, if the damn government had just kept funding the manned space program, none of this would have happened to him. All he'd wanted to do since he was a little boy was send people into outer space. Then he got to do it and made nice money, too. He'd been only one or two steps away from his final goal. Making space travel as routine as flying across the country. Then he would finally have felt it was safe enough for him to go up.

Arlo explores the stars, he thought. The idea still gave him a thrill.

Then, with the gravitational pull of a black hole, he was yanked back to reality as the door to the room opened and the two shit-kickers entered. Only they weren't dressed like poor white trash anymore. The one who'd been the cowboy wore a suit, something more expensive than Arlo had ever put on. The younger one wore an Air Force uniform. He'd seen plenty of those.

They had a woman with them, not the looker from the bar, but tasty just the same in an exotic way. His appreciation of her looks came to an abrupt end when he thought, "Oh, Christ, she might be a travel agent for the Guantanamo Hilton." That'd be all he'd need, getting locked up with the jihadis.

An involuntary shudder passed through Arlo.

Welborn sat opposite the prisoner and told him, "You hear what we have to say, you might want to moan a little bit, too."

Celsus sat next to Welborn and added, "Elvie Fisk gave you up. Man, that's about as low as you can go, a grown man having sex with a fifteen-year-old kid."

Arlo's mouth fell open. He looked at Welborn and Celsus. Their expressions said they'd lock his ass up for good and never bother about a trial. The woman who'd accompanied them stood in a corner. She looked like she'd just as soon shoot him.

"Now, wait just one damn minute," Arlo said. "She told me she was *eighteen* and showed me a driver's license to prove it."

With a sneer, the woman, SAC Elspeth Kendry, said, "Real geniuses, these washed-up rocket monkeys. They've never heard of fake IDs before."

Now, Arlo winced. He had asked to see the kid's ID, but once he did, he'd never questioned its authenticity. He just assumed he'd cleared a legal and moral hurdle. Why argue with success? Wasn't really a big deal getting laid, anyway, when you had it in mind to kill people.

Still. *Fifteen.* That was young enough to creep him out.

He shook his head and said, "I'm sorry. I honestly didn't know."

"You got any causes for future regret, Arlo?" Celsus asked.

Welborn followed that with, "How do you plan to help Colonel Harlan Fisk's Michigan Militia?"

Arlo looked at all three of his tormentors. The woman scared him the most. He recalled reading how American Indians, when they wanted to make a prisoner really suffer, would turn the poor sonsabitches over to their women.

"What's it going to get me, I talk to you guys?" Arlo asked.

"A life sentence instead of a death sentence, maybe," Celsus said.

"A cell of your own instead of just a bunk," Welborn told him.

"Maybe an extra scoop of ice cream once a month," Celsus said with a smirk.

"So not a hell of a lot," Arlo said.

"You want to hear the down side, dirt bag?" Elspeth asked with a snarl. "I grew up in the Middle East. I'll show you some of the things I learned there."

Arlo felt his bladder control start to slip. He had to clamp down hard.

The woman might make him clean up his own mess. Maybe with his tongue.

He hung his head and sobbed. It was all over for him. He was never going to have another happy moment in his life. His only concern now was how to minimize the pain.

He forced himself to look up, fear in his eyes that the woman might do something awful to him. Despite that, he forced himself to say, "It's the president. She's the target."

Arlo thought the admission would make him feel better, be a relief of some kind. Far from it. The cowboy in the suit looked as if he might strangle him where he sat. The other two might be happy just to watch. But nobody made a move.

Trying to explain his reasons for an attempted presidential assassination, he said, "The damn woman cost me my job, the only work I ever cared about. She ruined my life."

Arlo thought he had a nice tone of sincere outrage going, but when he saw the look of pure murder in the cowboy's eyes, a squeak of terror emerged from him. He tried to pull back but his freedom of movement was measured in inches. His cuffed hands ended his retreat.

The cowboy lunged at him and Arlo thought he might have died then if the Air Force guy hadn't grabbed his friend. Arlo would have covered his face with his hands if only his chain had more slack. Denied that opportunity, he had to face the naked hostility of the other people in the room.

"I'm sorry, all right?" Arlo yelled. "I'm sorry."

The cowboy pulled free from the Air Force officer and stomped out of the room.

Welborn said in a measured tone. "What can you tell us about whoever it is trying to kill the president?"

"I … I don't know. It's going to be a drone attack, but I don't know where or when. They kept that from me so …" A look of stupefied horror came over Arlo's face. "So, in case I got caught … Goddamnit! I'd tell you right now if I could."

The woman told the Air Force guy, "Give me a few minutes with him."

The Air Force guy gave Arlo a pitying look.

After he left, the woman took a curved dagger out of a pocket.

That and a whetstone. She started sharpening the blade.

It hissed like a snake as it slid down the stone.

Arlo screamed but no one came to save him.

As the woman stepped forward, she scared the pee right out of him.

Rock Creek Park — Washington DC

Yves Pruet and Odo Sacripant were waiting outside of Dikki Missirian's building on P Street when McGill and Leo pulled up. A cloud cover hid the sun and the air was too chill for comfortable café conversation. But McGill was in the mood for a bit of fresh air.

He got out of the Chevy and said, "Are you up for a brisk walk in the park, *Monsieur le Magistrat?* Stir our blood a bit."

"Bonne idée," Pruet said. Good idea.

The two Frenchmen got into the back of the Chevy with McGill. Leo set out for nearby Rock Creek Park. On the way, McGill handed a Beretta 92 to Odo.

"Strictly as a last resort," he told Pruet's bodyguard.

"D'accord. Merci." Odo slipped the weapon into a coat pocket.

Five minutes later, McGill and Pruet strode through the park side by side. Leo walked point, Odo took the rear guard. The weather being cold and gray, they had no other pedestrian company. The bare trees sheltered no one lying in wait for them. Their conversation belonged to themselves and no one else.

"I spoke with Gabbi Casale this morning," McGill said. "She said Père Louvel sends his best wishes."

Not batting an eye, Pruet asked, "To you or me?"

"Both of us. He's an inclusive guy from what I was told."

"You are disappointed I did not take you into my confidence?"

McGill shook his head. "We all set our own boundaries."

"For all the good they do."

McGill laughed. "You hang out with snoops, you can't expect much privacy."

"Odo warned me about that."

"I'm sure he also told you there won't be a happy ending if you kill somebody in this country. It would look bad for everybody, but appearances would be the least of your concerns."

Pruet said, "I've asked myself what price I might pay. I've yet to imagine one that is too high."

McGill thought about that. Pruet had just told him he'd sacrifice his life, if need be. He didn't doubt the magistrate's sincerity. Gabbi had told him the man who had died trying to stop the theft of the Renoir painting, Charles Louvel, had been a second father to Pruet. Possibly held in even greater affection than the magistrate's biological father. Someone like that wasn't lost to violence without provoking thoughts of reprisal.

McGill had no doubt he would feel the same way.

"The devil on the doorstep," he said.

Now, Pruet's face showed surprise, before it relaxed into a rueful smile.

"Père Louvel was unusually forthcoming with Madam Casale. For a fellow pledged to a celibate life, he still finds ways to enjoy a woman's company."

"Who could blame him?" McGill asked. "But he wouldn't have talked with Gabbi if you hadn't given him permission."

"I took Odo's warning to heart. I didn't wish to jeopardize our friendship any more than I already had. I sent word to extend Madam Casale every courtesy."

"That's good because Gabbi has an idea how accounts might be settled, back home in France, without you getting your hands bloody."

McGill's words brought Pruet to a halt.

"This is more than wishful thinking?" he asked.

"If you'll settle for something less than Fortier getting his head chopped off."

The magistrate looked cynically amused. "If my country ever brings back the guillotine, it will be for me."

McGill said, "All the more reason to give Gabbi a chance. She said she needs connections at the top art schools in Paris. You think you could manage that?"

Pruet remembered Duvessa Kinsale's claim to a connection at *L'École Nationale Supérieure des Beaux-Arts.* The magistrate felt things about to come full circle, the way criminal cases so often did. For just a moment, he allowed himself the hope that the devil might be kicked to the curb.

"Yes," he said, "I will help Madam Casale find the right people."

He was sure Papa would be able to give him names.

"Good. Let me know as soon as you can," McGill said. "In the meantime, would you like to get an advance look at the museum where Tyler Busby intends to exhibit his art collection?"

Surprised again, Pruet said, "I would like that very much. Can you arrange it?"

"I'm working on it," McGill said.

McGill Investigations, Inc. — Georgetown

Sweetie sat at her desk in the outer office of McGill's suite when he walked through the door. Deke Ky and Welborn Yates occupied visitors' chairs. Welborn was asleep and snored softly. McGill said hello to Sweetie, opened the door to his office and gestured to Deke to be the first to enter. Deke entering a room ahead of McGill was entirely appropriate to the news he brought.

"I'm back on the government payroll," he said. "Got my seniority back and credit toward my pension, too."

McGill waved Deke into a guest chair, as he took his own seat.

"Does that feel good or like a step backward?" he asked.

Deke took a deep breath, let it out before answering.

"It's more like putting on an old suit." Exactly what it looked like Deke had done. "The fit isn't quite the same and it's not really my style anymore."

"I appreciate what you're doing for me," McGill said.

Deke grinned. "Got a bump in pay grade, so that helps a little. Not that I need the money, but the recognition feels good."

Musette Ky, Deke's mother, had left a substantial sum and her house to her son before decamping to her native Vietnam. She'd earned her fortune by being the most clever criminal in DC's Vietnamese immigrant community. Deke hadn't been pleased about that. He'd kept his inheritance, but as far as McGill knew had yet to spend any of it.

"There is one consideration I'd like from you for my self-sacrifice," Deke said.

"Name it," McGill said.

"I want the same deal military service members get from enlightened employers."

"You want your old job back when your hitch with Uncle Sam

is up," McGill said. "Consider it done."

Deke said, "Truth is, I'd like that and a little more. Looking ahead, I can see how you and the president might be a little tired of this town by the end of a second term."

"Yeah, most likely."

"So, my point is, I'd be happy to work for Margaret, if she wants to keep the firm going, but I won't work under anyone else. If you and Margaret both leave, I want to buy the company name from you and run the business as my own."

McGill felt he must have looked as surprised as Yves Pruet had thirty minutes ago.

"You want to buy my name?" McGill asked.

"I figure it will have substantial value by then. You've already put this firm on the map."

McGill wondered if Deke would think to pay for the naming rights with his misbegotten legacy money. McGill wouldn't want that. Maybe, he thought, he could maintain a shamus emeritus relationship with the firm. Take a cut of ongoing revenue, consult a bit, but leave plenty of time to spend with Patti and his kids.

"I think we can probably work something out," McGill said.

"One last thing, if you and Margaret both leave, I'd like your last year on the job to be the transition period where you groom me to take over. You'd still be the boss, but I'd take over the administrative duties so I can be ready when I have to run things on my own."

McGill smiled. "You've really thought this through."

"I spent some time talking with my dad. He gave me pointers."

The last McGill had heard, Deke's father, Talbert Perkins, had been elected sheriff of Charleston County, South Carolina. It was always good to hear of a concerned father giving his son the sage counsel of an older man. McGill hoped his children would always be open to turning to him when they needed advice.

"Sounds like Sheriff Perkins helped you cover all the bases. If Margaret and I retire, you and I will work something out, along the lines we've just discussed."

They shook hands.

There was a knock at the door and Sweetie poked her head into the room.

"Welborn woke up from his nap. May we come in?"

U.S. Capitol — Washington, DC

Former Senator Roger Michaelson sat in the nearly empty visitors' gallery of the House of Representatives. He never really liked the chamber. Thought it resembled nothing so much as an ant colony. With its castes and classes; Democrats and Republicans, committee chairmen and back benchers. What it lacked was the organizing role of a queen. The figure to whom all were subservient.

In the old days, the speaker of the House filled that role. Not now. Speaker Peter Profitt knuckled under to the coalition of GOP and True South members far more than he led it. His only tool to hold the fractious group together was grinning, mealy-mouthed persuasion. If he had tried to exert top-down discipline by yanking members' committee chairmanships or assignments, he'd be out on his ear. Speaker no longer. Probably facing a primary challenge or retirement in the next election cycle, too.

What a madhouse, Michaelson thought. Four hundred and thirty-five members, having to raise funds every damn day, given that representatives faced election every other year. The way things were going, Michaelson could foresee the GOP disappearing entirely and soon. The mad-hatter voters in many districts would push scores of Republican members into the True South caucus. That or out of office entirely. The voters in the handful of districts not yet gerrymandered into single-party fealty would impel their representatives to take centrist positions incompatible with right-wing theology.

It wouldn't take many of those centrists tiptoeing over to the Democrats' side to give them the majority. Only Michaelson could see a schism coming on the left, too. If the Democrats became namby-pamby middle of the roaders, the die-hard progressives would leave them. The result would be …

Enough to make a man's head spin, Michaelson thought.

The great irony was, he might still be a member of the House if Patti Grant and Galia Mindel hadn't beat him in his first run for office. Wouldn't be a bad idea for him to send them a thank you note. Only Hallmark didn't make cards with the choice of words he'd use to express himself to the president and her chief of staff.

If they had, he still wouldn't have sent one.

That bastard McGill might tear him a new one again if he did.

Before Michaelson could dwell on that unpleasant thought, Representative Philip Brock sat down next to him. He slapped Michaelson's leg and asked, "So what'd you think?"

"Of what?" Michaelson asked. "Oh, I'm sorry. Were you speaking for the record just now? Must have nodded off for a minute."

Brock laughed and said, "Yeah, fuck you, too. You still flew all the way across the country and here you are, sitting right where I asked to see you."

"The body is willing," Michaelson said, "but the attention wanders."

Two guys in a pissing contest, Brock thought. Neither of them trusting the other. Welcome to twenty-first century American politics. Even if one guy was no longer in office.

The congressman said, "I don't flatter myself that you came all this way just to see me. So who bit on the chum I tossed off the back of the boat? Media or think tank? Outside propaganda or inside propaganda?"

"WorldWide News," Michaelson said.

"You're going to see them when you leave me?"

"Saw them first. Got a one-year deal to do commentary; buyout for the second year if they decide not to use me."

"Well, good for you," Brock said. "Having a job again will get you out of the house, raise your public profile, let you make a little money."

Michaelson nodded. "Yeah, all because you were such a swell

guy and brought my name up for a role Galia Mindel would never let me play in a million years. Honest broker between the right and the left, my ass. You've got something else in mind, but I'll have to find out what that is on my own because you're not going to tell me."

"If I intend to use you, why did you come here today?" Brock asked.

"Because you know an old jock like me wants to stay in the game, one way or another, and you knew I couldn't resist the challenge."

"That must make me pretty smart," Brock said.

"We'll see about that. I know you wouldn't want anything too obvious, like my becoming your public shill. You've got something sneakier in mind."

Brock did a respectably devilish laugh and got to his feet.

"Maybe I just wanted to challenge you to a one-on-one game of basketball," he said.

The congressman's midsection was on a line with the seated former senator's shoulders. The target of opportunity was too close for Michaelson to miss. He snapped the back of his right hand into Brock's groin. The move was so quick Brock never saw it, but he felt it intensely.

Getting to his feet, Michaelson kept Brock from doubling over by putting a hand firmly on the congressman's shoulder. Leaning forward, he whispered into Brock's ear, "You're not James J. McGill, asshole. You'd better remember that."

Brock crouched over, after Michaelson left, his hands on his knees.

Yes, the backfist blow to Brock's balls had been too fast for its victim to see.

But the tie-clip camera on the guy sitting across the gallery caught it perfectly.

Brock hadn't planned an assault on his manhood, but the blow worked nicely into his plans.

***

McGill's Chevy — Washington, DC

"We told Elspeth that Merilee Parker had seen the SOBs who are planning the president's assassination go into a room with Representative Philip Brock," Captain Welborn Yates told McGill, "but when Elspeth questioned Arlo Carsten, he said that Brock left the room before the others started talking about committing their crime."

McGill and Welborn sat in the back seat of McGill's Chevy.

Leo and Deke were up front. Each of them wore earbuds connecting them to their favorite tunes. So they could plausibly deny overhearing anything that passed between McGill and Welborn. If the time ever came when presidential pardons were required, McGill wanted to keep the number as small as possible.

They were taking Welborn home because he hadn't seen his infant daughters since Tuesday. Well able to empathize, McGill didn't want to prolong the separation any longer than necessary. Sweetie had gone off to track down Putnam Shady and have him wangle a pre-debut viewing of the art collection at Inspiration Hall.

"Did Elspeth think Carsten was telling her the truth?" McGill asked.

"She told Celsus and me she was sure of it. Neither of us doubted her for a minute."

"The interview took place at the FBI offices in Richmond?"

"Right."

"As far as you know, did anybody from the bureau see or record how Elspeth got Carsten to talk?"

Welborn said, "Unless they're a lot sneakier than they look, and I don't think they are, nobody saw how Elspeth did it. Former SAC Crogher got everybody together in the FBI video room, where the camera feed of the interview would go, and made sure no record was created. I had some reservations about working with Celsus at first, but he's turned out to be something else."

"How'd he get the FBI to go along when he no longer has any official standing?" McGill asked.

"Oh, he came right out and told them that, but he said he was still quite close to the president, and she'd know if they didn't play ball."

McGill gave Welborn a look. "He really did that?"

Welborn asked, "He shouldn't have?"

"*I* don't even do that. Threaten people with *my* connection."

"Oh … Yeah, you're right. I can see where that might not look good. You know, I think Celsus is still trying to sort himself out, between who he was and who he's becoming."

"Celsus Crogher is becoming someone new?"

McGill had trouble processing that line of thought.

"You should have seen him on the dance floor," Welborn said.

McGill nodded slowly. "Yeah, that's right. I'm supposed to ask if he can bring a date to the inaugural ball."

He thought that was actually a good idea. Having Celsus bring a date would make his dance with Patti look like less of a novelty act. He was sure Patti wouldn't object.

"Tell Celsus he can bring a date," McGill said.

He saw a look of doubt appear on Welborn's face.

"What?"

"You can speak for the president on this?"

"I can. Old married couples do it all the time. What, you and Kira haven't gotten to that point yet?"

Thinking about that, Welborn realized Kira didn't hesitate to speak for him. He, on the other hand … would start speaking for her, too. Starting immediately.

"Of course, we have."

"Then there you go. I'd never speak for the president on a matter of governance, but clearing Celsus to bring a date, no sweat."

Having things put into perspective, Welborn felt more at ease.

He got back to business. "Elspeth said Arlo told her there was one unlikely character in the meeting of the conspirators, a retired Catholic priest from Boston, Father George Mulchrone. Elspeth said she made Arlo confirm his presence a couple of times. He insisted Mulchrone was there, and he had been Representative

Brock's traveling companion."

McGill chuckled.

"What's funny, if I may ask," Welborn said.

"Well, it's like this," McGill told him. "We've got Mulchrone as a co-conspirator in a plan to assassinate the president. Let's say Brock brought him into the cabal by confessing the idea to him. The seal of the confessional would never allow Mulchrone to reveal that, but the only thing that might help Mulchrone get any consideration from the U.S. attorney would be if he ratted out Brock. I can't imagine a being between a bigger rock and a harder place."

Welborn thought about that. "The confessional seal applies to retired priests?"

"Oh, yeah. You never know, though, in Mulchrone's place, the Reformation might take on a whole new appeal. To heck with those old Catholic vows. Might be a good idea for the FBI to bring him in sooner rather than later."

Welborn thought so, too.

"You, Celsus and Elspeth did leave things on good terms with the FBI, didn't you?"

"Elspeth let them keep Arlo, gave them a full brief and didn't leave until Arlo signed a full confession for them. They're happy."

"Good," McGill said.

One fewer headache for Patti.

Leo pulled into Welborn's driveway.

The new father was out of the car before it stopped moving. His wife and daughters were waiting for him in the front doorway. Welborn filled his arms with twins and kissed his wife in front of the whole wide world.

Life as it should be, McGill thought.

Florida Avenue — Washington, DC

Sweetie entered the kitchen of the townhouse she and Putnam owned as he was speaking to someone on the phone.

"Yes, of course," he said. "Whatever's necessary. We'll make it work."

The call must've interrupted Putnam's lunch preparations, Sweetie thought. The salad was already made. Two baguettes, still warm, sat on the breadboard. The aroma of baking chicken came from the oven. Having gone out on his own, working as the head of ShareAmerica, the lobbying firm anyone could buy into for one hundred dollars a year, Putnam often came home for his midday meal.

He told Sweetie it was her doing. Having his largest meal at lunch meant he could eat lightly later in the day. Along with the regular exercise she'd inspired him to do, he'd not only shed the extra thirty pound he'd carried when they first met, he was actually starting to achieve muscular definition in various parts of his body.

He told her it was a slow-motion miracle.

At the moment, though, Sweetie thought Putnam was beset by a problem that neither a sensible diet nor a hundred daily pushups would solve.

Sweetie took the chicken out of the oven, sliced the bread, apportioned the salad into two bowls. She put out a place setting for each of them. She hardly ever drank alcohol during the day and imbibed abstemiously at night, but she took a bottle of Chardonnay out of the wine cooler and poured a glass for each of them. Leaving the bottle handy in case Putnam needed more.

Sweetie never had more than one drink a day.

"Yes, I'll speak with Margaret. Then I'll be right up."

Putnam said goodbye and put the phone down.

From the look on his face, there was only one question Sweetie could ask.

"Your family?"

Putnam nodded. He sat next to Sweetie and picked up his glass.

"Your mother or father?" she asked.

"My baby brother, Lawton. He died."

Sweetie felt her eyes moisten. She put an arm around Putnam, kissed him.

"I'm so sorry. How did you hear?"

"That was Sissy Jenkins calling. She and Emory got the news."

The Jenkins were the African-American couple who raised Putnam after his parents had fled the country one step ahead of the law. Putnam's parents, Charles and Mona, had perpetrated a nationwide scam that suckered horse racing bettors out of millions, selling them a "can't fail" way to pick winners. They'd taken Lawton, then a year old, with them.

"I thought you told me the Jenkins didn't know where your parents were," Sweetie said.

"They didn't, not while I lived with them. When it was time for Lawton to go to college, I just heard, he came back to this country under a new name. He brought a bank book with him in the Jenkins' names. Compensation for taking such good care of me."

"So your parents are still alive?"

Putnam shrugged. "They were at the time they sent Lawton to Johns Hopkins. Now? Who knows?"

"Lawton stayed in touch with Jenkins?" Sweetie asked.

"He did more than that. He married Sissy and Emory's daughter, LuAnne."

The name rang a bell for Sweetie. "She's that chef you like up in Baltimore. The one with the seafood place you invested in. What's the name of the place?"

"Great Catch. I always used to think of Lu as my kid sister."

Sweetie's eyes filled anew. "Used to? She —"

"Was in the same car with Lawton when the tire blew and the car went off the road and hit the tree."

A tremor ran through Putnam. Sweetie threw her arms around him, held him close, doing her best to absorb as much of his pain as she could. Her embrace couldn't keep a joyless laugh from escaping him.

"All these people I thought I knew. They sure could keep secrets, couldn't they? Sissy told me she and Emory never said anything about Lawton because they thought the FBI was still watching me, and for all I know they are."

The feds had watched Putnam through his college years, that he knew for sure.

He sighed and gently pushed Sweetie back to arm's length.

"There's one more thing, a pretty big thing. Lawton and Lu-Anne have a little girl. She's eight years old and her name is Maxine. Sissy said she and Emory just aren't up to raising a child that young anymore. She asked if I might help out. So, Margaret, my dear, how would you feel about becoming a mother?"

Sweetie was struck dumb.

Putnam said, "If you're not crazy about the idea, we could keep the kid in your old place down in the basement. Feed her our left-overs. Maybe take her out and walk her in the park a few times a week."

"Stop it," Sweetie said. "Of course, we'll welcome her into our home."

Putnam kissed Sweetie and said, "Thank you."

He got up and added, "I'm not too hungry right now. I'm going to wrap up my lunch and drive up to Baltimore."

"*We* will go to Baltimore." She kissed Putnam back to let him know they were in it together.

"How did I ever get lucky enough to meet you?" he asked.

Sweetie laughed. "You put an apartment-for-rent ad in the newspaper."

They put the food and wine away and were ready to leave in fifteen minutes.

Just before they stepped out the door, Sweetie thought she should let McGill know she'd be out of town. She hated the idea of leaving Jim shorthanded, but he'd understand the urgency of helping a child in dire need. He'd been there.

One thing she could do for Jim, ask Putnam about that favor McGill needed.

She did and Putnam said, "Sure. You drive and I'll make the call."

***

FBI Offices — Richmond, Virginia

"Daddy, the bastards got me," Elvie Fisk said into the phone she held. "Yeah, me 'n' Arlo both."

Deputy Director Byron DeWitt was the ranking FBI official in the room. With him were SAC Cecelia Kalman, head of the Richmond office, and Special Agent Bob Sanborn, whose job it was to monitor domestic hate and terrorism groups in the Southeastern United States.

DeWitt had taken the lead in speaking with Elvie.

He'd told her, "The advice you got earlier is something to keep in mind, Elvie. The more you help us, the better things will go for you."

DeWitt had dressed down for the interview. A leather bomber jacket hung over the back of his chair. He wore a derby blue long-sleeved polo shirt, Levis and scuffed cross-trainers. He had deliberately mussed his hair, wishing he'd kept it at its usual over-the-ear length instead of his new shorter cut. Even so, the kid was sharp enough to see the difference in appearance between him and the other suits who had been holding her prisoner.

"Y'all aren't gonna let me go, no matter what," she said.

"Of course not. You're going to prison, no doubt about it. The only questions are for how long and in what kind of facility you'll do your time. Some are less awful than others."

"I don't wanna be some bull-dyke's little bitch," Elvie said.

"See, you understand just what I'm talking about."

Elvie looked down at the table in front of her.

DeWitt waited her out.

She said, "Some of the guys I know have been to prison. They talk about what it's like. Some said it's just as bad in women's lockup. Maybe worse 'cause they might stick a mop handle or something inside you that's a lot longer than any guy's johnson."

"Terrible things have been known to happen," DeWitt agreed.

Elvie looked up at him. "Ain't you supposed to stop that?"

"Sure, that's what the corrections officers are supposed to do.

But then *everybody* is supposed to obey the law. That's not what you and Arlo were doing."

"We were fighting for our freedom," Elvie said, bristling.

"Freedom from what?"

"That bitch in the White House."

"The president was elected, twice. That's our system."

"She stole that last one."

"How'd she do that?"

"She got that Indiana woman to turn her way. Bought her off or somethin'."

"Who told you that?"

"My dad —"

Elvie bit her tongue. DeWitt was sure she was going for daddy before she caught herself.

"There's no proof of that," DeWitt said, "whatever your father might think. Aside from that, the president won millions more votes from the people than either of the other two candidates. Doesn't that make her the winner?"

"Nobody who thinks the way she does should ever win."

"Did your father tell you that, too?"

Elvie chose not to answer.

"What does your mother think?" DeWitt asked. "Does she feel the same way as your father?"

Elvie looked down again and said, "Mama and Daddy split up."

"Do you have any brothers or sisters?"

She shook her head.

"So it's just your dad and you. You're a good kid and you listen to him. You think like him and do what he tells you. You had to be thrilled when he sent you to get Arlo."

Elvie looked up smiling. "Damn right, I was. We'd have gotten away clean, too, it wasn't for that damn pickup truck. I never seen any truck go that fast before."

DeWitt nodded. "Did you ever ask yourself why your father sent you to get Arlo? Did he know you'd been sleeping with Arlo?"

The girl lowered her eyes but not her head, and told him, "He was the one who suggested it, and he sent me to get Arlo because he loves me, and he knows I'm the best damn —"

She caught herself a bit earlier this time.

And took the opportunity to fill the silence with her own question.

"Are you just some actor, mister? Someone these other assholes brought in to ask me questions. You look like you should be on TV. Tell you what, you get ten years knocked off my sentence, I'll do you any way you want."

DeWitt ignored the offer and said, "Did you ever think your father sent you to pick up Arlo because if you got caught you are not as important as anyone else?"

Elvie cleared her throat, as if she were loading up for another blast of spit.

She swallowed the saliva, not doubting at all a judge wouldn't like it all if she spat on *two* federal cops. The girl wasn't well educated, but she learned fast. She sat back in her chair and glared at DeWitt.

"My daddy loves me," she said.

"Okay. Let's see if he does. I'll give you a phone. You call him. Warn him that you and Arlo have been arrested. We won't interrupt you. I promise."

"Yeah, bullshit."

DeWitt offered a small smile.

"Can't blame you for not trusting us. How about this? I'll give you the phone, and then step back with my friends. That way you'll have at least enough time to warn your father before we can take the phone from you."

Elvie thought about that. Couldn't spot any trap. She nodded.

SAC Kalman handed DeWitt a phone. He placed it in front of Elvie.

Before he stepped back, though, he said, "Just so you understand what's really important to your father, tell him things will go a lot easier for you if he and his friends turn themselves in before they do anything stupid. You might even get out of a minimum security prison camp by the time you're twenty-one."

To Elvie, who was really seventeen, that sounded like a dream.

DeWitt stepped back. Elvie tapped the buttons to make the call. A dutiful daughter, the first words out of her mouth related the fact that she and Arlo were in custody.

When she saw no one rushing to grab the phone from her, she continued.

"Daddy, one a these bastards said they might lock me up for *sixty* years. Then this new one I'm talkin' to now says if you 'n' the boys don't do what you've got planned, give yourselfs up, they might let me go when I'm twenty-one."

The tone of Elvie's voice indicated her preferred choice.

She listened closely to her father's reply. None of the others in the room could hear it, but they didn't need to. The call was being recorded. Traced, too.

DeWitt and his colleagues had no trouble seeing Elvie's expression.

Her whole face sagged.

"You want me to soldier on? For sixty damn years?"

Harlan Fisk gave another reply to the daughter he'd already pimped out to his cause.

Tears welling up in her eyes, Elvie said, "Daddy, if they had you locked up, I'd do anything you asked me to."

Elvie's head jerked back as if she'd been slapped.

Her father had clicked off. She said, "Daddy?"

DeWitt stepped forward and took the phone from her hand. "Do you know your father's target, Elvie?"

The girl shook her head, her eyes unfocused.

"Tell me something, Elvie," De Witt said. "You're from Michigan, right?"

"I was born there."

"So why do you have a Southern accent?"

That one she could answer, and she no longer had any reluctance to do so.

"I was raised in the South. That asshole I was just talking to took me down there when I was little."

"To be near his friends, the guys with the guns who think they should be running the country?"

Elvie nodded. "There are three places where all the militias around the country go to train. One down South, one out West in the mountains and one up in Alaska somewhere."

DeWitt returned to his seat across from Elvie. She'd defected from the other side. She would tell him everything she knew if he worked her right. Did nothing to remind her of her father.

Once he had everything the girl knew, he'd have a talk with James J. McGill.

McGill Investigations, Inc. — Georgetown

Jim McGill sat behind his desk, alone in his office, his mind more than a little boggled. Sweetie had just called him, en route to Baltimore, and told him he, Yves Pruet and Odo Sacripant had been given permission to view the collections of paintings at Inspiration Hall tomorrow morning.

McGill had been about to crack wise and ask if he needed a secret password when Sweetie dropped her bombshell. Told him why she and Putnam were going to Baltimore. They were about to become parents.

The first thought that popped into McGill's head was that Sweetie was telling him she was pregnant. He knew that could happen later in life these days, but it had never occurred to him it would happen with Margaret Sweeney. It shouldn't have seemed so farfetched, but he just couldn't see it.

Then Sweetie explained the situation.

She told him about Putnam's family background, adding, "Putnam told me there were many times he wanted Mr. and Mrs. Jenkins to adopt him. They said they couldn't do that because his parents were probably still alive, and it wouldn't be right. But Maxine's parents are dead, and if she's agreeable to the idea, Putnam wants to adopt her. I feel the same way. We should all be a family."

McGill agreed, but counseled patience. "Maxine might not want to accept the idea her parents are gone. Could take her a while to see what you have in mind is the best thing."

"We know. We talked about that, too."

"God bless all of you," McGill said. "If there's anything I can do to help, let me know."

"We will. I'm probably going to be tied up for a while. Just wanted to give you a heads-up."

"Thanks. Good luck to all of you, Margaret."

McGill clicked off, amazed at how quickly life could change. It wasn't all that long ago Sweetie had been a single woman and content to remain so. Then she married the guy who'd rented a room to her. Now she was about to become a mother. McGill didn't see any little girl resisting Sweetie for long.

Putnam had come a long way since meeting her.

The two of them should make fine parents.

With thoughts of family in mind, McGill took his next phone call.

"Hey, Dad, what's going on?"

It was Caitie, calling from L.A., he presumed.

"I don't know. Why do you ask?"

"Well, a half-dozen new Secret Service agents just entered the soundstage where we're shooting today. They talked to the producer and the director and the guy who runs security for the studio. I went to say hi to them between takes, asked what was happening. They said they got a call from Washington, and they were just being careful. Do you know the real story?"

McGill tried to soft-pedal the situation. He and Patti had talked about increasing the kids' protection and, of course, they noticed the difference. Caitie was just the first to speak up.

He asked her, "The Secret Service didn't ask you to leave the shoot or try to shut down the production, did they?"

Separated by the breadth of a continent, he could still feel Caitie's sudden rise in tension.

"No, they didn't do anything like that. Why would they …

Dad, don't let them do that, please. Everything is going great. I'm doing really well. Andrew told me so."

Andrew was the film's director.

McGill's first impulse was to tell his youngest child there would be other opportunities. Then he thought to hell with that. Caitie shouldn't have to suffer because of any crazed assholes.

"Honey, with Patti's inauguration coming up, everyone worries a little more. That's all. As long as the Secret Service hasn't asked you to leave or the shoot to be held up, don't worry. But if something serious comes up and they want to move you fast, cooperate with them, okay?"

"Okay." Caitie's voice softened almost to a whisper. "I shouldn't be scared, should I? For me or anyone else here?"

McGill said, "No. The Secret Service is the best in the world at taking good care of people."

"I'd feel better if Deke was here."

"Maybe he will be. We'll see."

Then to take Caitie's mind off the chance of facing mortal threats, he told her Sweetie's news. Caitie squealed in excitement. So much so that she had to tell everyone on her end of the conversation that everything was all right.

"Dad, that's great. Sweetie's going to be a super mom."

"Yes, she will."

"Putnam will be a cool dad, too."

"No doubt. But keep a good thought for little Maxine. She's got some tough times ahead."

"I will. Hey, can I call her? Maxine, I mean. Introduce myself."

"After you talk with Sweetie, but give her and Putnam a day or two."

"Sure."

McGill told Caitie he loved her and she returned the sentiment.

Two more calls confirmed that Abbie and Kenny had their protective details supplemented, too. McGill decided to call Elspeth Kendry and get the specifics. Before he could, Patti called him. She didn't use her secretary, Edwina Byington, to place the call. She took the time to do it personally. That scared McGill.

"What's wrong?" he asked.

Patti told him, "The White House switchboard received a call threatening Abbie, Kenny and Caitie. The caller said if Elvie Fisk isn't released in twenty-four hours, our children will pay the price."

So, as it turned out, Harlan Fisk did love Elvie.

Ile de la Cité — Paris

Gabbi checked the security monitor to see who'd come calling at her apartment above the restaurant named Monsieur Henri. An elegantly dressed gray-haired man was at her door downstairs. She'd never seen him before. He didn't look threatening, but you never knew.

"*Oui?*" she asked.

"*Je suis Gaspar Lambert.*" *Monsieur Lambert* said he was from the Musée d'Orsay.

Gabbi buzzed him into the building and said, "Please take the elevator on your right to the second floor, *monsieur*." The third floor to Americans.

Gabbi's kid brother, Gianni, owned the building, had bankrolled the restaurant and made the two flats above it available to the big sister he adored. Gabbi lived on the first floor — the second floor to Americans — and did her painting in the space above that.

Gianni had a skylight installed on the top floor to provide Gabbi with an abundance of Paris' gorgeous golden light. In his mind, nothing was too good for her. Including the best security system anywhere, one he'd designed personally.

A computer science prodigy since middle school, Giancarlo Casale, after making his first billion, had decided he could get by on the licensing royalties from the patents he held, and decided to go into teaching. He would have been welcomed to any faculty in the world, but he decided to stay in his hometown of Chicago and work at the Illinois Institute of Technology.

In addition to his undergrad and graduate level classes, Gianni also devoted his Friday afternoons to sixth-through-twelfth graders from the metro Chicago area. He called the class for his younger students Introduction to Magic. Its purpose was to find and nurture the next generation of American genius. Gianni said the more unlikely the sources of that genius were the happier he would be. Minority, female, LGBT, economically disadvantaged and physically challenged applicants were encouraged to apply.

At her brother's request, Gabbi painted murals of all manner, genders and hues of young scientists doing things that bordered on the heroic and actual magic. The murals filled the lab in which the class was held. Gabbi refused to take a penny for her work.

She figured she owed Gianni more than he owed her.

Gabbi also believed doing a good deed was its own reward.

Sometimes, though, you got paid a dividend in the form of good karma.

Gabbi figured that was exactly what happened when *Monsieur Gaspar Lambert* presented himself at her studio. He was the archivist at the Musée d'Orsay, the Left Bank museum that housed the largest collection of impressionist and post-impressionist masterpieces in the world. If you wanted to marvel at and understand the works of Manet, Monet, Degas, Renoir, Cézanne, Van Gogh and many others, you went to the Musée d'Orsay.

Or, in Gabbi's case, *Monsieur Lambert* brought the museum to you.

Yves Pruet had spoken to his father, Augustin. The senior Pruet talked to a friend at the museum. The friend made a confidential request of the archivist, *Monsieur Lambert,* and now here he was. He'd told Gabbi it would be best if they met privately. She'd suggested her studio.

As Lambert stepped out of the elevator, he took his bearings, starting with Gabbi and moving on to each corner of her studio. He looked at the placement of the skylight in relation to where Gabbi kept her easel and nodded in approval. He stepped up to Gabbi, introduced himself and shook her hand.

He took two flash drives and a sealed envelope out of his coat pocket.

She accepted delivery and said, "Thank you, *monsieur.*"

"A favor to an old and dear friend, Madam. One whom I will never be able to repay."

"Of course."

Lambert looked around again and said, "You have a fine space, but I don't see any paintings anywhere."

"I've been working in the United States the past two months. I put everything in storage while I was away. It's just as well. Compared to the giants you see every day, my talent is very small indeed."

"That is not what I have heard. I had hoped to see some of your work."

"I have some of it tucked away here, if you'd like to wait a few minutes for me to take it out and find the right places to display it."

Lambert shook his head. "I would not put you to that inconvenience. If you ever hold an exhibition, though, please let me know." He gave her his business card.

"It would be my pleasure, *monsieur.*"

Lambert gave her a small bow and started toward the elevator.

He stopped, turned and asked, "If I do not ask too much, may I know the nature of the work you did in the United States?"

Gabbi said, "I painted the official portrait of James J. McGill."

"Le partisan de la présidente?" he asked. The president's henchman.

"Oui."

"Will you do *madame la présidente* also?"

"She told me possibly. But I've checked and no single artist has ever painted both portraits, the president's and the first lady's."

Lambert smiled. "Yes, but there has never been a woman president or her henchman before now. Oh, one more thing. I trust you will be able to find what you are seeking from the computer files. Please shred the envelope I gave you, unless you find the other information inadequate."

Gabbi gave him a questioning look.

The archivist said with a smile and a shrug, "If you open the envelope, Madam, I would feel obliged to repay a very large bribe."

McGill's Hideaway — The White House

McGill spoke to his daughter Abbie, home in Evanston, Illinois on winter break from Georgetown University, and his son Kenny, also under his ex-wife Carolyn's roof, along with their stepfather, Lars Enquist.

Abbie had told him. "Dad, it's almost like Patti's visiting the house or something. I've never seen any security like this that didn't involve POTUS."

President of the United States.

"It's not too much, is it?" McGill asked.

Abbie told him, "Patti called and said to let her know if they laid it on too thick. So far, it's okay."

McGill told his daughter, "Things will get better soon."

He was going to see to that personally, if he got the chance.

"Only four more years, right?" Abbie asked.

"Not even that for you, Kenny and Caitie. We'll get things dialed back to, well, what we've come to call normal."

"Don't do anything that puts you or Patti in a bad place."

Just like Abbie, McGill thought, always putting others first.

"Your advice is noted. Thank you."

That didn't keep McGill from thinking that this time a make-no-mistakes example might need to be made for all the bad guys to get the message. Not just for his children, but for Patti, too. You came at any of them, your affairs had better be in order.

Abbie said goodbye and passed the phone to Kenny.

"You doing okay, Champ?" McGill asked.

"Doctors can't find a thing wrong with me," Kenny said. He was in remission from the leukemia that had almost killed him. Every time McGill heard there was no sign of a relapse, he felt a weight lifted from his heart. Then Kenny added, "Some of the girls at school, on the other hand, think I'm somewhat less than perfect."

McGill said, "Girls at school? You've lost touch with Cassidy?"

Cassidy Kimbrough, daughter of Sheryl Kimbrough, the elector whose vote gave Patti a second term in office, had become fast friends with Kenny. The two of them had bonded over their respective life-altering traumas. Kenny's illness, Cassidy's burns.

"No, not at all," Kenny said. "In fact, I talked with her today. She was surprised when she and her mom got Secret Service protection."

McGill thought the fact that Sheryl and Cassidy needed protection was another reason to kick someone's ass.

Kenny told his father, "Cassidy asked me how I deal with it. I told her you show the special agents the respect they deserve, they'll let you see what cool people they are. Then it's pretty easy having them around."

"So you and Cassidy are good?"

"I think we'll always be friends. I'd like it to be more than that, but she'll be going off to Stanford soon, and there just might be one or two interesting guys out there. It'd be dumb to even pretend we both can wait until circumstance might bring us back together."

McGill continued to be awed by the way his children were maturing.

Kenny especially.

"Having a good friend is no small thing," McGill said.

"I know. Just like you and Sweetie."

"Exactly." Prompted by that, he told Kenny about Sweetie's news.

Kenny passed it along to Abbie and Carolyn and the call home ended on a high note.

McGill spent the next half-hour looking at the flames dancing in the room's fireplace. Patti had asked him if he'd mind losing the real thing, a wood-burning fire. She said a plan was afoot, one of her own doing, to reduce the carbon footprint of the White House. Part of the plan called for each of the twenty-eight fireplaces in the building to be switched over to clean-burning natural gas.

If McGill liked, Patti said, that process could be stretched out for a couple years.

McGill shook his head, but he asked that the fireplace in his hideaway be the last one to succumb to progress. His wish had been granted and at that moment the fire burned in a multitude of reds, oranges and yellows. Logs popped, cracked, fell and settled as the flames overcame them.

Lost in the hypnotic visuals and sounds, McGill thought about the problems, life and death matters, facing his wife, his children and himself. He didn't arrive at any immediate answers. But by the time Patti joined him, he'd thought of a couple questions to ask her.

She had Blessing, the head butler, roll in a cart with a tea service. Silver teapot. White House china and, bless her, a plate of Mint Milano cookies. While Patti poured the tea, McGill put another log on the fire.

He sat on the leather sofa next to his wife and asked, "Chamomile?"

"Yes."

"With just a drop of honey?"

"Yes. I believe I know most of your preferences by now."

"You do and you're kind enough to indulge them. Will the chrysin in the tea clash with caffeine in the cookies?"

Chrysin was an organic compound that relaxed muscles, relieved anxiety and led to deeper sleep. Caffeine was an alkaloid that acted as a stimulant. The stuff people used to put off sleep.

Patti said, "My hope is you'll have two cups of tea and one-and-a-half cookies. Tilting the balance in favor of a restful night."

"You'll have the other half-cookie, so we don't waste any food?"

"I will. The Secret Service is welcome to the rest of the cookies."

"Speaking of which, everyone we love is well guarded."

Patti nodded. "Elspeth is coordinating. She just gave me the word."

Reassured on that point, McGill picked up the one Mint Milano he could call his own. Patti broke another one so neatly he couldn't tell which piece was bigger. He would have taken the smaller part, but that was no longer an issue.

McGill asked one of the two questions he'd thought of earlier.

"If I'm not asking for classified information here, do you keep a personal schedule that even Galia knows nothing about?"

"I do," Patti said, "but I never put it in writing."

"So no one can happen upon it by either accident or design."

"Yes."

McGill finished his cookie and picked up his tea cup.

"Are you going to ask me why I do that?" Patti asked.

"I can make a pretty good guess."

"You know me that well, do you?" Patti finished her half-cookie, offered the remainder to her husband, watching him closely.

"Any time we're together, I pay strict attention."

"Are you saying you can't take your eyes off me?"

"My eyes and many other things."

Patti laughed. "You're incorrigible, and please don't ever change."

McGill made short work of his snippet of cookie. He said, "My guess is, whenever you can, you carve out a little time for yourself in your head. If at all possible, when the moment arrives, you seize it and push it into your real-world schedule."

Patti took a sip of tea and looked at McGill.

"If you were a spy, I'd have to have you shot."

"If I were a spy, I'd defect immediately. You wouldn't even have to ply me with Mint Milanos."

"I've heard that you were easy," she said.

"Only for you."

"So why did you need me to reveal my last remaining secret to you?"

"Putnam arranged for Yves Pruet, Odo Sacripant and me to get a special early look at Inspiration Hall tomorrow morning. I've read your official schedule and the one Galia keeps. There's nothing on either one about you visiting the new museum either before or after the official opening. I thought that was odd, as The Grant Foundation is a major donor to the place."

"And being a detective you solved the mystery," Patti said.

"So you are going to visit."

"Yes. I had an impromptu appearance in mind, to see the building and the art collections. My idea was to tell you and Elspeth tomorrow. Be there and gone like a will o' the wisp. Keep the mystery of the place intact until the official opening."

McGill took that in, did a walk around the information.

Patti knew her husband as well as he knew her.

"You think there might be an attempt made on our lives when we visit Inspiration Hall?"

McGill took Patti's hand and said, "If we're right and there will be an attempt to keep you from being inaugurated for a second term, we've got to ask what's the best target for the bad guys to hit before January twentieth. I was thinking they'll want to go after something that has special meaning for you. Like the museum Andy's foundation helped to build."

Patti nodded, her face grim.

"That would do it all right. So now, damnit, I don't see how we can go."

"Even if we don't, they could still hit Inspiration Hall for spite."

Patti put her tea cup down, closed her eyes and clenched her free hand.

"I don't want that to happen. I don't want Andy … his memory scarred that way."

Andrew Hudson Grant had died in the explosive blast of a rocket propelled grenade. Having a museum his legacy had helped to build also blown to bits would reopen the wound in the worst way possible. That thought ran through Patti's mind, until she blinked and looked at McGill.

"How would anyone other than you know I was planning to go to Inspiration Hall?" she asked. "I haven't even told Galia."

McGill knew that, having seen the schedule Galia had given him.

He'd been able to come up with only one answer, a dispiriting one.

He said, "You haven't told *anyone* in the White House what you were thinking?"

"Only you, just now."

"What about at The Grant Foundation? Did you tell anyone there?"

That was McGill's second question.

Hearing it left Patti looking stricken.

I-495 — Capital Beltway

Doctor Bahir Ben Kalil, personal physician to the Jordanian ambassador, cruised in the Virginia express lanes of the Beltway in his black Porsche 911. Next to him sat Representative Philip Brock. Ben Kalil didn't have an E-ZPass for his car; he had something better. Diplomatic plates. The Virginia State Police working the Washington suburbs knew better than to hassle diplomats. Their immunity was all but absolute.

In fact, when a foreign poobah obeyed the speed limit, as Ben Kalil was doing, the highway cops took it as a sign of respect and rarely even let themselves be seen in a diplomat's rear view mirror for longer than a heartbeat. Ben Kalil and Brock, on the other hand, were free to observe closely any vehicle they might find suspicious. At that moment, shortly before midnight, traffic was light and no other driver appeared to have anything in mind besides getting home.

The two men felt free to speak candidly.

His genitals still smarting from the blow Roger Michaelson had delivered to them earlier that day, Brock said, "I have to admit, I'm getting a bit edgy. I'd almost like to move things up. Get the job done sooner rather than later."

Ben Kalil flicked a glance at his passenger.

"So you'll call the president and ask her to move up her visit to the new museum?"

"Yeah, sure. She'll never suspect a thing."

Both men chuckled.

Ben Kalil asked, "This is just a moment of intuition you are feeling, my friend?"

What Brock was feeling, if someone could take a shot to his nuts in the gallery of the House of Representatives, there was no telling what else might go wrong.

But he said to Ben Kalil, "More like I've been thinking even John Wilkes Booth must have had a moment of stage fright before he shot Abe Lincoln."

"Yes, but if I remember my reading of your country's history, after Booth took his shot, he yelled, 'Sic semper tyrannus.' Thus always to tyrants."

Brock was impressed. Ben Kalil was not only a doctor and a jihadi, he'd also taken Sun Tzu's advice to heart. Know your enemy. Wouldn't do to underestimate the guy.

"Yeah, well, knocking off a president was a lot easier back then," Brock said.

Ben Kalil had to agree with that.

"If you are right, if you have perceived a threat to our plan at some subconscious level, we might well move to our first alternative. It would be less glorious, but a spectacular blow nonetheless."

"Yes, it would," Brock agreed.

Plan B was an attack on Inspiration Hall while Patricia Darden Grant was elsewhere.

Bringing enough of the building down that the rest would have to be demolished.

Using the Timothy McVeigh truck-bomb model.

Only this time the driver was prepared for in-the-moment martyrdom.

"Let's think about it a little more," Brock said. "Maybe we can go for all the marbles."

The two men began a second circuit of the Beltway.

***

Dumbarton Oaks — Washington, DC

Galia Mindel lay in bed, propped up against the headboard, rereading the latest report sent from one of her spies in the capital media pack. She'd learned only moments ago that Roger Michaelson was back in town. Had been given a job to do political commentary by WorldWide News. She hadn't seen that one coming.

Galia would have bet Michaelson was a spent force politically.

Hugh Collier had hewed to a more moderate point of view since taking over at WWN from the late Sir Edbert Bickford. So his hiring of Michaelson was also a surprise. The sudden change had to mean something hostile was afoot at the network.

Her spy thought Representative Philip Brock was involved in Michaelson's return. The man had been the one to raise Michaelson's name on Didi DiMarco's MSNBC show. Yes, but Brock was also the one who suggested that enough Republicans might be pried away from their alliance with True South to work with the Democrats in pushing centrist legislation through Congress.

Galia put her reading material on the nightstand and turned out the light.

She'd also seen the possibility of splitting the right-wing coalition in the House. So she had to credit Brock with some degree of political acumen and cunning. But she hadn't thought the time was quite right to move on the idea. Brock might well have quashed the possibility by going public with it early.

Of course, that might have been his goal.

She had a feeling the relative newcomer to Congress was playing a deep game.

Michaelson, she still felt, was little more than a pawn.

Drifting off, she felt it was too bad she couldn't directly hire James J. McGill to snoop on Representative Philip Brock … but she could at least point McGill in Brock's direction.

***

Saint Colm's Rectory — Saugus, Massachusetts

Father George Mulchrone left the front door to the rectory unlocked so he might hear the confession of the man who'd called him five minutes earlier. He couldn't offer the sinner reconciliation with the Lord at the parish church for the simple reason that the archdiocese had sold the church ten years ago and it had been replaced by a low-rise office building.

His excellency, the archbishop, had allowed Mulchrone to purchase the rectory as his retirement home. The price had been modest and Mulchrone had raised the sum by pooling his meager savings with donations from family, friends and former parishioners. As part of his deal, and as a means to avoid property taxes, the archdiocese recognized the premises as an "outpost of ministry."

That was, Father Mulchrone had approval to offer the comfort of four of the church's seven sacraments to those who might seek them. He was allowed to baptize new members of the faith, hear the confessions of those who had strayed, marry (heterosexual) couples with the case-by-case approval of the archdiocese and anoint the (deathly) ill.

As he had no church in which to celebrate a mass, he could not offer the Eucharist nor perform the Confirmation of young adults. It went without saying that he wouldn't ordain new priests, as that was the prerogative of higher clergy.

Mulchrone's budget allowed for a neighborhood widow to cook dinner for him, and for the woman's sister to tidy up the house every other Monday. Both of those good women were long since asleep in their own homes when the priest took the call asking him to hear a confession. The hour was late, but it never entered Mulchrone's mind to put the man off until the morning.

Letting someone face the perils of damnation for even a moment longer than necessary just wasn't in him. After telling the caller that his front door would be unlocked, the priest went into the large closet in the foyer. It had been divided into two equal parts with a seat for him and a kneeler for the penitent. A screen of sturdy black mesh allowed for communication while concealing the appearance of Mulchrone and anyone seeking absolution.

Mulchrone illuminated a small red light outside the makeshift confessional to indicate his presence within. He had to wait only a few minutes before he heard his front door open. The caller stepped into his half of the confessional. Mulchrone smelled body odor, tobacco and … fear, he thought.

"Are you all right, my son?" the priest asked.

"I've been better." The voice was deep and hoarse and there was anxiety in it. "You know who I am, Father?"

"I assume you're the man who just called me."

The truth was, Mulchrone recognized the man's voice. His odor as well. They hadn't been introduced or spoken to one another at the meeting in Virginia, but each had taken notice of the other.

"That's right. But do you know my name?"

"I know that you are a brother in Christ. That is enough for me."

There was no commandment saying: Thou shalt not equivocate.

"Well, I am that. I'm not Catholic, though. Do I still get that promise what I tell you goes no further?"

"Of course. Anything you say here remains with me alone."

Mulchrone thought to add he couldn't confer sacramental absolution, but he decided to keep that to himself. He'd answered the man truthfully. Or mostly so.

"That's reassuring, but what I want is for you to pass my message to our friend in Washington. You know the one?"

"I do."

"Tell him things are getting out of hand. Arlo Carsten has been arrested. We're going to try to bring things off the way we planned, but it'd be smart to have that fella with the truck up and running, too."

"I see," Mulchrone said.

"Yeah, it sucks, pardon my language, and that's not the half of it. Let me ask you something, Father. Does it bother you at all that the guy with the truck is from the other side?"

"It bothers me that things have come to this point at all."

"Ain't that the truth? Well, with any luck, we'll be able to hit our targets from above and at street level, too. And that'll set everything right. Assuming those suckers from the other side take all the blame, the way they're supposed to. Okay, Father, I gotta go. Give me two minutes to get out of your house and drive away."

"All right," Mulchrone said.

He heard the man step out of the confessional. The front door of the rectory opened and closed. An engine turned over and a car drove away.

The priest stayed where he was. He had prayed long and hard that moral order would be restored to the country he loved almost as much as his faith. But things only got worse. The decay accelerated. The faithful grew old and died. The young did not replace them. Churches and parochial schools closed. The call for sincere ministry went all but unanswered. He felt he was watching his world crumble before his eyes.

He didn't think anything would ever be set right again.

He didn't even feel he had the right to confess his own sins.

Without absolution, he was certain he would never see salvation.

Maybe the best he could hope for was to see a lot of old friends in hell.

Four Seasons Hotel — Washington, DC

Lying in bed, as he was at the moment, Yves Pruet was not given to wishful thinking. Foreboding far more frequently occupied his drowsing thoughts. He was sure that he would be dismissed from his position as an investigating magistrate soon after he returned home. The only reason he'd not been sacked sooner, he was sure, was some enemy in the new government had wanted him to get his hopes up. To think that all of his offenses against the dignity of those he'd failed to recognize as his superiors in government and society would be forgotten. Swept away by the passage of time and the press of new affairs.

Pruet thought no such thing.

He knew his enemies only hoped to inflict the greater pain of allowing him false hope.

Then they would crush him professionally and in any other way they could.

His government pension had been earned years before. Unlike so many people these days, though, he did not live for his retirement. He felt most alive when engaged in his work. Bringing some small measure of justice to a world inclined to turn a blind eye to crimes great and small. Stealing his pension from him would be petty theft for those who hated him.

He might have intended to put up a fight if he needed the money. His rapprochement with Papa, however, had relieved him of that burden. Not that he wanted to go into the business of making cheese any more than he had as a young man. Which was to say not at all. Nor would he be content to be given an allowance at his age. That would be an embarrassment.

Perhaps he might have to play his guitar on the Metro for the spare change of tourists, as his ex-wife, Nicolette, had once forecast. Should that become the case, he could imagine his former beloved gathering all their former friends, dressed in their finest attire, to watch him as he played, calling out requests and tossing one euro coins at him. Perhaps he could get a monkey to collect their offerings. That would entertain them all the more.

Then Pruet had hit upon an idea that amused him. Papa had finally come to understand that he was a first class investigator. He'd underwritten the trip to America for him and Odo. He'd even taken a personal satisfaction in helping his son with his inquiries. So, might Papa agree to fund his son in opening his own private investigations agency?

Such a thing would have been impossible for Papa to imagine a few years ago. It wouldn't have been a socially acceptable thing to do. But Papa had been quite impressed that he had been invited to dine, twice, with the most famous private detective in the United States, James J. McGill, once in Paris and once at the White House.

No one else Papa knew, even in his rarefied social circles, could claim that distinction. He had heard that Papa had told his posh friends that Yves was a personal friend of *Madame la Présidente.* To his own astonishment, Pruet had realized that was true. The lovely Patricia Darden Grant did enjoy his company, as he did hers.

So, with Odo and Gabriella Casale as his colleagues, it would only be sensible for Pruet to form a professional allegiance with the president's henchman. They would cooperate with each other, help one another whenever the occasion arose. Papa should have no trouble investing in that new business venture.

From outside his bedroom door, Pruet heard Odo cease his snoring. His Corsican friend had his own bedroom, of course. Tonight, though, he insisted on sleeping on the sofa in the living room of the suite. He'd said he wanted to be closer to Yves in case any intruder might think to visit them. It was just a feeling he had, Odo said.

Pruet chose not to doubt Odo, even at the cost of listening to him snore.

Now, that Odo had given Pruet a respite, the magistrate knew it was time to take his own rest. Having a new plan for his coming years, he relaxed and started to drift off. Then his mind formed another idea, even more compelling than the first.

It was a thought of poetic justice.

How he might punish Laurent Fortier.

By a means even more terrible than killing him.

The President's Bedroom

The most powerful woman in the world lay sleeping in McGill's arms. Looking at her, he was struck by the fact that every night Patti achieved the impossible. She looked even more beautiful asleep than awake. Her open eyes were gems not to be missed, but when her eyelids fell, he could see how she must have looked as a young girl, how she would look as an old woman. Both aspects bound McGill ever closer to her.

There was no way in the world he would let any act of violence steal her from him. Not now, not ever. Any such attempt would have to go through him first. Taking a sudden deep breath, Patti rolled out of his embrace, turning her back toward him. Letting him know, unconscious though she was, that he should get his sleep, too.

Most nights, McGill would have taken his cue.

That night, his mind wasn't ready to be stilled.

He lay on his back looking up at the ceiling, sorting his priorities, making his plans.

That was when he realized he would need an extra set of eyes when he visited Inspiration Hall with Yves Pruet in the morning. Not so many hours from now. For anyone else, finding the person he wanted might be a tall order. With the resources of the White House behind him, though, he was sure he'd find exactly the person he'd need.

Reassured, he closed his eyes and put an end to a very trying day.

CHAPTER 7

McGill Investigations, Inc.
Georgetown — Saturday, January 12, 2013

McGill sat behind his desk. He'd been awakened early that morning by a gentle tap on his shoulder from Patti. Still groggy from sleep, she told him, "There's a call for you." Her lack of wide-eyed alarm told him the kids were all right.

McGill took the receiver and said, "This better not be a telemarketer."

After a beat, a voice replied, "This is Deputy Director DeWitt."

"Up all night, are you?" McGill asked.

"As a matter of fact."

"You couldn't talk to me when I visited your office, but now you have something to say to me?"

"Only if you want to hear it."

That tease provoked a greater degree of consciousness in McGill.

He thought to ask, "By any chance, has Chairman Mao gone back up on your wall?"

Another pause ensued, followed by a question. "You don't read minds, do you, Mr. McGill?"

"Not as often as I used to, but I still have my moments."

"Yes, the Warhol serigraph is back on display."

McGill's mind brightened another notch. DeWitt contacting him now presented him with an opportunity. He asked, "Does the

Bureau's art crime team have a consultant on call who can spot forged paintings for you?"

"More than one," DeWitt said.

"How quickly can you have your best one get to my office?"

"Twenty minutes, if you can make it by then."

McGill looked at the bedside clock. It was five-fifteen a.m. Still dark as midnight.

In her first term, Patti used to rise at four-thirty. After re-election, though, she'd pushed that back to six-thirty, a move of which McGill approved wholeheartedly. Sleeping through your presidency, he thought, was possibly the best way to survive it. Just ask Ronald Reagan.

He told DeWitt, "Make it forty-five minutes. I'll see you and your art expert."

McGill had beat his own deadline by five minutes. Leo was parked at the curb downstairs reading Car and Driver and drinking coffee. Deke stood guard in the outer office, probably thinking of the new carpet and drapes he'd get for the office once he took over.

Sweetie was, with any luck, embarking on her first full day of motherhood.

Knuckles tapped at McGill's door. Deke opened it and said, "FBI."

McGill nodded and DeWitt entered his office. Closed the door behind him.

"Your art expert is outside?" McGill asked.

"He is, but he's not cleared to see or hear what I have to show you."

"Fair enough," McGill said. "Have a seat."

DeWitt took a guest chair. He laid his attaché case on his lap and took an iPad from it.

"You're familiar with this, how to use it?"

McGill said, "Each of my kids has one. They've taken me through the basics."

DeWitt handed the tablet to McGill. Before he delved into

Apple's latest marvel, he looked at the deputy director and asked, "Are you going to catch any grief for talking with me?"

"I don't think so. I'm not concerned if I do. My focus when we met the other day was too narrow. I'm sorry about that."

"Not a problem. For me anyway. You're sure you'll be okay talking to me?"

DeWitt took a moment to choose his words with care. "I have a fairly rare skill set. It occurred to me I might do better working as a contractor to the government rather than being a part of the chain of command."

McGill grinned. "That's what I thought, too, when the president was first elected. I'd be better off on my own than becoming a fed."

"I can see that," DeWitt said, "I haven't made a final decision yet, but I have one foot out the door and I'm leaning that way."

"In the meantime, you'll stay true to who you are."

"Yes, I will." He gestured to the iPad. "That video on the screen is my latest interview with Elvie Fisk. We finished just a little over an hour ago. She thinks her father had betrayed her. We didn't tell her about the threat he made against your children. We're holding her in isolation so there's no chance the news will leak to her. She said a couple interesting things in this latest go-round. I'll let you see what they are for yourself."

McGill tapped the screen and the interview video began to play.

He was stunned by how young the kid on the screen looked.

DeWitt saw his surprise and interpreted it correctly. "She's seventeen," he said. "We've verified that. Don't know if her petite frame is genetic or a matter of nutritional deficiency."

McGill nodded. He replayed the part he'd missed listening to DeWitt.

"The first thing you bastards better look out for is AR-13," Elvie said.

"Why's that?" DeWitt asked.

"You know how it is with us real Americans. We like our guns. We *love* that the law is on our side about keeping them."

"What's your point?"

"Well, that woman is gonna be outside when she gives her little speech, isn't she?"

DeWitt said, "You mean the president, when she takes her oath outdoors?"

"Right. Now, what that court says is Americans have the right to carry their weapons with them when they go about their business. Drop your gun in your pocket. Stick it in a holster under your coat, you're good to go. You also get to bring your guns into national parks now. And that grassy stretch of ground right next to where that woman is gonna speak? That's a national park."

Elvie showed DeWitt a cunning smile.

"How about that?" she said. "Bet you feds forgot that."

"We know that the National Mall is part of the park system."

"Yeah? Did you also know that ten thousand members of AR-13 plan to show up packing heat? If the local cops try to give them any shit about moving up close enough to make themselves heard, they better have those boys outnumbered. Outgunned too. They're gonna bring more than six-shooters, I'll tell you that."

McGill thought DeWitt had kept a fine poker face in light of that warning.

"What else might they bring?" the deputy director asked. "Something that Arlo Carsten might have had a hand in?"

Elvie shook her head, as if she were disappointed.

But not by DeWitt.

"You know, Arlo is so book smart it almost made my head hurt. He's sent people into outer space and brought them back again. He was real proud of that. Everybody he sent up came back down again in one piece. But if you closed the book he had his nose buried in, Arlo was more like a junior high kid than a grown man. I mean, I had him dancing to my tune, and there's not enough meat on my bones to interest any man who should be looking for a grown woman."

"Maybe he likes you for yourself," DeWitt said.

Elvie offered a mirthless laugh in response. "That's what I

thought for a while, too. Then I heard he actually got some hot old lady to talk with him in some bar. That was it for me. He's just another asshole like my old man."

"So how did Arlo plan to help AR-13 or whoever else might be involved?"

"That's just the thing. He wasn't working with the other guys. He palled around with them some. But he worked in this building all off on his own. Nobody but dear old Daddy and one or two other guys got to go in there with him."

"Did you ever hear your father speak of anything he and Arlo talked about?"

Elvie scrunched up her face.

"What's wrong?" DeWitt said.

"I did hear this one thing Daddy said, but it made no sense at all."

"What did he say?"

"He said something about Arlo working on hard pee. I know everybody's gotta pee hard now and then, but what the hell is hard pee?"

The video ended with a puzzled expression draped over Elvie's pointed features and the question left hanging.

McGill looked at DeWitt. "And the answer is?"

"The consensus of the technical people who've seen the video thus far is Elvie misunderstood her father's words. He said harpy, as in the mythological monster with the head of a woman and the body of a bird of prey."

It took a moment, but McGill made the leap.

"Bird of prey as in a drone?"

DeWitt bobbed his head. "Israel makes a drone called the Harpy. It can hover and attack pre-emptively. No human decision-maker needed."

"How the hell does that happen?" McGill asked.

"It's programmed to recognize and attack any radar signal that isn't included in its database as belonging to friendly forces."

McGill said, "There will be radar watching over the inaugural, right?"

"Yes."

"How close will any part of it be to the president?"

"You'll have to ask the Secret Service about that."

McGill pressed a hand to his eyes, as if struck by a blinding headache.

"Please tell me the Israelis keep this weapon to themselves."

"They've sold it to China, India and South Korea. Whether any of those countries have resold it elsewhere, we're not sure."

"Jesus Christ," McGill whispered, looking at the deputy director.

DeWitt told him, "I'm sorry to say, things get worse."

"How could they?"

The deputy director reached into his attaché case again. He brought out a small audio recorder. Put it on McGill's desk. DeWitt said, "This was delivered to FBI headquarters by a courier who is still being questioned." He hit play.

The two men listened to the voice of Senator Howard Hurlbert, who had fallen one vote short of becoming president. He spoke of assassinating the woman who had edged him out.

Ile de la Cité — Paris

Gabbi had worked so far into the night that she could do no more that stumble to the sofa she kept in her studio. She remembered falling in the direction of its cushions but had no recall of landing on them. Losing consciousness in mid-air, she thought, was not a habit to be cultivated. To emphasize that point, she awoke with a sore neck. She had a fuzzy head, too, though she hadn't had anything stronger than water to drink.

She seemed to recall that she'd made a good deal of progress last night. Was close on the heels of the notorious art thief Laurent Fortier. Catching that bastard would be a major coup for any investigator, much less one who had retired to daub oil paints onto stretched canvas.

She needed to clear her head before she could be sure she wasn't kidding herself about how successful she'd been. She grabbed the notes she'd made from the art table where she'd done her research. Took the flash drives and the sealed envelope, too. She went downstairs to her apartment, put everything into her safe. She'd never had a break-in. Likely never would with the security system Gianni had installed, but she was taking no chances.

She stepped into the shower stall and bracing herself turned on a torrent of cold water. She endured it for thirty seconds, until her head was clear and her teeth chattered. She moderated the water temperature, brought it up to warm and then bearably hot. The contrast to the previous chill made the heated water all the more pleasurable. Her mind was not only sharp now it functioned in top form.

The first conclusion she reached was she should stop crapping around and rip open the envelope Gaspar Lambert had given her. There was only one reason the archivist would have been bribed by anyone. To gain access to something that was restricted to legitimate scholars.

Wait a minute, Gabbi thought. Her basic assumption was that Fortier had an academic background, that he used it for personal gain instead of publishing his findings for public benefit. So why would he need to bribe *Monsieur Lambert* or anyone else? Well, she and Jim McGill had surmised that the name of Laurent Fortier comprised more than a one-man operation.

Okay, but for what possible reason would Lambert reveal to Gabbi that he'd accepted a bribe if he knew he was helping the most famous art thief in modern times?

There wasn't any reason that good. Doing a favor, even for someone very important to Lambert, didn't cut it. So, what was the answer?

Gabbi got out of the shower, dried herself and threw on an ensemble of old sweat clothes and pink sneakers. Her hair still damp, she retrieved her papers and the sealed envelope, sat down in her living room and reread her notes. One of the flash drives Lambert had given her listed the names of every legitimate scholar who had done research on masters of the Impressionist movement at the Musée d'Orsay over the past twenty-five years. That was the known span of Laurent Fortier's working career.

The number of researchers was legion and their distribution was global.

Matching the scholars with the artists and the works of art that were the focus of their research — the other flash drive held images of the relevant paintings — had taken all night and well into the wee hours. Just before she collapsed, Gabbi had winnowed the horde down to six names, all men with proper university affiliations and credentials. None of them, however, had published any learned articles, speeches, monographs or books on the subjects of their research. That raised the question she'd also voiced to Jim McGill.

Why do the grunt work if you didn't reap the professional glory?

The answer, of course, was because the greater reward lay elsewhere.

Stealing paintings that were worth millions of dollars. Or euros. Or any denomination you cared to name.

The idea hadn't occurred to Gabbi last night in the fog of her fatigue but now she thought maybe fate had intruded on the scholarly imperative to publish, perish or steal. The Grim Reaper might have come along and put an end to the best laid plans. Gabbi pulled up the Internet on her desktop computer and ran searches on the six names on her list.

Three of the men *had* died within a year of doing their research at the Musée d'Orsay. Given the pace at which scholarly writing proceeded, they were probably still busy composing their first outlines when mortality overtook them. One fellow died in an automobile accident. The other two had begun their research only after they'd been diagnosed with cancer. Either their prognoses had been overly optimistic or they'd chosen to die doing what they loved best.

A fourth scholar suffered from amyotrophic lateral sclerosis, aka Lou Gehrig's Disease. The illness had progressed to the point where simply getting through the day was a massive feat. Writing and publishing were no longer possible. Gabbi had to infer that even making the attempt to take on a new intellectual task must have been a heroic effort for the man.

That left only two names on Gabbi's list: René Simonet and Albrecht Hoffman.

Gabbi searched the Net for Hoffman first. She found photos of the man without any problem. He appeared to be somewhere in his fifties. Not the peak age for physical fitness, but Hoffman didn't look like he'd been an athlete at any point in his life. He was tall and emaciated, all long, bony limbs, hollow cheeks and sunken eyes. The only flesh on the man that Gabbi could see was the bulb at the end of his nose.

His unlikely appearance made it more than difficult for Gabbi to imagine him as a cat burglar whose exploits had grown to mythical proportions. Why he didn't publish the results of his research, she couldn't say. A political knifing by a superior at his university? A house fire that claimed years of preparatory work? A drinking problem?

Something. Maybe. But she didn't like him as her bad guy.

René Simonet didn't look like much either. About the same age as Hoffman, maybe even a year or two older. A cap of tight gray curls sat atop a nondescript face whose most striking feature was the gold wire-rim glasses he wore. A good foot shorter than Hoffman, he wouldn't cast a very long shadow. He was also thin, but not skeletal. More wiry. Maybe even strong.

Peering more closely at Simonet, Gabbi whispered, "Damn."

You wanted somebody who was nondescript, who'd fade from memory in the blink of an eye, who'd literally be able to lose himself in a crowd of people of normal height, he'd be your man. If he were as strong as she was coming to think he might be, he'd be able to clamber up a downspout quick as a simian, slip through narrow spaces, hide behind a sapling.

Unless her imagination was getting the better of her, Gabbi thought the guy would make a great thief. To cover her bases, though, she captured images of both Hoffman and Simonet. She put them into an email and sent it off to Père Louvel in Avignon.

She called the good father, too, in case he was the kind who didn't check his email ten times a day. He answered the call on the first ring.

"Father, it's me, Gabbi Casale. I just sent you an email with pictures of two men. I think one of them is the man you and Magistrate Pruet are looking for. Will you please forward the photos to your family's network of friends around France and ask if anyone remembers seeing either of them just prior to the time a family in the area might have lost a prized possession?"

That had been her bargain with Père Louvel. She wouldn't ask the name of the family or of the artist whose work was stolen. But if the locals had noticed a stranger in their midst, and they always did in small towns, she would get a fix on which one of these men had come to be known as Laurent Fortier.

Her money was on Simonet.

She hated to think think her whole theory was wrong and it was neither of them.

Père Louvel told her he'd just opened the email and would send it on to the dozens of families the Louvels had contacts with throughout the country. He would let her know immediately if he had any positive responses.

"Pray that I'm on the right path here, Father," Gabbi told him.

He responded, "That is always my prayer, *ma chère,* for everyone."

Gabbi said good-bye and her eyes fell on the sealed envelope.

If Simonet was her man, why would he have had to pay Lambert a bribe?

He was either a legitimate academic or someone who had been able to pass himself off as one. He'd gotten into Lambert's offices through the front door. Why should he have to enter through the back door?

Gabbi got hungry before she could come up with the answer. She'd slept too late to bother with breakfast. Monsieur Henri, the restaurant downstairs, served lunch. She called down to the kitchen and asked for *saumon fumé* — smoked salmon — and a green salad. A glass of wine as well. When your kid brother had bankrolled the chef, you got carryout when no one else could.

Even so, when the kitchen had just opened, you had to wait a few minutes.

Gabbi's stomach started to growl before then. She couldn't remember the last time she'd felt such strong pangs of hunger. That was when it hit her.

What if Simonet had been sick once upon a time? He wanted to do some research at the museum, but hadn't been up to it. Hell, three of the four names on her list who hadn't gotten around to publishing their work had fallen prey to illnesses that had either killed or disabled them. So why not Simonet, too? Not to the same extent maybe, but long enough to put him off his game for a while.

If he was determined to find some nugget of information, he might have sent someone, who didn't have his academic credentials, to the museum to learn something for him. That layman might have needed to grease his way past Lambert with a bribe.

For his part, the archivist wouldn't have thought he wasn't doing such a terrible thing. He was merely lending a helping hand to someone who was already approved to do research. But why then had Lambert described the bribe he'd been paid as very large.

That stumped Gabbi until she looked around her apartment.

Which wasn't really hers at all. Gianni owned the whole building. Her occupancy of the top two floors was a gift to her for being good to him when he was just a kid. For being cool, an artist in Paris. For helping him and his friends learn how to behave well with girls so they wouldn't end up being lonely geeks.

The scale of Gianni's largesse was what hit home for Gabbi. Being given a wonderful place to live and to work was truly a grand gesture from Gabbi's point of view, but for someone of Gianni's wealth it was just a trifle. So what was a very large bribe to Lambert might have been spare change to the person doling it out.

Just as it would be to her kid brother if she asked him to reimburse Lambert.

Lunch came and Gabbi, by custom, sampled everything and sent her compliments to the chef. Once she was alone again she opened the envelope. She recognized the name she saw.

Now, she was getting somewhere.

The Oval Office

McGill sat and watched Patti and Galia as they viewed Byron DeWitt's interview with Elvie Fisk on the iPad Patti held, and listened to the audio recording of Senator Howard Hurlbert speaking in plain language about assassinating the president. Neither woman reacted audibly to either presentation. Both of them, though, showed a range of emotions on their faces: anger, contempt and fear.

They were two hardened political pros, had been through eight political campaigns together, six runs for Patti's old house seat and twice now for the presidency. They'd gone undefeated. That didn't happen if you weren't as tough as armored plate.

Still, you heard a young girl speak of thousands of armed political zealots — traitors, as far as McGill was concerned — planning to show up bearing firearms at your inauguration and make their displeasure with you known to the world, you couldn't be blamed for worrying. On top of that, you heard the man you beat to become president talk about killing you. The rational response would be alarm.

Neither woman wept, lamented or rent her garments.

Patti hit the stop button on the audio recorder and looked at McGill sitting on the loveseat opposite her. Galia, sitting to the president's left, clearly had a multitude of thoughts racing through her mind, but she waited for the president and McGill to speak.

"Recommendations, Jim?" the president asked.

"Get the chairman of the joint chiefs of staff in here right away. Talk to the chief justice, right after that."

Galia felt the need to say, "The solicitor general should do that. He represents the government in matters before the Supreme Court."

McGill said, "All right, for the sake of form, do that. But the president should have a word in confidence with the chief justice. Let him know how grave the danger is here, that it's no time for half-measures."

The president said, "I agree. We'll make both the video and audio recordings available to the chief justice."

McGill wasn't finished. "Have the FBI assign agents to watch Howard Hurlbert. Don't let him slip out of the country. If the technical people can establish that Hurlbert's words were not cut and pasted together, that he really meant what we heard him say, he should be arrested."

Galia took a deep breath, and both the president and McGill looked at her.

She held up both hands to placate them.

"I'm not saying he wouldn't deserve that," Galia said, "but before we have Hurlbert arrested, we have to get airtight proof he was conspiring to assassinate the president. The standard we'll have to meet here is not just securing a guilty verdict in court, but demonstrating so clearly that Hurlbert is guilty that an overwhelming majority of the country will demand his head be taken off."

That was exactly the idea McGill had at the moment. He felt no need to wait for a trial, though, much less a verdict. For that matter, public opinion be damned. He neither shared nor intended to act on his feelings because he knew doing either thing would only make a bad situation worse for Patti and Galia.

The president had shared enough confidences with her husband to guess what he was thinking. To a great degree she shared his sentiments, but she couldn't act on them either. Not without destroying her presidency.

"Galia's right," she said. "My one-vote margin in the Electoral College gives Hurlbert a small measure of insulation. If I had him arrested without having indisputable evidence, I'd look like a tyrant disposing of a rival."

Galia said, "Worse than that. You'd leave yourself open to accusations that Hurlbert knew you'd won the election by deceit or other criminal means. You had to lock him away in an attempt to shut him up or at least destroy his credibility."

McGill asked, "Is that what you'd do, Galia?"

The chief of staff put a hand lightly on the president's shoulder and said, "If someone tried to lock up my candidate without solid gold evidence, you're damn right I would."

"Good to know," McGill said.

The president looked at her husband and her chief of staff. "I think it's safe to assume that Senator Hurlbert wasn't talking in his sleep when he spoke of killing me. He was in conversation with a co-conspirator. I think that's where we start. Recreate his public movements since the election, find out with whom he's been plotting."

"A good job for the FBI," McGill said.

"Agreed," the president told him.

Galia concurred.

McGill said, "The FBI will also need to see who's called on Hurlbert lately, at home or anywhere else he might have spent the night. In fact, I'd weigh any after-dark meetings more heavily than daylight get-togethers."

"Evil plans are hatched most often while good people sleep?" the president asked.

McGill said, "Sounds melodramatic, but that's been my experience. The big exception is a round of golf. Some guys come up with their craziest ideas on the links."

"I'll mention your suggestions to Director Haskins," the president said. "Do either of you have any idea, off the top of your heads, about who might have been conspiring with Hurlbert?"

"I want to say Roger Michaelson," McGill said, "only because the obvious answer is usually the right one. But that doesn't feel right to me. When Michaelson and I played our little game of basketball, we beat each other black and blue, but he never threatened to sic his lawyers, the cops or anyone else on me. But maybe I'm wrong."

Looking at Galia, he added, "Can you find out if Michaelson and Hurlbert were buddies in the Senate cloak room?"

The chief of staff nodded.

The president then asked for Galia's opinion.

"I agree with Mr. McGill. I'd be very surprised if it were Michaelson."

"You have someone else in mind?"

"Representative Philip Brock."

"Why him?"

"Brock raised Michaelson's name on Didi DiMarco's show. A source told me that Brock might also have played a role in Michaelson being hired by WWN."

That was news to both the president and McGill.

"Michaelson is back in town?" he asked.

Galia nodded. She told the president, "On a normal day, I'd have told you by now, Madam President."

McGill thought about the new development.

He said, "If Michaelson had stayed home in Oregon, he'd have a much lower profile. It would be much harder to pin anything on him. Having him here in Washington while this mess is playing out —"

"Is more than just a bit convenient," the president said.

"A straw man set up only to be knocked down," McGill agreed.

Galia said, "Meanwhile, there's Brock. He makes a speech in Virginia saying you didn't steal the election, it only looked like you did. The he goes on Didi DiMarco's show and says that was only a joke. He made a point of saying he doesn't have any ambition to reach for a leadership position in the House caucus, but then he suggests a way for the Democrats to form a majority coalition."

"You're saying the guy's slippery as an eel?" McGill asked.

"I'm saying if he was the one talking treason with Howard Hurlbert, he'd have made sure to edit out his half of the conversation. The part that might reveal his asking leading questions."

"What would be the point of all these machinations, Galia?" the president asked.

Galia told her, “Brock said on the DiMarco show that the True South members in the House would never work with the Democrats, and he’s right about that. But what better way would there be to get moderate Republicans to work with the Democrats than to discredit True South by making their founding father look like Lee Harvey Oswald. If Hurlbert were arrested, Congress would be in turmoil. Many members of True South would rebrand themselves under another name, but the chances are good that enough House Republicans would affiliate with the Democrats to prove they weren’t party to Hurlbert’s treason.”

McGill agreed with Galia’s take on the situation and said, “That would make Brock look good, like he’d seen realignment coming before anyone else. He wouldn’t have to campaign for a leadership position, it would come to him.”

The president said, “Howard Hurlbert doesn’t have Bobby Beckley to protect him anymore. Especially from his own worst instincts. I can see a sharp operator manipulating him.”

The president lapsed into silence, keeping her thoughts to herself.

Allowing Galia to fill the void.

The chief of staff said, “There would be risks in having the FBI watch Brock, too. Congress would not be amused to learn of a president ordering the surreptitious monitoring of one of their own. Doing it to a senator and a representative, that would cause an uproar. True South and everyone else will howl, including your new Democratic colleagues, Madam President.”

“But if Brock is behind Hurlbert’s treasonous ideas,” McGill said, “he can’t go unwatched.”

The president found merit in both points of view. The FBI, she said, would run light surveillance on Brock with a large cast of different agents and only where he might be doing business, the Capitol or his House office building. They would pay special attention to any meeting he might have with Hurlbert.

“That’s giving him a lot of leeway,” McGill said.

“It’s also where Galia comes in.” The president turned to her chief of staff. "Your unofficial snoops will have to keep their eyes open for Brock in any public venue, the way Merilee Parker did in Virginia."

McGill said, "That helps but it's still not dedicated surveillance."

"I know, Jim, but it's what we can do for the moment. If we come into possession of something else akin to the audio recording of Hurlbert making his threats, we'll step it up."

McGill nodded, accepting the political limits of the situation.

He said, "If Brock is as smart as we think he might be, he could be watching for a reaction from us. He might be laying low already, just going about routine business. If he spots someone watching him, he won't do anything incriminating. We want him to think he hasn't even shown up on our radar."

Galia said, "Yes, but if he's really so smart, would he buy that?"

McGill said, "The one weakness smart bad guys have? They're all too ready to underestimate the opposition. It makes them feel good to think the other guy is a dummy."

Galia conceded the point. "You're right. That's true in politics, too."

The president asked her husband, "When I speak with the chairman of the joint chiefs, how many battalions should I ask him to muster for the inauguration?"

McGill said, "That's best left to him, but frontline troops should be in the lead and they should be on the mall as soon as possible. Minutes after the chief justice issues an order forbidding anyone from bringing a firearm to the event. People who want a good spot at a public gathering stake out their places early. It's much easier to control a crowd before it coheres than when it's entrenched."

"I agree," Galia said, "we'll have to move quickly. With your permission, Madam President, I'll go contact the solicitor general right now. We'll need the chief justice to issue the no-firearms-on-the-Mall injunction before the military takes up its positions."

With a nod, the president gave her permission, and Galia left the president and McGill alone in the Oval Office. She looked at her husband, a personal question clearly on her mind, but she deferred it for the moment. Moved on to another point.

The president told McGill, "Using the military domestically is a very sensitive issue. After 9/11, my predecessor's attorney general wrote an opinion that it was the use of the military for *law enforcement purposes* that was prohibited not the performance of military functions such as fighting off terrorist attacks. Is that what you see happening here? A pitched battle at the scene of my public inauguration?"

"Well," McGill said, "what was it Elvie Fisk told the FBI? Ten thousand armed members of paramilitary extremist groups intend to take up a position close to the spot where you'll take your oath of office. The local cops better not try to give them any shit unless they have them outnumbered and outgunned."

The president said, "That was one young girl talking, possibly repeating braggadocio."

"Can we take the chance she doesn't have it exactly right?" McGill asked.

"No," the president said, "we can't."

The two of them spent a silent moment looking at each other.

The president came back to her personal question.

"You seem quite content to have me delegate tasks to all the proper authorities, Jim, but I know you. You're not an armchair general. What do you intend to do about all this?"

McGill said, "I still have to help Yves Pruet. As to the bigger picture … I'll find a way to keep busy."

They both knew he would tell her specifically what his intentions were, but only if she really wanted to know. Understanding that there were things a president — and a wife — were better off learning only after the fact. Patti nodded.

She said to McGill, "You know the line of movie dialogue I've always hated most?"

"Be careful?"

"That's it."

"Some things go without saying," McGill said.

Inspiration Hall — Washington, DC

Ethan Winger, the FBI's art consultant, was twenty-two years old, a prodigy and a dropout.

He'd applied to Yale, been admitted and spent one semester there. All to please his mother, Bonnie. She'd not only raised him successfully but also tended to the manifold needs of Ethan's father, Lawford. The elder Winger had taught painting in the fine arts program at the University of Iowa, his alma mater, in Iowa City, his hometown.

Lawford's talent, though, quickly outgrew his modest Midwestern roots.

That was despite the U of I having a highly regarded fine arts department. It wasn't, however, considered to be the equal of Yale's program. New Haven boasted not only the number one fine arts department in the country but also the top painting faculty. After exhibiting work in New York, London and Paris, to glowing reviews, Lawford Winger was invited to join the gang at Yale.

He asked for a week to consider the offer.

He shared his reservations with Bonnie. "I don't know if I'd be comfortable on the East Coast. We're doing fine here. Iowa City would be a good place for Ethan to grow up."

Their child was then two years old and thriving.

Bonnie, a sixth generation Iowan herself, said, "Okay."

Listening to the tone carrying the word, Lawford interpreted his wife's response as, "Damn!"

Bonnie had been Lawford's first: nude model and lover.

There was precious little he wouldn't do for her.

So he said, "Why don't we drive out there just to see what we'll be missing. Make a little vacation of it."

"Make me one deal," Bonnie told him. "If you see one person on that faculty who is even a notch better painter than you, you'll take the job."

"With the understanding that once I surpass that uppity bastard we can come back home," Lawford said.

They agreed to each other's terms and set out for New Haven the following week in their five-year-old Volvo, a car they'd bought with its reputation for safety in mind. In the fashion of artists and their models, though, they overlooked many of life's mundane details. Such as checking to see whether the tires on their safe car should have been replaced.

They were rolling east on U.S. 90 when a thunderstorm struck and the rain came down in torrents. The turnoff to highway 91 south, which would take them straight into New Haven, was no more than a mile or two ahead. Given the weather, though, they decided their best course was to spend the night right there in Chicopee, Massachusetts.

Grateful that Ethan was managing to sleep through the storm in the backseat, Lawford strained to see the next exit sign through the blurred smear of his windshield. Bonnie, who'd been trying not to let her teeth chatter in fright, told her husband, "I think there's something up there on the right. It's not moving."

Lawford had been trying to look farther ahead. He brought his sight line down. Saw what Bonnie had pointed out. A vehicle sat on the shoulder just ahead. It looked to Lawford like he should be able to pass by cleanly from where he was in the right lane. Not wanting to take any chances, however, he thought the better idea would be to move to the left lane.

He checked the driver's side mirror to see if he could make the move safely.

That was when Bonnie screamed.

Lawford looked back to the road ahead. The vehicle that had been on the shoulder, a rental truck, had pulled onto the road. Lawford swerved left, hoping to get around it. But the truck angled into the left lane. Lawford cut the wheel back to the right. His tread-bare tires hit a pool of standing water on the highway and the Volvo hydroplaned.

The car turned sideways and surfed along the highway for a hundred yards, before it came to a rise in the pavement and flipped. Over and over. Somehow it never collided with the truck that caused Lawford's desperate attempt at evasion. The rescue crew found the Volvo resting on its roof and thought they had three dead on their hands.

But everyone survived.

Bonnie and Ethan recovered from their injuries.

Lawford was quadriplegic, for six years. Through a recuperative process none of his doctors understood, he regained the use of his left arm. The one he used to paint. Ethan grew up watching his crippled father do magical work with his one functional limb. Early on, he came to imitate him, painting seated in a chair using his left hand.

The boy used his right hand for just about everything else.

In some form of cosmic compensation, Lawford Winger's son was the most accomplished student he had ever taught. As far as was possible, given their circumstances, the Wingers were a happy family. Living in Iowa City. Surrounded by extended family.

Then Ethan headed east to please his mother.

Wanting to earn money to send home, he became adept at finding jobs that used his skill set. When Uncle Ted, who worked for the FBI in Seattle, found out that Ethan not only had a matchless eye for doing his own work, but could also spot forged paintings with stunning accuracy, he put his nephew in touch with the Bureau's art crime team as a consultant.

Now, Ethan was riding with two Frenchmen to a museum he'd never heard of.

His assignment, being a rush job, paid a pretty penny, but at the moment another topic interested him more. He glanced at Pruet and Odo and said, "Let me know if I'm out of bounds here, but is it true France has more beautiful women than any other country? I've heard some talk that it does."

Ethan had yet to do his first nude, not without ten other painters in the room.

He was making decent money, even after what he sent home, and he was looking to spend a few months somewhere interesting, filling in the gap in his résumé. He'd thought about going to

California, Florida, the Caribbean … but before that morning France had never entered his mind.

Duh.

The two older guys gave each other a look. Then the tough-looking one who'd said his name was Odo told him, "For me, there is exactly the right number of beautiful women in *La Belle France*."

Pruet leaned forward and interpreted for the young man.

"*Monsieur Sacripant* is a happily married man, and he has every reason to be."

"Cool," Ethan told Odo. "Way to go."

The Corsican nodded, pleased by the compliment from his old friend and the implicit understanding of the young American. Once you found the right woman, who needed to count the others?

"What about you?" Ethan asked Pruet, being forward in the American fashion.

Of course, the young man had asked to be informed if he was out of bounds.

Pruet chose not to do that. He said, "I was married to a very beautiful woman, but it did not last. I am divorced, and I've chosen not to take a census of my alternatives."

Ethan turned red, realizing he'd put a foot wrong.

"Sorry."

Pruet was merciful. "I still have my eyesight, and I can tell you there are always many young women in the Latin Quarter who might make you act as foolishly as I once did."

Ethan beamed. France shot to the top of his list.

A minute later, they arrived at the museum and went inside.

Inspiration Hall's founding art collections, six hundred and twelve pieces, oil paintings, pastels, watercolors, sculptures large and small from around the world, were the bequests of three of the ten richest men in the United States: Tyler Busby, who held majority positions in oil, shipping and media companies; Darren Drucker, who was known as the greatest stock picker the world had ever seen and Nathaniel Ransom, author of the SoftKill debugging and computer security programs and owner of the company of the same name.

When Pruet, Odo and Ethan stepped through the front door, they presented their credentials — a note from Putnam Shady handed to Pruet by McGill — to a smiling man in a good suit who said he was the museum's publicity director. He asked them to please keep the details of anything they saw strictly to themselves until after Inspiration Hall's official opening. They said they would do just that.

They were offered the services of a guide, but they preferred a self-directed tour. In fact, they agreed to go their separate ways. The Frenchmen would start with the Busby collection. Ethan, a child of the digital age, wanted to see what Nat Ransom had brought to this party. They agreed to meet at the Drucker collection.

Pruet and Odo did not linger either to appreciate or study any of the paintings in the Busby collection. They conducted a survey that proceeded at a brisk walk. They were looking for a specific painting by Renoir. The original or the forgery they had seen in New York.

They found neither, and came to an abrupt halt, Pruet a bit breathless.

And far more disappointed.

He'd hoped to find his family's painting, demanding that it be taken down from the wall, filing charges against Tyler Busby with all the relevant authorities. He wanted the splash he made to be a media sensation that would carry the news to Paris overnight. *Le Monde* would announce his triumph to Papa with a banner headline.

Odo didn't need any of his police training to see how deflated Pruet was.

"Nothing is ever easy, *mon ami,*" he told the magistrate. "If it were, we would all grow lazy."

Pruet gave Odo a doleful look. "I could do with a year or two of indolence, thank you."

"You say that, but within a month you would begin to fidget. Another month and you would take up crossword puzzles. From there madness would be but a step away."

Odo had delivered his prognostication with a straight face.

Pruet told him, "If I remembered how, you might make me laugh."

"Very well then, if comedy is not the answer, let us return to police work. Having seen the forgery of your Renoir, and having made an attempt to buy it, we may have scared the villain who might otherwise have placed the painting in this museum as his little joke on the world. We *cannot* be sure who that villain is —" Odo raised a hand to forestall Pruet's objections. "We can't be sure who the villain is, but we *know* who the art dealer who displayed the forgery is. Let's go back to New York. I will have a private and very personal discussion with Madam Duvessa Kinsale. She will tell us everything she knows. I can assure you of that."

Pruet had reached the point where he would let Odo have his way.

"Very well, we will go back to New York. We'll collect our young American friend on our way out."

They found Ethan Winger examining a painting in the Drucker collection. He was jotting notes in a spiral bound pad. He was so intent on his work he didn't notice the Frenchmen's approach until Pruet cleared his throat.

Looking up at them, he wore a look of amazement.

"Do you *believe* this shit?" he asked.

Pruet and Odo shared a look of incomprehension.

"What shit would that be, *monsieur?*" the magistrate inquired.

"You mean, you didn't see any forgeries in the Busby collection? I found eight among the Ransom paintings, and two so far in the Drucker collection." He consulted his notes and saw he had the numbers right. "Yeah, eight and two, and I bet there are more in the Busby rooms."

Pruet leaned forward, his eyes now narrowed in keen interest. "You are sure you've seen forgeries?"

"Yeah, that's my job. Didn't anyone tell you?"

No one had. James J. McGill had been in a great hurry when

he left them at his offices, asking only that they take the young man with them to the museum. Not wanting to be rude, they had quickly agreed without asking Ethan Winger's role.

"No, no one told us," Pruet said.

Odo said, "You are very young. Are you … expert at you work?"

Ethan grinned. "I'm better than that. I'm a natural. Come on, let's take a look at the rest of this fun house."

He hurried off, Pruet and Odo quickly bringing up the rear.

They saw Ethan moving past the paintings of the Busby collection almost as quickly as they had. After the first half-dozen, he came to an abrupt halt and clapped an open hand against his face. His hand fell and he shook his head.

"What is wrong?" Pruet asked.

Before he responded, Ethan did a slow revolution, looking at the paintings all around him.

"They're fakes. They're *all* forgeries. Every last damn painting I see here."

"How can you tell?" Pruet demanded. "You all but *ran* past these paintings. You did not give them a *moment* of study."

A young man, Ethan didn't have much patience with people who doubted him.

He told Pruet, "You said you had a beautiful wife, right? If she were standing in a line-up of a dozen women who looked a lot like her and were dressed exactly the same way, how long would it take you to pick out your ex?"

Pruet shrugged. "I would know her immediately, but I *lived* with my former wife. I knew her intimately."

"And I know the work of all the painters whose work is supposed to be hanging in this place. My family, at great expense and effort, went to museums the way most people go to DisneyWorld. My father taught me how to look at paintings. To see how the artist went about his work, accomplished his goals. But he never had to tell me anything twice. I got it right away."

Ethan tapped his foot, looking for a way to explain himself

better.

He said, "Do you know anything about music?"

"I am a classical guitarist," Pruet said.

Ethan looked him up and down, nodded and smiled.

"That's cool. Then you should get what I'm about to tell you. Let's say you and another guy play the same piece of music. You each play it perfectly, note for note. But you play it with both passion and nuance because you're the composer. The other guy is playing the piece at a wedding reception. Could you hear the difference?"

"Of course. Immedi —" Pruet now saw what Ethan was saying. "You can really *see* art that way?"

Ethan bobbed his head. "I can see the love, the joy, the pain, the sorrow that went into every brushstroke. I can identify with it because I know what I feel when I paint. What I see here in all these forgeries is the work of one hand, a master craftsman. Who has *none* of the genius of the original artists."

Pruet and Odo shared another look. New York would have to wait.

McGill walked into the room, saw the tableau, three guys lost in thought.

"What'd I miss?" he asked.

The Andrew Hudson Grant Foundation — Chicago, Illinois

Presidential travel was often likened to moving a circus. Packing the elephants was never easy. The trip Patricia Darden Grant made from Washington to Chicago that morning was an exception. The president flew from the White House to Andrews Air Force base on Marine One, her personal helicopter. Instead of taking the 747-200B commonly referred to as Air Force One, she boarded a Gulfstream C37A, an executive jet with a lower profile than the iconic 747. By virtue of her presence aboard, the craft was given the call sign Air Force One.

The military's version of the plane had capabilities not available on the civilian version, worldwide military communications capability for one thing. A classified cruising speed for another. The usual two pilots were supplemented by a third as a safety precaution. A flight surgeon was also aboard. Lacking the defensive features of the presidential 747, two Air Force F-15s flew escort.

Not wanting to tie up air traffic at O'Hare and attract attention to her unpublicized visit, the president flew into Chicago Executive Airport, next door to the far busier airline hub. Disruption to commercial flights was minimal, nothing more than the usual need to circle O'Hare a time or two.

From CEA, the governor of Illinois, Edward Mulcahy, provided the president with helicopter transport to the Marcor Heliport just off West Chicago Avenue. From there it was a short straight shot east to Michigan Avenue and a brief jog south along the Magnificent Mile to the offices of The Andrew Hudson Grant Foundation. A column of six black Secret Service SUVs pulled up in front at spaces the CPD had kept clear for the president's party.

The cops also blocked off the sidewalk to allow the president, wearing a large brim hat and sunglasses to enter the building without delay. An elevator car, with three Secret Service special agents was waiting for the president and took her to the building's top floor.

The president and her security detail were greeted by more special agents and Joan Renshaw, The Grant Foundation's acting director. Joan was two years older than the president, just as Andy had been. In fact, Joan and Andy had shared the same birthday, August twentieth. The celebrations on that day often overlapped. Gifts were always exchanged.

Joan had known, and worked for, Andy for five years before he met Patti Darden.

Andy had described Joan to his wife as, "My Galia Mindel. She keeps the foundation running smoothly. Solves any problems that come up."

Each woman silently acknowledged the importance of the other to Andy and conducted herself accordingly. Their behavior with each other was unfailingly polite even when they were alone in a room. Underlying that air of propriety, though, was the feeling that it required an exhausting effort to maintain. One lapse of concentration might bring the whole facade tumbling down.

Despite the fact that Joan had failed to attend Andy's funeral service — explaining to Patti in a note that she had been too grief stricken — and declined an invitation to be a guest at Patti's wedding to Jim McGill — her mother was ill — Patti had kept her on at the foundation.

It would have been foolish to do otherwise.

She kept things running smoothly.

Solved any problem that came up.

The truth was, Joan's performance was as good as billed. Whenever Patti had a quarterly discussion with her to review the operations of the foundation, she found everything in perfect order. All funds were accounted for down to the penny. Every expenditure for operating expenses was meticulously noted and entirely legitimate. Each grant-in-aid from the foundation went to an organization, a cause or and individual that met with Patti's wholehearted approval.

In return for Joan's superb performance, she and every employee under her were the best paid people in the field of private philanthropy.

Even so, the lack of affection between the two of them remained constant.

They hadn't spoken of missing Andy to each other even once.

And now Joan trembled at the sight of seeing the president.

With all her Secret Service agents and all their guns.

Patti didn't greet Joan with an embrace or even a hello. She removed her sunglasses and said, "Why don't we go to your office, Joan? We need to talk."

Eiffel Tower — Paris

Gabbi Casale looked out at the Seine from the second level observation deck of the tower. Winter was the time to visit the

Paris landmark, if you wanted to avoid the tourist crush. The scarcity of visitors at that moment allowed Gabbi to hear the footsteps approaching her from behind. The sound stopped maybe ten feet from her position.

Without turning around, she said, "If you're trying to be ominous, you'll have to do better than that."

The footsteps began again, doing a shuffle step, moving into a cramp roll and finishing with a stomp. Gabbi looked to her right and saw Tommy Meeker, her replacement as the State Department's regional security officer in Paris, leaning against the rail the next to her.

"Tap dancing lessons are coming right along," she told him.

"Surprised these tired old legs can even shuffle after you make me climb six hundred steps to get up here."

"You couldn't spring for eight euros to take the elevator?"

"Eight point two euros, and I don't have a rich kid brother."

Gabbi said, "I would have reimbursed you."

"Now, you tell me. So how did the trip to Avignon go?" Tommy asked.

"Good. I learned some important things."

"You're working with James J. McGill again, aren't you? Helping him with a case?"

Gabbi flashed him a smile and said, "I'm a painter, you know that."

"Uh-huh. And what kind of help can I provide to my friend the painter now?"

"I'd like you to check the movements of a beautiful woman and locate the residence of a distinguished academic," Gabbi told him.

Tommy glanced at her and then turned his view to the city below them.

"Can't I do just the first part, and keep the woman if she's my type?"

"If you visit her in prison often enough, she might spare you some of her time when she gets out. Probably won't look quite so fetching by then, though."

Gabbi handed him a photo of Duvessa clipped from a magazine and mentioned a date. "I'd like to know if she used the Solférino Metro stop or the RER Musée d'Orsay stop that evening."

"I hope you're asking because you know she had a Navigo pass."

The prepaid monthly transit pass bore the user's photo, and allowed the use of the subway system by swiping a card past an electronic reader. Since 9/11, and facing its own threats from terrorists, France had become meticulous about collecting and storing records of those who moved about Paris and the country at large.

Being ever so polite to the country in which it had established its first foreign embassy, the United States had hacked French intelligence systems without ruffling any feathers or even letting their hosts know that they'd intruded at all.

Which was only fair as all of the allies of the U.S. tried to do the same to Washington.

"I'm assuming she did have a pass," Gabbi said.

"If she didn't, there won't be any security video from that long ago."

Gabbi nodded. "I know. Please see what you can find. The second half of the favor is by far the more important part. Find *Monsieur Simonet's* primary residence and you'll get a gold star in your personnel file. The French will send you a case of champagne, too. So you might want to make it look like you found him through a legitimate source."

Tommy looked at Gabbi, held his stare until she looked back at him.

"That sounds intriguing. And what might I get from you?"

"What do you want?"

"How about you string up a hammock for me when you go to Saint Bart?"

"I could do that."

"When do you leave?"

"As soon as I finish the favor I'm doing for someone, and don't ask who."

"I won't. Will you paint a portrait of me, too, while we're in the

Caribbean?"

"Sure, and if you want to buy it, I'll give you a discount."

Tommy laughed and said, "I'd better get cracking."

To help him on his way, Gabbi paid for his elevator ride back to terra firma.

En Route to Washington, DC

The president's Gulfstream C37A cruised smoothly at fifty thousand feet. Aided by a strong tailwind, the aircraft was doing better than six hundred miles per hours. The flight back to the capital would be a relatively short one. Over before Patti Grant could get the bitter taste out of her mouth, certainly.

The meeting with Joan Renshaw had ended just as badly as the president had feared it might. Good God, the things people did because of a tormented heart were enough to boggle the mind. Turn the course of history, too, if you weren't careful.

In both of her careers before entering politics, modeling and acting, Patti had laid down a strict code of conduct for herself: no married men, no man more than ten years older than her, no man who offered professional advancement in return for sex, no man who demanded sex in return for professional advancement, no man with drug, alcohol, ego or money problems.

Her rules severely narrowed her choices of companionship, but they also served her well. The few guys she'd dated — slept with — had left her with no regrets. Circumstances simply hadn't been right for commitment and marriage.

When she'd met Andy Grant, her baggage was small enough to fit into an overhead bin. From everything she saw, Andy was similarly unburdened. He had neither an ex-wife nor a spiteful girlfriend in his background. He was only two years older than her. He waited for Patti to make the first move sexually, not that he had to wait long. He enjoyed a beer at a ball game, a glass of wine or two with dinner, but that was all. He never did drugs because he enjoyed life just the way he found it.

He had tons of money but didn't let that keep him from being a regular guy. He said he grew up upper-middle class, studied hard, made a smart move or two and wound up rich. Big deal. You were born with a running start, he said, you ought to reach the finish line in pretty good shape. He'd dedicated using the bulk of his fortune to helping others. His generous spirit was what Patti had always loved most about him. He was good to everyone he met.

That had included Joan Renshaw.

Who mistook Andy's attentiveness, good humor and giving nature as an implicit pledge of love. One that had all but matured to romance, she thought, when Patti had turned up. Joan had told the president so in no uncertain terms that very day.

"Andy was *mine,* goddamnit, until you came along!"

Joan stood behind her office desk, tears streaming down red cheeks.

Patti watched from a guest chair, silent and still.

"We were together for five years," Joan continued, "working together every day. Making the world a better place. Making each other happy. The night he was supposed to come home from Los Angeles, he was going to take me out to dinner. He told me so. He was going to propose to me that night, I know it. Only he stayed on the West Coast another week."

Joan's eyes narrowed and her lip curled.

"When he did come back, you came with him."

True enough, Patti thought, and the night before they flew to Chicago was the first night they'd slept together. At Patti's initiative. Who knew? If Patti hadn't met Andy on his trip to L.A., maybe everything would have been different.

Everything. The president had to push that notion out of her mind.

She hadn't broken any of her rules. Andy Grant was a single man when she met him, and if his affection for Joan had been more than a matter of proximity and convenience he would have declined Patti's offer to spend the night with her.

At that moment, though, only one thing mattered.

She said, "Joan, did you tell anyone I intend to visit Inspiration Hall before it opened?"

Tears continued to trickle down Joan's face, but she stopped producing more. Her mood hardened. A cold gleam came into her eyes. She smiled without humor or warmth.

"I did," she said, a note of defiance in her voice.

"Why did you do that?"

"Because I was asked."

"What did you think would happen?"

"I don't know specifically. I just hoped it would be something bad."

"Did you think someone might kill me?"

Joan's smile broadened. "Only if I got lucky. You're the one responsible for Andy dying. If he'd stayed with me, he'd be alive right now."

Patti got to her feet.

She wanted to bash Joan. Because she might have been right.

Restraining herself, she asked, "Who did you tell, Joan?"

"Roger Michaelson."

Patti blinked. Then she had Elspeth Kendry take Joan Renshaw into custody, instructed that Joan be allowed to call her lawyer. She summoned the foundation's deputy director, told her she was in charge until further notice, and left to return to Washington.

The president might have dwelled a long time on the idea that she'd been responsible for her first husband's death except the C37A touched down at Andrews Air Force Base seemingly only moments after it had left Chicago.

Galia Mindel called. No doubt she'd had the control tower alert her.

She had important news.

The chairman of the Joint Chiefs of Staff was waiting to speak with her.

Chief Justice MacLaren had issued the injunction.

Anyone coming to the inauguration would not be allowed to bear arms.

Arlington National Cemetery — Arlington, Virginia

Father George Mulchrone rested on one knee before a headstone inscribed with a cross and and a biography succinct enough to fit the available space: DESMOND EDWARD MULCHRONE, SGT US ARMY, WORLD WAR II, FEB 9 1922, DEC 21 1944, PURPLE HEART, SILVER STAR. The retired priest would have liked to kneel before his elder brother's grave, but he if he got down on both knees, he might not be able to rise again.

Unlike most times these days, he wore his clerical garb, the black suit and Roman collar. Signs posted at the cemetery reminded visitors that they were treading hallowed ground and were expected to behave with dignity. For the most part, people did as they were bade. Conducted themselves with respect for the fallen and consideration for the bereaved.

Still, Mulchrone knew from experience, it was only normal for those with broken hearts to reach out to one another, looking for someone else who knew the pain they were feeling, but who might be just a bit stronger, able to offer a moment of informed solace. That was especially true when he wore his collar. He attracted Catholics like a magnet.

But not when he went down on his knee before his brother's grave.

In that instance, others afforded him an extra measure of privacy. That was what he wanted when he came to visit Dez. His big brother had always been his hero, eleven years older, impossibly big, strong and handsome to little George. More than that, he was always kind. Made time to joke with him, roughhouse in a gentle way, pretend to let his kid brother throw him to the ground and say *oof* when he landed.

He'd get to his knees and raise George's hand in the air, intone, "Undefeated and still champion, George 'Killer' Mulchrone."

George would giggle and bow to an imaginary audience that rained cheers down on him. A celebration always followed. Dez would take him into their parents' kitchen and buy him a "drink."

Chocolate milk with as much syrup as George cared to add to the glass.

Dez was one of the first guys in South Boston to line up at the recruiting office on December 8, 1941, the Monday after the attack on Pearl Harbor. He was only nineteen. Mom and Dad wanted him to wait. It might be a good, long time before he got drafted, they said. The war might be over by then. Dez wouldn't hear of it. He left the house after kissing Mom and shaking Dad's hand. George wanted to go along with his brother, his hero.

He knew the army wouldn't take a little kid like him, but he wanted to be with Dez every moment he could. His parents sent him to his room. He could still hear his mother weeping and his father trying to assure her that Dez would be okay. The army needed smart guys, he said, not just mugs with guns to do the fighting. Dez would get a job behind the lines, would probably become an officer, planning battles and such. The army would see how smart Desmond Mulchrone was. Just look how he'd gotten into Boston College.

George agreed with every word his father said. More than that, he knew how strong his brother was from wrestling with him. Those Japs and Krauts had better watch out. Dez would knock their blocks off. Despite every word of reassurance addressed to her, his mother couldn't stop crying.

George, himself, got a real scare right before Dez shipped out for Europe. He had George walk him to the taxi that was waiting to take him back to camp on his last day of leave. He'd already kissed Mom and Dad goodbye at the doorway to their house.

Before getting into the cab, Dez went down on one knee and took George's shoulders in his hands. "I want you to be a good soldier right here, Georgie boy. I'm giving you the job of keeping Mom and Dad's spirits up. They're going to be worrying about me, so you've got to do everything they tell you. Follow orders like they're your personal generals. Do things without even having to be told. Make them proud. Make them happy. Okay?"

George bobbed his head.

He told his big brother, "I don't know why they'd worry,

though. You're gonna be fine. You're gonna do great."

Dez lowered his head for a moment and when he looked up he said, "Pray for me, Georgie, that I will be all right. Pray for all us guys going out to fight. We're going to need it."

Desmond Mulchrone kissed his kid brother's forehead and got to his feet.

He came to attention and snapped off a perfect salute.

George did a credible imitation. Then Dez got in the taxi and was gone.

He died in the Battle of the Bulge. Despite George having prayed for him every morning and night since he'd left home. George could only conclude he hadn't known how to pray well enough, and decided he'd better become a professional in the matter. After a life in the priesthood, he still doubted his ability to have the Almighty grant the smallest of his entreaties.

He saw a shadow fall across Dez's tombstone.

He looked up and saw Representative Phil Brock.

Brock noticed the name on the headstone and said, "Family? I'm sorry for your loss. But I have to hand it to you. Who'd ever suspect anything we say to each other here?"

McGill Investigations, Inc. — Georgetown

McGill brought Yves Pruet, Odo Sacripant and Ethan Winger back to his office with him. On the way, he called Byron DeWitt and asked him to join them. They'd no sooner arrived than McGill took a call in the outer office from Patti and asked the others to excuse him for a moment. He went into his office and picked up the phone.

Patti told him Joan Renshaw was the leak at The Grant Foundation.

He told her of Ethan Winger's discovery.

They agreed to meet in either the Oval Office or the Residence, depending on the hour, and discuss what they should do next.

"Bet you never knew what you'd be letting yourself in for when you met me," Patti said.

McGill said, "Wouldn't have missed it for the world."

"You think Jean Morrissey would make a good president?"

"Sure, with some seasoning. If you resigned anytime soon, though, I think she might be prone to beating up members of Congress with her hockey stick."

Patti laughed and said, "Mayhem on an ice rink instead of a basketball court?"

"We each have our favorite sport. Let's see if we can hang in there a little longer."

"You'll give me a foot rub when you get home?"

"One toe at a time, if you like."

"You make me very happy, Jim."

"What's a henchman for?"

They said goodbye and McGill asked the others into his office. Pruet, Odo and DeWitt sat. Ethan Winger stood in a corner, just a bit unnerved by the company he was keeping. Deke stood guard in the outer office. Leo kept watch down on the street.

McGill looked at Ethan and said, "Just for clarity and the benefit of Deputy Director DeWitt who wasn't with us earlier today, will you please confirm your findings, Mr. Winger?"

Ethan cleared his throat, looked at McGill and then DeWitt.

"I found thirty-three forged paintings among those hanging in the Ransom and Drucker collections. In the Busby collection, I found only three paintings actually done by artists whose names appear on them."

DeWitt said, "I'm sorry. If I have it right, you're speaking of Nathaniel Ransom, Darren Drucker and Tyler Busby?"

"Yes," Ethan said.

"You were given access to Inspiration Hall?"

"You know about Inspiration Hall?" McGill asked DeWitt.

"The Bureau tries to keep up with what's being built in DC," he said.

McGill didn't miss the note of understatement.

To Ethan, DeWitt added, "You're sure you've got it right, how many forgeries there are? Are you really that good or are the paintings that bad?"

Ethan held his hands wide. "I consult for the FBI, remember? You called me."

"Because you were at the top of the list I was given. To be honest, I'm surprised you're so young."

Unruffled, Ethan said, "Okay. Let me take your questions in order. I'm sure I've got the numbers right. I am that good. The fake paintings are pretty good, too. Good enough to fool most people but not good enough to fool me."

McGill, Pruet and Odo paid close attention to the verbal jousting match.

"Where were you trained, Mr. Winger?" DeWitt asked.

"One semester at Yale and a lifetime with my father, Lawford Winger."

DeWitt was about to ask a follow-up question, but Ethan held up a hand.

"Look, I don't mean to be rude, but why don't we do this? I'll give you a list of three other experts who can look at the same paintings I did. You choose one of the people from the list. Don't tell me who you've picked. I'll bet you my life savings, forty thousand dollars, he or she gives you the same results I did without a single exception. How about that? Are you game?"

The conversation had morphed into a hand of all-in poker.

DeWitt was more than a fair player.

What he saw was the kid had the cards. He could take the bet, but he'd lose.

So he folded and turned to face McGill.

"Always nice to learn the Bureau hires good people. *I'll* bet you have an idea where we should go from here, Mr. McGill."

"I do, but I'll let Magistrate Pruet tell you his idea first."

Arlington National Cemetery — Arlington, Virginia

"Harlan Fisk came to see you?" Brock asked Father Mulchrone.

"He didn't tell me his name. Only asked that I pass the message on to you."

"That we might need the guy with the truck for the job?"

"Yes."

Brock didn't let any displeasure show on his face but he was more than a little ticked off. A large truck bomb could do the job, but it wouldn't have the same sense of menace, the same élan as using drones firing missiles. One more big bang from a truck — after the Oklahoma City blast — and every farm in the country might have to go back to using cow poop for fertilizer, but that was nowhere near as cool as making people look up in fear every time they heard a buzz overhead.

"The man who visited you gave you this message in your confessional?"

"Yes."

"So our secret's safe?"

"Yes."

Brock sighed. Sometimes you had to make do with the choice that was left to you. He would have to let Bahir Ben Kalil know it was time for him to fire up his martyr and scoot back home to Jordan, just to be safe, before the truck went boom. A hitherto unknown Middle East terror cell would claim credit. It wouldn't actually exist, of course.

Misdirection was the idea.

That and the exhaustion of government resources.

The domestic crazies would be disappointed their hands hadn't triggered the death toll, but they'd still be happy that the woman who'd *stolen* the presidency would get what she had coming. Per the last word from his friend, Joan Renshaw, at The Grant Foundation, the president was still scheduled to visit Inspiration Hall tomorrow.

If, God forbid, Joan's treachery were uncovered, she'd hang it on Roger Michaelson.

As for Brock, well, he'd done all he could to sow the seeds of chaos.

The spirit of Mikhail Bakunin that lay at the core of his being was pleased.

Bakunin having been a Russian revolutionary and the father of modern anarchy.

Of whom it was said, "On the first day of the revolution, he is a perfect treasure. On the second, he ought to be shot."

Brock intended to be in Costa Rica before anyone got around to shooting him.

He told Mulchrone, "Thank you for all your help. Again, I'm sorry for your loss."

Left alone at his brother's headstone, Father George Mulchrone was also infused by the spirit of another. That of his beloved brother. Who'd rushed off at the tender age of nineteen to help save the country he had loved more than life.

The retired priest looked down at the headstone.

He said, "There's only one thing for me to do, isn't there, Dez?"

Turn himself in, confess to the authorities what he knew about the truck bomber. He couldn't tell them about Brock or his drones. The congressman was a Catholic, had first spoken to him under the seal of confession. That conversation was inviolable. But he could talk about what he'd heard from Fisk. He wasn't Catholic. Hadn't spoken to Mulchrone in the context of a sacrament.

True, he'd lied to both Fisk and Brock about keeping his mouth shut.

That was a sin on his part, one he could confess.

He doubted he'd see Dez in the next life, which he felt fast approaching.

But there was no harm in giving it a try.

McGill Investigations, Inc. — Georgetown

"I am still of the opinion that Tyler Busby stole my family's Renoir," Pruet told DeWitt. "I had expected to find it at the new museum, but I did not."

Ethan piped up. "Maybe they hadn't gotten around to hanging

it yet."

Everyone in the room looked at him.

He shrugged and said, "Just an idea. We never asked if the exhibits were finalized."

McGill made a note of that.

The magistrate continued with his explanation.

"I first thought Busby meant to sell the forgery, perhaps to lead any investigators, such as myself, down a false trail. In order to savor the real Renoir, I thought he would have to build a private viewing room. A discreet place where his theft would not be subject to discovery. I thought it would be a reasonable idea to see if the man had construction work done at any of his homes in the past year."

DeWitt bobbed his head.

"I like your idea, *monsieur*," DeWitt said. "We can check for building permits. If we don't find any of those, we can check with the neighbors to see if they noticed any work being done. If they did, and no permits were obtained, that's a clear sign of a guilty mind."

McGill said, "It might be more subtle than that. A building permit might have been obtained for another stated purpose, a storage room perhaps, but the space will be used to exhibit the stolen art."

Everyone thought about that for a moment. Wondering how they might unmask such a deception. They couldn't go to a judge and ask for a search warrant on a hunch. Ethan came up with the solution.

He said, "What you need to do is find out what kind of lighting was put into any new construction. You'd light an art gallery differently than a shed or a garage. Check how much wiring went into the room. The number of light fixtures, too. That way you might even get a close count of the number of paintings the guy intends to hang in his little hideout. You know, in case he wants the Renoir to have some company."

McGill took all that down, too. He directed a smile of approval at Ethan.

DeWitt liked the young man's reasoning, too. He told Ethan, "That's good. Sorry I doubted you. There's still something that bothers me, though. Mr. Winger here said he knows other experts who could spot the forgeries he saw. Some of those people are bound to visit Inspiration Hall. What's to keep them from raising a stink?"

McGill sighed.

"What?" DeWitt asked.

McGill said, "I have an idea about that, but I have to ask Mr. Winger and *Monsieur Sacripant* to leave the room first."

Odo got to his feet without hesitation or complaint.

"C'est rien," he said. It's nothing. Colloquially, no problem. He opened the door to the outer office and extended a hand to Ethan. *"Mon ami?"*

The young prodigy left without a word, but not before directing a look at McGill.

As if to say, "Okay, buddy, let's see what you can do on your own."

McGill took no offense. He liked the kid's cockiness.

"Your farm team looks pretty good," he told DeWitt.

"But not quite ready for the major leagues?"

Pruet did his best to keep up with the American idioms.

Believing he understood what had been said, he told the others, "I think the young man was an asset."

McGill nodded. "He was, but what I'm about to say, I shouldn't even be telling you, *Monsieur le Magistrat.*"

"But you're going to," DeWitt said uneasily. "Maybe I shouldn't be a witness to that."

McGill said, "You're right. No need to put you in the soup. I'll come see you soon."

DeWitt nodded, got up and left, waving farewell to Pruet.

The Frenchman looked at McGill.

"Seeing you in your own milieu, *monsieur,*" he said, "I must conclude you can be as much of a problem to your government as I am to mine."

McGill laughed. "Probably more. I'm not on the payroll. I'm married to the boss. It's hard for people to find a handle on me."

Despite all his advantages, McGill's face turned somber.

"There are, however, people who will try just about anything to manipulate me or at least make me pay for what I do."

He asked for and received a pledge of confidentiality from Pruet. Then he told him in general terms about the threats Patti faced and how they had been extended to his children. Hearing the news, Pruet's mood also became grave.

"This is terrible," the magistrate said. "If there is anything I can do to help, you have only to ask."

"*Merci,*" McGill said. "There are a few more things I need to tell you. Patti was betrayed by someone who was quite close to her first husband." He told Pruet of Joan Renshaw's perfidy. "That led me to think that perhaps you've overlooked someone else when you decided that Tyler Busby was behind the theft of your family's Renoir."

With the sinking feeling he was about to put his foot into a trap, Pruet asked, "Who?"

McGill said, "If I remember correctly, you told me your great-grandmother's engagement to one of the Busbys —"

"Hiram Busby," Pruet said.

"Yes, her engagement to Hiram Busby was the cornerstone, I think you said —"

"Of a grand business alliance."

"Right. So you saw the Busbys as the injured party, and old Hiram probably had his ego as seriously bruised as his body was from the beatings the Louvels gave him. But did having Hiram's wedding to your great-grandmother fall through do any lasting financial harm to the Busby family? Assuming Tyler Busby still possesses the original versions of the forged paintings hanging in Inspiration Hall, I'd have to say no."

Pruet thought about that and said, "I must assume you are correct."

"So what does that leave?" McGill asked. "Hard feelings? If that's the case, would the Busbys have waited a hundred years to get even with the Pruets? Not likely."

Pruet couldn't argue with McGill's logic … and McGill had just told him how *Madame la Présidente* had been betrayed by someone she trusted. He knew where this should lead him, but he didn't want to put his conclusion into words.

McGill saved him the trouble.

He told Pruet, "You said your great-grandmother was originally an American, a Hobart. Have you thought to see how her marriage to Antoine Pruet affected the Hobart family? Did their financial fortunes take a dive. Might it have taken them a century to get back to the big time? Maybe one of your American cousins is the one who hired Laurent Fortier to steal your Renoir."

Pruet hung his head. Whether in sorrow or shame, McGill couldn't tell.

When he looked up, a new sense of resolve filled his eyes.

"I will ask the Louvels to see if any Hobart has visited our country home."

McGill said, "I don't think you'd need to have the Louvels look back more than a few years. This plan probably took a while to put together, but not all that long."

Pruet said, "I feel so … incompetent to have overlooked this."

McGill shook his head. "Don't. If not for Joan Renshaw, I wouldn't have thought of it either, and you're still going to wind up bagging a Busby, I'll bet. The thefts at Inspiration Hall had to be an inside job. Most of the world doesn't even know what the nature of the building is."

Pruet agreed. "A theft on such a grand scale and the commissioning of so many forgeries would also require a considerable sum of money to finance."

"Money, ego and a sense of entitlement," McGill said. "What's mine is mine and what's yours is also mine. I look at the way the forgeries are distributed at the museum, I can come up with only one conclusion. Most of the genuine Busby collection remained with its owner, and he cherry-picked the pieces he liked best from the other two collections. Assuming I'm right. You think we need to ask young Mr. Winger for his opinion?"

Pruet smiled. "Only if you wish to impress him with your understanding of the criminal mind."

"Yours, too," McGill said. "I think you're spot on about his need to build his own private gallery, not just for one Renoir, but for all the paintings he stole from the Drucker and Ransom collections, too."

Pruet said, "But *Monsieur DeWitt* pointed out the flaw in that. Busby will not be able to sustain his illusion for long."

"He thinks he won't have to," McGill said. He shared one more secret with Pruet. "Inspiration Hall is the target for the people trying to kill the president and me. They mean to bring the building down. Preferably on us. Tomorrow."

Thinking about that, McGill had an idea that might land a fly in the bad guys' ointment.

He asked Pruet to give him a moment of privacy and called Patti.

The Oval Office

In the time honored fashion of Washington mission creep, a meeting between two people, the president and the chairman of the joint chiefs of staff, grew into a meeting with six people: the president; her chief of staff, Galia Mindel; the head of the presidential protection detail, SAC Elspeth Kendry; the director of the Secret Service, David Nathan; Secretary of Defense, Patrick O'Connor; and chairman of the joint chiefs, Marine Commandant Barett Turnbull.

Galia was the one who had told the president, "On matters like this, it's best to have all your bases covered."

The president said, "Baseball has just four bases."

"Only because the federal government didn't invent the game," the chief of staff replied.

Patricia Grant sighed and yielded. Now, she and Galia sat side by side in rosewood chairs. Elspeth and Director Nathan sat on the sofa to their right. Secretary O'Connor and General Turnbull sat on the sofa to their left.

"Thank you for coming, gentlemen, Elspeth," the president said. She looked at those present and had a thought. Yet another person needed to be present. "Will you all please excuse me for just a few seconds. There's someone else who should be here." She went to her phone and asked Edwina Byington to have the vice president join them.

Less than a minute later, as if she'd anticipated the summons, Jean Morrissey entered the room. SAC Kendry gave her place to the vice president and stood behind Director Nathan. The president told her number two, "Thank you for coming on such short notice, Jean."

"My pleasure, Madam President."

The president proceeded to tell those present of the threat to her inauguration as described by Elvie Fisk, and Joan Renshaw's leak of her closely held plan to visit Inspiration Hall tomorrow. Then she asked for comments, starting with Elspeth Kendry.

"Off the top of my head, Madam President, I'd say you have to cancel your visit, but I have the feeling …"

For the first time in years, Elspeth felt the pressure of being in a room filled with people far above her pay grade. She wasn't actually intimidated. She just knew she'd have to choose her words carefully.

"What feeling do you have, Elspeth?" the president asked.

"That there might be other priorities beyond mine. Keeping you safe is not only first and foremost for me but …" Elspeth couldn't help herself. She had to speak plainly. "But to hell with anyone and anything else."

General Turnbull rewarded Elspeth with a tight grin.

Jean Morrissey had a sparkle in her eyes.

Everyone else kept a straight face.

"Thank you for your concern, Elspeth. You're right as usual. There are other considerations to take into account. We'll get to those in a minute. David, do you have anything to add from the

Secret Service's point of view?"

The director said, "Only that I couldn't agree with SAC Kendry more. She has it exactly right."

"Jean, how do you feel?" the president asked.

The vice president responded, "Madam President, I feel like putting on some brass knuckles and beating some bad guys to a pulp."

That got a laugh from everyone in the room.

Jean Morrissey continued, "Failing that, I'd be pleased to borrow one of your limos and show up at Inspiration Hall in your place. Nobody would ever mistake me for you, but we might get the creeps ready to jump by using your car and once they saw me, they might figure half-a-loaf's better than none."

"You'd risk your life for me, Jean?" the president asked.

"Yes, ma'am. I was already threatened. I'd place my faith in the Secret Service and our military. If the bad guys are planning to hit tomorrow, and if one of us doesn't show up, they might pull back, regroup and think up a new plan. We don't want that. Might turn out worse for everyone."

"Exactly what I was thinking," the president said.

General Turnbull raised a hand.

"Yes, General?"

"Ma'am, the vice president's courage would do any Marine or other uniformed service member proud, but from my information we may be dealing with hostiles who've gotten their hands on missile-firing drones. Is that correct?"

"That's the latest intelligence I've received as well," the president said.

"Then, Madam President, the other side might well not wait to see who gets out of your limousine. The vehicle itself might be the target. In which case, there would be no need for the vice president or anyone else to be in the vehicle."

"My limousine can drive itself?" the president asked.

"Not yet," Director David Nathan said. "We're working on a confidential pilot program with Google. The idea is that if your driver were ever injured and you needed the car to make a strategic departure — "

"An escape," Elspeth said.

"Yes, an escape," the director agreed. "Under the envisioned scenarios, your car would be able to get you out of harm's way without a human driver."

"But we don't have that technology in place right now?" the president asked.

"No, ma'am."

"So we'd need a volunteer, someone willing to risk his or her life, if the car should become the target," the president said.

"Unless you forgo the visit to Inspiration Hall entirely, Madam President," Director Nathan said, "and don't send anyone in your stead."

The president replied, "The museum itself might become a target. A gleaming new repository of Western culture might be as great an affront to the extremists as, say, two giant sculptures of the Buddha. Perhaps the time to strike would be on opening day when Inspiration Hall will be filled with any number of well-known visitors. Or it could be sometime later. Say a day when school buses are unloading children."

Now, Elspeth understood the president's view of the bigger picture.

"Yes, ma'am, it could be something like that," she said.

"That's unacceptable," the president said. She looked at the secretary of defense. "Patrick, does the military have any system to counter drone-fired missiles?"

"That's also in the works, Madam President, and also currently unavailable."

The president took a note from a pocket. She glanced at it and said, "Intelligence from the FBI's interrogation of Elvie Fisk suggests that the drones in the possession of our unidentified adversaries might be either Israeli Harpies or based on the technology of that drone. I'm told the Harpy will fire without a human command if it detects a radar signal that its database does not identify as friendly.

Is that correct?"

O'Connor looked to Turnbull.

"Yes, ma'am, that's correct," the commandant said.

"Well, then, knowing that and knowing the target, my arrival at Inspiration Hall or the building itself, couldn't we at least detect the approach of the hostile drones? Jam their video transmissions and use our radar selectively to misdirect the drones' missiles to some relatively harmless area? Say a river or an open field."

O'Connor and Turnbull looked at each other.

The secretary of defense said, "I'd have to check on that, Madam President."

Elspeth guessed the note the president had read and the idea it described had come from James J. McGill. The man was involved in this situation up to his eyeballs. Who knew what else he had in mind? The SAC would have to be ready for anything.

"Please do," the president said, "and now lets talk about the number and composition of the troops we'll need on the Mall in case Washington sees its first military skirmish since 1812."

Ile de la Cité — Paris

Gabbi Casale was getting ready for bed when the phone rang.

"You have a hammock at your place?" Tommy Meeker asked her.

"I have a guest room. I also have a hide-a-bed. Will that do?"

"Yeah. See you in fifteen minutes."

"I'll buzz you in, but come to the studio, okay?"

"Absolutely."

"Would you like something to eat or drink?"

"Now that you mention it, food sounds good. Can that fancy French chef of yours do something simple like an honest-to-God hamburger? Maybe with a side of *pommes frites* and a Kronenbourg."

"Sure. Would you like to split a chocolate mousse with me for dessert?"

"Love it. Be there soon."

Gabbi called the kitchen of Monsieur Henri's and placed the order. She slipped out of her pajamas and into her SAIC sweats. Whenever she was asked why the School of the Art Institute of Chicago would put its initials on athletic wear, she said the tuition at the school was a heavy lift for anyone not named Rockefeller.

Regular workouts with your accountant and banker were obligatory.

By the time Tommy arrived, Gabbi sat on a stool, doodling on a Strathmore art pad with a Staedtler 3H sketching pencil. Her friend and former colleague raised his nose as he stepped off the elevator. His meal had been delivered only a minute earlier. It was still hot and —

"My God, that smells great," Tommy said.

"Pull up a stool and eat," Gabbi told him.

The food had been placed on the worktable to Gabbi's right. Tommy sat just around the corner of the table from her. He removed the dome from the serving plate, grabbed the burger and took a huge bite.

Gabbi flipped the page of her pad and started to sketch the expression of bliss on Tommy's face as he chewed. It was a tribute to the chef that he didn't notice what she was doing until he swallowed the first bite. Then he asked, "You're drawing me while I eat?"

"Yes, I want to see how your face works. You asked for a portrait, didn't you?"

"I did." He looked at the burger in his hand. Didn't want to let it get cold. "Oh, go ahead."

Gabbi had to smile as she worked, doing her best to catch Tommy's expressions as he made small murmurs of pleasure. Unbidden, the thought entered her mind that people probably displayed the same range of expressions while eating that they did when making love. Not that she'd want to do actual comparisons. Well, okay, maybe just once or twice.

The burger disappeared in less than two minutes and the fries and beer followed quickly.

Gabbi flipped the page so Tommy couldn't see what she'd drawn and put the pad on the table. She popped the top of a small plastic cooler and took out a glass goblet of chocolate mousse. The kitchen, per her request, had provided two spoons. Gabbi handed one to Tommy.

Being a gentleman, he gestured to her to take the first bite.

She did, and said that was all she wanted. She told him to take the rest.

The first touch of the chocolate on his tongue brought back Gabbi's idea of erotic eating.

Forcing her focus back to the task at hand, she asked, "You've got some news? You didn't just stop by for a free feed and a place to crash, did you?"

Tommy interrupted his gustatory delight to reach a hand into a pocket and toss her a laminated photo. A replica of a Navigo pass in the name of Duvessa Kinsale. Gabbi took it in and looked back at Tommy. Now, his smile was informed by more than his taste buds.

"You got her," Gabbi said.

"Had to run around town, but, yeah. She went to the Musée d'Orsay on the night you thought she did. At least she got on the RER at the museum station that night."

Gabbi made a fist and said, "She was there, all right. This is a big first step."

"It takes more than that to run me ragged. I found René Simonet's lair."

"You didn't."

Tommy covered a huge yawn with his right hand. Noticing a dab of chocolate on a finger, he sucked it off and said, "I did."

"Where is it? Tell me where."

Tommy got to his feet. Did a big stretch. Blinked at Gabbi, regarding her through bloodshot eyes. "Maybe I should save that 'til morning. Keep you in suspense."

Gabbi dropped her voice to a menacing register and asked, "Do I have to beat it out of you, Meeker?"

"That might be fun," Tommy told her, "but I'm too tired to put up much of a fight."

He reached back into the pocket that had held the Navigo pass and brought out a slip of paper with an address neatly printed on it.

"Maison Simonet," he said.

Gabbi took in the information. Gave it a firm press into memory. Immediately had a second thought about what she'd seen.

"What if this is just the place he lives? What if he keeps the art he stole somewhere else?"

Tommy shook his head.

"Already thought of that. Checked to see if he owns or leases any other residence, storage facility or even somewhere else to park his car. Couldn't find a thing. Looking through a million records are why my eyes are so bleary. You think about it, there's also a perfectly logical reason why he wouldn't stash the stolen masterpieces somewhere else."

Gabbi said, "He wants them close so he can enjoy them."

"Right. Now, I have to use the *pissoir,* and then I must sleep."

Gabbi showed him the way to the guest room. It had its own *salle de bain.*

Once Tommy was tucked in, Gabbi had a choice to make.

Did she call James J. McGill immediately?

Or did she visit Simonet's house first and see what he had hanging on his walls?

FBI Offices — Richmond, Virginia

McGill swung by the J. Edgar Hoover Building and picked up Deputy Director Byron DeWitt and a crew of his technically adept colleagues and headed south. The feds had arranged for a Virginia State Police unit to lead their little caravan. McGill's black Chevy, with Leo and Deke in their customary places, followed the state cops. A black SUV filled with the FBI techies brought up the rear. The trip to Richmond lasted little more than an hour at the speed they traveled.

Long enough for McGill to pose a question he'd long wondered about to DeWitt.

"Why is it the FBI headquarters is still named after J. Edgar Hoover? The guy's been dead over forty years and he was a crooked cop when he was alive. Harry Truman said Hoover transformed the Bureau into his private secret police force and blackmailed Congress."

DeWitt smiled and said, "Yeah, those were the good old days, all right. I was in diapers, of course, when Director Hoover kicked the bucket, but maybe they keep his name on the building in the hope of returning to the glory days."

DeWitt gave a wink to McGill. Let him know he was just kidding.

The deputy director said, "Truth is, I don't know why they keep Hoover's name on the building. It has to suit someone's political purpose. Maybe you should ask the president or Galia Mindel. They'd know more than I would."

McGill tucked the suggestion into a corner of his mind.

Maybe the next time he and Galia were knocking back a few brews, he'd ask her.

When they arrived at the FBI offices in Richmond, former NASA rocket scientist, Arlo Carsten, was waiting for them, handcuffed to a table in an interview room. He wished to register a complaint with DeWitt, as the deputy director and McGill seated themselves opposite him.

"I haven't been given access to a lawyer," Arlo said.

DeWitt told him, "Look on the bright side. You haven't been waterboarded yet either."

The deputy director's tone was jovial, but a man in Arlo's position couldn't disregard DeWitt's use of the word yet. He turned to McGill, hoping to find someone who'd view his circumstances with greater sympathy. Then he realized who had come to see him.

"Hey," he told McGill, "you can't be here. You're just a private eye."

"Yeah, but I have friends in high places," McGill said.

Arlo shook his head, "This isn't right. This is *not* right."

McGill looked at DeWitt and said, "Doesn't it kill you when a creep like this, a guy who planned to murder you, gets irate when *his* rights get scuffed up a little? What would Chairman Mao do with this jerk?"

"Chairman Mao?" Arlo had read enough world history in school to recognize the name. "Isn't he dead?"

DeWitt ignored Arlo's question and answered McGill. "Put a bullet into the back of his head and make his family pay for the round."

"Jesus," Arlo yelped.

McGill looked at the bound man. "We don't do things like that, but maybe in your case, and those of your friends, we could make exceptions. As short of money as the government is, maybe making condemned prisoners pay for their own executions would be a popular idea in Congress."

Having lost his job to federal budget trimming, Arlo didn't see McGill's idea as being outside the realm of possibility.

"What do you want?" he asked McGill.

"Let's start with your recognition of who the aggrieved party is here."

Arlo hung his head. He wanted to say *he* was the one with the gripe. But he knew that wouldn't play well. His eyes still downcast, he said, "You are."

"The president and my children and then me," McGill told him.

Arlo looked up. "Kids? I never threatened anybody's kids. I wouldn't have anything to do with something like that."

"Of course, you wouldn't," DeWitt said, "you only have sex with seventeen-year-old girls."

"I told you. She said she was legal and ..." His voice trickled off to near inaudibility. "It had been a while for me."

"Yeah, well, enough about you," McGill said. "Let's talk about me some more. You say you wouldn't threaten anyone's kids, but what about Harlan Fisk? Would he really go that far? If he made a threat against my children, would he try to carry it out?"

Arlo looked as if his stomach had just turned sour.

"That's exactly what he did, isn't it? Because your feds caught Elvie and me."

McGill nodded.

"I think he would," Arlo said, "given the opportunity. He sort of looks at Elvie as his property more than his flesh and blood. But he values her all the same, and he believes in payback."

So do I, McGill thought, but kept the sentiment to himself.

DeWitt stepped into the pause in the conversation.

"Are your drones based on Harpy technology?"

"They are Harpies. Bought black market out of South Africa."

"Do Fisk and his clowns have anyone besides you who can fly the drones?" DeWitt asked.

Arlo nodded. "I trained two other guys. They're not as good as me, but you spend what Fisk did for those drones, you're not gonna leave them on the shelf."

McGill had something come to mind. The picture of Jean Morrissey running out of the VP's house? The one they thought had been taken by a drone and caught Jean square in their cross-hairs? That photo had been taken after Arlo was in custody. So the guys who'd done that had shown they weren't half-bad at their jobs.

McGill asked Arlo, "Don't any of you fools remember what happened to Timothy McVeigh?"

Arlo looked down again. "Things weren't supposed to work out the way they have. A bunch of assholes from one of those Mid-eastern outfits were supposed to say they did it."

DeWitt asked, "How are they supposed to make their claim credible?"

When Arlo looked up he wore a sly smile. "They've got a Harpy or two of their own. They think it's hilarious, their having an Israeli weapon."

"You know specifically who these other people are?"

Arlo shook his head. "Fisk might, I don't."

McGill said, "Okay. Now, you're going to tell us what ideas you might have for us to blind your drones and manipulate the way they respond to being tracked by radar. So we can make them shoot their missiles where we want them to go."

"What do I get for all my help?" Arlo asked.

McGill leaned over the table, cupped a hand around the back of Arlo's head and whispered directly into his ear.

When he let go, Arlo jerked away from him, sitting back as far as he could.

McGill sat back, too. Met Arlo's eyes with a hard stare.

"The navy," Arlo said, his voice tight with fear, "I've heard the navy's got a directed energy weapon, a laser gun, they can fire at drones and blind them."

DeWitt said "How do you —"

McGill held up a hand, cutting off the deputy director's question.

He didn't care right now who the source of Arlo's information was.

"That's a start," McGill said. "Now, tell us how to screw up the drone's missiles."

Arlo told them everything he knew, including some ideas he came up with that very moment.

The National Mall — Washington, DC

Odo wanted to see the National Air and Space Museum.

Not wishing to dwell on his own problems, and having spoken to the Louvels about seeing if any Hobart had visited Avignon in the recent past, Pruet decided to accompany his friend to the museum. The two of them took in many of the stunning displays illustrating humankind's escape from the shackles of gravity.

They started with the 1903 Wright Flyer, the first successful, powered, heavier-than-air flying machine. Moving along a historical time line brought them to the *Enola Gay*, the B-29 SuperFortress that dropped an atomic bomb on Hiroshima. The two Frenchman contemplated the horror of that day for everyone who survived it, including the crew of the plane. They moved on from a world war to the Cold War and the SR-71 Blackbird spy plane, the fastest jet aircraft ever built. They concluded their tour by viewing the space shuttle *Discovery.*

As they walked along the Mall back to their hotel, Odo told Pruet, “I would like to travel in outer space someday.”

“Visit other planets?” Pruet asked.

“No. I don’t think I will live long enough to do that. What I’d like to do is circle our own planet and possibly the moon. Behold all the beauty that surrounds us every day, marvel at what we miss because we are too close to it. Too much a part of it. See our natural wonders from a proper perspective and appreciate them as never before.”

Hearing Odo’s words, Pruet felt a tingling in his mind.

An idea was about to be born. He didn’t try to hurry it.

Odo asked, “Would you like to do that, Yves?”

The magistrate said, “I don’t have the courage. Sit atop a rocket the size of a tall building? Wait for an enormous engine to explode into life? Have gravity compress me to the delicacy of a crepe? The prospect does not intrigue me.”

Pruet’s description reminded Odo a great deal of making love to his wife.

He thought he would have to find a new woman for Yves when they got home.

Without getting specific, Odo said, “But think of the joy. Think of the marvelous view.”

That stopped Pruet in his tracks. He said, “*Voilà!*”

Which, in French, used as an interjection, means, “That’s it!”

Odo thought Pruet was pointing out a nearby threat. His hand darted under his coat for the pistol McGill had lent him, thoughtfully not asking for its return. Pruet put a hand on Odo’s shoulder, putting him at ease.

“I spoke figuratively, old friend. You gave me a brilliant idea.”

“How kind of me,” Odo said, relaxing. “Would you care to tell me what it is?"

"It is a way to have my revenge upon Laurent Fortier without killing him."

"Would the Louvels approve?" Odo asked.

Pruet shared his idea. Odo smiled, in the manner of a Corsican seeing justice meted out.

"Bien," Odo said. *"Très bien."*

The two men continued their walk, taking in the Washington Monument, so much like the Luxor Obelisk in *La Place de la Concorde* in Paris. Only in the American fashion of bigger being better, the Washington Monument was more than seven times taller. Even so, Pruet thought, grandiosity could have its place in a public space.

Getting back to matters at hand, he told Odo of the threats made against McGill's children and the anticipated attack on Inspiration Hall. Pruet had given McGill his word that he'd hold these issues in confidence. He did not consider telling Odo a violation of that pledge. As regarded professional concerns, neither of them withheld information from the other.

He was sure McGill operated in the same fashion with Margaret Sweeney.

"What would you do if someone threatened your children, my friend?" Pruet asked.

The mere thought was enough to give Odo's harsh features an even more brutal cast.

"I would be the last thing that villain would ever see, and no one else would find what little remained of him."

"I thought as much, and I do not see *Monsieur McGill's* response as being much different."

"Nor do I," Odo said.

"So he has the devil on his doorstep."

Odo told Pruet, "I do not think so. I will place my wager that God, the *Father,* would both understand and approve of any measure a man might take in defense of his family."

Perhaps Odo was right, Pruet thought.

In any case, it was not a point to argue with a Corsican.

"What about the attack on Inspiration Hall?" Pruet asked. "Do you think that will happen?"

Odo considered the matter. "If, as you say, the building holds personal significance for *Madame la Présidente,* then, yes, I think an attempt will be made."

"So you think Patricia Grant should stay away?"

"Oui."

"And *Monsieur McGill?"*

"That is up to him, of course."

Odo's concept of sexual equality was strictly situational.

"Any other thoughts on the matter?" Pruet asked.

Odo stopped to think. They'd reached the Vietnam War Memorial by now. They were close enough to read individual names on the wall. Both men shook their heads in sadness. Life was so much easier when you learned from the mistakes of others. France's loss in Vietnam might have been a lesson learned for America.

Odo looked at Pruet and then back to the wall.

He said, "Those tiny Communist bastards accomplished so much with so little. If I were *Monsieur McGill,* I would not overlook the chance that these terrorists he faces might not use their new drones and their missiles at all. They might rely on something far simpler. Something unexpected."

Pruet made a mental note to pass Odo's words of wisdom on to McGill.

Calder Lane — McLean, Virginia

Representative Philip Brock drove up the curving flagstone driveway and stopped in front of the lovely pale yellow house with the powder blue shutters. Pretty, Brock thought, but the place had more of a feminine look than a masculine one. But then he'd heard that Senator Howard Hurlbert's wife, Bettina, wore the pants in the family.

A thought occurred to Brock just then: best to be careful.

He put the car, a gray rental Ford with mud smeared artfully on the Vermont license plates, back in gear and idled forward to the far end of the house. There was a turnoff leading to a four-car garage out back. Above the garage was an apartment used by the married couple who served as Hurlbert's domestic help.

The senator had told Brock that his wife had taken the couple back to Mississippi and their main residence when she'd left on New Year's Day. Bettina could not abide northern winters. Not after she'd been denied the opportunity to become the country's First Lady. That was the story Hurlbert had told Brock. Caution told Brock to make sure the old soak had it right.

The apartment above the garage was dark.

Not even a nightlight showed in case a nocturnal whiz was needed.

Brock was satisfied the servants were elsewhere. Whether that was true of the grand dame of the house remained to be seen. He backed up the car, stopping it opposite the front entrance. He stepped out, went to the door and rang the bell. Not a praying man, Brock kept his fingers crossed that lovely Bettina was sipping a mint julep far, far away, and Hurlbert hadn't drunk himself into a stupor already.

He'd break into the house if necessary, but that was almost certain to trigger some sort of security alarm and force him to hurry. Increase the chances that something might go wrong. "Come on," he muttered, "come on, you old shithead."

He rang the doorbell again.

Brock wondered if Hurlbert might have forgotten to arm the security alarm. The answer to that question would depend what impulse had the upper hand that night, the senator's paranoia or his thirst. The way the guy was schussing down the slope of personal destruction, it was a fifty-fifty proposition. Turned out Brock didn't have to take any special risk. Hurlbert tottered to the door and threw it wide.

The senator squinted at his visitor through bloodshot eyes. He was smashed but still upright. Brock couldn't ask for more.

"Is that you?" Hurlbert asked.

Brock nodded. He was wearing a fedora over clear lens glasses and a trenchcoat.

Closing the door behind Brock, Hurlbert looked up at him and asked, "Damn, have you grown some, boy, or what?"

Brock only laughed, but he was wearing two-inch lifts in his shoes.

He gestured to Hurlbert to lead the way. In his McLean house, the senator liked to drink in the room he called his study. But the only point of academic interest was whether the old man would drink or spill more of his nightly bourbon. Genteel fellow that he was, though, he had stayed conscious long enough to receive his guest and to put out a second glass so Brock might partake of a drink, too.

There was enough Pappy Van Winkle in the bottle to be shared.

Brock had heard how highly regarded and hard to find the brand of bourbon was.

He was tempted to have a sip, but sensing there was nobody in the house other than himself and the senator, he decided it was best to get on with business and be gone.

Hurlbert had just taken his seat and finished filling his glass to the brim. He turned to Brock and asked, "Will two fingers do?"

Brock took a Beretta 92 from his coat pocket and with a gloved finger pulled the trigger three times, shooting Hurlbert in the chest.

"One finger will do," Brock said.

Then he thought: Christ, did I really just *say* that?

After not speaking a word. What a dumbass. He'd coached himself to stay silent in case Hurlbert had been dictating his memoirs or some other asinine thing. He clicked the gun's safety on so he wouldn't shoot his dick off and jammed the gun back in his pocket.

He got the hell out of there before he could open his mouth again.

McGill's Hideaway — The White House

McGill and Patti sipped hot cocoa in front of another wood-burning fire. The Michelin Guide would have to find additional stars to rate the cocoa, as they would with most of the treats available at the White House. The woodsmoke from the fireplace was aromatic without being overpowering. The leather sofa was seductively comfortable, as always.

Despite their deluxe comforts, neither McGill nor Patti felt at ease.

They'd share the news their respective days had provided.

Tidings of good cheer were nowhere to be found.

McGill did bring one hopeful note.

"Arlo Carsten says this new laser gun the navy has should be able to blast a drone right out of the sky not just blind it. He says it should be a simple matter of rewriting a bit of software so the laser targets Point B on the drone instead of Point A."

Patti put her cup down and called the secretary of the navy, told him what she wanted, listened to a reply, issued a new instruction that included bringing a dozen other people into the loop. Told the secretary not to disappoint her and said goodnight.

McGill took one look at his wife and intuited the gist of the call. "It's not a quick fix, rewriting computer code for a ray gun?"

"No, it is not. The weapon you were told about is still not operational."

"But there is a beta version?"

"Yes. The one the secretary of defense thought wasn't ready yet. It will be deployed overnight. The secretary of the navy was dying to ask me how I'd heard about the weapon, but he remembered who I am."

"The commander in chief," McGill said.

"That's right."

"So, boss," McGill said, "are we, in fact, going to look at a new museum and a bunch of phony paintings tomorrow?"

"Yes, we are."

"But since your limo might be a target, we'll take a different set of wheels."

"That would be prudent, yes."

"Maybe make it an early appearance before the bad guys are fully awake."

"I think that would be wise, too. Finish your cocoa and take me to bed, will you?"

McGill said, "Yes, ma'am. Right away. Before anything else worrisome happens."

Billy Goat Trail A — C&O Canal National Historical Park

The warning sign had it exactly right: 40-Foot Cliff. No Alternative Trail.

The trail was not recommended for anyone with a fear of heights or who suffered from a poor sense of balance. Absolutely NO bikes or dogs were allowed on the trail. No mention was made about lugging a small corpse up the incline.

After killing Senator Howard Hurlbert, Representative Philip Brock decided it would be half-assed of him to let Doctor Bahir Ben Kalil live. The good doctor might have been a fervent, if covert, jihadi at the moment, but even tough guys had been known to spill their guts after a few days, weeks or months of experiencing the hospitality of the CIA.

Ben Kalil could tie Brock to the coming attack on Inspiration Hall. And should Ben Kalil be found out and captured, wouldn't it be handy for him to have a United States congressman in his back pocket as a co-conspirator? At the very least, giving up Brock would get Ben Kalil a place of confinement with some creature comforts and a promise of no further enhanced interrogation.

So Brock had showed up at the five-star hotel, where Ben Kalil stayed when in Washington, and said he would drive him to the airport. They could talk about possible future plans on the way. They went to the hotel garage, a corner slot deep in shadow. Helpful fellow that he was, Brock even put Ben Kalil's Louis Vuitton

Zephyr 70 suitcase into his trunk for him.

Brock was counting on Ben Kalil having designer luggage, something more expensive than most young couples paid for their entire honeymoon trips. He was not disappointed in Ben Kalil's reaction when he said, "Holy shit, someone has put a gash in your bag."

The doctor ran to see the outrage. He leaned over the bag and shouted, "Where, where?"

Brock hit him a good one on the crown of his skull with a lug wrench, the old-fashioned L-shaped kind. Gave him another clout alongside his temple just to be sure and bundled him into the trunk. Ben Kalil had stood only five-four and didn't weigh a buck-thirty. He fit neatly.

Minding the speed limit and other traffic laws, Brock drove to the park. The visitors center was closed for the season. The park cops were suffering budget cuts like everyone else and as Brock cruised past the sign saying the park was closed, with his car's lights off, no one waved him over to the side of the road and said, "Naughty, naughty."

He parked with the car facing the exit and taking one last look around he opened the trunk. He was pleased that the dead man's thick head of hair seemed to have blotted up all but a few traces of blood and those had fallen on the sheet of plastic Brock had put down. To make sure there was no transfer of blood, saliva or snot to his clothing, the congressman put a plastic bag over his victim's head and cinched it tight. He pulled Ben Kalil's body from its resting place and closed the trunk.

Brock slung the body over his right shoulder, and hoped with all his heart Ben Kalil had packed several bricks of cash in his fancy bag. He'd changed his shoes to a pair of sturdy cross-trainers, not having any lifts in them. His faux spectacles were in the car's glove box and his trench coat was in the back seat. Now, he wore dark denim jeans, a navy blue sweatshirt and crew cap.

He had a small flashlight clipped to his waistband, but didn't think it would be a good idea to carry it lighted in his mouth for the climb. The sky was clear and the stars were bright, but there was only the slightest sliver of a waxing moon to help light his way. Brock told himself he'd just have to concentrate on finding his handholds and footholds; the lack of moonlight would help to conceal his evildoing.

In a moment of inspired improvisation, he used Ben Kalil's belt, also Louis Vuitton, to bind the dead man's right ankle to his left wrist. That turned him into a human loop. Freeing both of Brock's hands for the climb. With Ben Kalil draped over his shoulders, Brock could pretend that his burden was little more than a bulky scarf.

Which got really damn heavy by the time he was halfway up the cliff face. Got heavier still with each following foot of upward progress. He started to sweat despite the chill of the night. His heart pounded like a canon salvo Tchaikovsky might have worked into a composition. For one terrifying moment, a wave of dizziness rolled through his head and his eyes blurred.

He felt certain he was about to topple back to earth from the height of a three-story building. The irony of it, he thought. Ben Kalil would take his revenge after he was dead. But a jolt of adrenaline raced through Brock's body, all but setting his hair afire. His vision cleared, his balance stabilized and his muscles surged with blood.

He clambered up the final ten feet of the cliff with the speed and certainty of a mountain goat. He took five steps up the trail and collapsed, Ben Kalil's remains keeping him from cracking the back of *his* skull on the rocks. He lay there in the dead man's embrace until his heart slowed to a pace approaching its normal resting rate.

A memory came to him: Roger Michaelson smacking him in the balls. Telling him he was no James J. McGill. Turned out that bastard Michaelson was right. If McGill survived the next twenty-four hours, Brock knew he would have to get himself in much better shape. No way was he ready to deal with McGill right now.

Moving slowly, he got to his feet. He gave a soft hallelujah when he found that his flashlight still worked. Signs posted by the park service ordered hikers to stay on the blue-blazed trail in order to avoid difficult sections. But when Brock reached an area known as Pothole Alley, he once again veered from the straight and narrow of both morality and topography.

He had to climb over boulders and jagged rocks. The area was also laced with crevasses. The adventurous might hop over these gashes in the landscape, and Brock had thought to do this, too, hoping for just the right spot to dump his former collaborator. But the first cleft he came to was wide enough to give him pause, and then to say, "Fuck it."

He eased himself to his knees and shucked his burden. He unfastened Ben Kalil's belt, spread his limbs and stripped him of his clothing. Taking care, he manipulated the corpse so it went into the crevasse face down. The body banged back and forth on the rocks on the way down. One arm was dislocated almost to the point of being severed, but when Ben Kalil jolted to a stop his face remained hidden.

It was too cold for bug-life to be active, but Brock thought birds and other scavengers would further obscure the dead man's identity before anyone in authority could pry his remains free.

He ripped the labels from the man's designer clothing and tossed the garments into the crevasse after him. He kept the money he found in a wallet, better than six grand, and Ben Kalil's identification. Taking care he didn't slip and fall going down the cliff, he made it back to his car without anybody seeing him.

He drove back into town, once again being the careful driver.

Reviewing what he'd done that night, killing two men of high official stature, he wondered how he should be feeling. Guilty or gleeful? He felt neither. He was just going about his plan, to disrupt the life of the United States government as much as he could. Why? Well, because its day had come and gone. Anyone could see that. Hell, the Republicans had made downsizing the government and obstructing its most basic functions their core beliefs.

He was just trying to move things along faster.

Well, there was one personal note to his evening's activities.

That woman at the cocktail party who was disappointed that he hadn't killed anyone?

How would she like him now?

Lyon — France

The TGV wasn't fast enough for Gabbi when she left Paris this time. She used Gianni's, connections to charter a Dassault Falcon business jet — and charged it to her kid brother. Flying time between Paris and Lyon was only thirty-six minutes. There were times when the compact size of European countries pleased Gabbi no end.

On the other hand, the flight from Lyon to Geneva, Switzerland took only ten minutes. Gabbi worried about that. She didn't want Laurent Fortier/René Simonet slipping out of France on her, if he was back in the country.

If he was elsewhere, her plan was to lure him home.

Then, thinking of her own home, she called and left a message for the sleeping Tommy Meeker so he wouldn't think she'd run out on him without a good reason.

She caught a quick catnap while en route to Lyon and felt a little better for it when she landed. She rented a BMW 528 at the airport and plugged the address Tommy had found for René Simonet into the car's GPS system. In minutes, she was on her way to Annecy, sixty-one miles away.

Gabbi had never been to the town so she powered up her iPhone and asked Siri for a quick backgrounder on Annecy. The town was set on the shore of a lake having the same name. It was known for the scenic beauty of its mountain views, woodlands and lake. One of the shortest rivers in Europe, *Le Thiou,* ran through the town, earning Annecy the title of Venice of the Alps.

The town had received official tourist classifications as a village in bloom and a town of — perfect — art and history. It sat only a twenty-two mile *drive* south of Geneva. There was also highway access to nearby Italy.

Jesus, Gabbi thought, that bastard Simonet had planned well. Left himself all sorts of escape routes in the unlikely event anyone ever caught up with him. But she didn't fully appreciate the thoroughness of Simonet's planning until she parked the BMW, got out and took a passerby's look at the place where the man lived, a four-story peach colored building along the river just off the rue de Marquisats. A stone's throw from the castle in the middle of the river.

The place had to be worth millions of euros. Nice digs for an academic who never got around to publishing any of his research. But the building's *pièce de résistance* was the shop on the ground floor of Simonet's hideout: an art gallery.

Could the man possibly have had any more gall?

Gabbi took all this in at a glance. She had been trained not to call attention to herself, and walked past at a purposeful pace. Someone who had been called out late at night and was eager to return home. She was barely out of view, had Simonet been looking out one of his windows, when a thought stopped her cold.

If Simonet fled to Switzerland or Italy, his extradition would be demanded by France, and it would undoubtedly be honored. If Simonet went to Italy he would be returned as a matter of principle, as Italy had made it a priority to recover its own stolen cultural treasures. With Switzerland, the principle would probably be that the Swiss liked to be seen doing the proper thing. In either case, though, there were plenty of villains in Italy and bankers in Switzerland who'd lend Simonet any help he might need to disappear in return for, say, a genuine Renoir.

Gabbi knew she was going to need help, and lots of it, to put the clamps on Simonet. She found a room at the Hotel de Palais de L'isle and called Père Louvel in Avignon. He'd been sleeping, but he both remembered Gabbi's voice and knew she must have important news to call at that hour.

"Est-ce qu'oui, ma fille, comment je peux vous aider?" the priest said. Yes, my daughter, how may I help you?"

"Father, I've found the home of the man who killed your brother, the man who stole the Pruets' painting."

She told him she was in Annecy, had just walked past the thief's residence. But she would need help to make sure the man did not flee France. Père Louvel said he would come at once.

"Father, we'll need more than just the two of us. What I was thinking, those other families you talked about, the ones who lost their works of art? Why don't we gather as many of them as possible in Annecy as quickly as we can? They have an interest in seeing this situation resolved, too. And the more people we have on our side, the more likely the authorities will be to do the right thing."

Gabbi made that point in case Simonet had cultivated any friendships with the local power structure. She'd bet he had, but if enough families with the stature of the Pruets gathered to form an opposition, they should win the day. Père Louvel understood what she meant perfectly.

"Madame, votre armée amasse," the priest said. Madam, your army is massing.

CHAPTER 8

The National Mall — Washington, DC
Sunday, January 13, 2013

Harlan Fisk wore combat fatigues despite never having served in any branch of the armed forces of the United States. A Beretta 92, the official sidearm of the U.S. Army, was holstered at his right thigh. Just below that, a scabbard holding a U.S. Navy Seals Combat Knife — $77.83 at Amazon — was tied to his calf. His ensemble was topped off by a blood red beret.

Not intended to be misunderstood as an official naval rank, he called himself the Commander of the First Michigan Militia. Other than a moderate middle-aged bulge at his gut, he cut an imposing figure, standing six-foot-three and weighing two hundred and thirty pounds. His broad shoulders and calloused hands were the products of someone who had worked construction for twenty-five years, starting when he was eighteen.

With the recession, though, he'd been *out* of work the past three years. His unemployment benefits were gone. The savings he and his wife, Krissy, had put away were almost used up, too. Only thing that kept them above water was Krissy had kept going to school all the time they were married. Got herself an accounting degree. Worked as a CPA for a plumbing supplies company in Lansing. Started using her proper name, Kristine.

Truth was, Krissy made a decent salary, while he didn't earn a goddamn cent. There were times, thinking how his tiny little doll of a wife out-earned him so bad, that his face got as red as his beret. She'd refused to come down South with him while he and the boys trained. He thought maybe that had to do with more than her job. She had to be tired of him not making any money, and she was bound to find someone new while he was away. Maybe she already had. So he decided to make the most of her credit cards while he could, buying all the arms and ammo Visa would allow.

He'd been tickled how Elvie had insisted on going South with her dad. That was a good girl for you. Tiny and pretty like her mom, but tough as a Detroit pit bull. Did *whatever* he told her to do. He was sure as hell gonna get her back or that cocksucker married to that thieving bitch in the White House would learn what it meant to lose your own flesh and blood.

He'd been surprised at first that Krissy would let Elvie go without putting up a fuss about it. Then he realized it would be that much easier for his wife to find a new boyfriend if she didn't have a kid around the house.

The thought never entered his mind that if he wasn't arming himself and his friends for World War III he could have been living a comfortable middle-class life. Maybe get some new vocational training himself. He'd never been much good in school, though.

He had trouble adjusting his thinking to new realities, too. His old man had taught him how things were supposed to be, and that was that. A man supported his family; he didn't live off his wife. That wasn't right. It was a pussy thing to do.

The other guys in his militia knew that. Who was going to look out for them if they didn't look out for each other? Nobody, brother. Things had to change.

Maybe not go back to the way they were exactly. There were plenty of decent colored guys and the Mexicans he knew worked as hard as anyone on the planet. Anyone could see those things. That's why his militia was *not* just a bunch of white guys. Any asshole with a Nazi tattoo tried to sign up with his outfit, he got a boot right in his ass.

His fight was, there had to be some new way for a working

man to find work. Do something with his *hands* that would let him bring home a respectable paycheck. Let him take a measure of pride in himself. Not get fucked over every time the goddamn bankers and other white-collar crooks robbed the country blind.

Jesus Christ, it just wasn't right, the way the world was going.

Harlan Fisk was one angry, heavily armed man.

His deputy commander, a former GM line worker, carried two Colt AR-15s, one for the commander, one for himself. The weapons were bought legal, online. All of the two hundred and forty-seven men in his militia carried their firearms openly. Exercising their second amendment rights just the way the Constitution said.

A well regulated militia being necessary to the security of a free state, the right of the people to keep and bear arms shall not be infringed.

More than one of his men had those very words inked on his chest or back.

Some had it on both sides; you got to see the second amendment coming or going.

They *were* a militia, as well regulated and trained as any in the country. They weren't just a bunch of jerks with guns. They were Americans standing up for themselves and their rights. Those old boys who wrote the Constitution had known things might come to this.

Fisk knew about the injunction from the chief justice.

To hell with him. Damn judge couldn't choose where a man's rights applied.

Their objective was in plain sight now: the Capitol of the United States of America.

Beautiful damn building, all lit up in the night. Made your heart swell with pride.

Until you thought of all the lying, cheating scumbags who worked inside of it. Wouldn't be long, though, until the First Michigan was joined by militias from all over the country. Their strength would be measured in the thousands. No damn cops would be able to stop them. They'd put things right for the whole damn country.

Right now, though, it looked like the First Michigan was the first to arrive.

Fisk extended his right hand and his deputy commander filled it with his AR-15.

He had no idea he and his men were walking into a trap.

FBI Headquarters — Washington, DC

Deputy Director Byron DeWitt sat behind his desk and looked at the man sitting in one of his guest chairs. The guy had to be crowding eighty years old. He wore a black suit, a Roman collar and handcuffs. You got cuffed when you showed up at 935 Pennsylvania Avenue NW and said you were a part of a terrorist conspiracy to assassinate the president of the United States and bring down a major building in the process.

Other things happened, too. The Bureau checked to see if you were inebriated or under the influence of drugs, prescription or otherwise. Your stated identity was verified. Once these two bits of business were completed, your medical history was pursued to make sure you weren't a fugitive from a place of psychiatric confinement.

Jailbreaks were also looked into.

After these points were addressed, someone had to decide who would interrogate you. The extreme nature of the old guy's confession required that he talk to someone of eminence. Of course, the coot, if he'd known what he was doing, should have turned himself in to the Secret Service. The fact that he'd sought out the wrong federal law enforcement agency cast some doubt on the veracity of his claim.

The FBI simply could have transferred the guy to the custody of their federal brethren.

But like any cops — local, state or federal — they had an abiding curiosity about any crimes that had been or might be committed in their jurisdiction. The FBI was of the mindset that their jurisdiction was planet Earth. Given the current state of tension concerning the presidency being won by a single electoral vote, if the geezer had turned himself in at midday, he might have spent some time talking with the director himself.

Having surrendered himself the previous evening, and having been processed shortly after midnight, though, Mulchrone had caused DeWitt to get rousted from his bed.

"So you're a priest?" the deputy director said.

"Yes, but I'm retired from full ministry."

"What was your order, Father? What kind of priest were you?"

"Franciscan."

DeWitt smiled. "Founded by St. Francis of Assisi, a man of great humility and kindness. The new pope is a Jesuit but he chose the name Francis in honor of the saint, didn't he?"

Father Mulchrone returned the smile. "Why, yes he did. Are you Catholic?"

"No, I'm a Buddhist, but I admire the teachings of Jesus."

Mulchrone looked puzzled. "I'm not quite sure I see the connection."

"Well, Buddhists believe that you end suffering by eliminating ignorance. Whatever else people might think of Jesus, most would agree that he was a teacher of profound influence. If he wasn't, why would people still ask themselves, 'What would Jesus do?' They're seeking his wisdom. Hoping to end someone's suffering. The connection between these two great faith traditions seems obvious to me."

"I'd never thought about that," Mulchrone admitted. "I'm afraid my faith is the only one I've studied."

"Because it has served you so well," DeWitt said.

"Yes, exactly."

"And following your faith led you here to me today."

Mulchrone hung his head. "Yes."

"Obviously, though, it never instructed you to kill anyone."

The priest shook his head.

DeWitt said, "That was strictly a failing on your part."

"It was." Mulchrone's voice began to quaver. "For which I am grievously sorry."

That was the moment the deputy director took the man in front of him seriously. His remorse was true, deep and painful. It would be with him a long time. Probably for the remaining days of his life.

DeWitt asked, "Did you go to confession, Father, before you came here?"

Mulchrone looked up. "I did."

"Were you absolved of your sins?"

"I was, provided I do everything I can to help you."

The deputy director was a graduate of Boalt Hall, the law school at UC Berkeley.

He knew a hedged answer when he heard one.

DeWitt said, "Meaning there are things you can't do to help me. Because they would violate church law."

"Yes."

"Okay. Let's start with what you can do to help. Tell me whatever you can."

DeWitt had been recording Mulchrone since the priest stepped into his office. So he just sat back in his chair and listened. Heard the man say the new museum in town, Inspiration Hall, was going to be hit by a truck bomb tomorrow. One of tremendous power. The detonation was supposed to take place while the president and her husband were on the premises.

The public and the media might not have known the nature of the new building, but the FBI did. In post-9/11 America, you didn't get to build a large structure in the heart of a major U.S. city and keep its purposes hidden from the national security agencies. The wonder of Inspiration Hall was that none of the people who knew about it had leaked the news and spoiled the surprise.

What shocked DeWitt was that an aged priest who wandered in off the street knew in advance what the president would be doing on a Sunday when she had no public events scheduled. At least there weren't any on her official schedule that the White

House routinely shared with the FBI. The deputy director wondered if even the Secret Service knew.

For everyone's sake, he sure as hell hoped so.

He asked Mulchrone, "When is the president supposed to be at this location."

"Ten-thirty in the morning is what I heard."

"Who told you?"

"A man named Harlan Fisk. He leads the First Michigan Militia."

"How did he know?"

"I don't know his source of information."

DeWitt saw only painful sorrow in the priest's eyes. No hint of deceit or willful withholding of information. Not on this point.

"All right, Father. I'll make sure this information gets to the Secret Service. You may have just saved the lives of the president, her husband and who knows who else. But you're holding back other information on me. The only reason you'd do that is because you heard it in the context of a confession."

"I can't say a word about that," Mulchrone said.

"Because church law says so, but here's the thing, Father. If you're protecting one of the people behind an attempt on the president's life, and if that person sees tomorrow's plan fail, he might try again. Might even succeed. Then you won't have saved the president's life at all, and you'll be an accomplice to an assassination."

The horror of that idea registered in Mulchrone's eyes.

DeWitt added to it. "Then, of course, there's always the collateral damage. Maybe James J. McGill. Men, women and children who just happen to be in the wrong place at the wrong time."

The deputy director leaned over his desk.

"Remember what I told you, Father? My faith tells me that you end suffering by eliminating ignorance. If that doesn't get you out of the awful corner you've put yourself in, pay heed to what your faith instructs. Ask yourself: What would Jesus do?"

***

Montreal-Trudeau Airport — Montreal, Canada

René Simonet pretended to wait patiently to board the Air France flight to Paris, traveling under his own name. He knew of the name the police had given him, of course. Laurent Fortier. It had amused him the first time he'd heard of it. As the legend surrounding Fortier grew, it even pleased him. The police were looking for a larger-than-life figure of their own creation. That could only serve to insulate him from apprehension.

The police were a small concern compared to the way Simonet felt about Tyler Busby at the moment. The more he thought about the ten million euros Busby had deposited in his Swiss account — the one the American knew about — the less he believed it was hush money. What it really was, Simonet thought, was please-stop-thinking-clearly money.

As long as Simonet, Benedict and Duvessa had been in business with Busby, he'd never been anything but a hardheaded businessman, driving the hardest bargains for their services that he could manage. Busby was a former colleague of Benedict's and the two of them had contrived an offshoot of the sell-the-forgery-to-the-sucker scam.

Busby would buy the forgery and swap it for a genuine, albeit stolen, masterpiece that one of his plutocrat friends had bought from other art thieves. The other fat cat thought he was getting an item of equal cachet and monetary value while insulating himself from a charge of being the receiver of stolen goods. The people who Busby dealt with didn't give a damn about the intrinsic value of the art; they cared about power, status and ego.

The signature at the bottom of the painting was what they craved.

Only one of them, that Simonet knew of, had either the wit or the interest to see if the painting he'd received from Busby was the genuine article. Learning he'd been snookered, the fellow sent a thug to deal with Busby. The thug was met by Special Agent Osgood Riddick of the FBI and told to forget about vengeance and mend his ways. For emphasis, the thug was Van Gogh-ed. Lost an ear. He was sent back to his boss with the message that there was no telling what might be cut off *him,* if he kept making trouble.

That was the Tyler Busby that Simonet knew.

He didn't give away small fortunes to buy silence.

Armed with that knowledge, Simonet knew it was time to get back France and start looking for a new home, for himself and his art. The money Busby had put in Simonet's Swiss account was meant to lull him into a false sense of security. Give Busby the time to arrange for Simonet's disappearance and … *Mon Dieu,* Simonet saw what Busby wanted more than his life.

He wanted Simonet's *collection,* all the paintings he'd stolen the past twenty-five years.

If the man would put himself in league with terrorists to cover up his thefts from the Ransom and Drucker collections — as Benedict had hinted to Simonet — he would hardly leave Simonet's treasures unplundered.

That horrifying epiphany had no sooner occurred to Simonet than he asked himself how Busby would lead him to the slaughter. What lure would he use? There could be only one.

He was packing his bag to make his escape when Duvessa called.

She told him, "It's been too long since we've spent a night together. I've booked a suite for us at the Pierre tonight. Are you interested?"

Simonet said, "*Certainment.*"

He scheduled their tryst for three hours after he caught his flight to Montreal with a connection to Paris. The connecting flight had a mechanical problem, delaying its departure for four hours. Each minute had been agony for Simonet. He was sure his fate was closing in on him. He contained his rage only so he didn't draw attention to himself.

The announcement finally came that all was now well with the damn plane and boarding began. Simonet flew business class. The leg room was adequate and a passenger called less attention to himself than he would have in first class. He was about to doze when a cabin attendant came by to take his drink order.

She began to chat. Not wanting to make a bad impression, Simonet engaged with her, hoping the conversation would be brief. It was long enough for her to draw out of him that he was an art dealer. She liked that, his being a man of culture. She immediately offered him a free upgrade to first class.

He decided it would look suspicious not to accept, and so he did, saying thank you. The new window seat was much more comfortable than his old one. Rather than worry pointlessly, he decided to take comfort in the added sense of luxury. He would sleep peacefully all the way across the Atlantic. When he awoke, he would catch the quick flight to Lyon. He would make the short drive to Annecy.

And he would start packing his paintings.

Before they could be stolen from him.

The President's Bedroom

McGill sat in a chair opposite the foot of the bed where Patti slept. She lay on her side, unmoving, her respiration just barely audible. The picture of someone restfully asleep. For the moment, McGill's job was to see that no one disturbed the president's slumber.

He'd been out of bed for an hour now, after catching ninety minutes of sleep. He always drifted off these days after he and Patti had made love. They both conked out within minutes. Sex used to be an exercise of grand passion and racing heartbeats. Now, it was a marital sleep aid. That was just fine with him.

Nobody would ever be able to put that feeling of blissful peace in a bottle.

Having departed from their bed to put himself between his beloved and the evil schemes of the outside world, McGill's mood had darkened considerably. When Patti had first mentioned to him that she was going to run for the presidency, he'd said, "Who better?"

Now, as they faced a second four-year term in the White House, he thought, "Why us?"

In all his years as a sworn police officer, he'd never done anything worse to anyone than flatten a nose. Since moving to 1600 Pennsylvania Avenue, he'd killed two men, one of them intentionally, the other to save Galia Mindel's life.

Well, if he wanted to rationalize things, he'd saved his life, and Sweetie's and Elspeth's, when he threw a madman out a window. So he could justify his actions in both cases. That didn't keep him from having the faces of both John Patrick Granby and Damon Todd come to mind when he wasn't busy thinking of something else.

Having those two to contend with for the rest of his life was bad enough, but with hostile crazies threatening to kill Patti *and* his kids it wasn't hard to imagine adding to his body count. The name Harlan Fisk was at the top of his potential hit list.

Goddamn the man.

He involved his own child in a plot to kill the president and thought she should skate on that or McGill's kids would pay with their lives? The SOB needed to be firmly instructed on the error of his ways. As stupid and vile as his actions had been, the lesson might well be terminal. The thing was, McGill didn't dread being the one to administer it. If Fisk didn't see the light in short order, show actual penitence, McGill thought there might be satisfaction if not pleasure in putting him out of his miserable existence.

Make an example of him that would not soon be forgotten.

You come at me and mine, this is what will happen to you.

That thought made McGill muffle a harsh laugh with his hand. What was that saying Pruet had shared with him? The devil on the doorstep. McGill had the satanic bastard sitting on his lap, purring like a tabby cat as McGill's rage stroked him.

McGill had told the White House switchboard the president would not be taking any calls that night. But the phone he held in his hand started to ring. Someone who had the direct line and knew the coded suffix for the president's bedroom. A very short list. McGill tapped the answer button in less than a second.

He saw that Patti remained asleep.

He looked at the caller ID. Welborn Yates.

"Yes," McGill said softly.

"Mr. McGill? Sorry to disturb you. I just heard from a military friend on the Mall. Harlan Fisk and his militia are surrounded. We have air support overhead. But they haven't put down their weapons." Welborn took a deep breath. "The brass on the scene haven't relayed this information to the White House yet, as far as I know, but Fisk says his people are going to shoot it out with our guys unless … unless he gets to talk to the president or you."

Easy choice, McGill thought.

"I was just thinking of Mr. Fisk," he said. "Tell him I'll be right over."

Four Seasons Hotel — Washington, DC

Yves Pruet was softly playing Chopin's Nocturne in C-Sharp Minor. The piece had been written for the piano, but the magistrate managed it quite nicely on the guitar. He knew his playing did not rise to the level of a virtuoso, but it was not far from it. The guitar *Monsieur McGill* had lent him had a lovely tone. A Martin, borrowed from a young fellow at the White House, he recalled. Pruet would have to get his name, send him a token of appreciation.

He glanced over at the living room sofa where Odo lay drowsing. After returning from their walk that evening, neither of them had decided to retire for the night, as if they'd both anticipated that their sleep might be disturbed. Pruet had continued the discussion of going into the private investigations business and affiliating himself with *Monsieur McGill.*

"Of course, I will need help," he told Odo.

His bodyguard had yet to commit himself to the idea.

"I will find you a wonderful secretary," his friend replied.

"I was thinking of someone with practical experience."

"A police secretary then."

"Very well, if you are not interested," Pruet said.

"I would have my own office?" Odo asked.

"Of course."

"Slightly smaller than yours naturally, but with an equally good view."

"Perhaps just a bit more off center."

"My salary will be respectable?" Odo asked.

"Assuming anyone wants our services, yes."

"We will both take all the usual holidays?"

"As any good Frenchman would," Pruet said.

Odo nodded in approval. "I think we could make a go of it. Associating ourselves with *Monsieur McGill* will lend us a good measure of prestige, but …"

Odo paused to think.

"But what?" Pruet asked.

"We will need a woman. No, two women."

Pruet looked at his friend, not quite sure what he was proposing.

Odo told him. "We will need a female investigator to provide us with a woman's insights into our investigations, and we will need someone to run our office."

"D'accord," Pruet said. "You are a born executive."

"I have my moments," Odo allowed.

He stretched out on the sofa and closed his eyes. Pruet picked up the guitar and began to play. Softly. At a level that couldn't possibly disturb any other guest of the hotel. Also, his selection of compositions was meant to aid sleep not disrupt it.

Just look what it did for Odo. Finishing the Chopin piece, the magistrate felt as if he might finally be ready to turn in for the night. Then, of course, the phone rang.

He picked up the receiver, saw that Odo now had his eyes open, was sitting up, ready to jump into action in a heartbeat.

"Oui?" Pruet said.

"Monsieur le Magistrat?" a feminine voice said. "SAC Elspeth

Kendry. *Monsieur McGill, est-il avec vous?"*

SAC Elspeth Kendry calling. Is Mr. McGill with you?

Speaking English, Pruet replied, "I'm sorry, special agent. He is not here. Is something the matter?"

Pruet heard the note of irritation in her voice as she said, "Sometimes Mr. McGill forgets to leave word of his movements."

The magistrate could easily imagine the problems the president's henchman would present to those who sought to be his minders.

"If I should see him, would you like me to let him know you called?" Pruet asked.

"Thank you, no. I'll find him and have a chat soon enough. I'm sorry I disturbed you."

"C'est rien," Pruet told her. It's nothing.

"Who is not here?" Odo asked.

Pruet told him, and asked, "Odo will you please turn on the television? A news channel."

Odo found CNN, an American station available in Paris.

The magistrate and his bodyguard saw a view of two groups of soldiers, one surrounding the other. The men encircling the others looked tense but professional. The trapped group seemed scared and likely to either shoot or bolt. Hovering helicopters cast harsh light on all those below. Individual faces came into view, many of them revealing twitches and tics.

A caption at the bottom of the screen read: *Standoff on the Mall.*

Then the camera angle changed abruptly and a troubled newsman appeared and told his audience, "Our aerial reporting crew has just been ordered to leave the area, the sky, over the mall by the military. We've been told that it's for reasons of their own safety, so they won't risk being shot down by gunfire or surface-to-air missiles. But without an overhead view and with access to the Mall being denied at street level, there will be no news cameras to cover this crisis."

"This does not look good, Yves," Odo said, turning off the TV.

"Not at all," the magistrate agreed. "So where else might *Monsieur McGill* be?"

The two Frenchmen headed for the Mall, Pruet making Odo leave his gun behind.

Southeast Gate — The White House

SAC Elspeth Kendry, muttering to herself, headed out of the White House grounds in an armored black Chevy Suburban. She wondered if her predecessor Celsus Crogher had once been a bronzed god, leached of all his pigment by four years of having to deal with James J. McGill.

How the hell could the man who was married to the president, and the father of three young children, charge off without notice into what might turn out to be the worst act of armed conflict on American soil since the Civil War? That was what SAC Kendry wanted to know. Christ, for all she knew, Madman McGill might intend to draw all the hostilities his way.

That'd be just like him.

It wasn't just McGill who'd made her crazy. What the hell was she going to do about newly reinstated Special Agent Donald "Deke" Ky? She'd tried reaching him. Her call went to voice mail. Shit. That wasn't *ever* supposed to happen with one of her agents.

Then again, she hadn't checked her email before running out of the building.

Maybe Special Agent Ky had resigned again. Given her two seconds notice. Was once again a gumshoe working directly for the man whose neck she wanted to wring. Only she knew she couldn't take him. As tough and well-trained as she was, McGill was bigger, stronger and knew more dirty-fighting tricks — techniques, if you wanted to be polite — than anyone she'd ever met. And that was saying a lot.

She supposed she could just shoot him. Not fatally, of course.

Just hobble him. Slow him down a little.

That might put a crimp in her career plans, though.

Shit, shit, shit, she —

Slammed on the brakes as she was cut off just before she reached the Hamilton Place access road to Fifteenth Street. Some suicidal jerk in a Mercedes SLK hardtop had stopped directly in front of her. Elspeth had her door open and a hand on her sidearm when the driver's window on the SLK went down and she saw Deputy Director Byron DeWitt with his hands meekly raised in a gesture of surrender.

Elspeth heard footsteps charging up from behind her. She saw three uniformed Secret Service officers coming her way to provide backup. She shook her head and help up a hand. "It's okay," she said, "he's one of us, almost. FBI."

Those last three letters told the uniforms all they needed to know.

Uttering perfectly audible deprecations, they returned to their post.

Turning back to DeWitt, she found him out of his car and standing three paces from her. Elspeth said, "I'm in a helluva hurry here. You want to get your car out of my way?"

DeWitt said, "Sure, right away. I've just come from hearing the confession of an entirely believable plan to assassinate the president, but I'll find someone else to tell."

Elspeth ground her teeth.

"Move your car and get in mine. You can talk while I drive."

"All right. Where are we going?"

"The Mall. They're throwing a party and we're going to crash it."

The Residence — The White House

Galia Mindel didn't know where she was when her secretary woke her. She lay on her office sofa right where she'd fallen asleep. Once that fact registered, Galia knew something awful must have happened. She wouldn't have been disturbed otherwise.

Without saying a word, Ginny, her secretary, turned on the

television.

The sound was off but the caption, *Standoff on the Mall,* told the story.

Galia asked, "Does the president know?"

"I called the Residence. Blessing told me Mr. McGill left a strict do-not-disturb order."

"Damn," Galia said. Then she caught the underlying message. "What do you mean left?"

"Blessing didn't explain, but SAC Kendry called a few minutes earlier to ask if Mr. McGill was with you? I said no, and she cursed none too subtly. I thought I'd better see if anything was going on out there in the world."

Meaning beyond the White House perimeter, Galia knew.

She looked back at the TV screen. Had no doubt where McGill was.

Galia said, "Thank you, Ginny. You did exactly the right thing. Hold down the fort."

Her secretary nodded, but Galia was already hurrying off to the Residence. Like anyone with a cursory knowledge of the Second World War in Europe, Galia knew that Germany lost the opportunity to launch an effective counterattack on the Allied invasion of Normandy because nobody wanted to wake a sleeping Hitler so he could give the go-ahead.

Galia didn't think matters were quite that momentous now, but who knew?

Maybe the High Command in Berlin had thought: No big deal; we'll get 'em tomorrow.

She bullied her way past the Residence staff and the Secret Service. She caught absolutely no grief from the president for waking her up. The two of them sat side-by-side and watched an anchorman sum up the situation for two minutes.

Then the president said to Galia, "Get me a line to whomever is in charge on the Mall."

***

The Mall — Washington, DC

Deke Ky showed his Secret Service badge to get McGill and himself past the outer perimeter of Metro Police lines at the Mall. Civilian federal law enforcement personnel did double-takes when they saw McGill, but none of them tried to stop him either. The frontline Special Operations Command Marines needed a word with him.

"Who're you again?" First Lieutenant Quentin Cole asked.

McGill patiently repeated, "James J. McGill."

"And who're you with?"

"The president of the United States," Deke snapped. He was tense enough, helping McGill get through this minefield of government personnel. He didn't need the military gumming things up. "Mr. McGill is the president's husband."

McGill nodded. He told the lieutenant, "Mr. Fisk asked to see me. He's also threatened to kill my children. I'm here to change his mind."

Lieutenant Cole looked McGill up and down. "Are you armed, sir? I ask because we know that Fisk fellow ..." Cole inclined his head. "That's him right over there. He has an assault rifle in his hands and a knife fastened to his leg."

McGill looked at Fisk. Judged him to be a bit younger than he was. Maybe an inch or two taller, thirty pounds or so heavier. He watched the way the man shifted his weight from one foot to the other and back. Saw how he carried his carbine. Took note of the tension in his hands as he opened and close his fingers around the weapon.

The guy was on edge. Knew he stood a better chance of dying than seeing another sunrise.

McGill said, "I'm unarmed, Lieutenant."

Deke leaned forward and whispered to McGill, "SAC Kendry just arrived at the perimeter. You want to make your move, you'd better do it quick."

McGill nodded and told the young Marine officer, "I'm going

to talk to Mr. Fisk now."

"What if he doesn't want to change his mind, sir?"

"I'll either persuade him, Lieutenant, or I'll beat him into the ground."

Lieutenant Cole saluted McGill and received one in return.

Then McGill headed straight for Fisk.

Lieutenant Cole told Deke, "That sack of shit over there tries to use anything but his bare hands to defend himself, I'm gonna smoke his ass."

Deke didn't place much faith in the power of persuasion either.

He said, "Me, too."

Florida Avenue — Washington, DC

Sweetie and Putnam had brought his niece — their prospective adopted daughter — home the previous evening. Maxine had been anything but eager to leave her grandparents, Cissy and Emory Jenkins, but the old folks had told her she'd have to get ready to go back to school soon. Well, to enroll in a new school, that was.

The thought of losing all her school friends, too, reduced Maxine to hysterics.

Sweetie longed to comfort the girl, but Maxine wanted no part of her. Tall, blonde and formidable, Sweetie looked nothing like her pert African-American mother. The very idea of being turned over to Sweetie terrified the child.

The situation might have been hopeless, had it not been for Putnam. He stepped up when no one else could. He took a seat on the Jenkins' living room sofa and extended his arms to Maxine. She stared at him a good, long time. Sweetie thought she might flee from the room, maybe even the house, but with tears rolling down her cheeks she told Putnam, "You look like my daddy."

Putnam said, "I do?"

He saw Cissy and Emory nod. Maxine did, too.

"I didn't know that," Putnam said. "The last time I saw my brother, he was a baby. That was when my parents left me."

Sweetie saw Putnam's eyes moisten.

"Why'd they do that?" Maxine asked.

"They were in trouble," Putnam said. "They did some bad things and had to run away. They didn't want me to have to run, too. So they left me with your grandma and grandpa."

"You never got to see your mama and daddy again?" Maxine asked.

Putnam shook his head, and Maxine ran to him. He embraced her and she said, "I'm so sad, aren't you?"

"Yes, it's very hard, but Margaret and I will do everything we can to help you."

Maxine gave Sweetie a dubious look, then buried her face in Putnam's chest.

"Can we at least live in Baltimore?" the girl asked.

"We can visit every weekend," Putnam said. Looking at Sweetie, he added, "And your friends can visit us in Washington."

Sweetie nodded.

Maxine looked at her grandparents and asked if they'd visit, too. Cissy and Emory promised they would. After a tearful goodbye, the three of them left for Washington. Sweetie drove. Putnam sat in back with an arm around Maxine.

They put Maxine in their guest bedroom. Sweetie took Putnam aside as Maxine put up some posters and otherwise decorated her new quarters. Sweetie said, "Maybe I should stay downstairs in my old place just for a while. Give you time to help Maxine adjust."

Putnam said, "No damn way. Max will come to need you soon enough, and I need you right now. Max will come around, Margaret, I know she will."

They took the child for a walk, bought her dinner and an ice cream cone.

Sweetie didn't want Putnam calling the girl Max unless she was agreeable.

So as they returned to their townhouse, Sweetie asked, "Do you like to be called Maxine or do you have a nickname?"

The girl looked at her and said, "Mama and Daddy call me

Maxi; I like that."

"May Putnam and I call you Maxi, too?"

The girl looked at Sweetie, considered and nodded.

Then she asked, "Do you have a nickname?"

"My friends call me Sweetie."

The girl giggled and ran up the front steps. Putnam took Maxi to her room to talk with her before she went to sleep. After an hour, Sweetie looked in on them. Maxi was asleep in her bed; Putnam was curled up on the floor, a stuffed elephant tucked under his head for a pillow. Sweetie put a blanket over him and closed the door behind her.

She went to the living room, sat in her favorite chair and said her rosary.

Not ready for sleep after that and not knowing what else to do, she turned on the television, with the sound down, and saw a panel of reporters wearing their most serious faces and talking in grave tones. A caption beneath the panel read: Armies on the Mall.

By reflex, Sweetie asked herself: Is Jim involved in this?

Her answer was to jump up, leave a note for Putnam and rush out the door.

All but certain McGill was on the Mall and would be glad to see her.

The Oval Office

"The Secret Service won't let —" Galia Mindel started to say, attempting to repeat a warning she'd given the president several times already.

The president held up a hand to cut her off.

Despite having misgivings that left her trembling, the chief of staff knew better than to ignore a presidential order to keep quiet. The president was on the phone now, had placed the call herself and the party on the other end had just picked up.

"Jean? I'm terribly sorry to wake you, but I need you to get down here right away. The Oval Office, yes." The president listened for a moment. "Yes, I'm afraid it is that serious. After we're done speaking, I'm going to call the chief justice and have him be here with you."

Oh, God, Galia thought, she's really going to do it.

The chief of staff saw the president smile.

"Thank you, Jean. That means the world to me, but this is something I really have to do myself. No, I'll have left before you arrive. That's why it's important that you hurry."

Not allowing Galia an opportunity to speak, the president placed a call to Chief Justice Craig MacLaren and dragged him out of his bed, too. He promised he'd be at the White House within minutes. By the time the president put the phone down, Galia had tears in her eyes.

"To hell with the Secret Service," the chief of staff said, "*I* won't let you do this."

The president put her hands on Galia's shoulders, kissed her on each cheek.

"You are my beloved older sister," she said. "It looks like Jean Morrissey is becoming my kid sister, and she's more impetuous than I am. If it turns out that she needs you, I want you to be there for her. Promise me that, Galia."

The chief of staff bobbed her head and then sobbed, throwing her arms around the president. Patti let her hold on for a moment and then eased free from the embrace. She stepped behind her desk and picked up the jacket that she had draped over the chair.

It was a brown leather bomber jacket. The presidential seal lay prominent on its right breast. In an arc above the seal were the words Commander in Chief. The only place Patricia Darden Grant had worn the jacket before that night was at Camp David.

Tonight, though, she intended to leave no doubt what her role would be. She thought the jacket looked good with her denim shirt, Levis and her black AdiZero shoes. Her hair was pinned back and she wore no makeup. Even at a time like this, appearances mattered. You had to look the part to bring it off successfully.

Taking a moment to compose herself, Patti Grant got her

game-face on.

With her usual impeccable timing, Edwina Byington opened the door to the Oval Office and said, "Madam President, Marine One is ready for take off."

Just then an image of McGill appeared on the muted television in the Oval Office. The image was grainy and flickering. The media may have been denied their usual tools to bring the world into everyone's living room, but it looked like someone had figured out a way to make a cell phone do the job. The president saw her husband approach an armed man.

She strode out the door.

Jim had forced her hand.

The country and the world had to be shown.

The president of the United States fought her own battles.

The National Mall — Washington, DC

McGill knew he was walking toward Fisk. He could see the distance between them diminish, but he didn't feel his feet touching the ground. He felt as if he were gliding a millimeter above the winter-withered grass. He was sure that, if he wanted, he could set upon Fisk and have the man's throat in hand, crush his windpipe before he could bring his rifle to bear, much less get a shot off.

Not that Fisk was motionless. His feet looked rooted to the earth, but his head tilted over one shoulder and then the other. His arms drew close to his chest and then relaxed. His hands tightened and then loosened their grips on the assault rifle. His knees flexed, as if to relieve tension in his legs rather than leap toward McGill or run away from him.

McGill took all this in, along with the blur of figures in the background, the body of men who called themselves a militia and came to their nation's capital bearing arms, the better to express their political grievances. Or maybe to see how many people they could kill as a means of establishing their preferred order. They weren't McGill's concern right now.

He had eyes only for Fisk.

He stopped ten feet away from the man.

"Are you Harlan Fisk?" McGill asked.

Fisk brought his carbine tight against his chest, as if that would keep him safe.

He nodded and said, "That's me."

"You know who I am?" McGill asked.

"I do."

McGill got right to the point. "Did you threaten to kill my children?"

Fisk's Adam's apple bounced up and down in his throat, as if he had a sudden problem swallowing. He looked past McGill, seeming to search for a more distant threat.

"You think somebody's going to shoot you?" McGill asked. Then he laughed, "You're not worried that you're being recorded, are you? That you might incriminate yourself if you make an admission of a crime. Believe me, that's the least of your troubles right now."

Anger flared in Fisk's eyes as he put them back on McGill.

He flicked the carbine's safety off.

McGill said, "You're going to shoot me? You'll be dead before you can point your weapon my way."

Fisk looked past McGill again still searching, looking at the trees lining both sides of the Mall.

"If you're trying to spot snipers, don't bother. Those guys are too good. They have real-world experience. Nobody's playing games here."

Fisk stared at McGill, angrier than ever.

"What about you, coming out here unarmed?"

"I came here to talk because I was told you wanted to see me."

"I want you to let my Elvie go," Fisk said.

"Because of the threat you made, even if you won't repeat it now. That won't happen. But if you and your friends lay down your guns, give up without a fight or trying to run, things could look pretty good for Elvie."

Fisk gave a harsh laugh.

"You'd like that, wouldn't you? One man taking down the First Michigan Militia without firing a shot."

McGill shrugged. "Seems like the wisest course to me. That and you apologizing for making your threat. Saying it will never happen again."

Fisk squinted when he tried to find the snipers this time.

It didn't help. He looked back at McGill.

"Even if your snipers kill me, some of my boys will kill you."

McGill nodded. "And then *all* of them will die. Right here and now. Is that what you want? To be the fool who led all these other fools to their deaths? Be a hell of a way to go down in history. An example of exactly what *not* to do when you've got a grievance to express."

Fisk's face tightened. His lips curled as if he might start to snarl. McGill saw the guy just might be nuts enough to start a bloodbath. He thought it was time to go to Plan B.

"Okay," McGill said, "I can see how you feel. You've put in a lot of effort, you've come a long way. Just giving up, that would hardly be satisfying. You need to do … what? See if you can knock my head off my shoulders?"

Fisk said, "That'd be a real good start. Those other bastards behind you could lock me up, execute me if they want, I'd still feel okay about it if I pounded you first."

"Sure, you'd be a hero. People would remember you the way you want."

McGill leaned forward from his waist and said in a quiet voice, "So let's do it. Just you and me. Bare hands."

"I disarm, your asswipes will kill me for sure."

"And let your people kill me? The way you just said." McGill shook his head. "No they won't. If you won't fight me, it's only because you're afraid. Your people will see that, too. Then where will you be?"

McGill saw that Fisk was trying to sort out how he'd found himself in this box.

So he helped him, and said, "You know Elvie ratted you out, right? That's how the *real* military was able to spring this trap on you."

For a second, McGill thought Fisk would try to shoot him. He was deciding which way to move to give the snipers he *hoped* were watching and waiting their best shot. Then Fisk clicked the carbine's safety back on and tossed the weapon off to his right.

"The knife, too, if you're feeling manly," McGill said.

Fisk unstrapped his knife and tossed it to his other side.

Two of his people came and retrieved their leader's weapons, and backed off.

McGill took a step back, too. He expected Fisk to charge him.

He didn't. He looked at McGill, spread his arms and raised his hands to chest height. Moving in on McGill slowly, he smiled and told him, "I'm going to break you in two."

That being the case, McGill gave Fisk the best chance he'd ever get.

He rushed the bigger man.

As Deke Ky had informed McGill, SAC Elspeth Kendry and Deputy Director Byron DeWitt had arrived at the outer ring of security lining the Mall. The two senior officials had just badged and threatened the Metro cops into submission and were about to start forward when a woman's voice called out, "Elspeth! DeWitt! Wait a minute!"

They turned to see who wanted their attention. Rushing toward them were Margaret Sweeney and McGill's two friends from France. Before Sweetie could say another word, Elspeth held up a hand like a traffic cop and told them, "No, no damn way. You're all staying right here."

Sweetie looked at DeWitt.

He looked at Sweetie and turned to Elspeth. "This woman is McGill's partner, his confidant, probably more important to him than anyone besides the president and his kids. She might be helpful."

Elspeth looked as if someone had just cleaved her skull with a dull axe.

"You want to bring the French, too?" she asked, clearly hoping for a no.

"Strength in numbers," DeWitt said.

Elspeth looked as if she might scream when a new voice, this one gruff and masculine, asked, "Are we in time?"

Celsus Crogher and Welborn Yates hurried over to the others.

Each was wearing the combat fatigues of his former or current service.

Celsus said, "What the hell are we waiting for? Don't you know Holly G. is on the way?"

Elspeth's eyes bugged out. Then she had to run to catch up with the others as the man who used to have her job and the others bulled their way through the lines of security.

Harlan Fisk reacted just the way McGill thought a guy his size would. If you wanted to crush a guy in a bear hug and he was nice enough to step forward, you put the clamps on him and watched him turn purple, listened for his spine to crack as you crushed the life out of him. McGill could have gone chest to chest with Fisk and delivered half-a-dozen blows before Fisk's hands had the time to lock behind his back.

Problem with that strategy, though, is that any one of the blows he delivered to Fisk — throat-collapsing, cervical spine-fracturing strikes — might be fatal. In the flurry needed to keep Fisk from succeeding with his plan, Fisk would certainly be killed. McGill didn't want that.

Not yet anyway.

So before he collided with Fisk, McGill ducked to his left, swung both of his arms up in an arc, catching Fisk's right arm from behind, sweeping it aside like a windshield wiper pushing a leaf out of the way. Now, the upper half of McGill's body was outside Fisk's line of attack. Supporting his weight on his left leg, McGill slammed his right knee into Fisk's right quadriceps.

The man bellowed as if he'd been shot.

As Fisk started to crumple, his injured leg no longer up to the task of supporting his weight, McGill planted his right foot, pivoted and slammed the palm of his left hand into Fisk's right ear. For good measure, McGill kicked the outside of Fisk's right knee with his right foot.

Watching from a distance of twenty-five yards, Pruet said, "*Sacré bleu.*"

Literally, holy blue. Colloquially, holy shit.

Odo chuckled and did his best to mimic the flow of McGill's attack.

Deke Ky, Celsus Crogher, Welborn Yates, and Byron DeWitt all wore grim smiles.

First Lieutenant Cole, a complete professional, kept his eyes on all those guys on the other side carrying automatic weapons. Not a one of them looked happy. He heard his commanding officer through his ear bud. The CO had just given a heads-up to his snipers, who were in place and ready to rock 'n' roll. They were told who to take out first, namely the guys who looked like the second tier of militia leadership.

And any sonofabitch who raised a rifle to firing position.

Elspeth Kendry was as amazed as anyone at what McGill had accomplished.

As to her professional future, though, she thought she might retire soon.

Just like Celsus Crogher had.

Go live somewhere relatively peaceful. Beirut, maybe.

Fisk fell to his hands and his left knee; he couldn't place any weight on his right knee. His right leg trailed off limply behind him. His head drooped toward the earth and his eyes were squeezed shut in pain. He tilted his head as if trying to clear water from his right ear. That wasn't going to work, McGill knew.

The man was done fighting. His right leg was useless. Even if it had remained undamaged, the blow to his ear had ruined his sense of balance, certainly for the moment, maybe for good. There was no way in the world Harlan Fisk was any longer a threat to McGill or anyone else.

McGill thought he should feel good about this.

As far as he knew, though, Fisk was still unrepentant.

Maybe that was why he still wanted to hurt Fisk. Boot his head off his shoulders like an old-fashioned placekicker trying to put a football through the uprights from fifty yards out. The temptation was so strong McGill felt the devil had to be inside him now, hovering around his soul, looking for a place to land and claim it as his own.

McGill took a step back from Fisk.

Hoping the increased distance would calm him down.

Or maybe give him a running start for his kick.

Fisk took his head out of play by collapsing to the ground. Cries of shock and horror came from his men. Several of them started forward toward McGill. He looked at them without fear. His rage began to escalate. To hell with all these guys, he thought.

Then a voice, using a loudspeaker, got everyone's attention.

"Hold your positions or you will be fired upon."

Whoever had spoken did a fairly good imitation of the voice of God.

Fisk's men stopped their advance. Looked around. Saw they were about to be mowed down like ripe wheat if they continued forward.

McGill turned his gaze back to Fisk. Despite the potential consequences, he knew all it would take for him to bring a knee down on Fisk's spine, just the way Elspeth had done with Ozzie Riddick, only with greater force, would be for Fisk to give him one fuck-you.

Fisk didn't comply. He only managed to look up at McGill and offer him a smile. Like he knew something McGill didn't. Like he would have the last laugh.

Close enough, pal, McGill thought.

You just chose your own fate.

McGill took one step toward Fisk when he and everyone else heard a helicopter coming in low, loud and fast. A beam of light from above found McGill. He knew it wasn't a beacon from heaven. He didn't hear a fanfare of trumpeting angels; he recognized the engine note of the approaching aircraft.

Marine One.

The president was about to arrive. To save him from himself. As bloodthirsty and crazed as he might be, he wasn't going to kill a fallen man in front of Patti. McGill's head slumped now, and he, too, fell to his knees.

"Is that my husband?" the president asked.

Neither the flight crew nor the squad of combat Marines in the passenger cabin could make a positive identification of the man on his knees or the one lying face down. Traveling with the Marines was a Navy corpsman. Bodies were repositioned so the corpsman would be the second man out of the aircraft, after the Marine officer taking the point position.

The president knew better than to try to force her way to the front.

All she could do for the moment was worry and pray that Jim wasn't seriously hurt.

Marine One landed with a jolt hard enough to put some spring into the guys going out the door. The president had been told to wait until she was give the all clear sign before exiting the aircraft. She'd nodded, but everyone understood she wasn't going to wait long so they'd better be quick about their business.

She counted to ten, thought about taking a quick peek out the door.

Decided that wouldn't look good. Far too timid. She had a part to play here and being timid was not included in the character description. She descended the steps from the helicopter like she owned all that she surveyed.

The first thing she saw was Jim, on his feet now, and smiling at her.

He gave her a salute and said, "Madam President."

She walked up to him and responded, "Stalwart henchman. You're all right?"

"You saved me."

"You *are* hurt?" She turned to the Navy corpsman who was attending the fallen man she'd seen from the aircraft.

Before she could reset the corpsman's priorities, McGill touched her arm.

"I'm not hurt," he said. "I'll explain later."

SAC Kendry arrived on the run; Celsus Crogher was at her side.

The president smiled at them. "Elspeth, Celsus. Please don't say anything to me about leaving immediately."

"Never occurred to me," Celsus Crogher said.

Elspeth said, "Madam President, this is still a dangerous situation."

"I know, but I have some work to do. I'll leave as soon as I can."

One of the Marines who'd arrived with the president handed her a megaphone.

"We're ready, Captain?" she asked.

"Yes, ma'am. You won't need to go far. Your voice will carry."

The president gave her henchman a look. He understood.

The cluster of Marines notwithstanding, this was a solo act.

Harlan Fisk was taken away on a stretcher and Patricia Darden Grant filled the space he'd vacated. She looked out at hundreds of heavily armed fellow Americans who had come to tell her ...what? That she'd better get the hell out of the White House? Leave town and maybe the country while she was at it? If that was what they wanted, they were going to be disappointed.

She raised the megaphone and said, "If you lay down your arms right now, I will extend to all of you a presidential pardon for anything you've done tonight that directly involves your presence here. I will also meet with ten members of your rank and file at the White House to discuss any problems you might have with me or my administration.

"If you don't lay down your weapons, you will all be arrested. If any of you uses his weapon, the armed forces of the United States will return overwhelming fire. Chances are all of you will be killed.

"You will make your decision now. When I lower this megaphone, you must put your weapons on the ground. If you don't, we'll know you've chosen confrontation. I will step back and the military will take command of the situation. That's all I have to say to you."

Not rushing it, the president lowered the megaphone.

Many of the First Michigan Militia dropped their weapons immediately. Most of the others followed a heartbeat behind. There were three instances where hardheads had to be wrestled to the ground by their compatriots. Even so, not a shot was fired.

The Marines moved in to seize the weapons.

Squads of military police ran forward to form up the militiamen for processing and, barring any outstanding criminal warrants, for eventual release. They would have to get home on their own dollars. They would not be taking any firearms, knives or other weapons with them.

The president truly hoped they did send representatives to talk with her.

She would address any legitimate complaints as best she could.

She also wanted to know what potential enemies were thinking.

After being assured that everything was well in hand, the president walked over to McGill and asked him, "Can a girl give you a lift, handsome?"

Not giving a damn about protocol, McGill put an arm around Patti.

They climbed aboard Marine One.

Went home, hoping to get some sleep.

Unfortunately, SAC Kendry and Deputy Director Byron DeWitt joined them and said there were pressing matters that wouldn't keep.

Pruet watched McGill and *Madame la Présidente* depart. The magistrate said, "What a remarkable country, don't you think, *mon ami?*"

Not getting a response, he turned to see Odo was on his cellphone, apparently listening to someone speak, saying yes, yes several times and then finally *au revoir.*

"To whom were you speaking?" Pruet asked.

Odo said, "Père Louvel. He told me that Gabriella Casale has not only discovered Laurent Fortier's real name, she —"

"What is the name?" Pruet asked.

"René Simonet. She has also found out where he lives, Annecy, before you ask. Simonet, I was told, has a house and an art gallery there. He seems not to be at home at the moment, but the Louvels have gathered in Annecy, and they're awaiting representatives of other families who have lost art to For — I mean, to Simonet. The good father asked if we would care to join him."

"At once," Pruet said.

He took off at a trot. Odo could not remember the last time he'd seen his friend run. Assuming he didn't mean to run directly to the airport, Odo caught up, turned the magistrate around and pointed him toward their hotel.

The Oval Office

Galia Mindel didn't observe proper behavior either when the president returned to the White House, alive and well. The chief of staff grabbed the president and held her tight, crying, smiling and kissing her cheek. After a moment or two, McGill told his wife, "Let me know when I should pry her off you."

Galia shot him a look, but the president told her, "We do have some business to get to."

The chief of staff stepped back, and the chief justice moved forward to shake the president's hand. "Beautifully handled, Madam President. I'll be going now."

"Thank you, Craig. I'm sorry I disturbed your sleep."

He grinned and shook his head. "Always a privilege to see history being made."

The chief justice departed and the vice president took her turn with the president, hugging her briefly before stepping back. "Damn, I wish I'd been there with you, Madam President. If you don't need me any longer —"

"No, I'd like you to stay, Jean. You should be here for this briefing."

McGill raised his eyebrows, asking a silent question.

"You stay, too, Jim. Maybe you'll have an idea or two to offer."

The president ordered drinks, coffee or soda, for everyone. They all took their seats around the room and DeWitt repeated what Father Mulchrone had told him. Fisk, fearing the drone attack would fail without Arlo Carsten to supervise it, wanted to go to a fallback plan, a terror attack using a truck bomb. Old school but, as they all knew, horrifically effective.

"I've heard of this priest," Galia said, "if he's the Mulchrone from South Boston."

DeWitt said, "He is. He had a reputation as a real fire-and-brimstone guy. You toed the Vatican line or you burned forever and always."

"If he was so extreme," the president said, "that would explain his working with Harlan Fisk, but what turned him around?"

"He said it was a visit to his elder brother's grave at Arlington National Cemetery. Sergeant Desmond Mulchrone died a decorated hero in World War Two."

McGill thought the devil had been at the priest's doorstep, too, and the memory of his big brother had saved him.

DeWitt continued, "Father Mulchrone said he didn't know if the use of the truck bomb would change the target but he didn't think so. He said he didn't get the impression that the planning behind the attack was sophisticated enough to consider multiple targets."

McGill asked, "How hard could it be to go to Plan B, if you were still using drones? Seems like drones would give the bad guys all sorts of flexibility."

DeWitt said, "They would, if you had the right personnel to operate them. Without skilled operators, though, who knows what they might hit?"

Jean Morrissey said, "Somebody did a pretty good job snapping my picture."

The president nodded. "That's true. Jim, what do you think? Are the drones still in the picture?"

McGill said, "That's possible, yeah. Only how will taking down Fisk and his militia tonight affect things? Maybe we bagged the drone operators with all the others."

"Tech specialists don't usually muster out with the grunts," DeWitt said.

McGill said, "You're right, but unless the drone operators are *real* hard cases, they probably don't like their chances as much as they once did."

"You think they'll just call it quits?" the president asked.

McGill said, "If they were smart, no sure bet, they'd walk away from anything that could incriminate them. But some guys just can't bear to part with their toys. So, my take is we still have to plan against a drone attack, but I don't think it's as likely as it was."

SAC Kendry brought things back to what she saw as the main point, "Madam President, there's no way you or Mr. McGill can go to Inspiration Hall in a few hours. Even if there was no chance of a drone attack, we now know there's a truck bomb scenario."

"You're right, SAC Kendry," the president said. "We can't go."

Elspeth turned to look at McGill.

"I'm going to sleep in," he said. "Besides Inspiration Hall is filled with forgeries."

Everyone looked at McGill, and he explained.

Turning to DeWitt, he added, "I previously asked a party I'll leave unnamed to check on whether Hiram Busby had any construction work done on any of his homes in the past few years. Maybe the Bureau could expedite that little search. I think the original paintings Darren Drucker and Nathaniel Ransom donated to the museum are now in Busby's possession. It would be good to get them back and, of course, not let the forgeries that replaced them be either destroyed or removed."

DeWitt thought a moment. "It's going to be a good trick to find the bomber's truck before it gets to Inspiration Hall and keep him from detonating the bomb. That and find out if we're holding any drone operators other than Arlo Carsten. I'd better leave and get to work on all that right now." He stood and said, "Madam President, if you'll excuse me."

She nodded, but McGill had one more thing to say, "Why don't you let Welborn Yates and Celsus Crogher have another go at Arlo. See if they can't get him to be more forthcoming about the other drone operators and alternative targets for a drone attack? We still have an inauguration to consider."

With that, DeWitt and Elspeth Kendry got back to work.

Galia said she had things to do, too.

Jean Morrissey congratulated the president on a job well done.

She gave McGill a pat on the back. Said he did okay, too.

The First Couple went back to the Residence. They were asleep two minutes later.

I-495 — North Springfield, Virginia

Rutger Bierman drove a Ford F-650 box truck southeast on the Washington Beltway. Just ahead was the I-395 turnoff leading straight into the capital. The truck was rated as a Class 6 medium-duty vehicle with a gross vehicle weight rating of 19,501 to 26,000 pounds. Gross vehicle weight included the weight of the vehicle, fuel load, passenger load and cargo.

Rutger at his peak had weighed one hundred and nine kilograms — two hundred and forty pounds. With his blonde hair, blue eyes and mesomorphic build, he'd have given *Der Fuhrer* a hard-on, had he been born two generations earlier. Would have fit right in with the prevailing homicidal maniac spirit of the Reich, too.

Now, though, after the pain in his middle had turned out to be pancreatic cancer, causing him to lose weight and his skin to become nearly as yellow as his hair had once been, he was little more than half the man he used to be. Sixty kilos or one hundred and thirty-two pounds. He steered the truck onto I-395. The distance to Washington was thirteen miles. Sunday morning traffic was light. Travel time would be a matter of minutes.

The signage painted on the truck said it belonged to Special Moments Party Planners. "Let us make your occasion memorable." Six thousand pounds of ammonium nitrate detonated by an incendiary trigger device ought to make that Sunday a day no one would forget, Rutger thought. His GPS showed him the way to the location in Southeast Washington.

He didn't know what was there. He didn't care.

He would detonate his bomb and his cancer would be cured.

That was what Mama wanted, too. His father also would have been tickled, had he lived to see this day. Berti Bierman had been a member of the Red Army Faction, a communist, anti-imperialist group fighting what they described as the fascist German state of the 1970s and 1980s. Berti had survived participating in the gang's assassinations, bank robberies and kidnappings; he was shot while sleeping, though, by a comrade whose girlfriend he'd been shtupping. Not quite as slyly as he thought.

That girlfriend was Rutger's mother, née Brigitte Meisner. Since her conversion to Islam, she was known as Aalia um Asim. Meaning Aalia mother of Asim. Rutger's Arabic name was Asim. Formally, she also should have indicated the name of the man whose daughter she was, but Otto Meisner had been born and died an infidel, and had been a Nazi to boot. So he didn't make the cut.

Rutger thought denying Otto his due just because he was a fascist was wrong. Nonetheless, Rutger's jihadi stepfather, whose real name he'd never learned, gave him free rein to express the violent heart of his nature. That was, after he, too, had converted. Hence the name Asim.

For public purposes, Rutger was allowed to use his birth name. To maintain his cover as a decadent, atheistic Westerner, he was also allowed to drink, smoke and fornicate. He was also provided with a free apartment and a stipend. Life was good.

To pay the toll for all his privileges, Rutger had to beat the hell out of any German skinheads who had beaten the hell out of immigrant Muslims. Thus, revenge was had without casting blame where it belonged.

Rutger carried out his savagery with exuberance. Had his mother taken another path in life, of course, he likely would have been a skinhead. Things being what they were, he got to enjoy the irony as well as the brutality.

When he was diagnosed with the cancer, he was told he would die within six months. The pain would be terrible and the only available treatments would not cure him. They would make him feel even worse. All of which made him wonder what the hell good a pancreas was in the first place.

His doctor told him the pancreas helped to digest food and produced insulin. Food and insulin, he was reminded, were required to sustain life. That was a downer for Rutger. He'd hoped he could just cut the damn thing out himself. He'd always believed the most direct and forceful approach was the best solution to any problem.

Now he was stymied. He didn't have long to live and what time he had wasn't going to be any fun at all. So Rutger was receptive to the idea his stepfather brought to him: It was time to strike America and become a martyr.

If he did what he was told, his death would have great meaning and his mother would get a gift of one hundred thousand euros. Rutger agreed immediately. He was told he would be driving a truck filled with explosives. He would detonate it and he'd never feel any pain ever again.

As he came within ten minutes of the best hope he could have for as a happy ending, Rutger received a call on his cellphone. The same device would be used to send the signal to the detonator for the fertilizer bomb.

The man calling Rutger said one word: *Gewitter.*

German for thunderstorm.

Rutger almost drove the F-650 off the road. That would have made a hell of a mess, but without the incendiary device going off, there would have been no explosion. He brought the vehicle back into its lane, checked his mirrors and saw no police vehicle behind or ahead of him. His slip in composure had gone unnoticed.

Thunderstorm was the code word to abort the mission. A scout had preceded him in an innocuous American sedan to make sure all was well. He must have seen something he didn't like. Rutger didn't know who the scout was but he had to assume the man wasn't incompetent. If Rutger ignored the warning and drove into a trap, he might be killed before he could detonate his bomb.

If he was captured, he would he have live out the miserable remainder of his life in an American prison. Mama would get no money. She might even suffer if her husband thought Rutger had betrayed the cause. No good son could have that.

There was only one answer.

He would have to blow up something else.

Something that would please his stepfather.

Shannon International Airport — Ireland

René Simonet might have thanked God he'd made it across the Atlantic alive. Instead, he trembled with rage and residual terror from the flight he'd recently exited. The mechanical problem that had delayed his departure from Montreal, the one that had taken hours to correct, had reasserted itself en route. The port wing engine had to be shut down.

The captain relayed this tidbit when he announced the flight would have to make an unscheduled landing in Shannon, Ireland to guarantee the safety of all aboard. This guarantee did nothing to soothe the fears of the fellow in the seat next to Simonet. From the man's appearance, Simonet might have thought he was a minor bureaucrat, except that a government employee should have flown economy class. So maybe he was —

"I'm a risk management analyst," the man said.

He said he worked for a large insurance conglomerate.

"Would you like me to tell you how much losing an aircraft engine increases the odds that you'll not only have to put down at another airport but more likely crash into the ocean?"

Simonet said he would not like that.

Then the art thief said, trying to buttress his own confidence, "I thought all these modern airplanes are supposed to be able to fly with only one engine."

"They are," the risk analyst said. "Supposed to, that is. But if one engine malfunctions, would you like to know the chances the other one will, too?"

"No!" Simonet snapped.

From that point on, Simonet listened closely to the sound of the remaining engine, fearing that at any moment he might hear it falter. He looked for any sign of panic in the eyes of the cabin crew. He watched the progress line on the flight-in-motion map inch forward. Having a window seat, he peered down to confirm whether they were still above the open sea.

An atheist, he nonetheless prayed to see another dawn, the welcoming west coast of Ireland and the landing lights on the runway where they would safely return to earth. The rising sun came first and then the land mass that was the westernmost point of Europe. Not far now, he thought. Please, let us close the remaining distance safely.

The aircraft did, landed smoothly, rolled straight to the gate.

The captain apologized for the inconvenience. He informed his passengers that another plane would be sent to take them on to Paris. It should arrive sometime that afternoon; they would all be home in time for dinner. Lunch in Ireland would be compliments of the airline.

"What about drinks?" someone in economy bellowed.

The captain heard the question. "Very well, drinks, too."

A cheer went up from the cabin. Simonet did not join in the exultation.

He was determined to get home as quickly as he could, on some other airline. If they had been able to make London, he could have taken the Eurostar train, but no tunnel connected Ireland to the Continent. If there were no seats available on another flight, he thought he might go mad.

The only stop he made before beginning his search for alternate transportation was the men's room just off the arrival gate. He was standing at a urinal relieving himself when his seat-mate from the plane came to stand next to him.

Simonet paid him no attention.

Until the man told him, "I'm not really a risk analyst, you know."

Turning his head toward the man, Simonet said, "What?"

The man gave himself a shake, his business over quickly, and tucked back in.

"Here is my card," he said, placing it atop the urinal Simonet was still using. "You, *monsieur,* have just become part of my act."

Simonet could only gawk at the man as he walked away. As the door to the men's room closed behind him, Simonet turned to look at the card. The bastard had lied to him. He was a comedian. Had scared Simonet for his own amusement and, as he said, for his act. Simonet's fear would be ridiculed for the entertainment of others.

He would have throttled the bastard right there, if he could.

He would … break into the fellow's home, something he knew all about, and kill him at his convenience. It wouldn't be hard to find him. He had his card. Simonet took it with him when he left the men's room.

Had he been thinking more clearly, Simonet might have taken into account that a trip that had gone so badly thus far would best be not completed at all. There was no telling what might be waiting at journey's end.

The thought never entered Simonet's mind. He pushed on.

Richmond Detention Facility — Richmond, Virginia

Arlo Carsten had been moved from the FBI's Richmond offices to the federal lockup to give him a taste of what he had coming. He didn't like it one bit. People yelled and cried all night long. Sometimes it sounded as if someone was being murdered. The sole saving grace with which he might comfort himself was that he was alone in his cell.

But the small, grim place did have a second bed.

He didn't want to even imagine who might be put in with him. It was all he could do not to go nuts, especially any time he heard the footsteps of a guard approaching. Each time, he thought someone was being brought to share his space. Maybe even invade his most intimate spaces. There was no way he was going to be the tough guy behind bars.

He had to be lamest SOB in the whole joint.

When his stomach started to growl, he knew it must be getting near breakfast time. He heard the footsteps drawing near again. This time, the guard stopped in front of his door, and he did have someone with him, another guard. They shackled and hobbled Arlo, dragged him off to an interrogation room.

Waiting for Arlo were the two bastards responsible for him being locked up. The Air Force officer and the former cowboy who both now wore fancy suits. Arlo wanted to scream at them. Call them assholes and … no, he didn't even want to think about assholes. Not while his was at risk.

He did find the nerve to share a newsflash with them.

"That woman who was with you the last time," he said, "you know what she had with her? A goddamn knife. You know what she did with it?"

Welborn and Celsus looked at each other.

"What?" Celsus asked.

"She gave me a shave. Dry. The knife was so sharp it didn't even leave a knick. Smoothest damn shave I ever had."

"So you have no complaint?" Welborn asked.

Despite his predicament, Arlo had to laugh. Bitterly.

"She told me to hold real still because she didn't want to cut off an ear or slit my throat. When she finished, she took out this little makeup mirror. Let me see what a good job she did. Then she told me if I didn't tell her everything I knew she was going to shave my balls next, and that was trickier 'cause just about everyone squirmed when she did that."

Celsus laughed out loud and slapped the table.

Welborn told Arlo, "You know, we have that lady's number on speed dial."

Arlo's new prison pallor went three shades whiter.

"Unless you talk to us right now," Celsus said. "No bargaining, no bullshit."

"I'll talk, but I don't know what to tell you I haven't already said."

Welborn said, "Listen to what we have to say. Maybe you'll think of something."

They told Arlo about Harlan Fisk being taken prisoner, along with his men.

Celsus said, "Were the drone pilots, the ones who backed you up, members of Fisk's ground troops?"

The First Michigan Militia was still being processed; none had yet been released.

Arlo shook his head. "Unh-uh, no way. Those boys, the ones with me, had actual college science courses behind them. They knew their math and computers. The other guys were lucky if they had high school diplomas."

"What were their names, your little helpers?"

Arlo provided them.

"You know if those are their real names?" Welborn asked.

Arlo thought about that. "I was dumb enough to use my real

name but I'm not sure they did."

"What'd they look like?" Celsus wanted to know. "Give it to me in detail."

Arlo did.

"You know where they are now?" Celsus followed up.

"No."

Welborn said, "Did you ever talk about what would happen if all of you drone pilots went down?"

"Yeah, we did," Arlo said. "I wouldn't be surprised if that's what'll happen now. The plan was that the drones and missiles would be stored and locked up someplace safe until another opportunity came up." He hesitated before adding. "You know, something special."

Celsus said, "These other dipshits, the ones with the drones, they have any sense of initiative? Would they take things into their own hands? If they did, how likely would they be to hit what they were shooting at?"

Arlo took a moment to consider. "They were true believers. Not just in Jesus, I mean. They thought the president stole the election and they couldn't let that stand. They might give it a try even without Harlan Fisk to tell them to go ahead. I'd say it's fifty-fifty they'd hit their target. They're smart, but not experienced."

"You got anything else you think we should know?" Welborn asked.

Arlo shook his head, "If I did, I'd tell you, believe me." He took a second before daring to ask, "You think you can get them to continue letting me stay in a cell by myself?"

Celsus told him, "You plead guilty to whatever charges are brought against you, we'll see what we can do."

"I wouldn't be signing my death warrant, if I did that, would I?" Arlo asked.

Welborn told him, "The way things stand now, no. Your two friends get off a good shot, your charges will be amended, and you'll be out of luck."

Arlo nodded. "Get me a prosecutor, I'll plead right now."

The President's Bedroom

Despite their intentions to sleep until Morpheus set them free, the sun was up by 7:26 a.m. and so were McGill and Patti. They looked at each other and sighed. Both felt it was a sad state of affairs when you couldn't sleep in on Sunday morning only hours after you'd faced down a would-be insurrection. Well, giving credit where it was due, the Marines had helped, too.

"We're still not in Kansas, are we, Dorothy?" McGill asked.

Patti said, "I lost that state as both a Republican and a Democrat. All in all, I'd rather be in Oz."

McGill smiled and said, "Speaking of politics, how do you think our performances are going to play with the public?"

The president yawned. Took a moment to think and said, "The people who hate us will hate us more. They'll probably do fund-raising events on right-wing radio to buy new assault weapons for the people I pardoned."

"Maybe you could take up the cause to keep that from happening," McGill said.

"Gun control? Sure, just as soon as I can pick my own Congress. Failing that, maybe I'll wait until next month."

"Okay," McGill said with a smile, "you've earned a little down time"

"You're too kind. Looking at the other two-thirds of the political spectrum, I think we both helped the cause. From what Galia whispered to me, she's heard you used just the right amount of force on Harlan Fisk. The military people on hand were quite impressed."

McGill looked away for just a second, but that was long enough.

"What?" Patti asked. "You think you went too far?"

McGill shook his head, and needed some time to find the strength to confess what he'd been about to do to Fisk. He got it out because he knew it would be worse if he didn't. Patti looked at him, studied his face as if expecting to find something she'd never noticed before.

She shook her head. "I'm sure you felt the way you just told me, but I think if it wasn't me something else would have stopped you. I don't think it's in you to kill someone that way, Jim."

"I wouldn't have thought so, either. But, honest to God, I was so damn close. Just thinking of it scares me ... until I remember that bastard had threatened to kill our kids, and then he smiled at me like the danger hadn't ended with him going down. When I think about that, I wish you'd arrived a minute later."

"If you'd gone through with your intention," Patti said, "everyone might have started shooting and I might have lost you."

"And if I'd survived, I might have become someone else."

Patti put her arms around McGill. "Very well, I saved you. Hurrah for me. I wouldn't have it any other way."

She kissed McGill and said, "Overall, I'd say we both get bumps in the polls. The country will see we stand up for what we believe is right. Neither of us is a milksop."

"Not even close," McGill agreed.

"The use we made of the military was both judicious and effective. Chances for a peaceful second inauguration should have improved."

"From your lips to God's ear."

"Indeed."

"So you think we're good?"

"I do," Patti said.

Calder Lane — McLean, Virginia

Senator Howard Hurlbert had considered Cesara Muñoz, the housekeeper he'd hired after his wife had taken the family servants back to Mississippi with her, to be the perfect person for the job. She came with her own green card, so he hadn't had to finagle one for her. Her Hispanic surname let him look like he'd given a minority immigrant a decent job. Her Castilian bloodlines meant she was almost as white as he was. The fact that she came from Argentina and her family had been supporters of both Juan and

Evita Perón put Cesara on the right side — his side — of the political spectrum.

In her early forties, Cesara was too mature to be considered a young plaything masquerading as domestic help. Hell, she was a hard worker and did a fine job. As for her appearance, she was *almost* a looker. She certainly had a nice, toned figure for a gal old enough to have kids in high school. Had a handsome face, too.

But that was where the problem lay.

Poor Cesara's esthetic downfall was her upper lip. It was a bit too hairy. Truth was, she had a mustache a sixteen-year-old boy would have envied. More than once, Hurlbert had been tempted to offer to have that taken care of for her. Get it lasered or something. He'd gladly have paid just for the privilege of looking at her defoliated mouth.

What had stopped him was he couldn't figure out two things. How to make the offer without offending Cesara, and how to keep his wife, Bettina, from finding out, if Cesara bought the idea. Bettina thought the new housekeeper looked swell just the way she was. Even an old hound like Howard, she felt sure, wouldn't go sniffing after someone who might do commercials for Gillette.

When Cesara came to clean that Sunday and saw Hurlbert shot dead, her hand flew to her mouth in horror. When she took it away from her face, half her mustache came with it. No lasering necessary.

The off-putting feature was a product of artifice.

Hell, she'd have worn a goatee, if necessary.

She just wanted to do her job and be left in peace. Her strategy was facial hair. Her sister, a makeup artist, had given her the idea. But she'd never had to repair her 'stache before.

Had never found a murdered employer either. Not in the United States.

"Ay, mierda," Cesara said. Well, shit.

She went to the nearest bathroom. Washed her hands and her face. She would have to give a statement to the police; it would be better to do so with her own face. She came back out and looked at the senator. Someone had wanted him dead all right. Cost her a well-paying client, too.

Cabrón. Bastard.

Looking down at Hurlbert with the fetching face he never got to see, she used her cell phone to call the cops.

Lyon — France

Yves Pruet had none of the travel difficulties encountered by René Simonet. Tapping his father's deep pockets again, he chartered a Gulfstream with the range to fly him directly to Lyon. He was able to sleep soundly in the bedroom compartment of the private jet and awoke eager to bring Simonet to justice. Gabriella Casale met him at the airport in her rental BMW and they headed off to Annecy on the last leg of Pruet's trip.

"You are feeling well, *Monsieur le Magistrat?*" Gabbi asked.

Pruet looked at her and smiled. "I am well and hope to be better still quite soon. Has Simonet shown himself yet?"

"Not yet."

Pruet's skeptical side reasserted itself for a moment. "Do we know he will come at all?"

Gabbi told him, "He'll come."

"How can you be sure?"

"*Monsieur Simonet* made the mistake of stealing art from several influential families, one or two even wealthier and more influential than your own. In other words, he has powerful enemies. They've spoken to the authorities in Annecy and to the employees of the art gallery Simonet owns. We believe that the people who work for him are honest, were shocked to discover they were working for Laurent Fortier. But after we obtained a search warrant for Simonet's building, the top two floors were found to hold enough masterpieces to start a small museum."

"My family's Renoir?" Pruet asked.

Gabbi shook her head. "I'm sorry, no. You should talk with Père Louvel about that."

Pruet nodded and said, "Please continue."

"Simonet's chief assistant at the gallery made a phone call to him. She found him in Ireland. Told him there had been a fire in his building. It was put out quickly but there had been a lot of smoke. Possible damage to the upper floors was suspected but could not be confirmed because the doors were locked. Simonet replied he would be in the air soon and should be in Annecy …" Gabbi glanced at the dashboard clock. "About an hour after we arrive."

"*Bon,*" Pruet said, "I will be waiting for him."

He paused and then told Gabbi about his and Odo's business plans.

"Odo says we will need a female investigator," the magistrate told her.

Gabbi smiled and said, "You know, Jim McGill once asked me if I'd like to open an office in Paris for him."

Four Seasons Hotel — Washington, DC

After Yves Pruet had departed for France, Odo Sacripant availed himself of a few hours of sleep and a filling breakfast. He checked out at the front desk. He'd allowed a bellman to take his bag. He carried both the borrowed guitar, in its case, that Yves had played so beautifully and the Beretta that *Monsieur McGill* had so thoughtfully lent him, and that he, thankfully, had no occasion to use.

The lovely young woman at the front desk asked him, "Did you enjoy your stay with us, *Monsieur Sacripant?*"

"A delight in all respects," he told her.

She smiled and asked, "Would you like me to call a limousine for you?"

"The White House is sending a car for me, thank you."

A gleam of more than professional interest entered the young woman's eyes.

She was far too young and he was far too married for that to matter, but it still pleased him. He said, *"Bonjour, madame."*

"Bon voyage, monsieur."

Odo left the lobby with a spring in his step. In his earlier days, he would have stopped outside to have a cigarette. Marie never allowed him to smoke in their home, and after their third child was born had made him give up the habit altogether. He tipped the bellman and waited for Leo Levy to arrive, a very competent and amusing fellow, the former race car driver.

Odo had shed blood for La Belle France, but the more he saw of America, the more he liked it. The next time he visited, he would have to bring Marie and the children. Take them to California perhaps. See Hollywood. Surely, someone there would take interest in a Corsican private eye.

The doorman gave him an assessing look.

"Forgive me if I'm out of line, sir," the man said, "but would you care for a smoke?"

He took a pack of Marlboros out of his coat. Odo looked at it. A cowboy's favorite cigarette, he thought. He'd never had one and —

Odo smiled and shook his head. *"Merci, non."*

Marie would never have known, but he had too much to live for to go back to smoking.

He contented himself to breathe the clean, cold air.

Pennsylvania Avenue — Washington, DC

Having lost his primary objective, Rutger Bierman cast about in his mind for a new one, a target of opportunity that would be a stunning achievement. He would be the man who blew up — what? What did he know about Washington? Very little. This was his first, and last, trip to the United States.

He'd entered the country through Mexico, legally. The crush of people, Americans and Mexicans, entering El Paso from Ciudad Juárez, was like nothing he'd ever seen. People of all ages, sizes, shapes and colors. He was spellbound by the diversity. No one thought to comment on the sallowness of his complexion. What mattered was that his papers were in order.

As if a good German would have it any other way.

He smiled through his pain, used his few words of English to get past the border and found his way to the bus station. Took what seemed like an endless motor trip across a country so vast he could not begin to comprehend it. He felt more dead than alive when he arrived in Washington. At the bus terminal, before he was picked up, he found a tourist brochure for the city. On the cover was —

His new target. The White House. The palace where the American president lived. Stopping for a red light, he pulled the brochure out of a pocket. The address was right there under the picture of the building: 1600 Pennsylvania Avenue.

Rutger fed the information into the truck's GPS system. A map appeared on the screen, showing a red line between his present position and his destination. Rutger smiled, until car horns began sounding behind him. He looked up and saw the light was green.

For just a moment, he felt an impulse to detonate his bomb right there.

Take all the impatient swine behind the truck to hell with him.

Only he was certain his stepfather would think of that as a misuse of resources. Destroying the White House, on the other hand, that would have to earn Mama an even greater reward. And, who knew, maybe there would be wine and women waiting for him in the next life.

Beer and women, if he was really lucky.

Rutger stepped on the gas just in time to be the only vehicle through the intersection.

Karma wasn't instantaneous, but he was paid back soon enough. Despite what his GPS map showed him, Pennsylvania Avenue was blocked off to automotive traffic. *Scheisse.* Shit. He could see the damn building he wanted to destroy. He could also see the policemen with automatic weapons. If he tried to run the barricade, he would be killed immediately.

Having seen the grand building, though, he was determined

to get at it.

He would look for another point of access.

Four Seasons Hotel — Washington, DC

Leo was running late, and Odo felt an increasing temptation to change his mind and take the doorman up on his offer of a Marlboro. The cowboy cigarette, could it possibly be any better than, say, a Gauloises or a Black Cat? There was only one way to know for sure.

The thought brought him up short. The devil on the doorstep. True, one cigarette would not kill him, but if he found that he *liked* Marlboros and took to smoking them regularly, that might kill him. Leave Marie a widow and his children fatherless. That would be unforgivable.

Even if he had only the one cigarette, he would have to brush his teeth, gargle, shower, shampoo, have his clothes dry cleaned. Do everything possible to leave no trace of his lapse for his wife to find. The price, in inconvenience if nothing else, was too high.

And yet … Odo's eyes were about to track back to the doorman's pocket.

When he saw Leo's car turn into the driveway to the hotel.

It was followed not long afterward by a boxy truck.

Above the truck's cab were the words: Special Moments Party Planners.

Rutger Bierman sagged behind the wheel of his truck, feeling as if he'd been driving the damn thing his entire life. Would be damned to do so for eternity. He driven up and down more Washington Streets than he could recall. Now, at least, he was back on Pennsylvania Avenue, but he didn't know whether he was driving toward the White House or away from it.

Did that even matter, he asked himself? Having had some time to think about the situation, he'd decided the Americans wouldn't be so foolish as to block off access to the White House from one direction only to allow it from another. That would be stupid.

So, not only had his primary target been taken from him, the one he'd conceived of for himself was beyond reach. He not only felt like a failure, he was also becoming increasingly sure that this would be his last day alive. His whole body burned, ached and throbbed. Through all the pain, he recognized his very will to go on was being consumed.

If this was life, give him death and quickly.

But not so fast he didn't get to trigger his bomb, leave some lasting impression that he'd once been alive, had mattered to someone for something. He saw a sign ahead, Four Seasons Hotel. Was that a place where the rich stayed? He didn't know. But he saw a shiny black car just ahead of him pull into the driveway.

It looked like the kind of vehicle in which a member of the bourgeoisie might ride.

So maybe the hotel was the kind of place where …

His father, the man he'd never met, might like to cause some trouble.

Rutger followed the black car into the driveway.

Odo saw immediately that something was wrong. Leo had navigated the driveway smoothly. That was as it should have been. Odo had been up and down that stretch of pavement both in a car and on foot. It was perfectly smooth. Just what one would expect of a roadway leading to such a fine lodging place.

The driver of the truck, though, made abrupt pulls on his steering wheel as if slaloming left and right to avoid craters in the pavement. He was impaired in either his vision or his mind. Or he had something else distracting him.

Leo stopped McGill's Chevy in front of Odo, got out of the car and said, "Hey, Odo, sorry about —"

Odo hurried around the front of the Chevy and handed the guitar case to Leo, saying, *"S'il vous plait."*

He brought the Beretta out of his pocket, clicked off the safety and using both hands pointed the weapon at the driver of the oncoming truck. He remembered what he'd told Yves about the Vietnamese using simple means to prosecute their war. How drones weren't necessary to make your point. Long before they had come into global vogue, vehicles filled with explosives had been used in Vietnam.

Odo's uncle had been in the French army that had been chased out of that country.

He'd told his nephew his war stories, none of them happy.

Odo stepped forward, placing himself between the truck and the hotel. He was not sure whether the face of the driver would be Asian, Arab or … German! Odo recognized those Teutonic features the moment he saw them.

Grandpère Sacripant had been in the Resistance during the Second Great War. France and Germany might be allies for the moment. Others might have forgiven the Germans. Odo's family had not.

He held up his left hand and yelled, "Halt!"

The driver, who'd seemed to be looking for something on the seat beside him, lifted his eyes, and now he held something in his right hand. Odo couldn't see what it was. He saw perfectly, however, the twisted, malice-filled smile on the German's face.

He shot him four times before diving out of the truck's path.

Annecy — France

René Simonet threw open the door to the gallery he owned and entered the premises at a run. He came to a quick stop ten feet from Yves Pruet, who sat upon a wooden chair facing him. For a man in late middle age, Simonet managed to center his balance deftly, ready now to move to his right or left or spin and run. The problem with any of those maneuver was that the man facing him calmly held a handgun on his lap.

The fellow would have to be a truly miserable marksman to miss him no matter which way he moved. Especially should he charge straight ahead. Simonet stayed put and raised his open palms to his sides, as if to say, "What now?"

"Do you know who I am?" Pruet asked.

Simonet sighed and said, "Someone who knows who I am."

The magistrate nodded, and inclined his head to another chair. One Simonet had not placed in his gallery.

"Pull the chair over and sit in front of me.

Simonet complied and said, "You wish to interview me?"

"I am a *juge d'instruction*." An investigating magistrate.

"Pruet."

"Oui."

Simonet knew that ninety-five percent of the cases a magistrate referred to a court ended in the conviction of the defendant. He had no wish to live out his remaining years in a cell. The guillotine would be preferable, were it still available.

"If I tried to attack you, would you shoot me?"

"Yes, but not fatally."

"You are that good?"

"My bodyguard makes me practice far more often than I would like."

Simonet heard the ring of truth in that complaint.

The only thing worse than going to prison would be doing so as a cripple.

"What do you want to know?" Simonet asked.

"Why did you kill Charles Louvel?"

"Don't you mean, 'Did I kill Charles Louvel?'"

Pruet said, "If you lie to me again, even by implication, I will shoot you for my own pleasure. Perhaps in *les couilles*." The balls.

Simonet squirmed in his seat. Could this quiet fellow really be *that* good? Did he dare take the chance that Pruet was bluffing?

The thief said, "He was standing between me and freedom."

"Freedom to steal my family's painting."

"If you wish to be technical. My argument is Renoir belongs to the world."

"Charles Louvel belonged to his family and mine."

A look of consternation crossed Simonet's face as an unhappy memory came rushing back. "He was a stubborn old man, and he would not get out of my way. If I had run to another door, he would have cried out and brought the whole household down on me."

"So you thought you had a right to make off with someone else's painting?"

"As I've said, Renoir and all the other cultural treasures of France belong to the people."

"I see, and how large a part of our population have you invited to the top two floors of this building to view their common cultural heritage?"

Simonet started to rise. Pruet waved him back into his seat with his gun.

"Do not concern yourself about the paintings. There was no fire. No smoke damage."

The thief's face drooped and he said, "I have been betrayed?"

"By the people you deceived, yes."

"I paid them better than any —"

"You paid them with the proceeds of your crimes, no doubt. They feel terrible about that, too. Now, back to the matter at hand, Charles Louvel. He would not allow you to run out the back door of my father's house. Where his body was found."

Simonet drew himself up into a self-righteous posture. "Yes."

"I advise you to be careful with your attitude of indignation, *monsieur.* My temper is quite short."

"You would enjoy shooting me, wouldn't you?" the thief asked.

Pruet said, "I have another punishment in mind, something that will please me even more."

Simonet didn't understand what that meant, which scared him all the more.

Pruet said, "Back to Charles Louvel. He told you he wouldn't let you leave. You didn't want to put the Renoir down and wrestle with him, so what did you do?"

The thief's face and voice turned hard. "I deceived the old fool. I said I would take one last look at the painting, give it to him, and he would stand aside to let me leave."

"And how was your deception carried out?"

"The painting had been hung in a shamefully careless manner, hanging from two hooks by a thin braided wire. I pulled one end of the wire free from the frame. It required almost no effort. I *saved* that Renoir from a possibly calamitous fall."

Unmoved, Pruet asked, "What did you with the wire?"

"As I pretended to hand the painting to the old man, I looped it around his neck and garroted him. He died in Renoir's embrace. That was better than he deserved. He was unable to make a sound and raise an alarm."

Pruet said, "Very well. You are free to go."

Simonet blinked. Didn't believe Pruet for a second.

"You are joking."

"If you can get through the door by which you entered, you are free."

The magistrate raised his gun, waved it to prompt the man to go.

For just a flickering moment, Simonet had hope. If the magistrate had gone mad, who was he to argue with his good fortune? He jumped to his feet, spun and —

Saw a dozen members of the Louvel family waiting for him. The doorway was clogged. The sidewalk outside the gallery window was filled with a storm cloud of angry faces. To try to push his way through that mob, Simonet knew, was to invite being torn to pieces.

When he turned back to Pruet, he saw the magistrate was standing at the head of another furious crowd. There was no escape for him in that direction either. No way out at all.

Pruet said, "I have told all these good people to try not to kill you. I really do have something worse in store for you, should you live. Nonetheless, everyone here would like to have a word with you, and I could not deny them that courtesy.

Pruet stepped aside.

Watched as the thief's past closed in on him.

***

Dumbarton Oaks — Washington, DC

In a house not far from Galia Mindel's home, though three times its size, agents of the FBI's art crime team, operating under the specifications of a federal search warrant and observed by Deputy Director Byron DeWitt, swarmed through the house of billionaire Hiram Busby. Within minutes, they found a concealed entrance to a windowless new wing of the structure.

Natural light did flow into the half-dozen rooms through skylights fitted with linear polarizing filters on the glass, as Pruet had suspected. Aerial snoops would not be able to eavesdrop on what lay beneath the high-tech screen. On the walls of the six rooms were the authentic versions of the paintings on display at Inspiration Hall: the works Busby had supposedly donated and masterpieces looted from the Drucker and Ransom collections. Nothing like stealing from your rich pals, DeWitt thought.

The head butler of the house, one Corwin Alcott, told the FBI that Mr. Busby was not in residence. He provided a list of the man's other homes in the U.S. and abroad, but warned he might not be in any of them as he also had two yachts, two long-range business jets and often spent time in top hotels around the world.

Alcott, after some stern prompting, also provided the feds with all the phone numbers and e-mail addresses he had for his employer.

Asked if he knew what was hanging on the walls in the new wing of the house, Alcott said, "No, sir. None of the staff here has been allowed into that area."

All the servants on the property had their fingerprints scanned just to be sure.

DeWitt waited for the art crime people to finish their inquiries before he asked his only question, "Who handles the insurance on Mr. Busby's art collection?"

***

The Oval Office

The president and McGill watched the news broadcast on NBC. Brian Williams was anchoring the coverage. A banner on the screen read: Sen. Howard Hurlbert Murdered.

Williams provided such news as was available. "Senator Howard Hurlbert of Mississippi, the founder of the True South Party, who may well have been the president-elect if not for a change of heart by the last member of the electoral college to cast her vote, was found dead this morning in his McLean, Virginia home by his housekeeper, Cesara Muñoz. Ms. Muñoz told police she cleaned the Senator's Virginia home every Sunday morning. Today, when she showed up for work she found the senator dead, apparently from three gunshot wounds to his chest. She called the police, and in the hope of catching the killer, the McLean Police Department and the Virginia State Police have decided to share the details of the crime with the public.

"Reached at her Mississippi home for comment, a tearful Bettina Hurlbert, the widow of the late senator, characterized the killing as an assassination, and said she didn't want the federal government to play any role in the investigation of the homicide."

The network went to a commercial break.

McGill asked, "Seen enough?"

The president nodded. McGill turned the TV off.

A perfunctory knock sounded at the door and Galia stepped into the Oval Office.

"You saw?" the president asked Galia.

The chief of staff nodded. "It's only a matter of time before that woman accuses you of being behind her husband's murder, Madam President."

"The thought did occur to me."

McGill nodded and added, "Good thing the First Michigan Militia was disarmed before this news got out."

"We'll have to watch for more paramilitary activity."

"You're right about that," McGill told Galia.

"Before anything else happens," the president said, "I have to make a televised announcement condemning the killing and, Bettina Hurlbert be damned, assigning the FBI to head the investigation. Killing a member of Congress is a federal crime."

McGill thought, teach me to hope things were looking up.

The FBI would have to find the killer fast or … no, it wouldn't be a good idea for him to get involved, McGill realized. That would be made to look like a coverup, no question. He might even be accused of being the killer. Unless Hurlbert was shot while he was on the Mall. Might turn out that his alibi would be provided by Harlan Fisk.

The world grew more surreal by the day.

To underscore that point, McGill's cell phone rang. He'd forgotten to turn it off, as he usually did upon entering the Oval Office. He was about to let the call go to voice mail, but he saw it came from Leo, who never called unless a situation was critical.

He asked the president, "May I?"

She nodded. McGill clicked the answer button and said hello.

"Boss, we got one helluva situation over here at the Four Seasons. I'd swung by to pick up Odo Sacripant and give him a ride to the airport, the way we discussed. Well, I pulled into the hotel driveway just ahead of this medium duty box truck. Thing was, it had about three tons worth of a fertilizer bomb inside."

"Jesus Christ," McGill said, scaring both the president and her chief of staff.

"Yeah, if that damn thing went off, they'd be working three shifts at the casket factory, and I wouldn't be talking to you."

"The bomb was disarmed?" McGill asked.

"In a manner of speaking, yeah. Odo got a feeling something wasn't right. He stepped out in front of the truck and plugged the driver four times. The guy died with a cell phone in his hand. The feds think it was the bomb trigger."

It had been that close? McGill plopped down on a sofa.

The president rushed to join him. Galia hovered over both of them.

"Boss, Odo said you gave him the gun he used. That's what he told me. To everyone else, he doesn't know a word of English, and his French ain't all that good either. He did exactly the right thing, but he had to unload on the guy before he had *proof* of what he was gonna do."

McGill turned to the president. He was about to tell her another pardon might be needed, but he changed his mind.

"Boss, that ain't all," Leo said.

"What else is there?"

"Even without the bomb going off, only one thing stopped that truck from ramming the hotel. Boss, you, me and Deke? We're gonna need a new car."

The Residence — The White House

Patti intervened directly before Odo Sacripant was questioned by either the Metro Police Department or the FBI. He didn't have diplomatic immunity; he had something better. Someone who could make all his problems go away with the stroke of a pen. To law enforcement, however, the president said she knew how to speak the Corsican dialect of French and might be helpful in clearing things up before an international misunderstanding could arise.

McGill, who'd been listening in, told his wife, "You've been in politics too long."

But now he was the one who took Odo aside for a moment and spoke to him privately. Having delivered his message, McGill extended his hand to the Frenchman. Odo shook it and then embraced McGill and kissed him on both cheeks.

The First Couple and their guest had dinner in the family dining room: porterhouse steak, Chicago style mashed potatoes, fresh steamed broccoli and a chocolate sundae. Odo had requested a typically American dinner. As a bow to France, they drank a 2007 Les Lézardes Syrah with their meal.

"When I tell my wife of sharing this occasion with you and *Monsieur McGill, Madame la Présidente,* she will not speak to me for a month. She already thinks I'm far too lucky for my own good, and this will only confirm it," Odo said.

The president put a hand on Odo's forearm. "After saving an untold number of American and other lives today, *Monsieur Sacripant,* you and *Madame Sacripant,* and your children, are welcome to dine with us anytime you care to visit Washington."

Odo beamed. "You are much too kind, but I will accept your invitation because it is certain to fill *Monsieur le Magistrat* with envy."

McGill and Patti laughed.

"Yves is always welcome here, too. Have you heard from him after he returned to France?"

"Oui."

He told them of the capture of René Simonet.

"Unfortunately, he didn't find the Renoir belonging to the Pruet family, and *Monsieur McGill* tells me that it wasn't found at Hiram Busby's home either."

"I have an idea where it might be," McGill said.

"As do I," Odo offered.

Together they said, "New York."

Forsaking a *digestif,* McGill made a phone call to Detective Louis Marra of the NYPD Major Case Squad.

"Would you be up for doing me a small favor or two, Detective Marra?"

"Happy to. What do you need?"

"You think you could take a run past the Duvessa Gallery? Make sure the lights are still on."

"I can answer that right now. I heard a rumor last Friday that Duvessa was going someplace warm for the rest of the winter. Galleries don't close in this town on a personal whim like that, so I decided to have a look. Sure enough, place is dark, no lights on at all."

McGill thought about that. Byron DeWitt had shown him a

photo of Duvessa Kinsale with former Special Agent Ozzie Riddick. Riddick was still under arrest and in a hospital bed. Right there in Washington.

"You coming to town soon, sir?" Marra asked.

"Not me, but my friend Odo Sacripant might be there tomorrow. That's the other favor. Would it be all right if he checks in with you? You might help him get around town a little."

"Any chance we might recover some stolen art?"

"I think there's a good chance."

"Always happy to help out," Marra said.

The President's Bedroom

McGill and Patti both hoped they'd be allowed to sleep through the night. McGill was in his pajamas and Patti was still in her bathroom when the phone rang. McGill groaned.

He picked up the phone anyway.

"Dad, it's me. Patton's First Army and I are back in town."

His beloved elder daughter, Abbie. Who needed a small history lesson.

"General George S. Patton commanded the Seventh Army in Sicily and the Third Army in France and Germany."

"Yeah, okay. I bet neither of his armies had as many guys as mine does."

Of all his children, Abbie was normally the one who complained the least about the burdens of dealing with her security cocoon. He wondered what was up.

"So you're safe and sound but disgruntled?"

"Exactly. We all saw what you did on the Mall early this morning."

The media had not been present, but cell phone videos were on YouTube.

"By all you mean your mother and your siblings?"

"Lars, too." The second husband of McGill's ex-wife, Carolyn. The kids' stepdad.

"Sure, Lars, too. It all worked out okay, don't you think?"

"Yeah, but the first time Mom saw the video she didn't realize she was watching a recording. The outcome, what with all those guys and their guns, was in doubt."

"She was scared?"

"We were all scared, even after we knew you were okay. You *could* have gotten hurt or killed."

Abbie was right, of course, but McGill asked, "Would you believe I did it for you, and for Patti?"

"Of course, I would. Why else would you do it? Doesn't mean we can't be scared or it won't give us nightmares."

"I'm sorry, honey. I felt I had to do it."

"I know, but we're all still mad at you."

"Because of the risk I took."

"That and we haven't received our invitations yet."

"Invitations?"

"To Patti's second inauguration. We're going to be there, right?"

"Your mother and your siblings?"

"And Lars."

"Of course."

McGill lapsed into silence. He wondered if he should show his kids, his ex-wife and her husband the video the Secret Service had done. In which he and Patti got blown up.

"Dad?" Abbie said.

"Yes?"

"Caitie and I spoke on the phone. She says she's going to the inauguration, like it or not. She says she's already got the movie studio to agree to provide her with a private plane to fly her to Washington. She says she's going to show up and see who will dare to stop her."

McGill blinked. He could imagine his youngest child doing just that.

Who would stop her? Other than him or Patti, no one.

"Dad?"

"Yes?"

"Where does Caitie get off behaving like a diva? She *thirteen* years old. She hasn't even finished making her first movie yet."

"That's just who she is," McGill said.

"Yeah, well, when Caitie shows up, I'm coming with her. I want to see who'll try to stop me, and if we both come, you know what Kenny will do."

"He'll come, too."

"Right, and no way Mom will stay home with the three of us there."

"No, she won't."

"So what are you going to do?"

"Make sure I don't forget Lars' invitation," McGill said.

CHAPTER 9

White House Press Room
Monday, January 14, 2013

Aggie Wu, the president's press secretary, told the assembled newsies that the president and James J. McGill would both be speaking to them that morning but neither of them would be taking any questions. Aggie said she would be handing out copies of both statements, and there would be elaborations on what the president would say. Unspoken but understood by every reporter in the room was that if anybody didn't like her ground rules, they could be replaced by bloggers.

Like the smart children they'd once been, and occasionally still acted like, the newsies would save their grumbling for when they were back at the office or out tippling a few drinks.

The president entered the room followed by McGill. She stepped behind the lectern with the presidential seal on it. He took a seat at the side of the room.

The president gestured for the newsies to sit and began.

"I'm here today to speak to the American people of two matters of grave importance. The first is the murder of Senator Howard Hurlbert who was shot to death in his Virginia home. This was a vile and cowardly act. The perpetrator will be found, tried and punished as the appropriate court deems fit. The sooner this happens the better it will be for all of us. We will, however, not rush to judgment merely to ease the anger and heartache caused by

Senator Hurlbert's death. The first order of business for those investigating this crime will be to get things right.

"As to who will lead that investigation, it will be the FBI. Killing a member of Congress, by law, is a federal crime. So is killing a member-elect of Congress. So is killing a member of the president's cabinet or a cabinet nominee. And, of course, so is killing the president or the vice president.

"The law has been written this way to demonstrate that an attack on the individuals who embody the federal government is an attack on the nation as a whole, not just any state or region. There is no question that the FBI is the right law enforcement agency to bring Senator Hurlbert's killer to justice. I am sure once that has been accomplished the misgivings some people might have about how the matter is handled will be laid to rest."

The president had no trouble seeing that every reporter in the room wanted to jump up and ask, "What if it isn't handled to everyone's satisfaction? What if misgivings persist?" But Aggie had well and truly put the fear of banishment into them. Not a peep was uttered.

"Moving on," the president said, "I'm sure most of the people in this room are aware there was an incident involving the shooting of a truck driver at a local hotel yesterday. What I now have to tell you, and the country as whole, is the truck was filled with a bomb large enough to have brought most of that hotel down. The driver was a would-be suicide bomber."

That made all the newsies sit up straight. Now, they were *dying* to ask questions.

The look on Aggie's face told them: Better not.

The president continued, "It was a matter of great good fortune that a member of a police service of an allied country was on hand, saw the situation for what it was and killed the driver before he could detonate his bomb. That official was debriefed by the FBI earlier this morning. The information the FBI received was forwarded to government officials in the driver's home country. We expect the investigation there to lead to those ultimately responsible.

"Mr. McGill will now provide you with a few more details regarding this potential attack. For reasons of protecting the integrity of an ongoing investigation, he will speak only of matters that pertain to his direct involvement."

The president stepped to the side of the room. McGill took the microphone from its holder, stood to the right of the lectern. Nobody was going to get a photo of him standing behind the presidential seal. Or some creep somewhere would assert he was plotting to be the next in line.

"What I have to say is simply this: I gave the handgun to the foreign police official that he used to kill the terrorist. I did so because the official was in our country on another matter, a personal concern. He expressed the feeling to me that he might be in danger. He is a person who stood at my side in a moment of great danger. I knew he could be depended upon to act responsibly. As it turned out, he acted heroically.

"Even so, I should not have done what I did. I appeared this morning before a local magistrate. Taking the entirety of the situation into account, she sentenced me to forty-eight hours in jail, a suspension of my private investigator's license for thirty days and a ten thousand dollar fine. I wrote a check for the fine this morning; I will surrender myself to serve my sentence as soon as I'm done here today. Thank you."

With that, McGill and the president left the press room.

Between learning of a thwarted terrorist attack and hearing the president's husband was going to jail, the investigation of Howard Hurlbert's murder got a little breathing room from the media.

Rayburn House Office Building — Washington, DC

Sitting in his office, his feet up on his desk, Representative Philip Brock (D-PA), clicked off his TV, having just seen the president and McGill exit the press room.

"Damn, these people are good," he whispered to himself.

Howard Hurlbert's murder, a story he thought would dominate the news for weeks, got shoved aside the same morning the story broke. McGill, in a period of twenty-four hours had not only battered the leader of a large group of armed men, he'd also had a hand in preventing a horrific terrorist attack. Then, the cherry on top, he proved what a regular guy he was by copping to the gun charge and taking his punishment like a man.

The truck bomber must have seen or been warned off of attacking Inspiration Hall. Looking for a secondary target was the natural thing to do. But how he came to choose a luxury hotel where a foreign cop was staying, a guy who just happened to have a gun courtesy of McGill, a guy who stepped up and saved the day, Brock would never know.

He might have ascribed it to divine intervention, if he was a Catholic for anything more than political advantage.

The drones with their missiles were still out there, but the way things were going, Brock would bet the president's second inauguration was going to come off without a hitch.

Thinking about the brains, ruthlessness and luck of the other side, he wondered if he was overmatched here. The president said she'd get him for killing old Howard. Would she?

Would McGill help her do it?

Brock chuckled to himself. Took out the bottle of Pappy Van Winkle bourbon he now kept in his desk. Damn thing had been hard to come by. The taste, though, was worth the effort. He poured himself a glass and raised it.

The great thing about being an anarchist, he thought with a grin, life was never dull.

In a quiet voice, he said, "Game on."

Union Station — Washington, DC

Odo Sacripant waited to be called to board the Acela to New York. He could have flown but he preferred to see the countryside from ground level. He mused on the bargain he'd struck with *Monsieur McGill.* He'd told the FBI he had been fearful — no simple admission for a Corsican — and in turn *Monsieur McGill* would take all legal responsibility for the matter.

On the television in the waiting area for the train, Odo had just heard from *Monsieur McGill's* own mouth what the punishment had been. Two nights in jail? Unpleasant, but he was sure the president's husband would be given far from the meanest accommodations. The loss of a month's income and the ten thousand dollar fine? Something like that would cramp the Sacripant household more than a little.

Monsieur McGill had made it seem like a trifle, the way any strong man would.

Of course, he was married to a very rich and powerful woman.

That eased a great many pains. Still, the next time *Monsieur McGill* came to Paris, Marie would have to cook for him. *Madame la Présidente,* too, if she wished to come to dinner.

Business class passengers were called to board the train, and Odo stood.

As he did, the young art expert from Inspiration Hall walked over to him and extended a hand in greeting. Odo shook it and asked, "*Monsieur Winger,* you have come to see me off?"

Ethan Winger smiled and said, "Maybe. I've come to ask if you can identify *Monsieur Pruet's* Renoir as genuine, if you find it."

Odo said, "You make a good point. I cannot, but won't the police in New York have their own experts?"

"Sure, they will. But Mr. McGill thought you might like to have your own, me."

"*Oui, naturellement.* You have a ticket?"

"I do."

"*Bon. Partons.*" Good. Let's go.

And away they went.

Central Detention Facility — Washington, DC

McGill's first and only jailhouse visitors were Sweetie, Putnam and Maxine. Per his VIP status, McGill was allowed to remain dressed in his own clothes rather than a prison jumpsuit. He also had a one-man cell with Deke Ky or another Secret Service special agent sitting directly outside of it to make sure no jailbird tried to achieve historical notice by sticking a shiv into the gizzard of the president's husband.

Or, more likely, force McGill to cripple any dummy who thought he'd be an easy mark.

Sweetie looked at McGill, across the table in a staff break room, and told him, "See what happens when I take a little time off."

Putnam made an effort to repress a smirk, and almost succeeded.

Eight-year-old Maxine, who told McGill he could call her Maxi, asked, "Did you do something really bad?"

"I did something I shouldn't have done," McGill said.

"Are you sorry?"

"Maxi, I'm sorry I wasn't smart enough to think of a better way to do things."

"A way that wouldn't get you in trouble?"

"Exactly."

"Are you *really* married to the president?"

McGill grinned. "Yes, hard as that may be to believe."

"Margaret said we could visit you and the president at the White House."

"We'll do that real soon. I'm going to have some time on my hands."

Maxine extended her hand to McGill and they shook on it.

Sweetie said, "I think Maxi's seen enough of this place. I'll take her out to the car, if that's all right with her."

The girl nodded, gave Putnam a kiss on the cheek and left with Sweetie.

"So how's it feel to be a dad?" McGill asked.

Putnam shook his head and said, "It wasn't that long ago I thought I'd be a lifelong bachelor, a ladies' man and a general reprobate until the day I died. Which I figured wouldn't be all that long in coming. Then I met Margaret. Now we're married and shortly after that … it's not that I think I won't try to be a good father to Maxi. I just think she deserves better than me. That there's got to be a catch. I'll take my eye off her for just a heartbeat and when I look back she'll be gone."

McGill smiled warmly. "Welcome to the wonderful world of parental paranoia. Just do your best. Practice knowing the times when you shouldn't take your eyes off her. Margaret will help with that."

Putnam said, "Yeah, I'm sure. Well, listen, I talked with Deputy Director DeWitt. He was wondering if Hiram Busby, slick SOB that he is, might have tried to work an insurance angle on the phony paintings he stuck us with at Inspiration Hall."

"Didn't he *donate* the paintings?" McGill asked. "Wouldn't the museum insure the art work and collect the payout if everything went up in smoke?"

"That's the way it would work with the Drucker and Ransom collections. Their paintings were donated, and covered by the museum. But Busby's paintings were exhibited on an indefinite loan. I told DeWitt who the insurance carrier is on his paintings. So, yeah, if Inspiration Hall had been destroyed, and I understand that truck bomb might have been up to doing the job, he would have collected on the forgeries, most likely. While he enjoyed the originals at home."

McGill shook his head. "So the FBI's going to try to find Busby by following the money?"

"Yeah. See what else he might have insured with the same company. DeWitt thinks Busby could provide information about who set up the whole plot: kill the president, destroy the museum, get the whole country scared spitless again."

McGill nodded. "Putting Hiram Busby where I am now would be a good idea."

"Yeah. Well, I thought you'd like to know what's going on."

"Thanks, Putnam."

"You're not going to eat the food in here, are you? They'll spit in your soup for sure."

McGill told him, "The Secret Service will bring me White House carryout."

Grand Street — Manhattan

The NYPD, using an unmarked helicopter, did a middle-distance flyby of the loft building in SoHo. Both the pilot and the observation officer reported seeing two people inside the unit to which their attention had been directed. Both persons in the loft seemed to be moving with a sense of urgency, as if they feared imminent apprehension.

The location had been provided to the cops by former Special Agent Osgood Riddick. The deal he'd worked out that morning with the Department of Justice mitigated by degrees the sentence he would receive for both menacing James J. McGill and his role in aiding both art thefts and swindles committed by the man currently known as Giles Benedict and art gallery owner Duvessa Kinsale.

If either Benedict or Kinsale was taken into custody and convicted, Riddick's sentence would be reduced by X years; if both Benedict and Kinsale were caught and imprisoned, Riddick's sentence would be reduced by 2X; for every work of stolen art recovered an additional year would be eliminated from Riddick's sentence.

The Emergency Services Unit of the NYPD moved in quietly. A dozen plain clothes cops materialized from the pedestrians passing by the building. At the entrance to the building, they dropped the heavy civilian coats they'd been wearing, revealing NYPD raid jackets, automatic weapons and other tools of their trade. They charged up the stairs to the third floor loft.

Detective Louis Marra had told the ESU people they were dealing with a different type of hostage situation here. There could be paintings worth tens or even hundreds of millions of dollars in the unit. The bad guys, reacting in either anger or panic, might try to vandalize the art work. The ESU's job was to take the people inside the loft into custody before that could happen.

Keeping their fellow coppers safe was paramount, as always, but they should try not to shoot up any of the paintings, if they could help it.

Ten seconds after the ESU had made their charge, patrol units pulled up in front of the building and behind it. The unmarked helicopter was replaced by one flying the NYPD colors. Getting away was not going to be an option for the bad guys.

Marra parked his unmarked unit at the periphery of the police cordon.

Odo Sacripant sat beside him, watching and listening to their police radio.

Hoping and silently praying that he heard no gunfire.

Or police officers cursing in anger.

What he heard within ninety seconds of the ESU entry into the building was a voice announcing, "All clear."

Marra said to Odo, "Let's go see if they've got your friend's painting."

They had it all right, along with many others, several already boxed and ready for shipping. Odo put in a call to Ethan Winger. Marra went back through the ring of cops to escort him in. It took the young artist no more than a few seconds of study to break into a broad smile.

He looked at Odo and said, *"Merveilleux."*

"Marvelous, yeah," Marra said. "But is it a real Renoir?"

"They don't get any realer," Ethan said.

Annecy — France

René Simonet stood before the judge and admitted he was the art thief commonly known as Laurent Fortier. He confessed to killing Charles Louvel in the home of Augustin Pruet during the commission of an art theft, stealing a painting by Pierre-Auguste Renoir.

Simonet spoke clearly, but his voice quavered and his eyes darted about the courtroom.

All the people who had confronted him at his gallery were there. They hadn't killed him, hadn't even beaten him, but they'd manhandled him, screamed in his face, even spat in his eye more than once. Told him in no uncertain terms that if he didn't plead guilty they would tear him to pieces, burn the remains, dump the ashes down a sewer and piss on them.

The judge listened to the recording Pruet provided of Simonet confessing to Charles Louvel's murder. He asked all those present if they'd heard Simonet confess freely, without any form of coercion. All but one said they had.

The judge asked the exception what he'd seen and heard.

"Nothing, *monsieur,*" Augustin Pruet said. "I was late in arriving, for which I will never forgive myself. But I will say to you and all here that I have never been more proud of my son, Yves. He is nothing short of brilliant."

"Yes, well, your pride is understandable, *monsieur.*" He turned to Simonet and asked, "Do you have anything to add?"

The thief shook his head.

The judge told all those present, "We will have to go through all this again in a formal proceeding, but I will recommend a term of life imprisonment, and I'm sure that will be the final outcome. My congratulations to you, *Monsieur le Magistrat.*"

Pruet bowed his head in recognition. He handed a sheet of paper to the judge.

He read it and laughed. Looked at Pruet and nodded.

"Yes, I will recommend these conditions be imposed upon *Monsieur Simonet,* too."

The thief looked at the judge and asked, "What conditions?"

"For the crime of taking Charles Louvel's life, the state will take your freedom from you. For the crimes of stealing works of art from their rightful owners, the state will do its best to make sure that you never see any any form of art again. You will be allowed no printed or electronic media showing any art. The window of your cell will be covered in daylight, so you might never enjoy seeing another dawn or sunset. Your window will also be covered on clear nights so you may never again witness the movements of the stars and the moon. If, however, a night is stormy you will be allowed to see the fierce thrusts of lightning in anticipation of what your judgment will be in a courtroom beyond this world."

Simonet's face sagged. He would never see any form of art again?

Except that of his own damnation.

The terrible punishment Pruet had promised him.

He tried to run from the courtroom. He was seized immediately.

There would be no escape for Laurent Fortier this time.

Outside the court building, Pruet spoke with his father and Père Louvel.

The priest handed him a name written on a sheet of paper: Langston Hobart.

"Your cousin, a few times removed, I think," the priest said. "You asked for the name of any American relation who visited your father's home in the past few years. He is the one. Was quite fascinated by the painting of Antoine and Jocelyne. He mentioned that Jocelyne was his great-great grandmother."

"What will you do, Yves?" his father asked.

"Shall I lead my family on a trip to America?" Père Louvel asked.

Pruet shook his head. He said, "Let the war end here. If this Hobart fellow bought anything, I am sure it's nothing more than a forgery. If he thinks he is victorious, he is a fool, deceiving only himself."

Augustin Pruet and Père Louvel were unsure they agreed with Yves.

Until Odo brought the real Renoir back. Then they thought more of Yves than ever.

CHAPTER 10

The Oval Office
Wednesday, January 16, 2013

McGill forgave the president for not coming to visit him in prison.

"I didn't think the optics would be good," she said.

"Well, as long as you had a sound reason."

The two of them watched the new video the Secret Service had produced. This iteration took into account the events of the past nine days: a potentially hostile civilian militia had seen what they would be up against facing off against the United States Marine Corps; a would-be truck bomber had been violently dispatched to whatever afterlife might await him; the United States Navy's ray-gun prototypes had been fast-tracked for practical use.

In the fashion of Hollywood films, the Secret Service provided two endings to its opus. Audience feedback would determine which one made the final cut. In the first ending, the drones that were still missing and their substitute operators got off an attack, but the Navy's Buck Rogers ray-gunners shot them down before the missiles could be launched. In the second ending, no drone attack was attempted.

Rewinding the video, McGill liked the speech Patti gave and was pleased that nobody tried to either shout it down or shoot up the president.

"That's it then," he said. "I'm going to have to let the kids, Carolyn and Lars come to the inauguration. If that's all right with you."

The president laughed. "As if I'd say no."

CHAPTER 11

West Front of the United States Capitol
Monday, January 21, 2013

Despite the Secret Service's sanguine view of the current situation, McGill glanced heavenward while holding the Bible as Patricia Darden Grant squared her shoulders and prepared to take the oath of office to become president of the United States of America for the second time.

When the moment came for the president to speak, McGill looked right at her.

"I, Patricia Darden Grant, do solemnly swear that I will faithfully execute the Office of President of the United States and will to the best of my ability preserve, protect and defend the Constitution of the United States, so help me God."

McGill's heart filled almost to the point of bursting with pride.

Leaving him just enough room to wonder what regrets he might have later.

He made sure not to let Patti feel any of his misgivings as he kissed her in front of the United States and the world. He beamed at his children, Carolyn and Lars. One cause of concern became immediately apparent at that moment. The way Caitie was looking at Patti, there was no question in McGill's mind that his daughter was imagining herself at her own inauguration.

Well, hell, if she got that far, he'd leave it to *her* husband to worry about things.

The other person who caught McGill's eye was Celsus Crogher. He'd pleaded for and received one last chance to catch a bullet for the president if necessary. Good man.

Inaugural Ball — Washington, DC

Merilee Parker told McGill, "You're a heavenly dancer, sir."

"Thank you, Ms. Parker. You're quite accomplished yourself."

Only two couples were out on the dance floor.

The other was the president and Celsus Crogher.

As tradition required, the president's first dance had gone to McGill.

Then she'd kept her promise and let her former chief bodyguard lead her onto the dance floor. Now, Merilee Park looked at them and sighed. She turned to McGill.

"I thought Celsus was getting sweet on me," she said. "Now, I don't know if I'll ever get him back."

McGill told her, "Don't worry. I'll see that you do."

ABOUT THE AUTHOR

Joseph Flynn has been published both traditionally — Signet Books, Bantam Books and Variance Publishing — and through his own imprint, Stray Dog Press, Inc. Both major media reviews and reader reviews have praised his work. Booklist said, "Flynn is an excellent storyteller." The *Chicago Tribune* said, "Flynn [is] a master of high-octane plotting." The most repeated reader comment is: "Write faster, we want more."

The Jim McGill Series
The President's Henchman, A Jim McGill Novel, #1
The Hangman's Companion, A Jim McGill Novel, #2
The K Street Killer, A Jim McGill Novel, #3
Part 1: The Last Ballot Cast, A Jim McGill Novel, #4
Part 2: The Last Ballot Cast, A Jim McGill Novel, #4
The Devil on the Doorstep, A Jim McGill Novel, #5
Short Cases 1-3, Three Jim McGill Short Stories

The Ron Ketchum Mystery Series
Nailed, A Ron Ketchum Mystery, #1
Defiled, A Ron Ketchum Mystery, 2

The John Tall Wolf Series
Tall Man in Ray-Bans, A John Tall Wolf Novel, #1
War Party, A John Tall Wolf Novel, #2

Other novels *[continued on next page]*

Round Robin, A Love Story of Epic Proportions
One False Step
Blood Street Punx
Still Coming
Still Coming Expanded Edition
Farewell Performance
Hot Type
Gasoline, Texas
The Next President
Digger
The Concrete Inquisition

If you would like to contact Joe, or read free excerpts of his books, please visit *www.josephflynn.com.*

CPSIA information can be obtained
at www.ICGtesting.com
Printed in the USA
BVHW091656200122
626527BV00002B/47